**Praise for *New York Times* bestselling author
Megan Hart**

"Meticulously sensual details and steamy interludes make this an achingly erotic read."
—*RT Book Reviews* on *Flying*

"Hart's beautiful use of language and discerning eye toward human experience elevate the book to a poignant reflection on the deepest yearnings of the human heart and the seductive temptation of passion in its many forms."
—*Kirkus Reviews* on *Tear You Apart*

"*Naked* is a great story, steeped in emotion. Hart has a wonderful way with her characters.... She conveys their thoughts and actions in a manner that brings them to life. And the erotic scenes provide a sizzling read."
—*RT Book Reviews*

"*Deeper* is absolutely, positively, the best book that I have read in ages...the writing is fabulous, the characters' chemistry is combustible, and the story line brought tears to my eyes..."
—*Romance Reader at Heart*, Top Pick

"[*Broken*] is not a traditional romance but the story of a real and complex woman caught in a difficult situation with no easy answers. Well-developed secondary characters and a compelling plot add depth to this absorbing and enticing novel."
—*Library Journal*

"An exceptional story and honest characters make *Dirty* a must-read."
—*Romance Reviews Today*

Praise for Jen Christie

"Filled with conflict and suspense, [*House of Glass*] delivers everything readers of this genre need for a fulfilling escape into another time and place."
—*Goodreads*

"The writing is visual, lush and haunting just like the story itself. There's a dark and tortured hero, a dash of mystery and a heroine whose voice pulls you in."
—Author Stefanie London on *House of Glass*

Megan Hart is the award-winning and
New York Times bestselling author of more than
thirty novels, novellas and short stories. Her
work has been published in almost every genre,
including contemporary women's fiction,
historical romance, romantic suspense and
erotica. Megan lives in the deep, dark woods of
Pennsylvania with her husband and children.
Visit her on the web at meganhart.com.

Books by Megan Hart

Hold Me Close
Vanilla
Lovely Wild
Flying
Tear You Apart
The Favor
The Space Between Us
All Fall Down
Precious and Fragile Things
Collide
Naked
Switch
Deeper
Stranger
Tempted
Broken
Dirty

Visit the Author Profile page
at Harlequin.com for more titles.

MEGAN HART

AND

JEN CHRISTIE

Bound by the Night

and

House of Shadows

ISBN-13: 978-0-373-60228-5

Bound by the Night

Copyright © 2016 by Harlequin Books S.A.

The publisher acknowledges the copyright holders
of the individual works as follows:

Dark Heat
Copyright © 2016 by Megan Hart

Dark Dreams
Copyright © 2016 by Megan Hart

Dark Fantasy
Copyright © 2016 by Megan Hart

House of Shadows
Copyright © 2016 by Jennifer Grannis

This edition published by arrangement with Harlequin Books S.A.

For questions and comments about the quality of this book,
please contact us at CustomerService@Harlequin.com.

® and TM are trademarks of the publisher. Trademarks indicated with
® are registered in the United States Patent and Trademark Office, the
Canadian Intellectual Property Office and in other countries.

Printed in U.S.A.

CONTENTS

DARK HEAT

Megan Hart

These stories are for everyone
who knows to keep their toes under the blankets
so the bogeyman can't tickle them.

Prologue

Everything had gone dark.

And oh, there was pain, great slashing waves of it washing over her as though she'd fallen into an ocean of agony and was being swept away to drown. Blindly, Monica raked the air in front of her and found nothing but emptiness. Hot and stinking breath assaulted her. Then the ground came up to slam into the back of her head and the darkness became sprinkled with the sharp white points of painstars behind her eyes.

She rolled onto her hands and knees, already pushing upward. She had to get to her feet or it would open her throat with teeth and claws like razors. And this rancid cave, this pit, was not the place where Monica intended to die.

She'd lost her knife but swept the ground to look for it and found it with her fingertips. The slice of pain was brief but would ache and burn later. If she was lucky enough to survive being mauled, she'd take those scars gratefully. She found the hilt and grabbed it up as she got to her feet. She turned, slashing outward, nothing but blackness in front of her.

She hit something solid, the blade sinking deep, and Monica didn't wait but pulled it out and stabbed again. Sticky heat flooded her hands. She kept going. Something shoved her again, at the same time grabbing with thick, scaly fingers so she couldn't fall. Couldn't get away.

Teeth on her throat.

Her own voice, screaming.

Then, the blood.

Chapter 1

Monica Blackship woke with a gasp, her hands slashing at the air in front of her before she realized she wasn't in the cave but in her own bed. Alone, thank God. Though in the next moment as the sob wrenched out of her throat, she desperately wished she had someone to cling to.

Brad was gone. A whole month, by now. She didn't blame him, not really. He'd stayed longer than she would have if the situation were reversed. But that was the kind of man he was. The good guy, the hero. He'd tried to save her, but she was past saving. It had been too much for him, in the end.

Still, the bed was vast and empty without him, and though she wasn't *afraid* of darkness, it was so much easier to bear with someone else beside her. She gave in to tears. They leaked from the corners of her eyes and slid down to fill her ears, which was annoying as hell and effectively stopped her from totally surrendering to the indulgence of her misery.

She wouldn't be able to sleep again. The dream always meant the end of the night for her, no matter what time it occurred. Monica rolled to look at the clock, relieved to see that at least it would be morning soon. She wouldn't have chosen to be awake at this hour, but at least she could get up without feeling as though the entire night had been wasted. She could maybe even be a little productive—she'd pay for it later in the day when she couldn't keep her eyes open, but there was nothing to be done about it now.

She swung her legs over the edge of the bed, unable to stop herself, as always, from hesitating just that little bit as her feet hit the floor. Monsters were real, though she'd never encountered one that lived under the bed. It never stopped her from imagining the bite of talons severing her Achilles tendon, of writhing tentacles dragging her under the bed. She settled her feet firmly onto the hardwood planks and used her toes to find the soft edges of the braided rag rug her grandmother had given her.

She didn't turn on the lamp. She knew her way to the bathroom without it, and she'd learned long ago that anything that was afraid of the light was small enough to be dealt with in the dark. Monica shucked off her pajamas and turned on the shower, giving it a few minutes to get hot while she brushed her teeth to clear away the final sour taste of her nightmare. Once under the scalding spray, she pressed her hands to the tile wall. Willing away the bad dreams. Willing away the loneliness.

Monica had already learned there was only one surefire way to push the thoughts away. A good, hard old-fashioned hair-pulling, ass-slapping fuckfest. Brad had not quite been the man to give it to her—even after nearly four months of steady dating, he'd often been too timid with her. Afraid of hurting her. He'd wanted candlelight dinners, stuff like that. Monica had been honest with him from the start—she wasn't looking for that. At first he'd been happy to fuck her in the middle of the night when she woke up, sweating and gasping, reaching for him, but then things had changed.

"There's more to me than being your cock on command," Brad had complained.

Monica hadn't tried to dissuade him from the notion that was how she thought of him. Yes, Brad made a stellar cup of coffee and remembered to put the toilet-seat lid down, and yes, he knew how to match his belt to his shoes. For a lot of women he'd have been a perfect boyfriend, but she was so far from being any kind of perfect anything it would've been unfair of her to try to convince him to stay. Even if it did mean now she stood in a steaming-hot shower with her own fingers sliding between her thighs so she could find some sort of release. Some way to wipe away the horror that crept so regularly into her dreams.

Her fingertips stroked, moving faster. There was nothing of romance in this. Nothing of love. She knew her body well enough to push it into pleasure fast and hard and sharp, just the way she wanted it. Ecstasy spiraled upward, urging her to cry out. Shuddering, Monica climaxed. The pleasure didn't linger. In another few seconds she was simply shivering under the spatter of water, feeling empty inside.

At least the dream had been pushed away.

Dripping, Monica wrapped her hair in a towel and then grabbed another to use on her body. She caught a flash of her reflection in the mirror. You couldn't miss the scars, several long slashes sweeping over her belly. She could look at them impassively now. She put her hand over them, aligning her fingers with the marks. The official report had been a bear attack. The wounds didn't match anything familiar or animal; she'd spent a few nights in the psych ward before giving up her insistence that she hadn't been hurt by a bear. A beast had torn her open, but Monica had done her own work on her wrists and that sort of thing had a tendency to make people give you the side eye about everything else.

She touched those marks, too. The one on the right was precise. The one on the left, ragged. Four inches long, lengthwise, not across. She'd been serious about wanting to die.

"But not anymore," she whispered to herself, just to be sure the face in the mirror was really hers.

She would put on some comfy clothes and make herself some coffee and eggs and toast, she decided firmly. She would not text Brad to see if they could get together—he'd made noises about the two of them staying "friends," but she knew well enough how that would work. As in, it wouldn't.

She'd barely started the eggs frying when her phone rang. At this hour it could only be Vadim, which could only mean one thing. Monica thumbed the screen of her phone, not bothering with a hello.

"This is the job," Vadim said without a greeting of his own, and suddenly Monica wasn't sleepy any longer.

Chapter 2

Jordan Leone had no patience for rich fucks who thought a hefty bank account equaled free rein to buy and sell any other creature's life. Paul DiNero wasn't usually that sort. The guy genuinely cared for his animals, though his hard-on for the exotics meant he had quite a number of pets that weren't the cuddly kind. It was how the guy acquired the animals that lit a slow fire under Jordan's skin.

DiNero wanted what he wanted and he had the money to get it, even when legal channels failed him. Maybe especially when that happened, since that was often the only way he could procure the pets he wanted. He had contacts all over the world, from legitimate and licensed breeders to poachers to other collectors who were looking to sell off their animals or their offspring. Sure, the guy had a bunch of documentation proving his backyard menagerie was a private zoo used for "educational" purposes, but the fact was, DiNero's collection was for his own private pleasure and nothing else, and when he wanted something, that meant he was willing to put up with the sort of arrogant douche bags Jordan hated.

Today it was some guy with a weird accent that sounded French but wasn't. His greasy black mustache glistened from the bison burger he'd scarfed down while sitting on DiNero's terrace. His beady eyes narrowed while his mouth stretched into a grin Jordan wouldn't have trusted on a great white. He waved a languid hand.

"The price," he said, "is nonnegotiable."

"You understand I'll need to have my man here give the animal a full health check," DiNero warned, though he didn't look concerned. He'd dealt with this dick-blister before.

Jordan hadn't eaten a burger, even though the smell of it had flooded his mouth with greedy, ravenous saliva. His stomach clenched, not so much in physical hunger as in simple longing. He'd restricted his meat eating for over fifteen years, and though his vegetarian diet was self-imposed, he'd never quite managed to convince his body he wasn't missing out. He took a long drink of his beer instead, savoring the hoppy flavor.

"Of course, of course. I wouldn't have it any other way. Not for one of my best customers." The guy, whose name was something like Algiers or Algernon or maybe it was Addison, flicked his gaze at Jordan and gave him another smarmy smile.

DiNero nodded at Jordan and bit into his own burger. Juice squirted. Jordan had to look away.

"Go make sure my new girl is healthy, Jordan, while Mr. Efforteson and I chat about some things," DiNero said.

It was a dismissal, but Jordan didn't mind. With barely a nod at Efforteson, he headed for the stone stairs off the terrace, toward the driveway and the truck parked there. Unmarked, without even ventilation, the inside would be pitch-black and stinking of frightened animals, but Jordan had seen worse conditions. Sometimes when he'd had to travel to pick up a new pet, the sights he'd witnessed were so horrible they'd left him shaking and furious. Violent.

With a nod at the armed bodyguard, Jordan yanked on the truck's rolling door in the back and hopped into the bed. Inside were rows of cages, all empty but for the one at the back. In it, a cowering female silver Russian fox yipped and rolled her eyes as he approached. He soothed her with a low murmur and put out a hand for her to sniff, his fingers against the bars of the cage. The foxes had been bred for generations in Russia as an experiment at domestication, and now the animals were more like dogs than their ancestors had been. They'd gained in popularity as exotic pets, expensive and limited in where they could be legally kept, rare only because of how difficult it could be to acquire one. This pretty girl was a replacement for one DiNero had lost.

"Hey there, pretty girl. Sweet girl," Jordan soothed, settling close to the cage so the fox could get used to him. "I won't let anything happen to you."

Not like the other one, he thought with a hard swallow of anger. He'd fucking warned DiNero about fixing the barriers between the zoo and the bayou, but the man had been more concerned about keeping away nosy neighbors or thieves than anything else. Gators couldn't climb brick walls or smash them, either, but something had scaled the ten-foot wall. The barbed wire on the top had been torn and tossed aside like candy floss. This last time, the intruder had left behind a pen full of dead foxes.

Jordan opened the cage and the fox crept closer with a small yip. She'd clearly been socialized thoroughly, something DiNero wouldn't bother to do once he had her ensconced in the zoo. The fox had been bred as a house pet, but to DiNero she was an ornament.

"C'mere, little girl." Jordan stroked the soft fur, feeling for any obvious lumps or bumps. He gave her some cuddling time before scooping her up to take her outside. The bodyguard looked surprised, but Jordan ignored him to take the fox across the long expanse of soft green grass to the small bungalow he used as an office.

The fox yipped and buried her face against him when they went inside, but Jordan continued to soothe her with murmured words and gentle touches as he examined her. Her paws scrabbled on the steel tabletop, but she quieted when he gave a warning noise under his breath. She still trembled, but she wasn't trying to get away.

She looked good, at least as much as an animal could when it had been kept caged in the dark and improperly fed and watered for the past few days. But she was healthy, without any signs of abuse or genetic flaws as the result of inbreeding. Jordan finished the exam and slipped a treat from his pocket that the fox took eagerly. She butted her head against him, and he took her narrow face in his hands.

"Pretty girl," he said quietly. The fox licked his face.

Once she'd been put away in her own habitat, separated for now from the three surviving foxes for a quarantine period before he introduced them, Jordan made the rounds of the other habitats in this section. He'd spent long hours building most of them, re-creating different terrains or climates to provide the best possible housing for their inhabitants. The animals were under his care, and that meant their living conditions, too.

Veterinarian, handyman, lion tamer. That was his job here at DiNero's, and it was the best one he'd ever had. The man gave him a good salary and free room and board on the property in a tiny but cozy bungalow with full catering privileges from the main-house kitchen. Most important, DiNero usually left Jordan alone.

Until today, apparently. Jordan rounded the corner of a low stone wall meant to keep the prairie dogs from getting out—DiNero loved prairie dogs and would often spend hours feeding them peanuts and watching them pop in and out of their holes. Today, though, he stood with his back to Jordan. Efforteson wasn't with him. DiNero's companion was a woman, her long dark hair the color of black cherries. It fell in soft waves to the middle of her back, and when she turned, eyes like a summer sky opened wide beneath dark arched brows.

"Jordan, come say hello to Ms. Blackship."

Reluctantly, Jordan came closer. DiNero had been married four times, no children unless you counted the third wife, who'd thrown tantrums like a three-year-old. Now the man claimed he would never get married again, which only meant that he brought around his one-night stands to impress them with his menagerie, and Jordan had to make nice and pretend to give a damn.

"Monica," the woman said as she gave him a firm, brief handshake.

"She's the… Whattaya call it, honey?"

If the endearment raised her hackles, Monica Blackship didn't show it. She gave DiNero a flicking glance but then put her focus back on Jordan. "I'm a crypto-zoologist."

For one awful moment, Jordan thought maybe DiNero was trying to replace him. But then he understood, having heard the term somewhere. "A crypto…"

"I research unusual or what some might consider legendary creatures," Monica replied calmly. "Bigfoot. That sort of thing."

"You think Bigfoot jumped our wall and killed our animals?" Jordan didn't even care what DiNero might think of him taking any small part of ownership. "That's ridiculous."

"Of course it is. By all accounts, the Sasquatch is a vegetarian," Monica said without so much as a quirk of her smile.

DiNero chuckled. "Just like you, Jordan."

Jordan scowled, crossing his arms. "Sasquatch also doesn't exist."

"That remains to be disproven, actually." Again, that calm, almost blank look without a hint of any expression. It made him want to do something to see if he could shake her up.

"Hasn't been proven," Jordan added.

DiNero gave him a look. "Something came over our walls, Jordan. And you said yourself it wasn't human."

"I didn't say it was Bigfoot, either!"

"That's what Ms. Blackship is here to help us figure out. She works with an organization that studies this sort of thing." DiNero, who could be a pain-in-the-ass wisecracker most of the time, looked serious. "You know animals, dude. You know this is some kind of animal that keeps doing this."

Jordan involuntarily thought of the first slaughter he'd found three months ago. The scent of blood, the patches of fur. It was more than the loss of the animals, or even the money they'd cost. It was how they must've suffered that made his stomach tense and churn. He wasn't convinced whatever had killed the zoo animals didn't wear boots and kill with knives.

"Something didn't just kill them," DiNero continued, now facing the woman. "It ate them, we're pretty sure."

Jordan shook his head. "You don't know that."

Monica nodded. "I've seen similar cases. I'm thinking it might be something like a chupacabra…"

"The hell…?" Jordan snorted derisive laughter. "What the hell is that?"

"They're usually found in Puerto Rico and Mexico," Monica went on as though he hadn't spoken, and damn, if there was one thing Jordan couldn't stand, it was being dismissed as if he were nothing. "But there have been cases of them moving north, more and more often now. They typically prey on smaller animals, but several of the cases my colleagues have worked on dealt with what looks to be a different breed of chupacabra, maybe…"

"Hold on. There's more than one breed?" Jordan shook his head. "Please."

"Like dogs," Monica said. "Or wolves."

DiNero had watched the interchange with rapidly rising brows, but now he held up a hand. "Jordan, listen. Monica was sent here by a friend I trust. He's dealt with things like this before, and I want to know what's going on. What's breaking in here, what's eating my pets."

"So you can kill it," Monica said softly.

"Hell no," DiNero said. "So I can put it in my collection."

Chapter 3

It was better than a sleeping bag on the ground or a bedbug-ridden hotel room, that was for sure. DiNero had put her up in one of the guest bungalows scattered throughout the private zoo. Kind of a safari experience for his guests, she supposed and curled her lip. Monica had never liked zoos, seeing the animals in cages. Lions pacing and miserable. DiNero's menagerie was housed in better habitats than any she'd ever seen, but they were still kept captive. Not free.

In her lifetime before, when she'd been attending veterinary school, Monica had dreamed of getting a job at a big zoo. Maybe a circus. She wanted to work with exotic animals, not just dogs and cats. She hadn't finished school, because the attack had screwed that up for her, big-time. Yet she'd ended up working with exotic animals just the same, hadn't she? The deadliest ones, too, nothing soft or fluffy, because people never called for help when they came across a mewling, fuzzy bundle of fur with big eyes. Nope, the Crew got the calls only for the things that chewed your head off and spit down your neck.

Damn, she was tired.

She'd been up for most of the night because of the dream. Then she'd been on a plane from her place in Pennsylvania with a layover in North Carolina and this final stop in Louisiana. Then another four hours or so driving through the bayous to get here. Where here was, she didn't exactly know. Vadim had told her that DiNero demanded secrecy so he could avoid getting caught with his illegal collection. Personally, Monica had no interest in fucking with his animals, so long as they were cared for.

Which made her think of Jordan Leone. That long, tall drink of water was in charge here, and he'd made sure to let her know it. Not that it mattered, really. She was here to figure out what had killed a silver fox, four prairie dogs, a couple chimps and, more frighteningly, a tiger. The tiger had been, by Jordan's account, old and blind in one eye. Raised in captivity, it had come from another collection, where it had been treated like a house cat and overfed, allowed to live with its owner in a tiny two-bedroom cottage until it had pissed one too many times on the couch. It hadn't been full of much fight, Jordan had told her. But still. What could attack and kill a tiger and also drag it half a mile and through or over a ten-foot-high brick wall topped with barbed wire?

After pouring herself a glass of what turned out to be very good whiskey, Monica turned out the lights in the small kitchenette and then the equally compact living room. On bare feet, she crossed the bamboo floors with her glass in her hand and made her way out onto the small terrace. She'd brought a book but didn't feel like reading. The mosquitoes were going to eat her alive out here, she thought, but settled into one of the comfortable chairs and put her feet up anyway.

From here she had a good look directly across into Jordan's bungalow. She hadn't been given her choice of places to stay, and if she had, she wouldn't have picked one so close to his. He was a man who cherished privacy, she could tell that right off. He wasn't going to be popping over asking to borrow some sugar, that was for sure. And there were other guesthouses—she'd seen them when DiNero gave her the tour of the estate. So why this one, then?

It had something to do with Jordan protecting her, she thought with a low chuckle and a shake of her head. DiNero hadn't said as much, but he might as well have patted her on the head when he called her *honey*. She'd figured it out. He didn't seem to have a problem believing in her credentials or ability to find out what was stalking and killing his pets, but he didn't think she could defend herself. Monica gave an internal shrug. She hoped she wouldn't have to, but if she did, she doubted she'd need Jordan Leone's help.

Never mind those long, strong arms and legs. Those big hands. Never mind the muscles cording in his back and shoulders, clearly visible even through his shirt when he bent or lifted anything. Never mind that mouth…

Monica stopped herself. She wasn't here for that. Sure, he pushed just about every one of her buttons, aside from the fact he didn't seem to have a sense of humor. Oh, and that he obviously didn't like her at all, was suspicious of her being here and had no faith in anything she'd already proven to herself as truth. She could get over him not believing in Sasquatch, but Jordan had been blunt and up-front about his utter lack of even an inkling of belief in anything other than what he could read about in a textbook. A man like that wasn't for her. No way.

Still, it couldn't hurt to admire the shape of him through the sliding glass doors at the front of his bungalow as he moved around inside. Cooking dinner, judging by the good smells of onions and garlic in olive oil. She'd eaten at the main house with DiNero, slabs of steak as thick as her fist and wine she bet cost more than her rent. He'd have someone stock her fridge for her tomorrow, he'd promised. Until then, if she wanted a late-night snack, she was out of luck.

At least if she wanted food, Monica thought, watching Jordan's silhouette, and then she reined in her hormones and went inside.

Jordan woke early, as he always did, though this morning he'd actually needed his alarm to rouse him. He'd been dreaming, jumbled images that made no sense. Nothing he could remember, really, but for the first time in forever, he couldn't seem to shake away the sleep.

Breakfast didn't satisfy him, either. Granola and soy milk. Healthy, yes. Satisfying? Not when he really wanted a platter of fried eggs, a rasher of bacon, a fistful of sausages... Shit. His stomach rumbled angrily as he made himself some sourdough toast spread thickly with strawberry jam. Strong coffee eased the cravings a little bit, but not entirely.

It definitely didn't help that when he headed up to the main house to see if that woman DiNero had hired was ready to join him on the daily rounds, Jordan discovered Magnus had laid out a spread. DiNero's personal chef believed in hearty, down-home cooking. Gumbo, jambalaya, but also breakfasts that could feed an army. Jordan nodded at Karen and Bill, two of his assistants, who were helping themselves to the buffet on the sideboard, but he didn't dare get any closer to the food. He'd fall on it like…well…like a starving man.

He spotted Monica and DiNero on the terrace overlooking the yard. She looked fresh faced and ready to take on anything, her dark red hair pulled into a neat ponytail at the base of her skull. He gave her a grudging nod, noting her work pants and boots. At least she'd dressed appropriately.

"Morning, Leone. How the hell are you? I was just telling Ms. Blackship here about the elephant." DiNero gave Jordan a gator grin.

"We don't have an elephant," Jordan said.

DiNero waggled his brows. "Not yet."

Jordan sighed. He'd told his boss an elephant was too much to handle. The sheer size of it would mean a habitat that would require far too much upkeep, unless the man wanted the poor thing to be hemmed in. Not to mention that elephants were smart and could be vengeful if mistreated—not that Jordan would ever mistreat an animal, but you never knew how they'd been treated before. Elephants did not belong in a private zoo. Then again, he thought with a bland smile as DiNero kept blabbing away, no animals really did, even if it meant Jordan would be out of a job.

"Grab a plate," DiNero said.

"Already ate. Thanks." To Monica, Jordan said, "You want to come on my rounds with me today?"

She tucked a final bite of toast into her mouth and nodded, wiping her hands on a napkin. She swigged some coffee and stood. The way DiNero ogled her ass when she turned made Jordan want to punch the other man in the face.

"He's kind of a douche bag, huh?" she murmured as they left the dining room.

Jordan gave her a glance. "He's my boss."

"He's totally looking at my butt, isn't he? I can tell." She slanted Jordan a sideways smirk.

Jordan didn't answer her, but Monica laughed softly anyway. They'd just started heading for the golf carts when Jordan's third assistant, a white-faced and shaking Peter, ran toward them. Jordan knew before the other guy had even said a word what had happened.

"Where?" he asked.

Peter shook his head and pointed toward the mountain-lion habitat. Jordan took off running, Monica on his heels. In minutes they made it to the habitat, where Jordan skidded to a halt. The entire interior of the habitat had become an abattoir. There was no sign of either of the mountain lions.

"It took both of them." Peter sounded as if he was going to be sick.

Jordan knew how he felt. He ran his hands through his hair, stalking, pacing. He became aware of Monica next to him.

"Can you let me inside?" she asked.

Jordan nodded. "Yeah. We need to check everything out."

They spent the next hour doing that. Monica took notes on the drag patterns in the dirt and blood spatter while Jordan had Peter, Karen and Bill ready for the cleanup. All of them were silent as they worked.

"No signs of damage to the habitat walls. The lock on the gate looks picked," Jordan said.

"Scratched." Monica looked at him. "All around it."

Jordan shook his head. "An animal didn't do this. You can't tell me that something came and picked the fucking lock."

She tucked her notebook into her pocket and then pushed her hair behind her ears. "There have been instances of tool use in some—"

"I need to check the outer wall. See where it got in." Jordan wasn't interested in her lame theories about tool-using monsters.

Monica followed him. "Jordan, wait."

He stopped but didn't turn. He could tell that Karen, Bill and Peter were watching, though none of them said a word. Jordan waited for her to continue, but she didn't. After another minute, he stalked off.

There was nothing. No breaks in the wall. No holes. No bent barbed wire this time. The lock on the gate nearest the mountain-lion habitat had similar markings to the one on the habitat gate. Scratches.

"It's something smart," Monica said from behind him.

Jordan frowned and shook his head. "Smart enough to pick a lock? I'm telling you, poachers are doing this. Someone with a grudge against DiNero, maybe…"

"Poachers would take the animals. They wouldn't kill them. Would they?"

He looked at her. "About seven years ago, DiNero got into a fight with some Japanese billionaire over a rare breed of panda they both wanted. Neither of them had the right habitats for it, but they were going head-to-head over it anyway. DiNero won the auction. The billionaire had someone come in and kill the panda before DiNero could take delivery. Some people don't want anyone else to have what they want."

She gave him a long, steady look, then reached to touch his shoulder. Just briefly. Just once. "Jordan, I know this is killing you. Believe me, I want to find out what's going on."

He put a hand on the wall and leaned, shoulders hunched. "This is fucked up, Monica. I know DiNero brought you in here because he thinks you can help figure out what's happening. But I just can't..."

"You don't have to believe me," she said. "Honestly, if it's a chupacabra or a poacher, does it matter, so long as we find out and stop it?"

Grudgingly, he looked at her. "No. I guess it doesn't."

"We're going to find out what...or who...is doing this." She looked grim.

Though he hadn't known her long at all, Jordan had no doubts that woman meant what she said.

Chapter 4

Vadim's face was a little blurry for a moment on the computer screen before the picture cleared. He was sitting, as he almost always was when they video-chatted, behind his oversize mahogany desk. Behind him, bookshelves overflowed with textbooks and papers. He adjusted his glasses and leaned forward to look at her.

"Strong enough to drag a tiger over a wall but now picking a lock instead?" he asked.

Monica sipped some more of DiNero's excellent whiskey and nodded. "Yes. Maybe whatever it was got tired of the heavy lifting. It looks like it figured out how to get through one of the gates along the perimeter wall, then let itself into the mountain-lion cage. Both were missing. Some blood, some hair, but nothing else. No bones, even. If it's actually eating the animals, it's consuming them entirely."

"DiNero's man thinks it's human, eh? An inside job?

Does he have a grudge against his boss?" Vadim sat back in his chair.

Monica shrugged. "It's possible. DiNero is kind of a dick. But Jordan seems to really care about the animals. If he was somehow working with an outside source to steal the animals away from DiNero, he couldn't hurt them."

"He could be making it look as though they're hurt," Vadim pointed out.

"He could, I guess. Seems pretty elaborate to me. And he seems genuinely upset by what's going on. He runs a clean house here. The habitats are expensive and well maintained, not just cages. There's a wide variety of animals, but they're all really taken care of." She paused, sipping. "He's a little odd. The zookeeper."

Vadim grinned. "Handsome?"

"Ugh, stop." She made a face. Vadim was always trying to set her up with some Crew member or other. Then she laughed a little. "Very."

"I have Ted ready to head down to you once you think you might know what's going on. I'd send someone sooner, but…"

"I know. Too many investigations, not enough Crew. I got it. I'll be careful," she put in before Vadim could lecture her.

Crew rules stated that no investigator try to hunt something alone. They worked at the minimum in pairs. Her role here was to assess the situation and try to get a handle on what they were looking for. No use coming loaded for bear, as Vadim said, if they were really hunting rabbit.

Something told Monica this was no bunny.

"Have they added any security measures?" Vadim asked. "I warned DiNero that your safety was my priority. Not that of his collection. You're not to go off on your own, do you understand?"

He was nowhere near old enough to be her father, though he tried to act as much as a patriarch to the Crew as a leader. Sometimes Vadim's protective nature warmed her. Other times, like now, it left her with the urge to roll her eyes and stamp her feet like a teenager reminded over and over again to "drive carefully." Monica kept her expression bland.

"Don't give me that look," he said.

She raised both brows, innocence personified. Vadim sighed. Monica raised her whiskey glass. After a moment, he shook his head.

"Something that can haul away a tiger could certainly do a lot of damage to you, Monica."

She had, for a period after losing Carl, done many reckless things. But time had passed and her life had gone on, whether she liked it or not, because that was what life did. "I know. And believe me, I'm not... I'm not trying to get myself killed. I'm here to study and assess, and then the team will come in and we'll catch this thing."

"If we're lucky," Vadim said.

They both knew how infrequently the Crew got lucky. There was a reason why people kept repeating that monsters weren't real, after all, and it mostly had to do with how hard it was to find proof. Monica raised her glass again, draining it, and this time, Vadim signed off.

Chapter 5

Ten guesthouses, and DiNero put the woman in the one closest to his. Jordan fumed, though it was pointless. DiNero would do whatever he wanted. And, Jordan grudgingly admitted, it made sense to have Monica closer to him, if only because she'd be walking the zoo with him for the next few days.

He'd seen her out on the terrace earlier. Sipping a glass of whiskey he could smell across the lawn and through his open windows. He could smell her, too. The soap she'd used, the laundry detergent seeping from her clothes. Those were good, clean scents. So was the lingering scent of wine she'd had with dinner. She'd be mortified to know he could smell the meat she'd eaten still on her breath, though she'd covered it with toothpaste.

She made him *hungry*.

Damn it.

Dinner for him had been some pasta with olive oil and some fresh-baked bread. A salad. The food filled him up but didn't sate him. That was why, he told himself, he was up at nearly two in the morning to rustle around in his fridge for some scrambled tofu and cheese when he really wanted to gorge himself to bursting on a thick slab of beef still dripping with blood... Jordan shook himself. He shoveled the food in his mouth, barely tasting it, trying to fill the emptiness. When he'd finished, he rinsed his plate and looked out the kitchen window to the guest bungalow where Monica was staying.

Her lights were off, which made sense at this time of night. The bedroom window was open, though, like his own. He could hear her inside. The slide of limbs on the bedsheets, the whisper of her hair on the pillow. She murmured something sleepy.

He needed to stop being a freaking creep about it. Jordan shook himself and put the plate in the drainer, then froze, head going up, ears straining at the change in her voice. He couldn't make out the words, but the tone had changed.

Carefully, slowly, he put the knife and fork he'd been using in the drainer, too. Still listening. He closed his eyes, opening his senses.

Her scent had changed, becoming bitter. The low mutter of her voice rose, edging toward hysteria. Not quite screaming, but definitely in distress.

Jordan didn't think twice. He was out the back door and heading for the guest bungalow in seconds. He leaped the low brick wall of his back patio and landed hard on the other side, bare feet slapping at the grass DiNero paid so much to keep looking nice. He hit the guesthouse's back patio in three strides after that. She'd locked the door. One hit with his shoulder and the door frame splintered.

She was in the bedroom, and Jordan barreled through the door ready to battle whatever was attacking her. He'd been unable to save the animals, but there was no way he was going to let something hurt anyone or anything else. He skidded on the hard floor, moving too fast to stop himself when he saw the woman was alone.

She sat up in bed at the sound of him coming into the room. Her hands punched at the air. Her low cry changed as her eyes opened and she focused on him.

He'd been moving so fast that he'd ended up next to the bed. Breathing hard, he stared down at her. He looked everywhere, trying to make sure nothing was there ready to pounce on them both.

"Am I still dreaming?" she asked in a totally clear, absolutely calm voice that sounded nothing like the terrified cries he'd been hearing earlier. "Because if I am, goddamn, please get over here and fuck me."

She wasn't still dreaming. Monica hadn't ever been able to control what happened while she was—she had friends who could lucid-dream, and there was a whole squad of people in the Crew who dealt with the monsters that lurked in the realm of the subconscious. The words had tumbled out of her before she was fully awake, though, and she wasn't going to take them back.

The man in front of her had grumbled his way through their earlier introductions. He wasn't someone she'd ever have considered in a romantic way. She was here on a job, not to get laid. Yet of course right now, after the nightmare, which had been even more intense than ever, all she could think about was getting fucked right through the mattress. It didn't matter much who did it.

"Shit," Jordan said.

Shirtless, jeans hanging low on lean hips, bare feet. If she'd ordered him from a catalog, he couldn't have arrived in more perfect condition or with better timing. And, she realized as she took in the heave of his chest and the way his fists were clenched, he'd burst in here to…save her?

She was naked. The covers had come down. He could see her completely, and was he looking? Oh, yeah. He definitely was.

The dream was fading but her hands were still shaking. Now not just from terror. Her nipples had gone hard, and without thinking, Monica cupped her breasts. Not necessarily to hide herself from his gaze. More to draw his attention.

"Jordan," she whispered. "Come here."

He did, two hesitant steps until his knees brushed the edge of the blankets. He licked his lower lip, looking her over. His breathing had slowed, but only a little.

"Did you come here to save me?" Monica asked in a low, rough voice.

He nodded. "I thought whatever killed the animals was in here with you."

"Do you still want to save me?" She shuddered, closing her eyes for a moment to push away the memories. Without opening them, she added, "I need you."

The bed dipped beneath his weight. When his rough hands skimmed up her bare sides, Monica let out a small gasp and allowed herself to arch back onto the pillows. His breath gusted over her cheek and she turned her face, lips parting, waiting for him to kiss her. She thought he wouldn't.

But he did, oh, he did. Hard and fierce and sharp, the way she liked it. The way she needed it. His tongue stabbed into her mouth as his hand slipped to cradle the back of her head. Then his mouth was moving down her throat to nip and nibble and then, yes, oh God, yes, to scrape along her flesh in that beautiful burst of pleasure-pain she craved.

When his lips closed over one nipple, Monica threaded her hands through his thick dark hair, fingers tangling. "There. Yes."

She still hadn't opened her eyes again. She wanted to be lost in this, all the sensations sweeping over her. She gave up to him.

When Jordan's mouth moved lower, though, she tensed. His lips tickled the scars on her ribs and belly. She waited for the questions, but all he did was kiss her softly and then move lower to nip at her hip bone. When he parted her thighs, again she tensed, though this time not out of trepidation.

At his first slow, long lick, she cried out. She lifted herself to his mouth, but Jordan had moved to slide his hands under her ass and his grip stilled her. When she tried to move again, his fingers tightened on her skin hard enough to bruise. She didn't quiet at the sting. She writhed.

His tongue flickered along her clit, then switched to flat, smooth strokes that had her bucking beneath him in a few minutes. Desire was already building, surging. She always woke from the dreams desperate for sex, but this, oh, shit, this was amazing. Brad had been a competent, considerate lover. Jordan, on the other hand, was eating her pussy as if he meant to destroy her with his mouth.

Monica's orgasm tore through her, leaving her gasping. Her fingers tightened in Jordan's hair again, involuntarily yanking. He made a noise, something like a low…growl?

Startled, Monica opened her eyes at last. With her climax still washing over her, all she could do was ride it as, seemingly without effort, Jordan pulled away just enough to flip her over. Hard. Reckless. Not at all gentle—in fact, her head butted the headboard for a second before she managed to look over her shoulder.

He was on his knees behind her, already tearing open his jeans. His cock, thick and gorgeous, sprang free into his fist. His other hand slapped her ass as he gave himself a few strokes. He looked at her, eyes gleaming.

A flash of red.

In the next moment, he was inside her, thrusting so hard she again moved forward and only her hands pressed to the headboard kept her from hitting it. He fucked so deep inside her that she cried out, expecting pain but feeling only the hot, slick engulfing of his cock by her still-clenching pussy. Again Jordan thrust inside her. Again.

When his nails raked down her back, she screamed, breathless and gasping. His body covered hers in the next moment as he leaned to find her clit with his fingers. No soft strokes now. He pinched, jacking it as he fucked into her, and it was too much, too much—she was going over again. Spiraling. Exploding.

Jordan's growl this time sounded like her name, which sent one last wave of ecstasy pulsing through her. He shuddered against her and…oh, fuck, he bit down on her shoulder as his fingers gave her one last pinching stroke and he came inside her. Monica couldn't come again, not after that, but it was close.

Spent, she collapsed onto her face in the pillows. His weight pressed her for a few seconds before he moved off her to flop onto the bed beside her. Boneless, sated, exhausted, Monica couldn't move.

She ought to say something, she thought blearily but couldn't make her mouth form any words. The dream had always made her crave sex exactly how she'd just had it, but this was the first time she'd ever had it exactly how she needed it. She tried to roll over onto her back to at least see if she could get up and go to the bathroom, but her body refused to do anything but sink back into dark and dreamless sleep.

When she woke up to golden streams of late-afternoon sunlight streaming through the window, Jordan was gone.

Chapter 6

As much as Jordan might have loved to take care of everything all by himself simply so he didn't have to deal with other people, there was no way he could possibly manage to feed and clean the habitats of every animal in DiNero's menagerie. Not even if he worked twenty-four hours a day. That was why he had a small rotating staff of three workers who took care of the daily care under his charge, while he spent his days visiting each habitat to be sure the animals were safe, healthy and as happy as they could be in captivity.

The woman was supposed to be with him again today on his rounds. He didn't need her advice on how to keep his animals safe, he thought sourly, just some thoughts on what the hell was continuing to break through and attack them. So far, all she'd done was toss a lot of stupid theories at him. Nothing he could actually work with. Besides that, she hadn't shown up this morning, not a call, not a note, nothing.

He couldn't stop thinking about the taste of her.

He was hard now, thinking of it, and that pissed him off, too. For Jordan, sex over the past few years had been relegated to an occasional one-night stand when he traveled into New Orleans. He favored tourists, women in sundresses and wedge sandals, drunk on hurricanes. The ones who were shy or claimed to be, at least until he cut them from the pack of their squealy girlfriends and took them back to the small, barely furnished flat he kept just off Bourbon Street. Anonymous, brief, nothing but two bodies—or three, and once four—writhing and grinding until there was nothing but pure mindless pleasure. It was something he did with strangers, some who never even thought to ask his name. It was not something he did with women he ever expected to see again.

But he'd had sex with Monica last night, and he *wanted* to see her again.

By the time lunch had come and gone, Jordan had made his rounds. He checked in on the staff congregating in the small common room outside his office but didn't linger, even though today was Peter's birthday and Karen had brought a cake. Instead, Jordan headed for the perimeter wall, intending to walk the entire length of it to look for any breaks or to repair any damage. Also to check for any signs that the thing attacking the animals had returned. He'd made it all the way beyond the empty tiger habitat when the light scent of feminine soap lilted to him along the breeze. His nostrils flared, but he didn't turn. He could hear her and smell her. That didn't mean he needed to acknowledge her.

"Hey," Monica said from behind him. "Sorry I missed you this morning. I totally overslept. I never do that."

Jordan had been looking carefully over one of the spots that had been damaged to make sure the repairs were holding. He glanced over his shoulder. "No problem."

She stepped up closer, moving beside him. She pointed. "It came through here originally?"

"We found two holes in the outside wall after the first attack. Both broke all the way through, but this was the biggest, and neither one was big enough to get anything through. Even if *it* could squeeze, you can't squeeze a tiger. The barbed wire—" he gestured along the top of the wall "—had been completely torn away. Whatever it was tried to make it through, and when it couldn't, it went over the top."

"Any signs of blood here? Like something had cut itself?"

He gave her a flat look. "There was blood everywhere. Whatever it was came in and dragged away a full-grown tiger."

"There are a few things that could do that." Without looking at him, Monica moved closer to the wall to run her fingers along the patched section, then took a step back to look upward. "The other hole was smaller than this one?"

"Yeah. I can show you."

Wasn't she going to mention anything about the night before? Was she not going to say a word? She'd come on to him like a freight train, and now she was going to pretend it had never happened?

Fine.

He took her there and watched as she studied the

repaired spot. She pulled out her phone, took a few photos. Tapped some notes.

"So," he said, unable to stop himself. "What do you think it is?"

Monica looked up. "I'm still not sure. I came here convinced I was looking for a new breed of chupaca-bra or something similar, but now I'm thinking this is something else entirely."

Jordan snorted. Monica's brows rose. He shrugged.

"Is it really so hard for you to believe in the un-known?" She put a hand on her hip and gave him a hard look he thought was meant to shame him.

It didn't, though it did stir another, baser emotion in his lower gut. Jordan shrugged again. Monica sighed.

"Do you know there are thousands of new species of animals and insects discovered every year? The rain forest—"

"This isn't the rain forest," Jordan pointed out. "This is Louisiana."

"And every inch of it's been explored, huh?" she challenged, moving a step closer. "There are thousands of acres of land, all charted. Nothing could possibly be hiding away from the rest of the world, could it?"

"Nothing like what you're talking about. Something big and predatory would've been discovered before now, that's all I'm saying."

Monica frowned. "My grandparents live in New Jer-sey. Not Jersey Shore, but up north, close to New York. They have a postage-stamp lot backed up to another postage-stamp lot, with neighbors all around them. You could spit and hit two different highways. And guess what they have in their backyard every night."

"A lot of noise?"

"Smart-ass," she said but didn't seem angry. If anything, he'd made her smile. She shook her head. "Deer. They eat my grandma's garden and make her crazy. It's not a place where you'd think you'd see deer, but there they are, and why? Because they've been driven there. They don't have another place to go."

"You're saying whatever's attacking the menagerie has been driven here?"

"Could be. Land development, taking away territory. Chemicals in the water, changing the food supply. Something we don't even know about, like down in Florida, where those people are dropping off their ball pythons and anacondas that got too big to be pets, and now they're breeding and fighting with the alligators for dominance on the food chain."

"That's not happening here," Jordan said.

Monica gave him a solemn look. "Could be something else, then. Too many gators being taken, maybe this thing normally eats *them*, and now it's hungry. Whatever it is, it's discovered the menagerie, and it's not going to stop coming back unless we stop it." She paused. "Why is it so hard for you to believe?"

"I don't believe in monsters," he said flatly.

Monica laughed. "You're lucky, then. Because trust me, they exist. Or they did and have gone extinct. Or, like in this case, haven't been discovered."

"Maybe it's zombies," he said, deadpan. Scoffing.

She narrowed her eyes. "You mean like voodoo?"

"I mean like 'They're coming to get you, Barbara,'" Jordan said. "Voodoo is a religion."

She frowned again. "I wasn't trying to be offensive. Zombies like in *Night of the Living Dead* definitely are not real, I can tell you that much."

"No? But Bigfoot and the Loch Ness monster are, huh?"

She turned on him, finally, with a scowl. "I'm a cryptozoologist, Jordan. That means I search for the existence of animals whose existence has not been proven. Or things outside their natural realm. Do you know that just last year a half-sized cougar was discovered rummaging in the Dumpsters of restaurants in Hell's Kitchen? A cougar in New York City."

"That's not surprising, I bet there are lots of cougars in the city," Jordan said.

Monica laughed, and he discovered how much he liked the sound of it. "Not that kind of cougar. My point is, it might've been someone's pet that got too big or some kind of inbred cougar that managed to thrive in the urban environment. People had been reporting sightings of it for months before the Crew came in and was able to trap it. But first we had to prove it existed."

"A cougar is still a real animal."

"Yes. But there *are* things in the world we don't know or understand, whether you want to believe it or not. And they're animals, too. People can't turn into something else. No vampires, no zombies, no werewolves. There are monsters, but they're not human."

Not human.

Monica drew herself up and visibly shook herself. "Look, I'm here to do a job, so let me get on with it, okay? What's on the other side of this wall?"

"Bayou."

"I guess that goes without saying," she said. "Dumb question, sorry."

"DiNero put a lot of money into draining his land. Lots of money into landscaping. You wouldn't know there's anything out there besides more grass, I guess." Jordan tried to shrug off her words, but they clung to him, making his skin itch.

"I've never been to Louisiana before, if you can believe it." She gave him a small smile and another of those neutral but somehow assessing looks. She turned back to the wall, then glanced at him over her shoulder. "Can you take me over the wall? I want to see the other side."

Jordan paused. "Yeah. I guess so."

They spent the rest of the day that way. He took her outside the gates and showed her the places that had been compromised. She collected scrapings of the bricks. The soil. The water. She didn't tell him what she was looking for, and Jordan didn't ask. When finally she was satisfied, he brought her back inside. They'd shared scarcely more than a few words, which normally would've been perfect, except that the longer she went without paying attention to him, the more disconcerting he found it. They'd been driving in one of the estate's golf carts, so he pulled up into the small space between their bungalows and waited for her to get out.

What the hell kind of woman seduced a man and then proceeded to ignore him as if they'd never been naked and sweating and...

"Thanks," Monica said.

Jordan shrugged, stone-faced. "It's my job."

"Not everything you did was part of your job," she said. When he didn't answer her, she gave him another enigmatic smile and got out of the golf cart. "See you later."

He watched her go, waiting to see if she'd turn back. She didn't. But he was suddenly so damned hard it hurt to move. It made his hands shake, so he clenched them into fists on his thighs, but the hunger didn't abate. It rose within him, something fierce and unyielding, until all he could think about, all he could do, was get out of the golf cart and force himself to put on a pair of running shorts and go for a run.

Run. And run. And run.

By the time he got back, night had fallen. Golden light welcomed him from the windows of her bungalow, while his were cold and dark. Breathing hard, the coiled snake of hunger still hissing in his belly but low and quieter, Jordan paused to bend over and spit into the grass.

Her door opened. Her silhouette made him groan. She took a step onto the patio and was followed by the waft of something warm and delicious. His stomach growled.

Not human, he thought.

"I made dinner," Monica said. "Come inside."

Chapter 7

She'd begged supplies from the main house, despite the cook's assurances she didn't need to make her own dinner. But Monica liked to cook. It helped her think. While chopping and slicing and sautéing, she could let her mind wander over all the possibilities.

Too bad most of the possibilities had involved going another round with the taciturn and delicious Jordan Leone instead of figuring out what exactly was attacking the menagerie.

There *was* a science to what she did, though you couldn't get most people to believe it. Tracking prints in the dirt or analyzing blood samples or simply calculating what sort of musculature would be needed for something to be able to jump over a wall. What sort of claws could dig through brick, what kind of hide was thick enough to fend off the bite of barbed wire. The Crew kept files. Made reports. She and her peers compared notes. But still, so much of what they did had to be based on speculation. When you couldn't prove something, that was all you could go on.

Vadim had sent her down here thinking she might be looking for a chupacabra. Never mind it wasn't killing goats and it was out of the normal territory associated with that beast—there weren't many things that could do whatever *this* thing was doing. Yet after looking over the pictures of the slaughter and having Jordan take her around the estate, Monica wasn't convinced. She'd been on a couple cases hunting chupacabras before, and while they could certainly cause a lot of damage, there'd never been one she'd seen or heard of that could drag away a full-grown tiger or even a half-sized mountain lion, for that matter.

Which meant this was probably something different. Something they didn't know about, hadn't ever seen. The tingle of anticipation had been with her all day long, and being so close to Jordan all afternoon hadn't helped much.

So, she cooked.

She'd never had jambalaya and wouldn't have dared to try it here in the land where it was considered comfort food, so she'd settled on something she knew without a doubt she could pull off. Nothing fancy, just pasta with a fresh tomato sauce and lots of onions, peppers and garlic. Fresh-grated parmesan. The cook had given her a loaf of sourdough bread, which she'd cut into splits and baked with some more parmesan and olive oil. Adding a salad of mixed greens and lots of extra veggies, she had a complete meal. Enough for two, as a matter of fact, which had been her plan all along.

"You didn't have to do this," Jordan said from her doorway.

"I wanted to." She waved him into the small dining area. A table set for two. The plates were white ceramic, heavy and serviceable and far from romantic...but romance wasn't what she really wanted. Was it?

For a half a minute, she was sure he was going to refuse her, but then he shook his head and moved toward the table. He took a seat. Then he looked at her.

"I should... I was running."

"I saw you." She'd watched him head off and return hours later. Sweating. Panting.

"I should shower first."

"Sure," she said. "If you want to."

He didn't move. Monica smiled and set the bowl of pasta in front of him. Jordan fell on it like a starving beast, scooping a huge portion and digging in without so much as a second look. She served herself, eyeing him casually, though in reality she was taking in his every move.

"Good," he grunted around a mouthful of bread.

"You were hungry, huh?"

Jordan paused. Chewed. Swallowed. He reached for the glass of red wine she'd set out and drained half the glass before answering her. "Yes."

"Good," Monica echoed him and set to eating her own portion. She hadn't been exercising as he had, but she managed to put away a decent amount of pasta before she sat back in her chair to rub her belly.

Jordan had cleared his plate, plus the salad and most of the bread, and was looking hopefully toward the kitchen. "Is there more?"

"Yes. Plenty. Help yourself." Monica watched him

get up. The view from the back was as nice as the one from the front.

He caught her looking when he came back. She didn't pretend to be embarrassed. He frowned, settling into his chair.

"I'm not on the menu," he said. "In case you were hoping for dessert."

Monica burst into laughter. "Oh. Was I that obvious?"

"No, actually, you're not obvious at all." He sat back in his chair and gave her a look so stern it made her sit back, too.

"Erm," she said finally when it was clear that was all he was going to say. "Sorry?"

Jordan swiped at his mouth with a paper napkin and flung it down, then got up to pace a little bit. "I mean, what the hell was last night?"

Before she could answer, not that she had any clue what to say, he'd turned on his heel and stalked over to her. He should've been intimidating—and he was, or he would be if she hadn't faced actual monsters, not just some guy with his boxers in a twist. When he leaned to get in her face, though, she did pull back a little.

"I thought you were in trouble," he snapped.

"So you figured you'd save me?" Monica snapped back. "Well, that's noble and all, but I promise you, I can take care of myself."

"I've seen what that thing can do. You haven't, not firsthand."

She put a hand on his bare chest, no longer sweaty. He'd taste like salt, she thought. And fuck, that made her want to lick him.

"I've seen other things, Jordan. I'm not a shrinking flower—"

His hands gripped her upper arms, tight. She was up and out of the chair before she knew it. She thought he meant to kiss her, and she was already opening her mouth for it, but instead, he shook his head. His dark hair had fallen over his eyes.

"The next thing I know, you've got me fucking you," he said in a low, rumbling voice. "And that's it. Nothing after that. Not a damned word about it, all day long."

"I made you dinner," Monica whispered, torn between being flattered he was so upset and apologetic for so unexpectedly hurting his feelings.

Jordan let her go and stepped back. He was still breathing hard. Light flashed in his eyes. He turned away from her, shoulders hunched. Fists clenched.

"Why are you even here?" he muttered. "It's ridiculous. DiNero has too much fucking money."

That stung. Monica rubbed at her arms where his fingers had left marks. "Look, I know what I do must seem crazy. But really, there are things out there that people refuse to see."

He swung around to look at her, brows furrowed, mouth curled into a sneer. "Sure. Like a goat sucker?"

"Among others. Yes. You work with animals—is it so hard for you to imagine that there are creatures we don't know about?" She put her hands on her hips. "Something came through that wall. Multiple times. Something killed those animals. And something, if we don't figure out what the hell it is, will come back again and again and continue until everything in this zoo is dead, probably including the people. Because it can, Jordan. It simply fucking can."

"Keeping the animals safe is my job. Not yours."

"Yeah, well, DiNero hired me to figure out what it

is, okay? So once I do that, I can tell you what to do to keep them safe. My crew can come in and hunt it down, and if DiNero wants it alive, maybe we can even figure out how to tell you to take care of it. I'm sorry I stepped on your toes, if I did. And I'm sorry about last night… No, fuck that," she amended. "I'm not sorry about last night. I needed you, and you were there. I'm glad you were. Believe it or not, I appreciated it."

"Great. So I did you a favor?" Jordan's scowl twisted further.

She stepped closer to him. He backed up. She took another. This time, he stayed. She'd seen a look like that before. It turned out she'd been developing a habit of wounding men's pride, and that broke her more than anything else had.

Monica closed her eyes for a second. Thinking of Carl. How much she'd loved him and how long it had been since she'd felt that way about anyone. Maybe she never would again.

"I had a nightmare. I was attacked some time ago, and sometimes I dream about it," she said in a low voice.

"Okay." He eyed her warily. "And that's my problem?"

Oh, he was going to make this difficult. "In the dreams, I relive the attack. When I wake up, I can't get out from under it. The only thing that really helps me is to…fuck."

"What kind of attack?"

"I was hiking with my husband," Monica said flatly. "We'd gone into some unknown trails, stupid, I guess, but we thought it would be fun. Isn't that how horror stories always start? We thought it would be fun at the time?"

"I don't like horror stories."

Monica laughed bitterly, then shrugged. "Something came out of the woods. Slashed at him. Knocked me out next, so I didn't see what happened. It dragged him into a cave, where it killed him. It took me next. I woke up next to his body. When it came back, I fought it and killed it."

She said it matter-of-factly, not because the story didn't move her emotionally, but because it was the story she'd told the police and the wildlife officers and everyone else, the same story so many times the words themselves came by rote. It was the only way she could tell that story without breaking down.

Monica rubbed her arms again, this time against the chill of gooseflesh that had risen there. The food in her belly shifted uncomfortably. She couldn't look at him anymore.

"What was it?" Jordan asked.

She shook her head. "They said it was a bear."

"Bullshit," he said.

She did look at him then. Her chin went up. "I don't know what it was. I never figured it out. But I knew it was something, not a bear. It had scales. It could see in the dark. It had claws…"

She shuddered and went silent.

For a moment, neither of them spoke. Then Jordan said quietly, "I'm sorry."

"I'd been studying to become a vet. I decided to focus on figuring out exactly what sorts of thing could have done that to my husband. I'm going to figure out what did this to your animals, too."

"But you still dream about it at night."

She nodded.

Jordan took a step closer. He pulled her into his arms

again, this time more gently. Her face pressed against his hot bare skin, and though he might've grumbled about needing a shower earlier, all Monica breathed in was warm male. She closed her eyes. His hand stroked over her back.

"I'm sorry," she said. "I didn't mean to hurt your feelings."

Jordan, typically, didn't say anything. The steady thump of his heart beneath her cheek skipped a beat or so, though. His arms tightened around her.

After a minute, Monica pushed away. She cleared her throat. Jordan stepped back. They stared at each other.

"I need a shower," he said finally. "But after that, if you want to come over so we can talk about what you think this thing out there is…"

She nodded, hiding a smile. Stiffly, he backed away from her. She waited until he'd gone out the front door before she went after him to watch him cross the small piece of lawn between their bungalows. She could not figure him out. Not at all.

Chapter 8

The glass of red wine he'd downed had lit a fire in him that wasn't going to go out. The whiskey wasn't a good idea, not after last night and the wine and the conversation he'd had with Monica earlier, but then again, Jordan didn't always make the best decisions. He downed one shot before getting in the shower, where his cock got hard as soon as he tried to soap up. He took another when he got out. His hair was still wet and he'd barely put on a fresh pair of jeans and a plain white T-shirt before she was knocking on his front door.

"I brought dessert." She held up one of the cook's chocolate cakes. Jordan knew it by the scent of the icing. "I got it from the main house."

"Looks good. C'mon in." He stepped aside to let her pass. He'd managed to tame his dick, but barely. When she brushed his belly with her arm, he felt it stirring again.

They sat at his dining table. He'd put out a box of cheap chocolate doughnuts and made coffee, though the caffeine was going to do a number on him, as well. All of this was. Shit, he was going to need another run.

She'd brought along her tablet to show him some of the things she'd been working on, and before he knew it, they were side by side on his couch while she ran through lists of what she was putting together. She smelled so good. It had been a mistake to invite her here, Jordan thought. He was too hungry.

"But I don't know." Monica shook her head, then tucked a dark cherry curl behind her ear. She flicked her finger along a line of photos she'd pulled up. There was no denying the edge of excitement in her voice. "None of these things match the patterns. I've run through all the databases, and really, just…nothing."

"You love this, don't you? The unknown."

She looked at him. "Love it? I'm not sure. I've always thought of love as something that makes you happy."

"Me, I've always thought it was something that made you miserable," Jordan answered.

Monica laughed. "How many times have you been in love, Jordan?"

He didn't have an answer. He'd been homeschooled since the age of fourteen, when his parents had yanked him out of public school at the first signs of what they both had prayed would never come true. He hadn't gone to the prom, basketball games. Hadn't played in the band. He'd gone to college too wary of other people to trust anyone enough to fall in love.

"I thought so," she said when he didn't answer. "Sure, love can make you miserable. But it also makes you happy. So happy."

For a second, her gaze went faraway. Unexpectedly, Jordan envied the man who'd married her, the one who'd made her look that way. The one who'd died, he reminded himself.

Monica shrugged off her expression. "Anyway. I have some calls and messages out to some of my colleagues, but at this point, I'm looking at something big. Something strong. Something that lives in the bayou."

"Anaconda? Python? Something like that?" He shook his head. "I know there's a huge problem with that in Florida, but I told you, not so much here."

"Snakes don't have claws."

"Gator?" He laughed at the idea, but Monica looked thoughtful.

"Something like that," she said. "You can laugh all you want, Jordan, but I'm good at what I do, and based on what I've seen and what you told me, I wouldn't put something like a gator off the list."

"Gators can't climb walls."

She smiled. "I said something *like* an alligator. But it's definitely smart enough to figure out how to get through that wall and get what it wants."

He was silent for a moment, thinking. "You really believe all this stuff about things that go bump in the night."

"I believe in things that go bump in the sunlight, too."

He glanced at her to see if she was making a sexy innuendo, but all she gave him was that same blank, assessing look that was starting to make him crazy enough to want to do something to wipe it off her face. He frowned and scooped up another of the chocolate mini doughnuts from the box he'd put out. They were fat coated in fat with another layer of fat on them, but he needed the calories, or else he was definitely going to give Ms. Blackship a surprise she was not going to like.

Her gaze followed the movement of his hand to the box, then to his mouth. Heat filtered through him at the way her eyes lit up, just the barest hint, and the way the tip of her tongue crept out to dimple her top lip.

She caught him looking. "You don't believe in any of this stuff. I know."

Jordan shook his head. "I work with real animals. Real things. You're asking me to believe that some kind of monster is coming out of the bayou and slaughtering them? I'd be more likely to believe some kind of poachers—"

"Except poachers would take the animals alive. If they were going to steal and resell the animals, they'd want them alive. Even if they only wanted the pelts," she added, "they wouldn't slaughter them on-site."

"No," he admitted grudgingly. "I've been thinking about it, and you're right."

She leaned forward a little. "DiNero believes it. That's why he called the Crew."

"Then I guess that's all it matters, huh?" He leaned back.

Monica smiled a little. "Yeah. I guess it does."

They sat in silence for a minute or so that should've been awkward but was only quiet. It had been a long time since he'd sat with a woman this way, without idle chatter and inane small talk, stupid words to cover up the fact both of them were thinking only of how to get in each other's pants with the least amount of effort. He couldn't stop thinking about her flavor.

"Look," Monica said abruptly. "About last night."

"We don't have to talk about it."

"No. We do. I don't want you to think—"

"I don't think anything," Jordan interrupted. "We're both adults. It happened."

Monica shook her head. "But you didn't like it."

"I didn't—" Jordan cut himself off. "What the hell?"

She laughed gently, tipping her face up. "I mean you didn't like that it happened. Not that you didn't like…it."

Jordan scowled. "It was unexpected. That's all."

"It won't happen again."

That did not actually make him feel any better. If anything, the thought that he would never again be inside her tightened a knot in his lower gut. He didn't have words for her, though, just a low grunt.

"I *am* sorry," Monica said. "You were there, and I needed someone."

Jordan gave her a long, steady look. "Gee, way to make a fella feel special."

Monica ducked her head, looking embarrassed for a second, before popping up with the first genuine, full-fledged grin he'd seen on her. It lit her entire face. She was pretty, but that smile, that fucking smile… She was beautiful.

He kissed her.

He could have stopped himself. Years of therapy, of learning self-control, of discipline, of fighting the hunger—he could've done anything but kiss her. She was in his arms the second after that. She opened for him immediately. Her arms went around his neck, her fingers threading through his hair.

He picked her up as easily as he would a bag of feathers. She moaned softly into his mouth. The hum of it sent an arc of electric desire straight to his already rock-hard cock. He settled her on the table and pushed himself between her legs. She moaned again when he pressed his erection against her. She wore a flowing pair of thin batik-printed pants that provided little barrier, but his denim jeans were majorly cock-blocking him.

In seconds, without breaking away from her mouth, he'd yanked open his fly and pressed himself against her again. For a moment, they were at an impasse, but then Monica lifted herself up, fiddled with something at her hip and released a tie he hadn't noticed before. The pants opened somehow in that magic way of women's clothing he'd never understand. She wasn't naked beneath, but a good tug tore her panties away. She cried out, a sharp sound that mimicked pain—except Jordan knew the sound of pain.

He was inside her in the time it took to breathe once, twice. She cried out again, and this time, there was a tinge of true pain in the sound. He wanted to slam deep inside her but eased out, only to have her grab him by the hips and pull him back.

"Look at me," she demanded in a low, urgent voice.

He did and lost himself in her gaze. She took his hand and slid it between them to get his thumb against her clit. She was slick, and his thumb slid easily against her. She bucked and gripped his hips again. Her back arched. Her mouth opened.

"Fuck me," she whispered. Then louder. "Please, fuck me."

The table creaked as they rocked. The hunger built inside him, and the only way to slake it was to take her. Her mouth. The heat between her legs.

"Mine," Jordan heard himself say but as though from far away.

He felt it when she came, her body clutching his and forcing him over the edge into an orgasm so powerful that he saw gold stars flickering around the edges of his vision. He captured her mouth once more, the kiss at first fierce in the last few ripples of his climax, then softening.

In the silence that followed, he heard her breathing shift. He looked into her eyes again, not sure what he expected to see there. Or what he wanted to see.

Monica curled her fingers in the front of his shirt and pulled him to her to brush his lips with hers. "Jordan."

That was all she said. One word, his name, a wealth of meaning in the two syllables, if only he could figure out what it was. Or if he wanted to.

They disengaged. She tidied herself, and he did the same. Neither speaking. She didn't need to ask him where the powder room was, since the layout of their bungalows was the same. By the time she came out, he'd changed into his running clothes.

"Oh," she said.

"I need to go for a run."

"Jordan…"

"What?" he asked roughly.

"What just happened?"

"You ought to know," he told her. "You were there."

"That's not what I mean, and I'm sure you know it."

"What can I say?" he said with a shrug. "I needed someone. You were there."

Chapter 9

Bastard, Monica thought, even though she knew she'd deserved it. Why did she seem to pick only the men who got bent out of shape about what could be pure and simple passion if only they'd let it? She was still bruised and tingling from the ravishment Jordan had so delightfully provided on his dining room table only an hour or so before, but though her body was sated, her mind was anything but. She'd tried to sleep but couldn't, and for once, not because she was afraid of the nightmares.

She'd been watching from the window to catch a glimpse of him coming back, but so far, nothing. Instead, she sat on her uncomfortable couch and made more lists. She'd signed in to the Crew database again to compare what she'd been able to find out with what others had logged in their experiences. So far, not much was making sense. Then again, not much ever did.

Dark had fallen, and with her window cracked, she

could hear the familiar far-off noises of the animals in their habitats and night-active insects. Low-grade anxiety plagued her. A crackle of tension, as though there was an oncoming storm. Or maybe it was simply that she'd been here two days already and hadn't figured out what she was looking for.

Or she was fooling herself, she admitted reluctantly, and her need to pace was directly related to the man who still hadn't come back from his run.

Jordan Leone was trouble. Bad news. Which was probably why she wanted him again, Monica thought with a sigh and a smile so twisted it almost hurt. She rubbed at her face and tried to shake off the lingering feeling of his touch, but all she could think about was the way his mouth tasted.

She wasn't going to accomplish anything this way. No amount of note taking or database studying could help her if she didn't get out there in the field and do her own research. DiNero had hired her for a job, and she meant to do it—because the sooner she found out what had been killing his animals, the sooner she could get out of here and away from Jordan.

She put on a pair of thick khaki work pants with a lot of pockets and her heavy waterproof hiking boots, laced tight over thick socks. Her knife went on her belt, along with several others in different utility pouches. She tucked a notepad and pen sealed inside a plastic waterproof pouch into a pocket. She added a flashlight and a package of matches, both waterproof, and a small wax candle. A couple granola bars and a bottle of water went in another. They weighed her down, especially the water, but she'd spent forty-eight hours in a pitch-black cave, desperate enough to drink just about anything; she never went on any scouting mission without at least a minimum of supplies.

Finally, she pulled her hair into a tight tail at the base of her neck, threw on a baseball cap and shrugged into a denim jacket. She'd be sweating in seconds the moment she stepped outside, but the protection for her arms and upper body would be worth it. She didn't have a map of the menagerie, but DiNero had laid it out to be easily navigated, so it wasn't as if she had to figure out a maze. All she had to do was follow the paths.

She knew how to move quietly, though she wasn't trying to be sneaky. She paused at the first cage she came to, peeking inside at the flashing eyes of the silver fox. It yipped softly at her and came close to the bars of the cage, but Monica didn't reach to pet it. She crooned to it gently, though, watching the fox's ears flick forward and back.

"You're okay, pretty girl," Monica said and moved on.

She wasn't sure what she was looking for, exactly, just that she'd exhausted her resources and needed to come at this from a different angle. She'd worked on a team once that had set a bait trap, something she hesitated to do because it meant sacrificing an innocent living creature. She didn't think DiNero would go for it anyway, at least not with one of his pets. Which meant what, she thought as she walked, waiting for another attack?

Fortifying the walls could work to prevent another slaughter, but it was no guarantee. It also meant they'd never find out what had been doing it, unless the thing showed up someplace else…like a playground, Monica thought with a shudder. Sour bile painted her tongue at the thought of a case where the Crew had successfully managed to chase off a Chimera that had been repeatedly ransacking a poultry-processing plant, only to have the thing show up in the backyard of a nearby day-care center. She hadn't been on that team, but everyone had heard about it. The news had said it was a pit-bull attack.

That was why, she thought as she moved on, people like Jordan didn't believe.

Following the curving brick path, she caught sight of DiNero's house. Lights blazing. The sounds of a party inside. She hadn't been invited, didn't care. She paused, though, to admire the mansion and wonder what it was like to have so much money you could drop a few grand without a second thought. Most of what DiNero was paying her went back to the Crew to fund travel and other expenses, but she got her fair share. It wouldn't buy her a mansion but it was enough, as Carl would've said, to keep her in Cheetos and beer.

For a moment, grief rose in her throat, choking her. Her husband had been full of sayings like that. Most of them had made her laugh, even when his tendency to try to make everything a joke was making her angry. Suddenly, fiercely, but not unexpectedly, she missed him with a deep and wretched longing that would slaughter her faster than any monster ever could—if she succumbed to it.

There, right there, she almost did. She almost went to her knees on the bricks and wept. It was too hard, sometimes, to keep herself from giving in to sorrow. She had ways to manage the terror that came from the dreams that were really memories, but this…oh, this was something else, and nothing could make it pass but time.

Monica did not go to her knees, though she did close her eyes against the burning slide of tears. At the taste of salt, she let out a low, shuddering sigh. She rode the pain for a moment or two before steeling herself and shaking it off.

Carl had died, and nothing could bring him back. The most she could do was honor him by doing her best to prevent more death. And that was exactly what she intended to do here.

Chapter 10

Jordan had lapped the entire perimeter of DiNero's estate, eyes open for any signs of destruction in the wall but finding none. He'd exhausted himself, sweating, panting and finally aching, before he slowed to a walk. The night air was thick and humid, but he sucked it in greedily. No scent of anything weird, just the familiar mingled smells of the animals and, from farther off, dinner coming from DiNero's house. The guy was having another party, which meant that sooner or later Jordan could expect a call to give a tour. DiNero loved showing off his pets.

For now, though, Jordan walked to clear his head and soothe his muscles. He wanted a hot shower and something to eat but didn't dare go back just yet. He'd managed, barely, to fend off the hunger he'd tried to satiate with Monica.

Monica.

Damn, the woman had managed to get under his skin. He'd been stupid, he knew that, but no matter what she said, he *was* only human. Not even his twisted, tangled combination of DNA could make him less than that.

Still, there was shame, instilled in him for as long as he could remember by parents who'd wanted anything but this for their only son. They'd never tried to make him embarrassed about what he'd inherited; if anything, their staunch and devout insistence that he could learn to control his "condition" had been meant to make him feel better about it. But all they'd ever managed to do was repeatedly underline how different he was. How he could try and try, but he would never be the "same."

That made him want to run again, but there was no getting away from the past. He'd learned that long ago. No way to run away from himself. The best he could do was learn to control it, the way his parents had taught him. To keep the hunger at bay.

And still he felt it constantly, always under the surface. Waiting to rise to something as simple as a steak or a beautiful woman or a thousand other things that tempted him to give in to his baser impulses. Not human, Monica had said, but she had no idea.

No matter what happened to him, Jordan thought grimly, he was always a man. Nothing could take that away from him. He wouldn't let it.

For a moment, he leaned against the wall to feel the heat left from the earlier sunshine. It felt good, heat upon heat. It slowed things down. Made him languorous rather than agitated. He let himself press against it, then took a seat in the soft grass DiNero had spent a fortune to grow and maintain. If there was one benefit to his condition, it was that the night bugs left him alone.

If he stayed here a little longer, maybe she'd be asleep by the time he got back. Her windows would be dark. He wouldn't be tempted to go in and see her... Jordan's eyes drifted closed.

"Maybe we'll be okay," his mother said to his father when she thought Jordan couldn't hear. "His birthday was last week. He's fourteen now. Surely if it was going to happen, we'd know about it by now."

Jordan had been sneaking into the kitchen for a late-night snack, his rumbling stomach making it impossible to sleep. Summer, school out, nothing but the possibilities of a whole three months of freedom ahead of him. He had plans with Trent and Delonn tomorrow, video games and a bike ride to the gas station, where they might try to talk to some girls. Maybe. At the sound of his parents' hushed whispers from the back porch, though, he stopped. He hadn't turned on the light, so they had no idea he was there.

"It's going to be all right, bébé," his father said.

Jordan froze. Dad never called Mom that unless they were arguing about something and he was trying to make up to her. Had his parents been fighting? The soft sound of sniffling made his stomach twist. Mom was crying?

"I just want him to be all right, Marc. I'm so worried..."

His father made a shushing sound. "I know. Me, too."

"We should have been more careful." Now his mother sounded fierce, angry. "We knew the risks. We were stupid. Arrogant and reckless!"

"Hush, bébé, don't. You're going to make yourself sick."

"I *am* sick," his mother said. "Sick with worry. Jordan's the one who will pay the price for us being careless... My sweet boy. Oh God, Marc, what will we do if he has it?"

"We'll love him anyway," his father said. "What else could we do?"

The sound of his mother's sobs should've chased away any lingering hunger, but Jordan's stomach only ached more. What were they talking about? If he had what?

Last year, Penny Devereux had been diagnosed with leukemia. She'd had to miss almost the entire school year, and when she'd finally come back, she'd worn a scarf to cover her bald head. She'd been thin and pale, and she still laughed a lot, but she wasn't quite the same.

His parents had gone silent, but Jordan caught a whiff of smoke. That was bad. His mother only lit up when she was superstressed. She'd been trying to quit. Now she was smoking, right there with his dad, who hated it. Something was very wrong.

It didn't stop him from going to the fridge, though. It was as though a phantom hand pulled him, actually, an impulse he couldn't fight. He was so hungry he thought he might faint from it, that and the anxiety from over-hearing what he knew they didn't want him to know.

He'd come down hoping to snag a piece of leftover birthday cake or some of his mom's homemade tapioca pudding, but what his hands pulled from the fridge's bottom shelf was the plastic-wrapped platter of un-cooked burgers his mom had put together for tomor-row's dinner. Without thinking, Jordan tore the plastic off. Handfuls of soft ground beef went in his mouth. He barely chewed, shoving the food past his lips and licking his fingers. He couldn't get enough.

The lights came on. His mother cried out. Jordan turned, as guilty and embarrassed as if she'd walked in on him in the shower or doing what he'd just discovered he could do under the tent of his sheets late at night. No, this was somehow worse, because somehow he knew it was related to what his parents had been saying.

Something was wrong with him.

"Put that down!" his mother cried, but she wasn't angry, as she ought to have been. Fear had widened her eyes. He could hear it in her voice.

He could *smell* it on her.

"Jordan, give me that." Dad was calmer, pushing past Mom, who clung to the doorway and burst into tears.

No. Mine. The thoughts rose unbidden, and though Jordan would never have dreamed of disobeying his father, he backed up still clutching the platter. His mouth hurt. He tasted blood, and not from the meat but from his own gums. He ran his tongue along his teeth and felt the burn and sting of a wound opening—he'd cut it on something sharp.

His own teeth.

Mine.

The thought rose again, but this time, he tossed the platter to the floor. Raw meat splatted on the linoleum, and he backed up with his hands in front of him. There was more pain. He clenched his fists. More cuts, fingernails long, sharp. There was blood.

He would carry the scars on his palms for the rest of his life.

"You're going to be okay, son. It's all going to be all

right," his father said, but the look on his face told Jordan that nothing was going to be all right.

Not ever again.

Jordan woke with a startled gasp, hands in front of him. He'd clenched his fists and winced automatically at the expected sting of his nails pressing his flesh, but the years of self-discipline had worked. He wasn't going to run off into the night and start making mayhem.

Still, he got to his feet with the memory of those long-ago burgers coating the inside of his mouth. He spat, then again, but he could still taste them. He still wanted them. He would always want them, the way he'd always want to run and punch and break and devour.

With a low groan, he closed his eyes and breathed deep. He focused. Not full-on meditation, which he did every day, but still a forced pattern of breaths that was supposed to relax him. A minute passed. He opened his eyes.

At fourteen, everything had changed for him. His parents, recessive carriers of a set of genes that had combined in him to make him different, had never planned to have children. And if he'd been a girl, he'd never have ended up this way, since only males manifested the condition.

Monica had said werewolves did not exist, but Jordan could've told her otherwise.

Chapter 11

Monica had just decided to turn back and head for home when the first muttered cackling reached her ears. DiNero kept a bunch of peacocks that were allowed to roam freely over the estate. They weren't particularly exotic, not compared to the big cats or rare Russian foxes, but they were pretty. And they screamed, Monica discovered when the sound rose.

She didn't think twice but ran toward it, changing direction when another scream came. Her boots pounded the bricks, but then she dodged off the path and ran through the grass, past several habitats and into darkness. There was light from the house in the distance but she had to blink rapidly to try to get her night vision working. It didn't happen fast enough. She tripped over something and went sprawling.

It was a dead peahen, its throat slashed and long runnels carved into its body. Just beyond it lay another, a carcass rather than a bird, most of it missing. Monica rolled with a small groan and pushed up from her hands and knees, already expecting something to rush at her from the darkness.

Instead, she heard another chattering set of screams from the distance. She didn't want to run with her knife in her hands—that was a good way to end up stabbing herself. The best she could do was hope that whatever was killing the birds wouldn't see her before she saw it.

The menagerie hadn't been set up in grids or blocks, so she had to circle around one of the habitats, this one with a tall, domed cage. Inside it, small gray monkeys screamed and chattered. None of them appeared hurt and she couldn't see any breaks in their cage, so she kept going. She was heading for the exterior wall, heart racing, when something hurtled at her out of the darkness.

Something growling. Something with eyes that flashed red and sharp teeth that snapped at the air in front of her, coming so close she felt the breeze of it on her eyelashes. Claws raked her side, pulling the blow at the last second so she could roll away with her shirt flapping in shreds. Pain stung her, but she was still able to get her hands up to push away the thing on top of her.

Too dark here to see more than shadows. All she could do was twist and turn, getting an arm up to keep the snapping jaws from getting at her throat. Monica screamed, anticipating the crunch of teeth on her forearm, but it didn't come. She kicked upward and out, connecting.

The thing, which smelled of grass and dirt, growled but didn't retreat. It fell on top of her again, crushing her into the ground. She felt hair and limbs and another press of teeth, but by then she'd fought her knife free of the belt sheath. No hesitation, Monica slashed upward. Her aim was off, but she still connected. Her knife stuck and she pulled it free. This time, the thing howled and backed off.

She needed light, but back here close to the exterior wall, she was in a giant blind spot. Her head spun from hitting the ground, and bright sparks of pain made everything a blur anyway, but she did see a shape, a head and a half taller than she was. She smelled blood. She slashed again, her grip weaker this time, but the thing smacked her knife from her hand.

Whatever it was hit her in the face, not claws but a curled…fist? A hand? All she knew was the crisp feeling of hair on her face and the solid thunk of flesh on hers. The blow drove Monica to her knees. She rolled, and the next hit her shoulder hard enough to drive her face forward into the ground again.

This time, she didn't get up.

She was in the cave again. Pitch-black. The stink of death. Rattle of bones. Carl was dead; she'd seen him in the last flare of her light before it had been smashed. Her husband was dead, and she would be next, unless she fought.

She fought.

Fists and feet and teeth. Her knife. Slashing. Blood, pain, screaming.

Everything blurred.

She woke up screaming, throat raw. Something held her down and she writhed, fighting it until she realized it was the soft weight of a comforter. She'd been sweating beneath it, wearing only panties and the tank top she'd gone out in earlier. Her hair had come free of the elastic and tangled over her shoulders.

For the first few seconds, Monica still didn't know where she was. Then it came to her—the bungalow at DiNero's menagerie. She'd gone out, then she'd heard something…the peacocks, screaming. She swallowed hard at the thought of the beautiful birds being torn apart.

She'd gone to find out what had happened. Something had attacked her. She had to get up.

She winced and cried out softly when she swung her legs over the edge of the bed. Her head pounded, the back of it tender and swollen where she'd hit the ground. A stinging line on her throat had come from the thing's teeth, she remembered that much. Another set of four slashes on her side hurt, too, but they'd been cleaned and bandaged, so she couldn't see how bad they were. They didn't feel deep enough to be terribly serious, she thought and wondered why on earth she hadn't been torn to ribbons.

The thing had been big and strong and angry, and yet it had not actually tried to kill her. It couldn't have. She'd have been dead if it had. She was certain of it.

As it was, her entire body ached. When she got up and went into the bathroom, her reflection showed a pattern of bruises already gone black. She eased up the tank top to look at the bandages, which had been expertly applied. Gauze and medical tape, not adhesive bandages. The edges glistened with antibiotic ointment. She pulled her shirt back down and turned to go back to the bedroom—and let out a shriek.

She'd punched Jordan twice, first in the nose and then in the throat, before she could stop herself. He stumbled back with a shout, and Monica muttered a stricken apology.

He watched her warily, his eyes watering. She hadn't made him bleed—at least there was that. She might've laughed at the look on his face if everything didn't hurt so bad and if she weren't so freaked out by what had happened. That and the dream. Always the dream.

A strangled sob had forced itself out of her throat before she could stop it. She found herself pressed against him, though if she'd reached for him or he'd pulled her close, she didn't know. What she did know was that his hand stroking her hair felt good, as did his arms around her. Even the pressure of his body on her aching bruises lessened the pain.

When he picked her up and carried her to the bed, she expected him to lay her down, but instead Jordan sat on the edge of it and held her on his lap. Monica was no small woman and had never been fond of being made to feel delicate, but something in the way he cradled her only made her bury her face against the side of his neck.

"How did I get back here?" she asked against his skin.

Jordan hesitated before answering. "I found you. What the hell were you doing out there by yourself?"

She bristled at his tone, but when she tried to pull away, he held her close. "You're hurting me."

"Sorry." He loosed his grip, but not enough to let her go. "You're going to be sore for a while."

"No shit," Monica said. "Something attacked me."

"You shouldn't have been out there alone," Jordan said.

"I can take care of myself," she snapped.

Jordan slid his hand to the back of her neck and buried his fingers in her hair, tipping her head back hard enough to make her gasp—and yes, it made her body ache, but that wasn't why. His eyes narrowed.

"Obviously, you can't," he said in a low voice.

Monica didn't try to struggle. Part of her knew he was right. Her role here had never been to hunt down the creature on her own, but to determine what it was so the Crew could come in and work together on it. Still, she pushed at his chest, though she couldn't get away from him.

"I was out walking, trying to think. Then I heard the peacocks screaming," Monica said. "What did you expect me to do? Not try to see what it was?"

His mouth was very close to hers, though how it had happened, exactly, she couldn't say. He was going to kiss her, and yes, she was going to let him. Because that was what took away the pain and the fear, and because in his arms she could forget that she'd gone up against something that might've killed her, and this time, despite how hard she'd fought, she had not killed it. Something had saved her, and it had not been herself.

She couldn't think of it. And he wasn't kissing her, so she pulled his mouth down to hers. She gave him her tongue. At his soft groan, Monica pressed herself against him, writhing and ignoring the pain.

He pinned her wrists suddenly and held her away from him. "Monica. Don't. You don't really want this."

"Want? Maybe not," she said. "*Need*, Jordan."

And she did need it. Needed to fuck away the memories and the pain and the fear, the anxiety. She shifted, twisting, to straddle him. He still held her wrists, keeping her from pushing against his chest, but that didn't stop her from grinding her crotch down on his.

"I don't want to hurt you," Jordan said.

Monica slowed but didn't stop the steady rocking of her hips against his hardening cock. "I can handle it."

She leaned to flick her tongue along his lower lip. He didn't release his grip on her wrists, but he did soften. Then he pulled her toward him. He kissed her, hard, until she gasped.

"I'll hurt you," Jordan said into her ear, then slid his teeth along her throat.

His tongue stung the cut there, and she hissed. He gave a low growl and nipped her. Monica jerked, the pain so mingled with pleasure she couldn't be sure which she felt more of.

She shoved him back onto the bed. Still kissing him, she pushed up his shirt, ran her hands up his sides. He jerked when she did, and that was when her fingers encountered the soft padding of gauze bandages.

Head spinning, confused, Monica sat back. "Jordan? What...?"

Oh God. Oh my God. She tried to stumble back, to get off him, but he'd again grabbed her tight. Panic flooded her.

The smell of grass and dirt, the flash of red...the same as she'd seen in his eyes. She'd used her knife against the thing that had attacked her, and now here he was with wounds in the same place... She fought him, but held her tight. His breath covered her face, and she closed her eyes instinctively, waiting for the press and sting of teeth, this time slashing her throat open instead of nibbling.

"Monica, look at me."

"What the hell are you doing?" she cried. "What are you?"

He let her go so fast she fell back, but they were still

tangled together, so she had to fight her way free of him. Panting, dizzy, she backed up from the bed, trying to think about what she could use to defend herself against him, but all Jordan did was sit there.

"What are you?" she asked again in a low, strangled voice.

Jordan shook his head, shaggy dark hair falling over his eyes for a moment before he gave her a grim look. "Why don't you tell me?"

He'd seen the looks before. Disgust, fear. His parents had tried to shield him from most of it, but that hadn't been much better. Isolated from friends and even family, Jordan's high school years had been lonely and full of self-doubt. It had taken him years to learn how to keep the hungers at bay—for food, for sex, for violence. But he had, and damn it, he didn't deserve to be treated like some kind of serial killer for something he couldn't control.

"I don't know," Monica said in answer to his question.

He thought she meant to bolt, but for now she was staying still. Fists clenched. Every muscle tense. He could smell her anxiety, and it made his stomach hurt.

"No?" he asked, deliberately snide. "Here I thought that was your job."

Her eyes had been wide, but now they narrowed. "Are you the one...?"

"No!" Angry that she'd even think it for a second, Jordan got off the bed. It stung to see how she moved away from him, so wary. Her gaze flicked to the knife he'd laid on her dresser.

He was on her before she got even two steps toward it. He could've hurt her if he'd tried, but he wasn't trying. She didn't struggle. She looked up at him instead.

"You attacked me," she said.

"I didn't know it was you. It was a mistake." The excuse sounded lame, but it was the truth. "I heard the peacocks screaming, the same as you. I thought I could find what was killing the animals. I thought I could…"

"Kill it? With your bare hands?" Beneath his fingers, Monica's arms stiffened, and he let her go. She stepped back from him, but only a step.

Jordan's fingers curled, the tips pressing the faded scars on his palms. "I could've tried."

"This is crazy. It's crazy," she repeated and continued almost as though she were talking to herself, "People don't become things. It doesn't happen. Lycanthropy is a mental disorder, sure, but it's not…real. You can't really be…"

"I'm real," Jordan said flatly and pushed past her toward the door, where he paused to look back at her. "I've got a fucked-up genetic disorder that makes it hard for me to control my impulses. It forces physical changes, and most of the time, I can stop them, but sometimes I can't. Sometimes I don't want to, like last night, when I was thinking I could finally get whatever's killing the animals. But I am real, Monica."

She shook her head. "I don't… I can't…"

That was it. He'd had it. This woman had blown into his life like a fucking hurricane. He'd never asked for it.

"Fuck this noise," Jordan said. "All I ever wanted was to do my job and be left alone. You can believe in monsters, but you can't believe in me?"

He didn't realize how much he'd wanted her to answer him until she didn't, but all she gave him was her silence. His fingers curled again, pressing old wounds before he could force them to open. Then without another word, Jordan left her there alone.

Chapter 12

"It's reptile, we're pretty sure of that." Ted pushed his glasses up on his nose and waved expansively. "Based on the blood samples you gave us and some of those markings, I compared it with a case Boris and I were on last year in Miami. Rangers had found a bunch of gators slaughtered, figured poachers, of course, but we hunted what turned out to be a monstrous fucking... Hell, it was a dinosaur, I'm telling you."

Monica couldn't sit still. She had Ted and Vadim in her bungalow, both of them chowing down on the deli platters DiNero's cook had sent down, but she couldn't take even a bite. Not with Jordan mere steps away in the next bungalow.

You can believe in monsters, but you can't believe in me.

"You're sure it's reptilian?" she asked finally. "It couldn't possibly be something else? Something we haven't seen before?"

Vadim looked up from the sandwich he'd been piling high with meat and cheese. "What is this? You have something, Monica?"

She opened her mouth to spill it all, but at the last moment, her jaw shut with a snap of her teeth so hard on her tongue that tears sparked in her eyes. Secrets tasted like blood, she thought. She poured herself a glass of DiNero's whiskey and sipped it, relishing the burn.

Ted shoveled a handful of chips into his mouth and kept talking. Monica liked Ted a lot, but right now with him misdirecting Vadim's attention from her, she kind of loved him. She pretended she hadn't heard Vadim ask her anything at all.

"The patterns are almost identical," Ted said. "It could be something else, I guess, but I think we should go in armed for dino."

"What happened to the one you went after in Miami?" Monica asked.

Ted sighed. "It went down in the swamp, sank like a stone. Gators were on it before we could even get close enough to try to net it or anything. But it only took a couple shotgun blasts. Thing looked like a raptor of some kind. It wasn't much bigger than a gator—I mean, I've seen ones that were a lot bigger. But it stood on hind legs and worked with its front ones. Definitely smart enough to work at a lock. I could've kicked myself for not trying to tranq it, but when something with teeth the size of your fist is coming at you…"

"That's the nature of our work," Vadim put in. "If it were easy to prove what we find, we'd be out of our jobs, eh?"

He gave Monica a long, steady look that she had to pretend she didn't notice. Everything in her world had turned upside down. She couldn't stop turning it over and over in her head. Jordan, his touch, the sound of his voice, the way he'd made her feel.

There'd been more than a few men after Carl. She'd lost herself in physical sensation to keep herself from feeling anything else, and it had worked, in the short-term. But Jordan had been the only man so far who'd entirely chased away the remnants of the memories, left nothing lingering behind.

Sex was only sex, though.

"Monica?"

She tore herself away from memories of Jordan's hands on her and faced Vadim. He'd been there for her, too, in many other ways that had saved her. He and the entire Crew had believed her when nobody else did. They'd helped her find a purpose to her life. Their work, their passion, was hunting myths, and here was one practically right in front of them. She could offer up living, breathing proof of something Vadim had told her wasn't possible. But what would he do with that knowledge?

Would he hunt Jordan?

Chapter 13

"They're going after it," DiNero said, no mistaking the excitement in his voice. Like a kid on Christmas Eve. He knuckled Jordan's arm, then punched the air and did a little shuffle. "C'mon, man, this is awesome!"

Jordan bent back to the silver fox, who'd been cowering in the corner, frightened by DiNero's antics. "Shh, little girl. Hey. Calm down, okay? You're scaring her."

DiNero looked chastened. "You're putting her in with the others now?"

"Yeah." Jordan lifted the fox, who nestled into his armpit, hiding her face. "I think she'll be all right there."

DiNero couldn't have cared less about the fox. He was all about the thing Monica's team was here to hunt. He'd ordered Jordan to start construction on a new habitat—never mind they had no clue what the thing needed to survive, much less if they could even capture it alive. It was a bad idea, all around—that was what Jordan thought, but DiNero hadn't asked him his opinion.

Jordan hadn't seen Monica in three days. Not since the night she'd figured out he was something other than what she'd thought he was. He kept waiting for the Crew to show up on his doorstep with lit torches and a silver bullet. Not that it needed to be silver to kill him, he thought grimly. A regular bullet would do it.

Leaving DiNero behind, Jordan took the silver fox to her new habitat. There he sat with her for a while as the others, a sweet red fox and another couple of silvers, sniffed them both carefully. All of the foxes in DiNero's collection had come to the menagerie tamed and socialized, but that didn't mean they couldn't reject a newcomer. Jordan sat quietly while the foxes checked out the new girl. He'd brought treats. He relaxed, not wanting to transmit any anxiety toward them. Eventually, the red one came over to investigate again, and he scratched it behind the ears.

"Does he have a name?"

Jordan didn't turn at Monica's quiet question. "DiNero doesn't name them. I just call him Red."

"Of course. Can I come in?"

He shrugged. When she sat next to him, he didn't turn to face her. The silver fox had ventured off his lap, and at Monica's entrance, the others ran away, too. She didn't say anything at first.

"Are you going to tell them about me? Your crew. Am I going to show up in your database?"

She made a soft noise. "No. I don't know."

"DiNero thinks he's going to keep this gator thing you're hunting."

"Ted would be happy not to kill it if it means he gets to study it," she answered.

Jordan looked at her. "It killed a tiger and mountain lions. You really think you're going to take it alive?"

"No. I don't know that, either," she added. "Maybe. I haven't been able to think much about it."

He studied her, thinking he wouldn't ask her why, but the words came out anyway. "Is that so?"

When she moved toward him, he didn't recoil. Something in his expression must've told her how he felt, though, because she sat back. She looked tired.

"I'm sorry if you thought I was cruel, Jordan."

"About what? About using me to get over some kind of trauma, or about reminding me my life's a fucking mess, or what?" He tossed a treat toward the new silver fox, who took it with a small yip.

"About everything. I did use you, and I'm sorry. And I do believe in…you."

He looked at her. "Sure. Like you do in Bigfoot."

"No. Like I believe in you. A man who cares very much for those he's vowed to protect." She tipped her chin toward the foxes. She touched her side, briefly, where he'd slashed her. Her gaze met his, frank and open.

"I didn't mean to do that," he said in a low voice.

"I know you didn't. But I did mean to do it to you."

"You were fighting for your life, or you thought you were. I could've hurt you really bad. I could've…" He swallowed, hard. "I could've killed you."

"But you didn't."

He shook his head. "I'm not an animal. I do know what I'm doing. Even when the hunger gets too big."

"Do you actually change? I mean…"

"Do I turn into a wolf?"

She looked a little embarrassed. "Yeah."

"No. Not like in the movies. My teeth are sharp. My nails grow fast. If I don't shave twice a day, I'm a fucking lumberjack by midafternoon. I'm strong all the time. Adrenaline spikes it. Certain things trigger me. And then it can be hard not to just—" he shrugged "—rampage. Gorge and destroy and fuck."

She made a small noise. He looked at her. She bit her lower lip as though struggling for words.

"I work with myths and mysteries," she told him. "It's in my nature to want to know more."

Jordan looked at the foxes playing. Not at her. "I'm not the only one, you know. It's a family thing. My parents were both recessive carriers. It's a nasty secret we keep. You want me to spill out everything about myself? About my family? I hardly know you."

"I know that." Her soft intake of breath told him his words had hurt her, but he forced himself not to care.

"Just because I fucked you doesn't mean I owe you any damned thing." Jordan got to his feet.

That was when all hell broke loose.

Chapter 14

Ted and Vadim had set a trap and caught themselves a dinogator. Six feet long on its hind legs, talons like razors, teeth sharper than that. A hide so thick handgun bullets bounced off it, but Ted had come prepared with tranquilizers this time, and a dart to the underbelly had felled the creature. DiNero was out of a prize, though, because much like in Miami, the moment the thing went down, it was surrounded by gators that swarmed to devour it.

"Nature's way of cleaning up her messes," Ted said morosely to Monica as he and Vadim packed up their van. "I've never seen alligators act like that."

"Pheromones. Something like that. Put them in a frenzy. Hell if I know." Vadim shrugged and shook his head. "But where there's two, there must be more. You'll get another chance, Ted."

DiNero had been disappointed, of course, but it

seemed he was consoling himself with moving forward on purchasing an elephant instead. Monica didn't think that was the smartest decision the man could've made with his money, but it was probably better than trying to keep some swamp monster in captivity. The upward bump in her bank-account balance was all she really cared about anyway.

Well, that and something else.

"You're sure you don't want to ride back with us?" Vadim gave her a curious look as he shut the van's back doors. "Road trips can be fun, eh?"

Ted waggled his brows. "I have a great playlist. And I convinced Vadim to spring for three-star motels this time around. Not just two."

"Wow, the offer is so tempting." She laughed. "I think I'll stick with my original plans, though. I've never been to New Orleans. While I'm down here, I thought I'd like to check it out. Drink a hurricane or two. Tour a cemetery."

"Suit yourself." Vadim shrugged. "Don't get suckered into a ghost tour."

Monica snorted soft laughter. "Like I can't do one of those for free just about anytime I want?"

Ted got into the van, and Vadim pulled her closer for an unexpected embrace. Even more surprisingly, she didn't merely allow him the hug but returned it. Pressed to the big man's chest, Monica closed her eyes. She didn't want to cry, but damn if she didn't feel close to tears.

"Sometimes this job can be very hard," Vadim said into her ear. Monica nodded against him. He squeezed her gently. "But remember, we don't fear the unknown. We make it ours. Yes?"

She pushed away to look at him. "Cryptic."

He grinned. "There's more to life than hunting things in the swamps, Monica. But you sometimes have to be as fearless in seeking out life as you are about looking for the chupacabra."

Vadim squeezed her again before stepping back. From inside the van came a loud thumping bass beat. He sighed and shook his head.

"Are you sure I can't convince you to come with us?"

"I'm good." Monica eyed the van. "Especially if that's Ted's playlist."

Waving, she watched them drive off, then headed for the bungalow to pack up her things. A rap on the door had her heart racing; she tried not to act disappointed when she opened it to find DiNero, not Jordan. DiNero didn't seem to notice. He bustled in with the same high energy he'd had the whole time.

"He ran off!"

"We told you there was no guarantee we could catch it alive," Monica began, but DiNero stopped her with a look. "Who?"

"Leone. He took leave. He didn't even give me notice—he just said he's off to his place in New Orleans for a few weeks. He left Karen in charge, but I have a group of guests coming to stay next week, and damn it, I need Jordan here. Nobody can show off my animals the way he can."

Monica frowned. "He...left?"

"Yeah, said he needed a vacation." DiNero shook his head. "I think it's because he doesn't want me to get the elephant."

"Maybe." She paused, wondering if she ought to offer him something to drink. It was his own booze, after all. DiNero put his hands on his hips, staring at her. She tried to think of what to say. "Um…"

"Well, it's a clusterfuck, that's all. I need someone who can really handle the animals. I mean if they're sick or whatever."

"Hasn't he gone on vacation before?"

"Yeah, but I…" DiNero looked her over. "He always gave me notice, and I brought in another handler until he came back. And he was only ever gone a few days before. Shit, what will I do if he doesn't come back?"

Monica didn't have a lot of patience for people who worked themselves into a lather for no real reason, but now all she could do was shake her head. "He'll come back. Why wouldn't he? He loves his job here. He loves working with the animals. He's…happy here."

She wasn't sure if that was true, actually. He'd seemed content enough, here out of the way. What had he said to her? All he wanted was to do his job and be left alone.

Shit.

She'd chased him away, she was sure of it. "Where did you say he went, exactly?"

"He has some place in New Orleans that he keeps. I don't know exactly where." DiNero sighed. "And you're heading out, too? Great."

"My job's done. You don't need me here."

DiNero gave her a long, assessing look that left him about three seconds away from getting a knee to the nuts. "Now that you're off the clock, so to speak…"

"Don't even." Monica shook her head and put up a hand. "Do not."

DiNero grinned. "Worth a shot, huh? Can't blame a guy for trying. I mean, I know I'm no Leone, but I have a lot going for me other than brooding good looks and sex appeal."

"I'm sure you do, but what makes you think I'm even interested in him?" Monica crossed her arms.

"Shit, girl, you almost set the bayou on fire every time you looked at each other. You think I didn't notice?" DiNero shook his head and shot her a grin. "I've never seen that man give anything that much attention in all the years he's worked here, including every animal I've ever owned."

She frowned. "That's just…"

"He's got a place near Bourbon Street," DiNero told her. "And I'd like him to come back. It's worth another donation to your vacation fund if you can convince him."

"I don't hunt people," Monica said flatly. "If he wants to come back, he will."

DiNero held up his hands, looking apologetic. "Fine, fine. Again, can't blame a guy for asking. I guess I'll just have to beg him myself."

"No," Monica said. "You know what… I'll see what I can do."

Chapter 15

Long days. Long nights. Booze and women and the rich copper taste of rare steaks.

Jordan had glutted himself on all of it. Sex and meat and all the things he tried so hard to deny himself because giving in to the hunger only made it that much harder to deny it the next time. He'd smashed the mirror in the bathroom, and now he took slow, lingering satisfaction in the way the glass glittered on the floor because he hadn't cleaned it up.

There were other things he could've done, too. Crashed a car. Robbed a bank. Gotten in a fistfight with a motorcycle gang. The possibilities for mayhem were endless and alluring, and fuck it all, if he hadn't had any sense of conscience, he'd have done all of it. Run wild in the streets, howling at the moon.

Instead, he wallowed in his small sins, all he allowed himself to indulge in. Tonight it was a glass of very expensive wine and a steak the size of his head, with all the trimmings. Later, he thought, he would find himself a woman or two or three and spend the night's last hours reveling in naked flesh.

Except there was already a woman on his doorstep when he got home.

He knew her at once by her scent, and his lip curled. His dick got hard, too, immediately, and he hated himself for that. And her a little, too.

"How long have you been here?" he asked.

She shrugged. "A few hours. Where were you?"

"Eating an enormous dinner. Drinking too much. How'd you find me?"

Monica stood when he came closer. She seemed to have been waiting a long time. She stretched, and fuck if watching her body move didn't make him want to take her right there against his front door.

"I hunt down mythical beasts for a living," she said. "You have an address and a credit-card statement and utility bills. You were easy to find."

"What do you want?" He was a little drunk, not so much from the wine and the food but from seeing her again. Smelling her. He wanted to taste her with a real and physical longing.

"You," she said simply.

Jordan heard his own low rumble in answer. She would think he was an animal for sure at that sound, he thought, but he couldn't take it back now. Monica took a step closer.

"You," she whispered again, offering her mouth.

He wasn't going to kiss her. But there she was, soft and curvy, and that hair, that fucking hair spilling down her back and over his hands, and then she was in his arms and her mouth was on his and his knee pressed between her thighs, and in another second or so, he could be inside her, if he only…let…go.

"No," Jordan muttered without moving away from her.

Monica pressed herself against him. "Take me inside. Fuck me. Then feed me. Then we'll talk."

It was the finest offer he'd ever had, but he hadn't spent so many years learning to control himself to give in now, just like that. "What the hell do you want, Monica?"

She linked her fingers behind his neck. "I can't stop thinking about you. I still dream, Jordan. And when I wake up, I reach for you. Not just anyone. You. I don't know why."

He reached behind her to unlock the door and push them both inside. He had a moment to feel ashamed of how he'd let the place get filthy. Maybe she wouldn't notice in the dark.

"I'm not just a curiosity," he told her. "What do you want to do, study me? Put me in a collection the way DiNero does with his pets?"

She shook her head, following him into the small kitchen, where he poured them each a drink. "No. If I wanted to do that, I'd have told Vadim about you."

"You didn't?"

"No. You're not a freak or a curiosity. But I do want to learn more about you. Not just how you are in bed, which is very, very good, by the way." She leaned to kiss him again, but briefly. "Jordan…you're special."

"Sure I am."

She put her hands on his hips and pulled him closer to her. "Maybe it's just sex. Maybe it's only that. Or maybe it's something else. I'm willing to see if there's more to us than that. The best you can do is try."

He backed her up against the kitchen counter but stopped himself from putting her on top of it and ripping her panties off, pushing up her skirt. Sinking into her heat. He shivered from the thought of it. Made a low noise.

"DiNero sent me here to find you. See if you'd come back." Monica hopped up on the counter and drew him between her legs. "I told him I'd see what I could do."

"So that's why you're really here." He slid a hand between them, his thumb rubbing her through her panties. This time, she was the one who made the noise.

Her back arched a little. Her voice became raspy. "I know you love working there. Maybe not the guy himself, but the job? You love it. Don't let me take that from you."

"You think you could take anything from me?" He bent to nip at her neck, angry in a way but also so turned on he could barely think straight.

When she took his face in her hands and held him still so she could look in his eyes, the entire world shifted. "I don't know about taking, but I'm hoping you'll let me try to give you something."

His throat dried. "What's that?"

"Me," she whispered and kissed him again. "It's really all I have."

There was no holding back then. Her skirt went to her waist, her panties torn free. He was deep inside her right after that, and her nails raked his back through his shirt. They fucked hard and fast, rattling the cupboard doors. Her body clenched around his, sending him over the edge, and she cried out his name.

Breathing hard, Jordan blinked, a realization flooding through him. He shook his head, not sure what to think. What to do.

"What?" Monica asked him.

"It's… I'm not…hungry. Anymore."

She gave him a curious look, then one of understanding. She pulled his mouth to hers again, her hand cupping his chin to hold him there for the kiss. Her other went behind his neck.

"I understand," she told him. "You feed me, too."

Later, after a shower and cleaning up the glass and another meal, this time of fresh pasta and salad and bread, they sat at the table together. She'd been quiet, mostly, and that was fine with him. He was still trying to think about where this was going, or what it meant. She'd made him an offer. Just try, she'd said. But could he?

"I didn't think you'd want this," Monica said, indicating the plates in front of them.

He looked at her. She wasn't meeting his gaze, and he thought he knew why. "No?"

"You said you'd had a big dinner. I didn't think you'd want to eat again," she said.

He waited for her to look at him, and when she did, he took her hand and pulled her onto his lap. "There's something you should know about me, Monica. Something that might make a difference in what you asked me."

She looked solemn, slightly frowning. "Okay."

He kissed her hard enough to make her gasp. "Even if I'm not hungry, I can always eat."

It took her a second or two before the light of understanding filled her gaze, but when it did, she laughed.

She kissed him, softer than he'd done. She nuzzled his neck, making him shiver.

"So let me feed you," she told him. "And we'll see how the rest of it goes."

* * * * *

DARK DREAMS

Megan Hart

Chapter 1

Stephanie Adams wasn't going to wake up.

Not if she could help it anyway, even with the low bleat of her phone alarm begging for her attention. It would get louder. There'd be another. She'd set a total of six alarms on her phone, each progressively closer together. She also had an additional four alarm clocks, the old-fashioned windup kind, set to sound at similar intervals. One of them had been designed for hearing-impaired users and featured a blaring white light that was supposed to sear her eyeballs into opening.

She was *not* going to wake up.

Not now, not so close to this, the end of things, and surely it had to be the end, didn't it? Almost six months of work, she'd come so close, and now she was finally going to find him. Crouching low on the dark and shifting carpet of pine needles that were part of her anchoring spot, Stephanie curled her fingers in the prickly coolness. She breathed in, out, each breath a conscious effort because here in the Ephemeros, she didn't really need to breathe. She sipped at the air instead.

She could smell him. She didn't know his name. Hadn't seen his face. All she had was the softly drifting scent of him, not a cologne or a soap or any sort of perfume. It was the tang of sweat and blood and dirt; it was something else all tangled up with that and woven into a tapestry of sight and sound, left behind every time she'd managed to get close.

Everything worked together here in the dream world. Tasting sounds, seeing smells. That sort of thing. For the lucky ones who could control what happened to them and around them, too, the dream world was a playground. For those who couldn't, it could sometimes be less fun.

"Where are you?" Stephanie murmured as she let her fingers draw patterns in the gritty soil before she stood to dust off her palms on the seat of her leather trousers. Leather—she'd have laughed at herself if she weren't concentrating so hard on staying here instead of being pulled into consciousness. In the waking world, Stephanie would no more have worn leather than she would've slapped a baby. "Come out, come out, wherever you are."

The buzz of her alarm threatened to pull her from the dream world, but she forced herself to stay here. Damn it, why had she come so close to catching this creep now, when she'd had to schedule an early meeting that couldn't be missed? It was the only reason she'd set the alarms in the first place, so she'd be sure not to oversleep.

She'd spent months tracking the shaper who'd been

wreaking havoc, using information he'd gleaned here
from unwitting shapers in the Ephemeros to empty their
bank accounts and run up credit-card debt in the real
world. Of all the cases she'd worked, it was far from the
worst or most dangerous trick a power-hungry shaper
had pulled, but Vadim had been adamant that this was
a problem for the Crew to solve. You couldn't have
people taking advantage of what they could do in the
dream world. It messed with the balance of things in a
way Stephanie would never pretend to be philosophi-
cal enough to understand.

Again the alarm pulled at her awareness, but she
fought off waking. Here in her anchoring spot, where
she was strongest, she was able to hold on to her dream
self a lot longer, but even so, the edges of the world had
started rippling. Stephanie had spent too many hours
asleep and dreaming when she could've been living to
let go of this now. She had to find him and stop him,
before he caused any more trouble.

She sent out a small push of energy to reshape the
landscape around her. Out of her forest, into what she
thought of as the dark desert. Ringed by black mountains, the sky permanently the color of tar, this space
was as close to emptiness as she could manage to
shape without losing herself in the void. Just beyond
the mountains, which would always be miles out of
reach no matter how fast she ran toward them, blue-
white lightning sliced apart the sky. Once, she'd seen
a face peering through the cut in the atmosphere. Big
fingers, pulling apart the edges. Fathomless eyes. Just
the once, but that had been enough, because she'd never
been able to convince herself she had not glimpsed the
face of some god.

Now Stephanie pushed again, a nudge, sending out small tendrils of her will to draw the rogue shaper closer to her. Like a flower tempting a bee, she thought as the next steady, blaring throb of an alarm began pounding her ears. *Come closer*, she thought. *Come and find me.*

She'd flown in this world. Leaped high and floated down. She'd sunk to the bottoms of oceans without fear of drowning. She hadn't faced much in the Ephemeros that scared her, and yet her heart now beat faster as at last she felt the answering push-pull of the other shaper. Anticipation, not fear, though she clenched her fingers into a fist and straightened her back, squaring her shoulders. Ready to fight.

The dreamers who'd faced him in their nightmares had described him as various entities. Vampire, werewolf, dark wizard. He'd played upon their fears to wrangle their personal data, which he'd then used in the real world to access their bank accounts, credit cards. Identity theft, and nearly untraceable because he hadn't actually hacked into anything. He simply forced them to give him what he wanted to use, and in the dreams, they did.

"Come here," Stephanie whispered again. She shaped a park bench. A stone path. A tree. She sent out small and seeking threads of her will and felt the Ephemeros respond around her.

And then…there he was.

A shadow. Tall, lean, but unmistakably male. No features that she could make out, but he wore an outfit that looked similar to hers. Leather pants, jacket with a flare at the tail, or maybe it was a shirt with a vest. Hard to tell against the black of the mountains behind him.

Stephanie straightened. "Come here."

"Who are you?" The voice, low and raspy and rumbly, sent a vibration straight to the core of her stomach and then upward to the pit of her throat, making her feel sort of sick.

He wasn't trying to push her or even to shape anything around them. Stephanie let her forefinger make a small circle, sending a spiral of sand spinning into a dust devil that danced toward him but fell apart before it made it even halfway. The other shaper, the one they'd been calling Mr. Slick, didn't even move.

So, he wasn't threatened by her. Okay, then. Well, she'd faced worse than some dude with a boner for charging up other people's credit cards to keep himself living in style. She'd faced shapers who killed the sleepers they attacked in dreams. This guy was going to be a piece of cake.

Chocolate cake, thick with fudge frosting, a cherry on the top, ice cream nestled in the layers, whipped cream, candy, French fries, no, soft pretzels, pretzel sticks dipped into the sweetness, salt and sweet, and oh my God, she was so hungry, what was this in front of her, a plate, a tray, a trough, and Stephanie was going to dive face-first into the decadence and eat and eat and eat and…

White light blasted her eyelids, painting them with a reverse sort of lightning. She woke with a start and a low cry, her hands moving to shove her mouth full of all that delicious food, which of course was not really there. She sat up in bed, the blankets tangled at her waist, and let out a muttered curse.

"Bastard," she said. "What a dirty trick."

Then she let out a long series of sputtering laughs, because damn. How had he known exactly how to push her so she wouldn't know she was being pushed? That hadn't happened to her in a long, long time.

Sitting up, she swung her legs over the bed with a small groan. Then, scrubbing at her face and yawning, she stretched. Her phone rang and she glanced at it, thinking she wouldn't answer, but it was Vadim.

"Hey, boss."

"Terry says there were ripples last night. Are you just getting up?"

Terry was working a case in which the shaper was killing sleepers in the dream world. It didn't always kill them in the real world, though it caused comas, heart attacks and strokes. If there were ripples, Terry would be sensing them, for sure. But Stephanie's case wasn't nearly as serious—it was important, as they all were, but it wasn't going to kill anyone.

"I got close. Saw him. Spoke with about six potential victims who said they'd been approached by, in turn, a scary clown, a ventriloquist dummy, a shark, a vampire, and two said it was their ex-wives." She laughed through another yawn. "Funny what really scares people."

"Did they give up their information?"

"The frightened husbands did." She chuckled again. "I'll add it to the data sheet. I have a meeting with Kent this morning. I have to get going."

They signed off. Stephanie scribbled down the information she could recall from her dream. She'd have to tell Kent she'd gathered this data from "sources" and let him think it was something to do with computer searches and stuff, but that was the nature of her job. It wasn't as if she could stroll into his office and tell him she'd met these people in a dream, after all. He'd think she was nuts.

Chapter 2

Kent Gordon woke with a start, just before the sound of his alarm. He rolled with a groan to turn it off, then buried his face in the pillows. He did not want to get up. He wanted to stay in bed all day long.

Wallowing.

In the bed that had been theirs? With another groan, he swung his legs over the side of the bed and got himself moving. Carol had been gone only a week, not even long enough for the scent of her to vanish from the sheets, although he'd washed them. Twice.

In the shower, Kent bent his head beneath the spray and let the hot water pound away at the knots in his shoulders. In the kitchen, he made himself a cup of terrible instant coffee because Carol had always been the one to get the first pot brewing. He grabbed a frozen egg sandwich, nuked it and burned his tongue.

"Shit!" He spit the mess into the sink and stayed there

for a long moment with both hands on the stainless steel, head bowed. Waiting to…

What? Grieve? Mourn? Celebrate?

Whatever he was supposed to feel about the end of his four-year relationship, he wasn't feeling any of it. All Carol's leaving had done was point out to him how empty he'd been for a long time, and probably how empty he was going to stay for a lot longer.

It was not the best way to start the day, that was for sure, but a glance at his calendar when he got into work made it a little better. He had an appointment with Stephanie in about twenty minutes. Just enough time to grab a cup of marginally better coffee and a stale doughnut from the break room before getting back to his desk and pretending as if he wasn't just waiting for her to walk through his door.

He'd been working, on and off, with Stephanie Adams for the past six months. She was one of the investigators on the fraud cases that had been plaguing Member's Best for close to a year now. It had started with a few random account issues. Unauthorized withdrawals or transfers. Charges to the credit union's debit or credit cards, stuff like that. The incidences had started becoming closer together and for greater amounts, which was when the board had called in an outside team to check for security breaches. They'd found no evidence of hackers. Nothing could be traced. It was becoming a real problem for the credit union, which had more than twenty branches throughout Pennsylvania.

Kent was not technically supposed to deal with stuff like this. His job was to oversee the general management of all the credit union's branches. The board had decided that also meant liaising with the investigator to coordinate data regarding the thefts. Which meant he'd spent a lot of time with Ms. Adams over the past six months...and spent a lot of time ignoring that he liked her. Because, Carol.

Who'd left him.

Today Stephanie wore a pair of slim-fitting dark jeans topped with a black mesh sweater that hung off one shoulder. Black Docs on her feet, accented with a set of sparkly pink shoelaces. She slung her thick parka over the back of one chair and took a seat in the other, already pulling out a notepad from her shoulder bag.

"Morning," Kent said mildly.

She looked up, a small crease in her brow fading as she smiled. "Hi. Morning. Sorry, I'm a little distracted. Got some news."

"Bad news?"

She paused, then settled her notepad on one knee while she looked at him. "No. Why would you think...?"

"Sorry." He shook his head, feeling dumb. "You meant news about the fraud. Not personal."

"Oh. No. Nothing personal. But thanks for asking, in case it was." Again she paused to look him over. "You okay?"

"Yeah. Sure." Kent forced a smile and leaned back in his chair.

Stephanie shook her head. "You don't seem okay. Did something else happen? Another account hacked?"

"Not so far today," he said. Then he blurted out, "My girlfriend left me."

"Oh, good! I mean, goodness," Stephanie said. "Goodness me."

It was such an odd thing for her to say, spoken in

such a brightly robotic tone, that Kent laughed. Loudly. "What?"

"Oh, I just… That sucks, Kent. I'm sorry. Um…" She coughed, not meeting his gaze.

For a long few seconds of awkward silence, he simply stared at her while she fussed with her notepad. Good, she'd said. Good…as in…she was happy he was single, or what?

There'd been more than a few times in his life when Kent wished he was not so easily led by the ideas his little head got, despite what the one on his shoulders tried to tell it. Today was one of those times, and he cursed himself for it—he'd been single for, like, six freaking days, and even though it had been more like six weeks since he'd last gotten laid, that was no excuse.

Even if Stephanie did have the biggest, bluest eyes he'd ever seen. And that great laugh, coupled with a smile that would've made a priest say hallelujah and not because of a sermon. She was smart, too, on point with everything they'd ever worked on, even if she hadn't yet been able to figure out who was stealing from the Member's Best accounts.

"Right," he said slowly. "So…should we talk about your updates, or…?"

"Right, right." She coughed again, still not meeting his gaze as she fiddled with the notepad. When she did look up, she seemed uncomfortable to find him staring at her.

It of course made Kent feel like an ass to have been caught, so he looked away and it was a comedy of awkward silences and half-started sentences for the next minute until finally Stephanie laughed and shook her head. She cleared her throat.

She slid the notepad across his desk. "I've put together some possibilities of what's been going on. See, at first, the perp was just taking small amounts out of accounts here and there. Nobody even noticed, or they chalked it up to some glitch, right?"

"Yeah." He leaned to look at the names, dates and numbers on the pad.

An hour passed while they talked and Stephanie outlined what she'd been working on. How she'd been trying to connect the dots. She'd scooted her chair around to his side of the desk and was pointing at the notepad.

"Find the pattern," she said. "If we can do that, we'll find the douchecanoe who's doing this, and hopefully before he really hits anyone hard."

We, she'd said, and Kent hadn't missed that. Not that it meant anything beyond the work relationship, of course. But still. It was nice to hear.

"Hey, I'm going out to grab some lunch," he said with a glance at her. Sitting this close, he imagined for a moment he could feel the brush of her hair on his cheek. "You want to come out with me? We can keep looking for patterns."

She tucked a strand of her dark hair behind one ear as she looked at him now, a small smile curving her lips. "Sure. I have some time. Where should we go?"

"How about The Gold Monkey?" It was a quiet little Middle Eastern place around the corner.

"Perfect." She grinned at him, not moving away. Their eyes met. "I'm starving."

Chapter 3

"It wasn't a date," Stephanie told her friend Denise on the phone as she got out of her car and headed into the Morningstar Mocha to pick up a couple bags of their specially blended herbal tea. She was a coffee fiend, no doubt, except when she was working a case that meant she had to spend more of her time sleeping than any one person should've been able to.

Denise handled scheduling and travel arrangements for Crew members who needed, as Stephanie had, to relocate in order to pursue cases. Stephanie had known her for years, though this was the first time she'd ever been assigned close enough to hang out with her in person. It had made the Pennsylvania winter a little more bearable for California girl Stephanie.

"He told you his girlfriend left him, then he asked you to an intimate little venue for fondue. Fondue is not work-related material, Stephanie." Denise's voice dipped low for a second, crackling, before getting clear again. "Sorry, I've got someone on the line waiting for hotel reservations in Moscow. My Russian's pretty rusty. If I break off with you, it's to deal with that."

"I can let you go. I don't have any updates or anything. I mean, yeah, he's cute. And now he's single. But so what? I'm out of here as soon as I bust whoever's doing this stuff, and I'm back to Los Angeles. And he'll be here. So." Stephanie shrugged, though Denise couldn't see her. "I mean, anyway, he's a normal."

"Hey. I'm a normie!"

"You are so not normal," Stephanie said with a laugh. Denise had no paranormal talents, true, but she'd been working with the Crew for long enough to have seen some seriously strange stuff. That left marks.

Denise rattled off a long string of something that sounded like Russian before saying, "I have to go. Fill me in later!"

"There's nothing to—" Too late—Denise had disconnected.

Inside the shop, Stephanie ordered two bags of the tea, then leaned on the counter to wait. She pulled out her phone. No messages, not that she was expecting any. No new email, either. She casually thumbed open a Words with Buddies game, but it wasn't her turn to play any of the rounds.

She people-watched instead.

She'd made the Morningstar Mocha one of her favorite stops, so she already knew a few of the regulars. Carlos was still tapping away on his novel over there by the windows. Tesla worked the counter, her spiky blond hair tipped with bright purple now. Her boyfriend, Charlie, had stopped in to bring her something in a brown paper bag that made her giggle, and watching them kiss, Stephanie had to turn away because that was a story that didn't need her to make anything up about it.

There was another face, a kid of about sixteen, sitting in the back corner with a laptop open in front of him. The back of it was adorned with stickers from indie bands Stephanie had enjoyed a few times herself, mostly courtesy of her older brother, which made it a little strange to see them as decoration for someone at least ten years younger than she was. Still, it was going to be a few more minutes before her tea was ready, so Stephanie wandered over to take a closer look.

"Oh, wow," she said. "Bangtastic Frogmen? Really? I didn't think anyone else had ever heard of them."

The kid, pale, eyes faintly circled by shadows, looked up at her through the fringe of black hair. A girl, not a boy as Stephanie had first assumed from the thin frame and baggy clothes. The girl gave Stephanie a blank look.

"Huh?"

"The…sticker." Stephanie gestured. "Bangtastic Frogmen?"

The girl tipped the laptop's lid to look at the assortment of stickers, then closed it firmly and put her hands on top of it. Her fingernails were bitten to the quick, so raw in places that Stephanie winced. "It's… Yeah. They're great."

Great was not how Stephanie would've described the group, which had prided itself on being actually awful. Out-of-tune instruments, mumbled and incoherent lyrics. They'd made one album, so far as she knew, and while it had been played to death for a few months in her circle of middle-school friends, it had quickly been replaced by something a little more boy band. She eyed the girl.

"Front of Desperation? You listen to them, too?"

The girl began to put the laptop away, keeping her gaze from Stephanie's. "Look, I just have the stickers, okay. I'm not a fan or anything. I just liked the way they looked."

There was a ceramic mug on the table, one of the refillable ones. You could spend all day in the Mocha on a $2.99 cup of coffee, if you were so inclined. This girl had that sort of look. Come to think of it, there was something familiar about her, as though Stephanie had seen her before. Yet when she tried to remember if the girl was a Mocha regular, she somehow looked less familiar.

"Okay, no big." Stephanie tried on a smile the girl didn't return.

Behind the girl, on the wall, a large clock spun its hands. Frowning, Stephanie glanced at the menu pinned to the bulletin board next to it. For a second, literally one, the letters jumbled and merged, making it impossible to read. Automatically, Stephanie tapped her wrist three times with her forefinger, a trick she'd learned long ago to determine if she was awake or dreaming.

Awake.

But… "Hey, wait a second," she said to the girl, who was now slinging her laptop bag over her shoulder and trying to inch past her.

"Tea's up!" came a voice from behind the counter, and Stephanie turned. That was her order.

When she turned back, the girl had slipped out the front door and disappeared. Stephanie looked again at the clock and the menu, but both were fine. She was standing in the Morningstar Mocha for real, not in the Ephemeros, and she was drawing curious looks. She shook herself, just a little, and turned to the guy behind the counter.

"Who was that?"

He looked past her toward the door's jingling bell overhead. "Who?"

"That girl. The one who was sitting there, in the corner."

The guy shrugged. "I don't know. There was a girl?"

"She must've been sitting here for a while. She had a refillable mug." Stephanie pointed toward the table where the girl had been sitting but then let her hand fall to her side. "She had a Bangtastic Frogmen sticker."

That earned her a weird look, so she took the bag of tea and peeked inside. She didn't really like the way it tasted, but it did wonders for putting her to sleep when her body fought it. "Thanks."

"I love the Sleepytime. Puts me right out." The guy grinned.

Stephanie returned the smile absently, still thinking about the kid in the corner. Out on the street, heading for her car, she tried again to look and see if she could find the mysterious teen, but nope. The girl had vanished.

He had no reason to call her. They'd already had a meeting. Work related. Lunch had been a nice gesture; it didn't mean anything.

He wasn't ready to date. For sure. Right?

Grumbling to himself, Kent forced his way through a lackluster microwaved dinner and some bad TV, ticking off the seconds until he could make it into bed and give up to unconsciousness. If he were a drinking man, he'd have taken a few shots to help him along, but he made do with counting sheep.

He found himself unable to stop thinking of Stephanie instead.

When his phone buzzed, he snatched it up off the nightstand, thumbing the screen before he really paid attention to who was calling him. "Oh," he said. "Carol."

"Just calling to check in on you."

Kent frowned. "I'm fine. Thanks."

"I wanted to tell you that I'll be sending someone to pick up the rest of my stuff that I left in the guest room. I'll be at my mom's for a while." She paused. "How are you, really?"

He closed his eyes, thinking of the brightness of Stephanie's laughter and how nice it had been to sit with her at lunch, enjoying the moment without any resentments hovering between them. No bad memories and all the possibilities of making good ones. How long had it been since he'd felt that way?

"Carol, I'm fine."

"If you're sure." She didn't sound convinced.

That, finally, pissed him off more than her sneaking away while he was at work had. "Look, I'm sure you think that I can't survive without you, but the truth is, I think this is going to be good for both of us. Great, in fact."

She didn't have much to say to that. He took little satisfaction in her silence. It felt more like a standoff than anything else, and he was pretty damned tired of that feeling.

"Good night, Carol," Kent said finally. "I'll make

sure to have your stuff by the front door for when the guy comes for it."

"You know, you can call me..." she began but trailed off as though waiting for him to jump in with an answer.

This time, he didn't say good-night.

This time, Kent said, "Goodbye."

Chapter 4

Girls' Night In. Denise had brought a bottle of wine and they'd watched a couple chick flicks, chatting most of the way through them. By nine o'clock, though, Stephanie knew it was time to get to work.

Just one problem. She wasn't tired at all. The wine had worn off, which was good, since she needed to be on top of her game in the dream world if she wanted to make sure she got a lead on this creep.

"Can't Vadim prescribe you something?" Denise had never been able to shape anything in the Ephemeros, though she knew and believed it existed.

"He could, I guess. But I don't want to rely on sleeping pills or anything to get me under. Makes it too hard to wake up if I have to, for one thing. But it also affects me inside, just the way it would out here. I mean, it makes me dream, but it interferes with the shaping." Stephanie dragged a chip through the remnants of the queso dip and crunched it with a sigh. "I could try a food coma, I guess."

Denise laughed. "Sure. But what else works? Booze?"

"Same as pills. Sure, it puts me under, but it makes it hard to work. And then there's the hangover to deal with."

"Ew. Gross." Denise's nose crinkled. She looked at the clock on the wall. "It's early, that's all."

"Yeah, I know, but this guy's targeting the elderly. A lot of them are asleep by now and then up at the odd hours."

Denise nodded. "My grandma's like that. She'll be asleep in her chair by seven, but then she's up at three and can't get back to sleep until six or seven in the morning."

"Yeah." Stephanie crunched another chip, then sat back on the couch with a sigh. "Anyway, there's no telling who this guy will target next, of course, but I'm having better luck earlier in the evening."

"I guess I should let you get to it, then." Denise slapped her knee and stood with a stretch and a yawn. She looked down at Stephanie with a slow, wicked grin. "I have a tried-and-true way I use to fall asleep when I can't. But I'm not sure I should tell you what it is."

Stephanie got up, too, to follow her friend to the front door. "No fair. What's the secret?"

Denise shrugged into her coat and tied her scarf around her neck, then gave Stephanie an arched brow. "Sex."

"Yikes. Well, I guess I'm out of luck on that front," Stephanie said. "Seeing as how it's been a long dry spell for me."

"Orgasm," Denise clarified. "Surely you can have one or four of those all on your own."

Shit, she was blushing. Actually blushing. Stephanie cleared her throat. "Um...well, sure, I guess I could..."

"Don't tell me you don't..." Denise paused, clearly surprised. "Stephanie! Really?"

Awkwardly, Stephanie shrugged. "I do. Sure. Sometimes. I just...haven't. In a while."

"Shew, if I don't get off every other day or so, I'm a raging bitch. I have to keep my portable boyfriend charged at all times." Denise shook her head.

"I like sex," Stephanie said. "I've just been...busy."

"Never too busy for a little self-maintenance," Denise declared and pulled her scarf tighter around her throat as she dug for her gloves. "And I bet it will help you fall asleep for sure."

It was an idea, Stephanie thought as she put the few dishes they'd used in the dishwasher and went around checking the locks and turning out the lights. She'd had some of her best sleep after sex, that was true, even though it had been too long since she'd actually had any. As for self-maintenance, she thought as she went into her bedroom to put on her pajamas, well...it had just started to seem hollow after a while. The seduction of her hand or even the vibrator she kept in her bedside drawer was fine, but it couldn't beat kissing and being kissed. It couldn't replace lovemaking.

Still, the more she thought about it, the better the idea became. Except, just as she wasn't particularly sleepy, she also wasn't particularly turned on. Maybe she should just try to do some non-dream-world work, she thought as she settled against her headboard with her laptop on her knees. That boring stuff would surely help her into sleep, wouldn't it?

In minutes she'd pulled up the data files on her current job. The dates, times and amounts of withdrawals from the accounts, along with the interviews she'd done with the victims. All of them had admitted to sharing their personal financial information with someone in a dream and had been hit a day or so after.

This was about the least sexy thing she could think of doing. At least until she scrolled through her files and pulled up one more. This one had a photo included. His pertinent information, including his contact numbers and his Connex account. She hadn't connexed with Kent Gordon, only because she didn't bother much with social media sites, but she could stalk him a little bit there on what he'd made public.

She did.

It was harmless, Stephanie told herself as she clicked on his profile-picture photo album. It wasn't as if she were showing up beneath his window blasting a song from a boom box. She wasn't hurting anyone or anything by taking a casual peek at… Oh, shit.

"Shit," she breathed.

The photo was nothing anyone would notice as special. In it, Kent stood with his hands on his hips, his shirtsleeves rolled up to the elbow—those forearms, God. Stephanie let her cursor drift over the photo as she let out a long, hard sigh. She had such a thing for forearms. And big hands. And steel-rimmed glasses. And hair going just the tiniest bit gray at the temples…

Damn it, she had a thing for Kent Gordon, that was just the sad truth, and had for months. Since the first time she'd seen him, as a matter of fact, though the fact he'd had a live-in girlfriend had made him off-limits. Her name was Carol. She was blond and blandly pretty, and she posted inane memes and pictures of her lunch, which Stephanie knew because she'd also creeped a few times on Carol's Connex account.

Except now Carol and Kent had broken up.

It was still harmless, Stephanie told herself, logging out and putting the computer on the nightstand. She turned out the light and sank into the pillows, her hands flat on her belly. Everyone did it. Creeped around on social media sites, looking at pictures. That was why she didn't have any accounts.

Her internal clock ticked, loud as any she could've hung on the wall, and the passing minutes began to annoy her. The harder she tried, the less likely it was going to be that she could fall asleep. She should get up. Clean something. Pay some bills. Hell, she could do a little workout.

Or, she thought as her fingertips ran lightly across her belly, then lower, over the thin fabric of her boxers, she could try something else.

Oh, it had been too long, she thought with a sigh as her fingers slipped into her bottoms and she found her soft curls. A little lower, deeper, she delved inside. With a small gasp, she slid another finger in. Her thumb pressed her clit. She stayed that way for a moment, listening to her body. Gauging her response.

Her nipples had hardened, and she tugged her shirt up to free her breasts to the chilly night air. She kept her bedroom cooler than the rest of the house out of habit from California's much warmer temperatures, but in Pennsylvania, February meant it could be downright cold. It wasn't the temperature that had tightened them,

though. It was the thought of strong male forearms sprinkled with dark hair, exposed by rolled-up shirtsleeves.

She couldn't do this. Couldn't get off to a real person, a guy she was working with. A guy with a super-
recent breakup, Stephanie scolded herself, even as her
fingers moved a little faster.

Okay, so she wouldn't think about Kent. She would
imagine someone else, another lover with long legs and
broad shoulders, dark hair. Lean features. Glasses.

God, how could she have passed up this pleasure
for so long? She was wet now, fingers easing in deeper
before slipping out to circle her clit. Her hips bumped
upward when she stroked herself.

One hand on her breast, squeezing her nipple. Eyes
closed. Hips rocking. Fingers stroking. The pleasure
built, higher, stronger. Fierce. She slowed the pace,
wanting to make this last.

Unbidden, she drifted into fantasy. Not a dream—
she was still awake—and though she tried a tentative
push to see if she'd perhaps fallen asleep without realizing it, no handsome man appeared at the foot of her
bed with his cock in his hand. She opened her eyes to
peek again, to be sure, but nope. Nada.

He would, though, she thought. He would crawl up
the bed and cover her with his body. He'd kiss her.
Slowly at first. Then harder. His hand would slide beneath the back of her head to twist in her hair. His other
would slide between them to stroke her clit, the way she
was doing now.

"Oh," she breathed. "Oh, fuck. Yes."

A little faster now. A little harder, deeper, her fingers curling. Oh, she wished she had thought to invest
in some penetration toys, something that would fill her

better than her hand. It felt so good, though, she didn't want to stop. Couldn't stop. Not when each wave of pleasure was cresting. Pushing her to the edge.

She thought of him again, though she refused to let her mouth shape the sound of his name. She couldn't stop herself from imagining his lips on her. Those big hands. He would cover her entirely. He would fill her.

Fuck her.

Hard.

Fast.

With a small gasp, she came, writhing in the tangling sheets. Her back arched. A low, stuttering groan hitched out of her. It felt so damned good she didn't stop stroking, feeling the pleasure build again. Sending her over the edge one more time while she muttered a long, mumbled string of fucktalk that would've been embarrassing except she was alone.

At the end of it, breathing hard and sweating, blinking away the final remnants of her fantasy, she was all by herself.

She did, however, fall asleep.

Languid, relaxed, Stephanie felt soft warmth under her fingertips and smiled before she opened her eyes. She was in the Ephemeros. Still on her own bed and in her own room, but where the walls of her bedroom should have been, there was only empty space.

She sat up and swung her legs over the edge, shaping the forest. Birds chirped, far off, just the sound of them. She didn't put much effort into creating the birds themselves, which was the only way there'd be any. Animals dreamed, but they had their own Ephemeros to play in, so far as Stephanie could tell.

She drew in the scent of pine. Sun dappled its way

through the branches and speckled the fallen needles. This was her favorite entry point, built from a child-hood memory of the smallish patch of woods behind her grandmother's house, and she worked on it a little bit more each time she entered the dream world so she could keep it as her anchor.

She didn't have a lot of time now that she was on a case, so she quickly focused on shaping a bit more of the curving path. A few more trees. She took another lingering breath and stepped onto the path.

Naked?

With a startled laugh, Stephanie looked at herself. She almost always represented in the same outfit when she was working a case. Slim-fit black leather trousers, black silky T-shirt that clung to her like a second skin, a black corset-vest. Sure, it made her look like a Goth girl, but it was practical, served as armor and didn't impede her movements if she ever had to run—and she often did. The last thing she wanted to worry about when she was hunting down a perp was having to change her clothes.

But now, naked, she stepped with bare toes on the springy needles of the curving path. She lifted her face to the pine-scented breeze and closed her eyes for a second. It felt good to be naked here. Free. And, in the aftermath of the dual orgasms, she still felt sexy.

She was pushing it, too, she realized after a moment or so when the birdsong trilled and yet the forest began to fade. Someone was coming, beckoned by the unsubtle throb of her fading arousal. She was broadcasting sex, and it was going to pull in some unwanted attention if she wasn't careful.

Unless that was the way to catch this thief, she thought

for a second as she concentrated just hard enough to shape herself into her regular outfit. Lure him in with sex? He'd been targeting the elderly, both genders, but that didn't mean he wouldn't be immune to a little good old-fashioned catfishing, right?

Maybe she needed to make herself seem a little more...vulnerable.

Gone in a second was the leather, the kick-ass attitude. Replaced by a soft gown with frilly lace at the throat and sleeves. Stephanie shaped her hair longer, to her waist. She kept the bare feet, thickening her soles should she step on anything sharp but keeping the look of innocent damsel.

"Where's your candy house?" she murmured, opening herself to the Ephemeros's shifting, pulsing will. "Let me take a taste."

It was hard to resist the impulse to shape the space around her, but Stephanie kept herself still, curious to see what the collective unconscious was going to build tonight. It turned out to be a Victorian mansion, complete with gardens and a hedge maze and rooms full of people dancing and drinking...and fucking.

So it was going to be that kind of night, she thought as she moved through a room decorated all in red. An orgy. She wasn't shaping any of this, but how much of it had she contributed to, Stephanie wondered as she eased around a naked trio writhing on a velvet couch.

It was tempting to give in to this. The sensuality. The outright sexuality. The steady thrum and throb of music beat through the house. People moved to it. She moved to it.

And there, through the crowd, she caught a glimpse of a lean silhouette in black leather, whispering in a woman's ear. The woman wore a Regency-era gown, though her hair was totally '80s punk rock. She nodded, listening with a rapt expression to whatever the guy in black was saying to her. When he turned his face a bit, the gleam of fangs was the proof Stephanie was waiting for. That was her guy.

She moved forward, ducking around a bunch of people using toys and tools she'd only ever seen on the internet, and although the pull of their will was strong, she managed to resist it. Right before she got to her goal, though, she bumped into someone, hard enough to send them both back a couple steps. Intent on getting to the perp, Stephanie stepped to the side. So did the man in front of her.

She looked up, intending to push a little to get him out of the way and send his attention in another direction, but what she saw stopped her. "Kent?"

Of course, it wasn't impossible for them to meet here. If he was asleep at the same time, as he probably was, and with the strength of what was rippling through the Ephemeros tonight, it was no wonder he'd gravitated toward the orgy. And boy, did he look good.

"I can't," she said by way of apology when he took her hand. "I have…work…"

"You could dance with me," Kent said with a glance around them at the people who were dancing…or naked variations of dancing. "That would be all right, wouldn't it?"

She wanted to. Opening herself to the Ephemeros had left her vulnerable, but it was more than that. It was him.

"I can't," she repeated, threading together a little shield to keep herself from jumping him right there.

Over his shoulder she could see the man in black leather bending closer to the woman in the Regency gown. "I want to, but I'm working."

Kent nodded but tugged her hand to pull her a step closer. "Right. Working."

She was pushing up on her tiptoes to kiss him. She wanted it. Wanted him. Her arms went around his neck. His lips, so close she could feel the gust of his breath on her face. Her mouth opened.

"This isn't real," she warned.

"It's as real as we want it to be," Kent said. "Isn't it?"

At the last second, she turned. It wouldn't have been the first time she indulged in a little hanky-panky in the dream world, but doing it with him felt wrong. He wouldn't know what they'd shared, and she'd have to face him across a desk with the memory of his mouth on hers and pretend she didn't know how he tasted.

His hands moved to her hips, nudging her against him, and oh, he was hard against her, and she was going to kiss him, she was going to open for him and let him inside her, and they were going to dance and dance and...

She said his name.

With a gasp, Stephanie forced herself awake. Shit, she'd lost herself. Worse, she'd lost the perp. Heart pounding, sweating, she fell back onto her pillows and licked away the taste of salt on her lips.

She'd been pushed again. Mr. Slick was clever, she gave him that. He'd seen her coming and used what she wanted against her, only this time, instead of chocolate cake, it had been Kent Gordon.

Chapter 5

Kent hated coconut.

He hated the scent of it, the taste of it. He hated the hairy round shape of coconuts and how they sometimes fell out of trees and hit people on the head. There wasn't much in this world that was guaranteed to send Kent over the edge, but coconut would be it. And there it was, tons of it shredded all over the top of his birthday cake.

"Mom," he began, then stopped, because how could he tell her that he wasn't going to eat one slice of that monstrosity, much less take the rest home, as she'd already planned for him to do?

"It's a new recipe." She beamed, all four feet ten inches of her.

Kent didn't have the heart to remind her of his coconut aversion. It would hurt her feelings, first of all, but more than that, would remind her of how precarious her memory had become. Most days they could both pretend that she was simply a little scatterbrained, the way she'd always been. There was going to come a day, he thought, when it wouldn't matter if she was reminded about what she'd forgotten, because she wouldn't be able to remember that she'd ever known what it was in the first place. He didn't want to think of that.

Instead, he patted his stomach. "I'm so full from dinner, Mom. I'll take it home and have a piece later, okay?"

"Make sure to give Carol a piece. It's really too bad she couldn't make it tonight." A shadow passed over his mom's face, and she shook her head. "Oh. No. I'm sorry, honey, I forgot. You two broke up."

Since it had happened only a couple weeks ago, he couldn't really fault her for not remembering. He still sometimes forgot himself, at least until he came home to the empty, silent house and found nobody waiting for him, not even the dog. Carol had taken Lucky with her when she left.

"She wasn't good enough for you anyway," Mom said before Kent could answer.

He shrugged. "Things happen. That's all. I don't hold a grudge."

"No, you never did that. That's a good thing." She smiled again and put the lid on the cake box, which was a relief because now at least he no longer had to smell it. "I'll just put it away for you to take home anyway."

Mom protested when Kent insisted she sit to catch up on her programs while he cleaned the kitchen. It didn't take long. Mom kept a spotless house, even with the enormous meal she'd prepared for his birthday feast. Enough food for ten people. She'd make sure he was sent home with plenty of single-portioned meals to last him for the rest of the month, and he'd take them, because hell if being an unexpected bachelor didn't mean he'd been more apt to indulge in Chinese takeout eaten on paper plates than any kind of healthy food.

Kent put the paper grocery sack of plastic containers on the kitchen table and peeked into the living room to check on his mother. She'd dozed off in front of the television, as he'd expected. It was getting close to 10:00 p.m., well past her normal bedtime, but he'd been late from work and so dinner had been delayed.

"Mom," he said gently with a touch on her arm, trying not to startle her.

"I only have my pension," she said drowsily. "But of course you can have it, if you need it."

Kent paused. "Mom?"

"It's not much, lovey, but I want you to have it. No, really. Yes." Mom reached a hand as though to touch someone. Her fingertips brushed the front of his shirt.

Kent took her hand. "Mom. You're dreaming."

Slowly, her eyes opened. With a furrowed brow, Mom looked at him. Then smiled. "Hello, lovey."

"You were sleeping. Why don't we get you upstairs?" Kent laughed a little. "Must've been some dream."

Mom frowned. "I don't quite recall it."

She didn't struggle to get out of her recliner, though Kent stood by waiting in case she did. Physically, Mom had few issues beyond a bit of arthritis. It might've been easier, he thought as she made sure he'd appropriately packed up all of his leftovers, if she were frail. He could've done something for her to be really helpful, instead of simply suffering through watching her slowly deteriorate mentally.

"Give my love to Carol," she told him at the door as he bent to kiss her.

Kent smiled. "I will, Mom."

In the car, it hit him, though. The long lonely night ahead of him. A trunkful of food he would eat standing over the sink. A birthday cake covered in coconut.

A night of frustrating, sexy dreams featuring Stephanie Adams.

As far as birthdays went, it had been a pretty shitty one. It got worse when he slipped his phone from his pocket to put in the center console while he drove and saw the missed text from Carol. He didn't want to read it, but he did.

Happy B-day!

It was a nice thing for her to do. To remember. Carol was nice. The life they'd had was nice, at least, Kent had thought so until he came home to find her half of everything moved out and a note on the table telling him that she'd gone to stay with her mother while she looked for a new place to live.

He missed her, of course, but as he pulled up to his driveway and saw the dark windows, he thought that maybe it wasn't Carol he missed as much as simply... someone. They'd been together four years, most of them good, and he'd happily have gone on for four more, or forty, probably. Being with Carol had been easy, not a challenge. It hadn't been much work.

That was the problem. He hadn't put much work into things. That was probably why they'd ended up splitting. You had to put the work in.

Too little, too late, that was the problem. He could think of a hundred ways he might've been able to salvage things with Carol, but none of them mattered now.

He could've answered her text, too, though at the moment he saw no point in it. What was she going to do, chat with him about the day? Ask him again if he was recovering without her? That was only going to rub it in about how terrible a birthday it had been.

His stomach rumbled. Dinner at Mom's had been good, but though he'd told her a little white lie about being too full for cake, the truth was he'd left plenty of room for it. And damn it, it was his birthday. Why shouldn't he celebrate it, even if he had to do it all by his loser, lonely self? It was Friday night. He was hungry. The food in the trunk would keep with the temperatures as cold as they were.

Instead of pulling into his driveway, Kent kept on going.

Chapter 6

"I'm not gonna make it." Stephanie held back a yawn as best she could, but no matter how she tried, she couldn't stop it. Her jaw cracked. Her eyes felt filled with sand.

Denise frowned. "C'mon, Steph, wake up. It's not even eleven."

"Yeah, but I've been up since about three this morning." After the sexy dream with Kent, her frustration about losing sight of her target had kept her awake no matter how hard she'd tried to fall back to sleep. Nothing had worked. Now she was tired, angry with herself and cranky.

"Damn. No closer?"

"No, I'm closer. I actually saw him last night." She paused. "But then I got interrupted."

Denise's brows rose. "By what?"

Stephanie definitely didn't want to tell her friend

what had forced her out of the dream. Not only was it an embarrassing failure in her control, but it would let Denise in on the whole crush she had on Kent. Stephanie pressed her lips together.

"Ooh, he was in your dream, huh?"

"He was… A lot of people were…"

"Last night I dreamed I was schtupping my high school biology teacher," Denise said with a chuckle. "In some crazy hedge-maze thing. Man, that was wild."

Stephanie said nothing.

"You were there!" Denise slapped the table and tipped her head back to laugh so loud it earned her several appreciative looks from the guys at the table behind them. "You and Mr. Bank Manager?"

"Keep your voice down!" Stephanie shook her head. "It was nothing. It was a dream."

"Sure it was. Because nothing that happens in dreams is real," Denise said with a deliberately blank expression that quickly shifted again into humor. "Uh-huh."

"That doesn't make it okay. Anyway, I'm beat." Stephanie fought another yawn. "At least tonight I won't have trouble getting to sleep."

Denise sighed and looked around the bar. "Fine. Slim pickings here tonight anyway."

"The job's kicking my ass. That's all."

Denise frowned and leaned a little closer. "What's Vadim say about it?"

"He says keep hunting." Stephanie took a small sip from her beer, letting the flavor roll around in her mouth before swallowing. Last week she'd had a drink in the Ephemeros that had tasted of flowers and chocolate, a combination she doubted would be any good in the real world but which had been almost orgasmic in the dream. "Got a couple new reports that tie in to that same guy."

"You need a break." Denise looked serious. "I know you think of yourself as some kind of lone wolf, but really, you need someone helping you out."

Stephanie laughed. "Lone wolf?"

"You know what I mean." Denise didn't join in Stephanie's humor. "You think you need to take care of it all on your own, but it's dangerous. Too much time in there, and—"

"Yeah, yeah, I know. I might not come out." Stephanie shrugged. She knew it was possible, but she couldn't let it freak her out. She was more likely to end up in a coma from getting hit by a bus than from letting her time in the Ephemeros get away from her.

"Just because you think you're invulnerable in there doesn't mean you are out here," Denise said.

Stephanie gave her friend a grin meant to ease her worries. "I'm fine. I promise. Soon as I figure out who this guy is out here, I'll be done with this case and I can take a vacation."

"Promise?"

"Yes. I promise."

Denise sighed again. "Maybe we can go away for one of those all-inclusive deals. What do you think? A week or so of sun and fun and hot guys in thong bathing suits?"

"Oh. God, Denise, ew." Stephanie laughed.

"What? They'd be European. Totally hot. With accents," Denise added, laughing, too. Her gaze cut away after a second, looking over Stephanie's shoulder, and her giggles became a sly smile. "Oh. Hey. Look who's here."

Stephanie glanced behind her, not expecting to see that familiar long, lean body. Kent Gordon's profile was angular, his dark hair touched just the tiniest bit with silver at the temples. His steel-rimmed glasses flashed as he settled on the bar stool and nodded at the bartender.

Pretty much her ideal guy in every way.

"You should go say hi." Denise nodded.

Stephanie turned away, hoping he wasn't going to turn around and see her there. "Ugh. No."

"Why not? You told me you thought he was cute! You're having sexy dreams with him! He took you on a date."

He *was* cute. That was the problem. "He asked me to join him for lunch. I told you, it was so not a date. And I have to work with him."

"So?"

"So, I haven't exactly been bringing him anything he can use," Stephanie said. "And what can I tell him? That I've been searching for this guy who stalks people in their dreams to steal their money in the real world but I haven't quite managed it yet?"

"You could just tell him you're still investigating. That's the truth," Denise pointed out with another glance over Stephanie's shoulder. "It's not like you work *for* him. He's just your point of contact at the bank. Vadim's the one in charge. He should take the heat."

"Yeah, but I'm the one who has to come up with a plausible explanation for how we're going to nail this guy, something to explain to Kent and the board at Member's Best that doesn't make me look like an incompetent idiot."

"Part of the job," Denise replied unsympathetically.

Stephanie laughed. "Wow, thanks. Yes. Part of the job, but look. You know I can't get involved with a normie."

"There you go with that normie business again. God. I'm a normal, and you like me!"

"You," Stephanie told her friend again, "are so not a normie."

Denise rolled her eyes and tipped her beer toward the bar. "Well, I can't do what you can do anyway. And you never know. Mr. Sexy-Pants Bank Manager might be a shaper."

Stephanie stole another look at him. He'd ordered a beer, the same as her, though he didn't appear to be drinking it. The same as her, really, she thought as she turned the bottle in her hands and felt the slosh of liquid against the glass. She'd been nursing the same one for an hour. It was warm.

She could go up to the bar. Order another. Sit beside him, smile, toss her hair…

"Shit, Denise," Stephanie said. "He really is cute, huh?"

"Yes!"

Still, Stephanie shook her head. "I have to get home and get to work."

"All work and no play," her friend said. "I'm going to run to the restroom. Don't leave."

"Sure." Stephanie stifled another yawn while she waited, glancing up a few minutes later when a figure moved to slide into the booth across from her. "Ready to get out of here? Oh. Hi."

"Hi," Kent said with a small smile. "Your friend told me you were here."

"I am." It was a stupid thing to say, but there it was. Stephanie coughed a little, embarrassed at feeling caught this way. She twisted in her seat to look around for Denise, though she had a suspicion she'd been set up. "Did you happen to see where she went?"

"She left. She told me to tell you she'd call you tomorrow. She…um, she told me you like scrambled eggs for breakfast." Kent echoed Stephanie's awkward cough.

Her jaw dropped. Then she slapped a hand to her forehead, closing her eyes for a moment before looking at him. "That sounds like Denise. Sorry."

"No, it's okay." She'd seen Kent smile before, but not like this.

This smile warmed her all the way to her chilly toes. It spread a flush up her throat and into her cheeks that she sincerely hoped he didn't see. That smile made her want to crawl across the table between them, straddle his lap, take his face in her hands and kiss the breath out of him.

Whoa.

"It's my birthday," Kent said suddenly.

Stephanie's brows rose. "Happy birthday, Kent."

"It hasn't been the greatest," he told her, not sounding as if he were complaining, just being honest. "I'm not usually the guy who makes a big deal out of it, but you know, at least on your birthday you should have cake, right?"

"You didn't have cake? That sucks." Stephanie frowned, holding back another yawn threatening to squeak out of her. She was getting so sleepy that it would've been easy to convince herself she was already dreaming. She shot a quick glance at the menu to be certain she could read the words there. The fastest way for her to tell if she was indeed inside the Ephemeros was that letters and numbers no longer held their places but squiggled all over and refused to be read.

He nodded. "Yeah. My mom made me a cake covered in coconut frosting. She forgot I didn't like coconut."

"That really sucks." Stephanie frowned. The beer had been a mistake. She should've had coffee or a cola, even an iced tea. Driving home was going to be hard.

"Yeah. She's having some problems with her memory." Kent paused. "Now that I've unloaded my whole sob story on you…"

"It's okay. Birthdays should be fun and special. I don't blame you for being a little cranky about it."

They stared at each other across the table.

"I know a place that makes a killer chocolate raspberry cheesecake," Kent said finally. "Would you go with me?"

Her eyes were full of sand and she wanted to make this table a pillow, but at the sight of Kent's hesitant smile, she sighed. Oh, she was so going to kill Denise later. A little bit anyway.

"Far be it from me to turn down a guy on his birthday."

Kent's widening grin sent another of those disturbing sets of tingles all through her. He got out of the booth and reached for her hand. And, as she had last night in the dream world, Stephanie let him take it.

Chapter 7

It hadn't been much of a date. Or a date at all. Had it? Just as lunch hadn't been more than just, well…lunch… Damn it, now that he was home alone with a stomach full of cheesecake and too much coffee, all Kent could do was overthink things.

Over the past few months, he and Stephanie had met about once a week in the office and had shared dozens of emails, a few phone calls, once or twice an instant-message conversation on the computer to update him on some new developments. She had a terrific laugh. He knew she was originally from California but was renting an apartment locally, because they'd talked about their mutual love for the big fancy grocery store chain that had been putting in a location near his office. He knew she liked punk rock and indie music, because he'd caught a glance at her playlist once when she'd set her phone on his desk. She was smart, quick-witted and kindhearted, and he knew all of that because for the past six months, he'd been pretending he wasn't completely into her.

Now it was all he could think about.

After her friend had not-so-subtly mentioned to him on her way to the bathroom that Stephanie was sitting by herself, Kent had not intended to ask her out. He'd made his way over to say a friendly hello, that was all, but…well. A crappy birthday, a recent breakup, the stress about his job and Mom… Stephanie had given him a friendly smile and that laugh, and he'd been a goner. He'd asked her to join him for dessert on impulse, figuring she'd give him a gentle excuse. It wasn't a workday lunch, after all. She could've easily given him an excuse. Even when she agreed to go with him, he hadn't expected to have such a great time.

Something had told him she'd been surprised, too. They hadn't kissed or anything like that, it not being a date and all, but she'd hugged him. She'd smelled good. She was warm and soft, and she'd pressed her cheek to his at the end of the night in a way that had reminded him of the dream. That kiss. The feeling of her against him.

Ugh. With a groan, he forced himself to roll facedown to press himself into the pillow and try not to pay attention to the semi starting to throb in his pants. He wasn't that much of a creep, was he? But as his dick got harder the more he thought about the way her hair smelled and how she'd felt against him, Kent had to admit that maybe he was.

He wasn't in any good place to even be thinking about dating someone, not with the lingering scent of Carol's perfume still haunting him from unexpected places like the linen closet and the back bedroom upstairs that she'd used as an office. It didn't matter that things had been over with Carol long before she'd walked out. It didn't matter that he'd been noticing Stephanie for months.

"See you," Stephanie had said just before she got into her own car outside the restaurant and drove away.

Had she meant at work or something else? Kent let out a low mutter of frustration. When had he gotten so bad at this? Before Carol he'd certainly been no Lothario, but it wasn't as if he'd ever been afraid to ask a woman out.

"That's it," he said, determined. He pulled out his phone and found Stephanie's number.

Hey, it's Kent, he typed. I had a great time tonight. Maybe we can do it again sometime?

There. Sent. More casual than a call but not quite as impersonal as an email. He glanced at the clock. Just past one in the morning. If she answered him right away, that was a good sign, right?

She didn't, though, and five minutes later he'd begun to regret sending the text at all. Oh, well. Nothing to do about it now except feel like a jerk and go to sleep.

Except he couldn't. Not with the steady pressure in his boxers, his erection straining the front. He ran a hand over the soft material, cupping himself for a minute. Pretending he wasn't going to jack off for about thirty seconds before... Fuck, why pretend when he knew exactly what he wanted.

Well, it might not be what he wanted, but it was what he had. He shucked off his boxers, then stroked himself fully erect. He bit back a groan, arching into the pleasure. Lower, he used his other hand to cup his balls. He set the pace easily, steady and rhythmic. No teasing. Nothing fancy. He was going to get off, that was all.

That was the intention anyway, but as his mind filled with the memory of soft hair, sweet perfume, a lush body pressed to his, Kent found himself slowing. Stroking, languid, then palming the head as he pushed upward into his fist. Fuck, it felt good. Closer, closer, he edged himself.

He'd started off wanting a quick, easy climax, but now he wanted to linger. Savor. He wanted to lose himself in desire and keep himself teetering right there, in that place where nothing mattered but the feeling of flesh on flesh. Where he could let his mind run free and imagine all the things he wanted to do, and tell himself later he was swept away with lust. That it didn't matter.

He muttered, low, a small curse. He fucked his fist a little faster, then slowed to squeeze just behind the head to keep his orgasm at bay for a little longer. With his other hand, he slid his thumb down the seam of his balls, pressing that sweet spot that would not only help him fend off the climax but also make it that much more intense.

Up, up, tighter, twisted. The pleasure built and surged, and Kent rocked with it. Until finally, there it was, that moment of no return. Like that initial crest of a roller coaster in the front car, looking over that precipice before the first screaming, delighted plunge. Ecstasy burst through him. His cock pumped, spurting his belly with hot fluid. Spent, gasping, he let the last final strokes finish him off.

Blinking, Kent stared at the ceiling while his heartbeat slowed. The stickiness on his skin prompted him to roll a little to grab a cloth from the nightstand. Cleaned up, he settled back onto the pillows and closed his eyes. He sought sleep.

When he couldn't find it, he contented himself again with thoughts of Stephanie's laughter and the curve of her smile.

Chapter 8

The sly beep of an incoming text tugged at Stephanie's subconscious just as she was turning around in her usual entry spot into the Ephemeros. She ignored the text. She had only a few hours before dawn, and while she wasn't going to have any trouble sleeping far past that, all of the times she'd encountered the thief had been during local "normal" sleeping hours.

That didn't mean he was actually in her area or time zone, just that he was sleeping during those times. Experience had taught her, though, that it was likely the shaper who was pulling these stunts was in fact pretty close to her. It was why Vadim had sent her here to Central Pennsylvania to find him. She could've worked remotely from California, sure, but it would've meant a fucked-up sleep schedule for her.

Sinking deeper into the dream, Stephanie focused on her representation. She'd worked cases where she'd had to use a different sort of face and body, even a few times a different form altogether, and she liked the challenges of forming and keeping those changes. This case hadn't required her to be anything other than who she was, at least beyond the fashions. So far, though, that hadn't worked out so well for her. The closest she'd come to getting near the perp was the night she'd represented in that romantic gown, and look what had happened.

Kent.

What had that all been about tonight? Cheesecake. Laughter. He'd very carefully not tried anything even remotely romantic. Should she have been relieved or offended? Maybe she ought to have been a little more aggressive. Made the first move.

She didn't have time to worry about that now. She was going to find out the real-world identity of Mr. Slick tonight if she had to travel the entire Ephemeros to do it. Then she'd be done with this job and that would mean the weird work issue with Kent would no longer matter. Of course, it also meant she'd probably be heading back to California.

She'd worry about that part later, too.

For now, Stephanie stretched, loving the way her muscles and bones worked together inside the dream world. Nothing hurt, nothing cramped or ached. Sure, she could get injured if she wasn't careful, but she'd been doing this for such a long time that the only way she really got hurt was if someone did something to her before she could stop them, and not something nice like shaping a platter of dessert in front of her or tempting her into a kiss she really wanted anyway.

On her last case she'd ended up going face-to-face with a woman bent on terrorizing her cheating husband into a heart attack while he slept—that bitch had been righteously crazy, and while Stephanie couldn't blame her for wanting revenge, murder was still murder even if you committed it while you were sleeping. That woman had claimed not to know she was shaping anything, but her innocence had been a farce, proven when she'd turned herself into a mass of seething snakes and launched herself at Stephanie. The bites had been excruciating, leaving scars, but nothing Stephanie hadn't been able to handle. She'd managed to wrestle them into a knot and shove them inside a box, slamming and locking the lid until the woman had begged for release.

Of course, her remorse might not be lasting. That was the problem with punishment in the Ephemeros. You couldn't make it stick, not without doing major harm to the sleeper's real-world body. Putting someone in a permanent coma to keep them imprisoned in the dream world was a last resort, saved for only the worst sorts of criminals.

Stephanie's goal on this case was to find out Mr. Slick's real-world counterpart and then send the information to Vadim. Other members of the Crew would connect him to the actual thefts. It might require some fancy finagling of records or "proof," because it wasn't as though they could go in and explain how he'd been using dreams to manipulate people into giving him their financial information so he could simply take what he wanted without leaving a trace. But it was Vadim's job to assign a Crew member skilled in creating those sorts of tracks, not hers.

Her job was to find out who he was.

When she had, she was going to take a long vacation, just as she'd promised Denise. Someplace warm, with lots of drinks and food and dancing, and she would stay up late every night and barely sleep at all.

Stephanie settled deeper into the dream world with a concerted push of her will. She was aware, as always, of her sleeping body. Her head on the pillow. The weight of the blankets. The white-noise machine. Those things were her touchstones. Her way back in the unlikely event she found herself lost in here. It had never happened to her, but she knew it could.

Every shaper she'd ever met knew the stories of others who'd lost their way and couldn't wake up. She'd never met one, had not in fact met anyone who ever had, but like urban legends about bodies stuffed beneath hotel mattresses and spider eggs in bubble gum, there was always someone who knew someone who'd heard about someone else. Unlike the spider eggs, Stephanie believed in the real truth of being made incapable of getting out of the Ephemeros.

It was also not likely she was going to come across Mr. Slick tonight, it being so close to morning, but she figured she had to try. Where might he be? How about a place where a lot of other people were still clinging to their dreams before the alarms went off. So she opened herself to the push and pull of the collective will that shaped the dream world and let herself be drawn toward… What would it be tonight?

The last time it had been that Victorian mansion. Sometimes it was a dance club, others an amusement park, a shopping mall, a stadium. The places where people congregated in the real world were often represented in the Ephemeros, too, sometimes with bits and pieces of all those sorts of locations all in one. Tonight it was a park, a big one, with green grass and trees and benches and sweetly curving paths on which some people strolled in old-fashioned clothes and others rode bikes or skated on wheels they'd manifested from the bottoms of their feet.

She saw a few people manifesting with wings or horns or tails, a few curious creatures that looked like beasts but that she knew were really people who wanted, at least for a night, to be animal and not human. She saw no sign of her target. Maybe he'd had a run-in with the Crew before now and recognized her, or maybe he was just wily, because he always managed to disappear before she could get to him.

"Hi," said a man from beside her. He was dressed like Bert from *Mary Poppins*, the Disney version. Striped pants, white jacket, pink bow tie. A cartoonish penguin kept step beside him, a part of his manifestation and not a separate entity.

"Not tonight, buddy. Sorry." Stephanie shielded herself from the sleeper's hesitant attempt at shaping her into the matching nanny to his chimney sweep. What sort of dream *that* guy was having, she had no desire to discover. She tried hard not to judge what people dreamed about, but damn, there were some things she really didn't want to know.

He was easy enough to put off. So was everything else going on. She didn't feel any other shapers here right now, at least none who were working hard to mold the Ephemeros to their will. Like herself, they were going along with whatever the collective unconscious wanted. She didn't try to seek them out. She did, however, send out a firm but discreet push.

Have you seen him?

She shaped it as a text message and a photo of Mr. Slick's silhouette, appearing in identical phones in every hand she could reach within the scope of her talents. When no answers came, she moved through the park, shaping and sending without much hope of an answer. She hadn't set herself an alarm, but others clearly had, because one by one many of the locals began fading away. Not all of them, obviously. There were always going to be people sleeping and dreaming all over the world at all different times. But for the most part, those in her part of the world were beginning to wake.

With a sigh, Stephanie sent out one more push. She should wake up, too, so she could accomplish some things in the real world and get back to sleep tonight at a decent time. First, though, she thought she might enjoy herself a bit.

That was when the answer came in, of course, just as she was getting ready to shape herself a warm and sunny spot on a sandy beach. Her phone vibrated in her hand. She looked at it.

I've seen him.

She spotted him at once, a tall man with angular features and the phone she'd shaped in his hand. "Kent?"

He smiled, and while his representation in the dream was slightly different tonight—he was a little more muscular, dressed a little better, his hair a little longer, that smile was exactly the same. "Hi, Stephanie. Did you get my text?"

"You've seen him?"

"Not that one. The other one. The one I sent you earlier, about what a great time I had tonight."

Neither of them had taken a step, but they now faced each other with only a few inches between them. He'd done that, and she'd been so surprised to see him that she hadn't resisted his push. It was the same as it had been in the mansion. Stephanie laughed lightly.

"Oh…no. I'll get that one when I wake up. But thank you. I had a great time with you, too." Honesty was so much easier here, where people might shape themselves to look different but almost never lied about how they truly felt.

"Good. I'd like to take you out on a date," Kent said.

Stephanie laughed again. "Sure. If you ask me, I'll say yes."

"Yeah?" He grinned.

She shrugged, knowing that whatever they talked about in here, he was probably not going to act on it when he woke up. He'd play it off as a dream. Not real.

More important, she had a case to work on. "So. You've seen him. This guy."

She pushed another grainy photo onto Kent's phone. It was the best she had. He looked at it, then nodded.

"Oh. Yeah. He's been around here. What's he done?"

"He steals money from people by making them give up their private account information in the dreams, then uses it in the waking world to access their credit cards and stuff." She tilted her head to study him, wondering if he'd put the pieces together.

Kent in the waking world had seemed like a pretty smart guy, and he maintained that here. "He's the guy who's been hacking into Member's Best?"

"Yes. And probably lots of other places, too. Where have you seen him?"

"He was talking to that woman over there." Kent pointed.

Stephanie looked. The woman was sitting on a bench, feeding a covey of colorful pigeons. Not the most exciting dream she'd ever witnessed, but again, she wasn't going to judge.

"Hey," Kent said as she moved toward the woman. "Wait a second!"

Stephanie glanced at him. "I'll see you in your office on Monday. Ask me out on that date. I'll say yes. I promise."

With that, she moved away from him, heading for Mr. Slick. "Hey!"

He turned. At the sight of her, the fangs he'd been sprouting shrank into his gums. He took a stumbling step back. The woman he'd been talking to made a small noise of relief.

"Can I go? Can I please go? Please, I want to get out of here!"

Without looking at her, Stephanie said, "Yes. Get."

The woman moved away but remained, a shadow standing in silence. Mr. Slick didn't move at all. He had no face, not really, just an amorphous blob of features struggling to rearrange. Into what? Something that would scare her?

"You might as well forget about it," she told him. "I know what's what in here, and you're not going to scare me. So why don't we have a little talk about this business with the bank accounts? What do you say? I promise you, it'll be much better for you if you cooperate."

Mr. Slick's laugh was low and bubbling, like something rising from a mud puddle. A mouth appeared, or the semblance of one. "I know you."

"Do you?" Stephanie kept her gaze on him while she used her will to weave an invisible net, sticky, thinking she might at least bind him in place with it long enough to get some answers.

"Yes. I do. I've seen you before. But you don't pay attention to me, do you? Just that once. But every other time, I'm just…" Mr. Slick stopped and shook his head. Features formed and disappeared. He grew taller, thin, long arms and legs. Menacing.

"You mean out there? In the waking world?" Carefully, she twitched her fingers to toss the slightly glimmering strands around his ankles without alerting him to the binding. It wouldn't hold him long once he knew about it, but she hoped it would keep him in place a little longer anyway.

"Yes. Nobody pays attention out there. In here, I'm…somebody important. I do things. People give me things!"

Stephanie tugged the binding the tiniest bit tighter. It would trip him up, at the least, if he tried to run. "You steal things. That's what you mean."

"What difference does it make? Out there, nobody gives me anything!" Mr. Slick's voice wavered, getting thin.

The air between them wriggled, like the heat waves coming off a summertime road. Mr. Slick himself grew thin, transparent. Not waking, but definitely disappearing.

"Stay right there," Stephanie warned. "I need to talk to you."

"I don't have to talk to you! You're not my… You're not anything to me!"

Gone was the tall silhouette of the vampire, the werewolf, the slick thief in black leather. Replacing it was a smaller frame—black hair, pale face, dark eyes, a red slash of a mouth—but something nevertheless familiar about it. And then he was pushing her, hard, slamming her with a vibrating force that was not physical and yet might as well have been, because it sent her stumbling back.

She lost hold of the binding. She caught her balance before she could fall on her ass. Her heart raced, expecting an attack, but Mr. Slick only pushed again. Harder this time, sending Stephanie back another few feet.

"You can't stop me! I can do what I want, and I'm not hurting anyone! They can all make more money!"

"You are hurting people. You're stealing, and whether or not they can afford it, it's still wrong!"

Mr. Slick pushed, this time slapping a sticky piece of tape over Stephanie's mouth. "Shut up. Shut up."

Stephanie ripped away the tape, wincing at the sting of it. She rubbed her lips and decided to try a different approach. She held out her hands and spoke gently.

"Look, it's not like I can prosecute you for this. You have to know that. If you stop now, I won't be able to trace you in the waking world. You won't be caught. You just have to agree to stop."

For a moment, it seemed as though it might work, but then Mr. Slick shook his head. He'd shrunk, no longer a few feet taller than Stephanie, now a few inches shorter. Slighter. The air around him still shifted and turned, making it impossible to see who was behind the representation.

"I can't stop," he said, almost pleading. His voice had shrunk, too. Grown softer. Sweeter. "Don't you get it? It's all I have, really. When I take stuff from people and get away with it, it makes me feel like at least someone fucking notices me."

And then without another word or hint of warning, Mr. Slick disappeared.

"Shit," Stephanie said, defeated.

Behind her, the woman made another low noise. "I thought it was a soul sucker. Gonna suck my soul."

"Yeah, well. Something sort of like that, sure. What did he ask you?" Stephanie turned toward her.

"My first pet's name and the name of the street I grew up on."

"Did you tell him?" Stephanie asked.

The woman nodded, looking confused. "Was that wrong?"

Stephanie sighed, feeling the pull of morning in her own consciousness. "You should know better, even in a dream. What's your name?"

The woman told her right before Stephanie woke, and she wrote it down. Then she lay back in the bed for a few more minutes, puzzling over everything Mr. Slick had said. Stephanie knew him? From where?

Chapter 9

Kent had not been able to forget about the dream. Here it was, Monday, and he was still thinking about seeing Stephanie in that weird park and how she'd promised him that if he asked her out, she would say yes. Was he really going to do it?

"Hi," he greeted her as she knocked on his office door and peeked around it. "C'mon in."

"Sorry I'm a little late." She shot him a small apologetic grin as she settled into the chair on the other side of his desk. "Traffic."

"No problem." Small talk. Stupid. But he couldn't just blurt out a date request here in the office. "I was just about to go out and grab a coffee, though. Why don't we take the meeting there?"

She gave him an odd, fleeting look but nodded and stood. "Sounds great. I have some updates, but they won't take long. And I could always use a coffee."

"And a piece of cheesecake?" Too much, he told himself, but Stephanie didn't seem to think so.

She laughed. "It's a little early for cheesecake. You could convince me to eat a muffin, though."

"Done."

They chatted, more inane small talk, as they left his office and headed around the corner to the Green Bean, where they both ordered hot drinks and blueberry muffins, then took them to a small table in the corner. Watching her warm her hands on the cup, Kent knew there was no way he was going to actually ask her out, dream or no.

"I think I have an idea of who he might be targeting next," Stephanie said, surprising him.

"You do? How?"

She waved a hand. "Oh. Algorithms. Um…patterns in his previous marks."

That sounded plausible and yet something in the way she said it gave him pause. "Huh. So what do we do about it? Do we let the potential victim know? That could cause some concern. I mean, if we start scaring our customers, they might simply close their accounts. I don't think the board's going to be on…board."

Carol would've rolled her eyes, but Stephanie laughed at his play on words. "No. I agree. We can't warn them. But you can be prepared for any suspicious activity and handle it if it comes up, before the customer even knows."

"But you have no idea who's doing it? No closer to catching him? Or her," Kent added, to be fair.

"Or…her?" Stephanie paused as though considering that. "No. Sorry. Working on that. But I can give the name of who might be his next target. You can monitor her account."

"I guess if that's the best we can do…"

She blew on her coffee and sipped, then set down the cup to give him a serious look. "I know it's not the best result, but believe me, Kent, we're getting closer. Last night I…"

"Last night you what?"

"I got very close," she said. "Tracking him down."

Kent had never asked how she did that. He'd always assumed it was with some computer program or something, because even though there'd never been any trace of hacking with any of the thefts, that had to be what was going on. He drank some of his own coffee and watched her tear a bite of her muffin.

"So," he said after a half minute had passed and neither of them had spoken, "did you have a good weekend?"

"It started off great," she told him with a grin. "Late-night cheesecake and all."

Kent smiled. "Oh, yeah?"

"Yep." She leaned forward a bit to say, like a secret, "It was nice. Really nice."

"So…" *Do it*, he urged himself. *Just ask her already.* "Maybe you'd like to do it again?"

"Oh, yes. For sure. I said so, didn't I?" An expression fluttered across her face, there and gone so fast he couldn't determine what it had been. "I mean, in the text. I answered your text."

"You…did?" Kent pulled his phone from his pocket to check, but no, there'd been nothing. "It didn't come through."

She smiled, brow furrowing. "No? Huh. Weird. I guess you thought I must've been blowing you off."

"No. I mean… Yes. I figured you were going to pretend I hadn't sent it, that's all. I wasn't going to mention it."

They looked at each other across the table, both silent again but this time smiling. Stephanie's eyes seemed very blue as she looked at him over the rim of her coffee cup.

"Would you like to go out again?"

"On a date?" she asked, her tone of voice making it clear she already knew the answer.

Kent nodded. "Yes. On a real, official date. I'll pick you up at your house and everything."

"Flowers?" Stephanie asked.

This woman was going to kill him, he thought. In all the best ways. Dead as a doornail.

"Flowers, if you like," he told her. "Candy, too."

She laughed and covered her mouth with her hand for a moment. Her eyes gleamed. She leaned across the table, just a little. "You got it. Friday night?"

"Yes," Kent said, and some weird impulse made him add, "You promise?"

For a second, he thought he'd gone too far. Too fast, too creepy. What had felt like flirting might've come across as too desperate.

She smiled, though. "Yes. Sure. I promise."

He had no reason for the feeling of relief at her answer, but it was there anyway. "Great. Pick you up at six?"

They chatted about the details for a minute or so longer before Kent caught sight of the time and realized he had to get back to the office for a meeting he was going to be late for. They parted ways in the credit-union parking lot with a half hug he refused to let him-

overanalyze. It wasn't until later in the afternoon that he remembered he had never found out the name of the customer Stephanie thought was going to be the thief's next mark.

Chapter 10

"It's going," Stephanie said in answer to Vadim's question about her progress. "Slowly. I get so close, but this guy... It's like he knows just how to avoid me."

"He's probably been doing it for a long time." Vadim, tall, bald, intimidating, nodded at her from her computer screen. "Do you need backup?"

She shook her head. "No. But if it goes on much longer, more people are going to get duped. I feel bad. I should've figured him out by now."

"All things in their time." Vadim peered at her. "You look tired."

Stephanie laughed. "Gee, thanks."

"You've been spending too much time shaping and not enough time simply dreaming," her boss declared. "You should take tonight off."

"I'm fine," she protested but stopped at his look. "I know the rules, Vadim."

Everyone needs to dream," he told her. "Without proper dreaming time, your brain does not count the hours you're unconscious as true sleep. And without enough sleep…"

She grumbled, "Yes, I know. You go crazy."

"It's no joking matter, Stephanie. You are too good to lose to madness." Vadim frowned. "I insist you take tonight off."

She couldn't enter the Ephemeros without being aware that she was dreaming, but she could definitely spend more time relaxing and enjoying the dream world rather than actively working it. "Fine, but if I get even a hint of that guy anywhere around, I'm on it."

"Of course. But other than that, take a break." Vadim gave her a small, tight smile. "I am envious of you, of course. To be able to manipulate the dream world. It's a true talent, one I wish I could cultivate."

She didn't blame him. She'd learned in toddlerhood that she could shape and push the Ephemeros and couldn't imagine not being able to control her dreams. With another few minutes of casual chat, she and Vadim ended their conversation and disconnected the call.

Here it was, a full night off. For a moment, Stephanie thought about calling Denise to see if she wanted to head out on the town, maybe for a hump-day happy hour, but then decided against it. She was going to spend the night at home pampering herself, she thought. A couple glasses of good wine she usually couldn't otherwise indulge in, because too much alcohol made it hard to function in dreams as much as in the waking world. A steaming bubble bath. A good book. Chocolate. Oh, yeah, she had a couple pieces of decadent, expensive chocolates she'd been saving for a treat, and if a night off decreed by your boss didn't count, she didn't know what would.

The only thing that would make it better would be a sexy guy joining her in the tub, Stephanie thought as she settled into the apartment's vintage claw-foot with her wineglass and the chocolates on a plate. She hadn't had an orgasm with another person since just before she got assigned to move here, and that had been a rendezvous with Tomas in the Ephemeros. She and her friend with benefits had been spending quality sexy times with each other, on and off, for decades, though they'd never once met in real life.

She should look him up. Wine, the warm bath, her own slick fingers running over her wet and naked flesh...too many nights without enough quality sleep... She was going to doze right there in the tub. Doze and slip into dreams.

She appeared in the Ephemeros in a warm, bubbling pool of deep-gray-and-blue water faintly scented of lavender. Naked. A little thinner here, a little rounder there, Stephanie noticed with a small chuckle as she stretched in the lovely warmth and let herself float on her back. Above her, a trillion points of light pricked the black velvet of the sky.

Dream, she told herself. Dream, dream, dream.

She did let herself send out some feelers, a little push here and there. Looking for Tomas. When he didn't respond, looking for anyone.

Stephanie had no problem finding sex in the Ephemeros. In here, she could experiment. Take chances she never would while awake. She could be whoever she pleased, do what she liked. It wasn't always emotionally

...ng to wake up alone after a rampant nightly bout of fucking, but it satisfied her body anyway.

Why should tonight be any different, she thought as she stood to get out of the pool. Her skin gleamed in the starlight. Her nipples peaked at the soft, sighing brush of night air against her nakedness. Why shouldn't she look for a lover here, have her way with him and move on?

Because of Kent, she told herself with a rueful shake of the head. Because she had a date with him in two days, and he was the first real-world guy she'd had any interest in for a long time. Fucking someone else in here wouldn't be cheating even if they were in a long-term relationship, so why, then, did she feel so hesitant to keep sending out her signals into the Ephemeros's vastness?

"Stephanie?"

Turning, she shaped a gauzy dress of ribbons that clung to her wet skin. It did nothing to hide her tight nipples or the shadow between her legs. If anything, a dress like that was meant to draw the viewer's attention to just those places. She'd shaped it without thinking.

"Kent? What are...? Oh. Wow." She shook her head and covered her breasts briefly with her hands. When she tried to shape a different sort of gown, though, one more modest, the pull of his will stopped her. She paused to look at him. "No?"

"You look beautiful."

"Of course I do." She laughed. "It's a dream."

It could be tricky, telling a sleeper they were dreaming. Most of the time, they didn't believe it, and that was fine, unless there was a reason to convince them, like if they were in danger or something. She watched Kent's face carefully to see if he was shocked.

He smiled. "I should've known, right? A woman

as beautiful as you wouldn't give me the time of day otherwise."

"That's not true." She moved a step closer and put a hand on his shoulder. He was warm. "I said yes when you asked me out."

He looked faintly surprised, as though he'd forgotten. "Oh. Right. But now I'm sleeping. I have to wait a couple days to see you again."

"You're seeing me right now," Stephanie said with a laugh and let herself sink deeper into the dream.

She could've shaped them into anything or anywhere using the force of her will. Instead, she opened herself to whatever it was Kent wanted to dream about. She had the night off, after all.

And he was very, very cute.

Yet when he moved to kiss her, as she had the first time he tried, she turned her face at the last second so his lips caught her cheek and not her mouth. Sure, he wouldn't think of this as real, if he remembered it at all, but she was thinking of Friday and their date and the possibilities ahead of them.

"Wait," she whispered as he pulled her closer. God, he smelled good. He felt good, too. She could've blamed the wine, but no. When he tried to kiss her again, she shook her head. "Wait, I want it to be real. Not just a dream."

He pulled away to look at her, his expression serious. Then he slayed her with that smile again. "Aren't you supposed to get what you want in dreams?"

"Yes." She took a step back. Then another. Crooked her finger to get him to follow. "What you really want is to wait."

"I can't argue with that." He followed.

took his hand and walked with him through a landscape that shifted and changed with every step. Colors swirled. Neither of them were holding anything in place. Their fingers linked, that was real. Their conversation, words she would not recall in the morning, that was real, too.

"Look," Stephanie said and waved a hand to make a field of flowers grow in front of them. "Try it."

Kent wiggled his fingers, but nothing happened. They both laughed. He tried again, sprouting a dandelion he then plucked for her so she could blow away the seeds. They walked. Night was heading toward morning, and she didn't want to wake up.

They'd been laughing about nothing important when Kent stopped so short that Stephanie kept walking for a few steps before she looked up. "Kent?"

"Hey, I know her," he said. "Who's she talking to?"

She looked to where he was pointing. Her happy, giddy mood vanished when she saw the elderly woman sitting in a recliner, leaning forward to listen as a man in a long black leather coat whispered in her ear.

"Oh, shit. It's him!" she cried and leaped toward them.

That was when the wave came up and swept her away.

She woke, spluttering, her head beneath the water of the tub. Cursing, she got out, coughing. That had been stupid. She dried off and put on some comfy pajamas, her earlier good feelings about the dream with Kent fading. No matter how nice it had been inside, there was never any telling what it would be like for real.

Worse, she'd once again let Mr. Slick slip through her grasp.

Chapter 11

He'd been waiting all week for Friday, but not for this reason. Another account compromised. This time it had been his mother's.

The credit union was insured, of course, but that didn't help make him feel much better when he'd pulled up Mom's accounts after she'd called him questioning why her automatic bill payment hadn't gone through from her checking. Kent had spent all morning trying to figure out where the money had gone, how it had been withdrawn without a trace. His stomach sick, he'd transferred a couple thousand of his own money into Mom's account to cover the rest of her bills. Fortunately, the thief hadn't drained her savings or money-management accounts, and Kent worked quickly to change Mom over to all new accounts, but in the end it didn't make him feel much better.

He'd called Stephanie immediately but got her voice

mail. He hadn't left a message. He'd spent the rest of
the day fielding inquiries from the board and sifting
through data files to see if he could catch any signs of
other thefts. Nobody called to complain, so he supposed
everything was all right, but for how much longer?

By the end of the day, his head hurt from clenching
his jaw. His stomach churned from the stress. He got
out of work too late to go home and shower or change.
He was going to be late picking her up.

He wasn't even sure he wanted to.

It wasn't Stephanie's fault, and he knew that. She was
one investigator working on a case that Kent could see
was unusual. But if she'd done her job by now, his mom
wouldn't have had her checking account wiped out.

Sitting in the parking spot in front of her apartment,
he pulled out his phone. He should call. Make an excuse. Send a text?

Too late—the curtain of her apartment door twitched,
and the door itself opened as Stephanie peeked out. He
could see her smile from here. Shit. She waved him in.

He'd make an excuse, Kent thought. Say he was coming down with something, which was what it felt like,
sort of, to stand on her front mat and think about telling
her he didn't want to go out with her, after all.

He opened his mouth, but before he could say a word,
Stephanie pushed up onto her tiptoes to put her arms
around his neck. Her cheek pressed to his, she said
softly into his ear, "I'm so sorry about your mom. We
are going to catch this son of a bitch. I promise you,
Kent. I'm going to make it my mission in life to track
him down and make him sorry he ever lifted a single
cent from anyone."

His arms had gone around her automatically. His

eyes closed. He pressed his face into the softness of her dark hair and breathed in the sweetness of her perfume, something light and fresh. Citrus. Damn it, she felt good in his arms, and her words had taken away some of his earlier frustration.

Stephanie stepped back from him, though she let her hands run down his shoulders to rest lightly on his forearms. His hands had anchored on her hips. She looked up at him, her brow furrowed, her mouth thin.

"If you don't feel like taking me out, Kent, I get it."

It had been what he'd been thinking all day long, but when he was faced with her actually saying it, all he could do was shake his head. "No. Look, it's not your fault—"

"It is. If I'd caught this guy before now," she said, "your mom would've been okay. So would all those other people."

His fingers curled a little on her hips. She wore soft leggings and a slouchy sweater, but beneath that, he could feel her curves. "It's not your fault he's a thief."

She tipped her face to look up at him. "I've been on the case for six months. It's long past time I caught him. That's all. You might not blame me, but I take responsibility. So if you don't want to go out…"

"No. I asked you out. We should go out."

Neither of them moved. A flash of a dream came to him, the two of them walking through fields of flowers, hand in hand. He remembered her laughing.

"I…dreamed about you," he said. "Night before last."

Stephanie's smile was like watching a flower bloom. "I know you did. I was there."

Kent shook his head a little. "Okay, this is weird. What's going on?"

He saw the hesitation in her expression and waited for her to give him some lame explanation, but Stephanie drew in a short, sharp breath. She took another step back. Squared her shoulders.

"He's using their dreams to get their information," she said. "And I've been trying to find him in the dream world, but I haven't been able to yet."

Stephanie had told only three people in her life about the Ephemeros who hadn't already known about it. The first had been her high school boyfriend, her first love. She'd had a vulnerable moment after the night she lost her virginity and spilled her truth to him. He'd broken up with her the next day.

The other two had been strangers on a train. Both had been sleeping and had shown up in her world because of the proximity. They'd woken, startled, and given her guilty glances very much alike despite their not knowing each other any more than they'd known her. Her explanation of why the three of them had been having the same dream had spilled out of her on a whim. Rodney and Darryl had gone on to become a couple. They sent her Christmas cards every year.

Now she sat across from her kitchen table with Kent staring at her, and she waited for him to get up and walk out. Call her crazy. Tell her to never darken his doorstep again.

Instead, he said, "Can I do it, too?"

"A little, yes. More than that, I don't know. I mean, everyone shapes their dreams—it's just a matter of if they know it and can do it on purpose." She got up to refill both their mugs of coffee. She'd pulled a frozen cheesecake out to serve, too. Funny how she'd never have bothered to pick up a cheesecake at all before last week, but it had ended up in her cart because of him.

He nodded but said nothing. He leaned forward to put his elbows on the table, then pushed his glasses up on his nose. "Huh."

"Yeah." She laughed. "Crazy, right?"

"So when I dreamed about you…"

"The dream world is a real place. It's called the Ephemeros," she told him, picking her words carefully. "What happens in it can affect people in the real world, though most of the time, it doesn't. When we met there, it was because we were both asleep at the same time, and though geographical proximity is not at all required, it's usually a factor in who meets up. But you can dream about anyone, anytime. It doesn't necessarily mean that actual person is in there with you. It just means you've shaped them, or that you've put out a…well, like a signal. And someone who can shape not only themselves but also everything else comes along and helps your dream be whatever it needs to be."

"Someone like you?" Kent asked.

She nodded. "Yes. Someone like me."

"You can make dreams come true?" His smile tipped a bit on one side, rueful. Contemplative.

"Yes. I can. There are people who do it all the time."

He wrapped his hands around the coffee mug. "Hmm. Why?"

"Because dreams are important," she said. "Without them, without living out whatever it is we do inside them, well…we go mad. I mean, literally crazy."

"I want to try it."

Stephanie dug her fork into the cheesecake and let herself savor a bite before answering. "Okay."

"Okay?" Kent seemed surprised. "Just like that, okay?"

"Well, sure." She shrugged. "It's not like there's a secret club that you have to apply for membership to. You either can or you can't."

"Can you teach me?"

"I don't know." She thought about that for a few seconds. "I know it's possible to practice shaping and to get better at it. But I'm not sure you teach someone to do it if they can't already. Kind of like telling a good story. You either can or you can't."

"The other night, in the field. I made a flower, didn't I?"

She laughed. "Yes. You did."

"On purpose."

"Yes." She hesitated. "The other part is knowing you're dreaming. Have you ever had one of those dreams, where you knew it?"

"Yeah," he said, sounding eager. "Once, I dreamed I was being chased by a shark, but I knew it was a dream and I turned around and punched it."

"Yikes. Brave," she said with a grin. She let out a small breath, then said, "I know you were angry at me about your mom. I really am sorry."

"It just makes me all the more determined to catch this jerk. And this is your job? I mean…you do it all the time?"

"When needed. Yes. I shape in dreams to help sleepers along, to help them reach their goals in the dreams, whatever they are, but that's not my job. It's a responsibility." She shrugged. "I'd been doing that without really knowing why for years before Vadim approached me about joining the Crew. The money's good. The work isn't usually hard. And this really shouldn't have been that difficult for me. I guess I… Maybe I wasn't trying hard enough."

"I'm sure you take your job seriously, Stephanie."

"I like being here," she said suddenly, as though daring him to challenge her. "I like working with you. I think maybe I didn't try hard enough because I knew that once the job was over, I'd have to leave."

They stared at each other quietly.

"Sorry about the date. I really did mean to take you out," Kent said. "To be honest, I've been thinking about it for a while."

"You didn't bring the flowers," she told him with a small grin. "Or the candy. How about I take a rain check?"

He sat back in his chair. "Deal. So…how do we catch this asshole?"

Chapter 12

"This isn't the first time I've ended up in a woman's bed on a first date," Kent said in a low voice. "But it's definitely not the way I'd expected things to go."

Beside him, Stephanie giggled. She'd lent him a pair of oversize sweatpants and a T-shirt, then tucked them both into her bed. They'd been staring in silence at the ceiling for about ten minutes while he tried to fall asleep by timing his breathing to her steady, even breaths. It hadn't worked.

"You're a little naughty. I like that." She turned to face him.

He rolled, too. Their knees touched. He wanted to touch more than that but kept himself from it.

"I'm not tired," he said. "Sorry."

"Me neither."

"You don't have any tricks?" He settled a little more into the pillow.

"Deep breathing. Um…" Stephanie laughed and pulled the covers up over her nose for a second. "Orgasm?"

It was not what he'd expected, and he laughed even as several muscles tensed in places he hadn't been paying much attention to for the past few weeks. "Um…"

"Sorry, sorry." She laughed a little breathlessly. "It's true, but a little too much. I know."

"I'd be game, if you are," Kent said.

Her laughter eased and she pulled the blanket away from her face. "On the first date, huh? What a player."

"I'm the furthest thing from a player you could ever meet," he told her quietly. "I think you know that by now."

Silence.

"Yes," she said finally. "I know."

Did she move first? He thought so, although he was moving, too. The kiss was light, soft, gentle, the hint of her breath tickling his lips until, oh, damn, her mouth opened and she drew his tongue in against hers with a low groan that got him hard as rock within half a minute.

She broke the kiss with an embarrassed laugh, though she didn't pull away. "I thought it would be good, but I didn't know how good."

"So…how long have you been thinking about this?" He let his hand slide up to rest on her hip beneath the blankets. She wore a pair of lightweight boxers and a man's T-strap undershirt. There was the tiniest bit of bare skin between the bottom of the shirt and the top of the drawers. When he touched her there, she shivered.

"Oh, for about six months." She pressed her face to the side of his neck. "Since the first time I walked into your office and saw you with your shirtsleeves rolled up. I have a thing for sexy forearms. And guys in glasses."

Heat spread through him. He let his fingers trace more bare skin, easing up the hem of her shirt. Then over her belly, pausing at the small dip of her navel. Across her ribs. Higher still, to just below the curve of her breast. He stopped.

Stephanie let out a low, shuddering sigh. "You can touch me, Kent. This is real. We're really here. We can do this."

He wanted to. Everything about it felt right, even if the smart part of his mind, the part resisting the heat pooling in his groin, told him it was probably going to end painfully in the long run.

As if she felt his hesitation, she nuzzled against his throat, nipping lightly with the perfect amount of pressure to make him squirm. "If you don't want to…"

"I do." He pulled her closer so she could feel how much. "I just…"

She moved to look at his face. "It's soon. I know. You just broke up with Carol. I won't be sticking around. It's not something to jump into. I understand. But what if we just look at it as something to try? I mean…no strings, no promises?"

"Is that what you really want?"

Her brow furrowed. "Truth? No, not really. But I'm not saying I think we should jump into something serious right off the bat. As far as sex goes, I'm not exactly a prude about one-night stands and that sort of thing. I don't hop into bed with just anyone, either."

He stroked a fingertip over her eyebrows to smooth the crease, then tucked her hair behind her ear. "I like you a lot, Stephanie."

"I like you, too."

He kissed her again, tasting her sweetness until she gasped and moved against him. She shook a little. She pressed her head to his chest, and he tightened his arms around her.

"There are other ways to fall asleep," she whispered.

He kissed the top of her head. "But that's not really what this is about right now, is it?"

Her shoulders shook as she laughed. Her breath heated his skin through the T-shirt's thin material. When she put her hand flat on his belly below the hem of it, the warmth of her fingers made him draw in a long, slow breath. His cock throbbed. When she slid a hand lower to cup him, he couldn't hold back the small groan.

He didn't move, though. Uncertain if this was the direction they should go, if they both really wanted it, if they'd be making a mistake. It didn't feel like one. It felt like the best shot at happiness he'd ever taken.

Kent was right. This had nothing to do with sleep and everything to do with orgasms. More than that, too. It was something Stephanie had wanted without admitting it to herself for months.

"Sometimes, in dreams, you jump without knowing you have a place to land," she murmured into his kiss as she slid a hand into the sweatpants she'd lent him and found his hard, thick length. She stroked, gratified and aroused at the way he drew in a gasp at her touch. "But sometimes, when you jump, you fly."

Kent pulled her closer, his kiss getting deeper. His tongue thrust against hers as his hips moved, too. She tugged the sweatpants a little lower on his hips to free him, almost too nervous to look at his nakedness now that she had the chance. Then she didn't have to, because they were kissing so hard and fast all she could think about was how good he tasted, how delicious, how his touch was making her crazy.

He rolled them both to get on top of her, nudging her knees apart with his. One hand slid behind her neck to cradle her. The other moved up to cup her breast. He thumbed her nipple erect, then pinched it lightly, making her cry out into his mouth.

He pushed himself up to tug his shirt off over his head; Stephanie pulled off hers while he worked, too. For a moment, she wished for the Ephemeros to give her bigger boobs and a flatter belly. For a second, she shielded herself from his gaze. Kent ran his hands up her ribs, tickling a little, then let his palms go flat on her skin.

"You're gorgeous," he told her.

She believed him.

Arching, Stephanie put her arms over her head to curl her fingers around the headboard's spindles. She closed her eyes, smiling, as Kent let out a low whistle of appreciation. Her nipples tightened at more tickling touches as he moved his fingertips over her.

It was easy to feel beautiful in the dream world. Even sleepers shaped themselves into loveliness. Stephanie had long ago translated her ability as a shaper into confidence out here where it wasn't so easy to whittle away a few extra pounds or to add curves. Even so, it would've been easy to worry, this first time, if her nakedness pleased him.

Kent gave her no reason for doubt. He bent low over her, whispering compliments in her ear as he traced her body with his fingers, then, moving lower, his mouth.

Over the curves of her shoulders, down her arms. He placed kisses on the tender insides of her elbows and her wrists. He kissed her palms and curved her fingers over wetness he left behind.

He kissed her belly, murmuring her name and words of awe. Sending her higher. Over her hip bones, each one, pausing to nibble while she wiggled. Her thighs, her knees, her ankles. Kneeling over her, he took each foot and kissed her toes, laughing while she protested. Then he slid the sweatpants all the way off and knelt between her legs, fully naked.

Kent put a hand on his cock, lightly stroking. She pushed up on one elbow to get a better look. It was her turn to compliment.

"You work out?" she teased, letting one foot drift up to nudge his hard belly. "Mmm, abs."

"Good genes," he told her.

She arched again, offering her body to him. "Kiss me, Kent."

He did, but not on the mouth. Again he bent to trail his lips and tongue over her thighs and belly, pausing to blow sweet, hot breath through the lace of her panties. Automatically, her hand went to thread through his hair, the silken feeling of it tickling the back of her hand as she lifted her hips to meet his mouth.

He'd slipped her panties off before she knew it, then knelt again between her legs. Gently, he parted her to his questing tongue, which flicked lightly over her clit before he pressed the flat of it to her and stroked. Kent settled onto his belly between her thighs, both hands sliding beneath her ass to lift her to his mouth as he feasted. It was not what Stephanie had expected.

It was so much better.

"Oh," she said. "That's…"

"Good?" he said against her, looking up with a smile. He kissed her there, softly. Then again. He found her clit and sucked it gently before ducking back to the steady, slow stroking that was edging her closer and closer to going over.

She could've resisted, tried to make it last, but when she wriggled and whispered his name, the sound of his groan made it impossible for Stephanie to ask him to wait. She needed this, and him, and oh, fuck, he was giving it to her.

Hovering on the edge, Stephanie rolled her hips, mindless with the pleasure. Kent eased off, blowing soft puffs against her clit until she let out a frustrated gasp that became a laugh. Then a sigh. She looked down at him, her fingers toying in his hair.

"So close," Stephanie whispered. "It feels so good."

She touched his face. Eyebrows. Cheek. She stroked a finger over his lips. He closed his eyes for a second, his gaze hazy when he opened them again. He bent back to her.

Stephanie let him take her away. All the way. Up and over, pleasure coiling inside her so tight she thought she might surely break from it before it could explode. She came with a low cry, then his name. Her body moved; she came again, each wave throbbing through her while she clutched at the sheets so fiercely she pulled them free of the mattress. She fell back, panting.

Silence.

Stephanie licked her lips and breathed. She blinked as the world came back into focus. Kent hadn't moved from between her legs, though he now rested his cheek on her thigh. One hand had moved from her ass to cup her pussy, the warmth strangely comforting and still arousing, even if she didn't think she'd be able to go another round. At least not right away.

"Wow," she said after a few more seconds of quiet broken only by her still-ragged breathing. She moved a hand over his hair, tugging briefly before letting her touch land on his shoulder. "That was..."

He laughed and pushed up on his elbow to move over her body. He kissed her mouth. He covered her with his weight, his cock thick and hard against her thigh.

"That was amazing. You were so... God, Stephanie. Fucking out of this world." He stopped and looked concerned for a moment. "This is real, isn't it? We didn't fall asleep. I'm not dreaming."

She'd have laughed except she could tell he was serious. She pulled him to her for another kiss, then sat up a little to point at one of the clocks on her nightstand. "No. See that? The clock. Can you tell the time?"

"Yeah."

"Time, clocks, words, numbers, those things generally don't work right in the Ephemeros. The easiest way to tell if you're dreaming or awake is if you can read or tell the time." She snuggled closer to him. "This is real."

Kent pressed himself against her for another kiss. "Good. I thought... Never mind."

She reached between them to take his cock in her hand, squeezing gently but enough to make him shiver. She looked at him. "What?"

"I just thought this had to be a dream, that's all. Because that's how it feels, too good to be true."

If she'd ever had a sweeter lover, she couldn't think

about it now. She kissed his mouth, her hand moving slowly. "No. This is real. And it's good. And it's going to get better."

Chapter 13

"I don't know how it could— Oh, shit. Oh. Yeah."

She'd slid down on the bed to take him in her mouth, and Kent closed his eyes, head tipping back at that instant ecstasy. Her mouth was magic, her tongue stroking while she sucked the head of his cock before taking him in deeper. She cupped his balls, fingers stroking that perfect spot, exactly how he liked it best. As if she knew him already.

Stephanie hummed a bit in the back of her throat, the vibration adding a wave of pleasure on top of what was already pretty fucking fantastic. He thrust, then caught himself, not wanting to choke her, but damn, she only made another low noise and gripped him at the base as she took him all the way in. He couldn't stop himself from putting his hands on her head, not trying to guide her or change her pace. He simply needed to touch her.

At his touch, Stephanie paused. Then she took his hand and slid it deep into the fall of her thick dark hair, curling his fingers with hers to give him a good grip. She moaned when he tugged.

"Damn," Kent breathed. "You are so…"

She sucked harder, then slid her mouth off his cock long enough to look up at him and say, "You taste so good."

No woman had ever said such a thing to him. He'd had women who suffered through sucking dick, a few who'd claimed to love it and some who'd refused it outright. Not one of them had ever made him feel as though his cock in her mouth was a delight, a treat. A gift.

She looked up at him with a small smile that hit him right between the eyes with all the unerring and vicious accuracy of cupid's pointiest arrow. This was…more, Kent thought. More than sex. This could be something real.

He wanted to tell her, but when she went down on him again, the best he could manage was a few muttered words that sounded a bit like her name. She did that humming thing, and he lost the ability to even form words at all.

All he could do was relax and let the pleasure wash over him. She eased him higher and higher, then teased a bit until he gasped aloud. Kent would never have believed a woman laughing around his cock could feel so good. It made him laugh, too, not with humor exactly. More like joy.

That was how he felt when he was with her. Filled up with joy. And that was the last coherent thought he had before orgasm flooded him, making him mindless and thrusting and writhing under her skilled mouth and hands.

It went on forever, until spent, he fell back against the pillows and wondered if he was going to catch his breath. When Stephanie crawled up to snuggle against him, her face pillowed in the curve of his shoulder and her hand flat on his chest, Kent turned to kiss her forehead.

There should be words, he thought. He should say something. Yet in the quiet, filled only with the sound of their breathing, he discovered that at least in that moment, speech was unnecessary. All they had to do was hold on to each other. That was more than enough.

Kent fell asleep before she did, which wasn't a surprise to Stephanie, who'd found that most men did. Especially after a blow job. Contented and replete, she was happy to press her face to his bare skin and feel the slowing beat of his heart under her hand.

She did need to put herself under, though. Time was wasting, and she had all day tomorrow to think about what they'd done and what it meant, or what it didn't. Right now she had a job to do, and that meant using a few of her favorite tricks to get herself into the dream world.

She counted back from a hundred, slowly, breathing in and out. She had to do it three times before finally, on the final count of five, she found herself in the forest. She was alone, as she'd expected, though an easy push-pull of her surroundings sent out seeking tendrils to find Kent. It was the sex, she thought as she stepped through the trees, searching for him. It had connected them in a way nothing else ever did.

"Hi," Kent said from behind her. "Stephanie. Hello."

She turned with a smile. "Hey. You're here."

"I am. So are you." He'd represented in jeans and a denim shirt, rolled up in that way she loved. He tilted his head to give her a curious look. "I feel like…"

"You're dreaming," she told him.

"I'm dreaming," Kent agreed. He reached for her, pulling her close. He kissed her, sweetly. No urgency.

She could get lost in this, but not right now. "We have to find the guy who's been stealing."

"I know. I just wanted to kiss you again. You taste like berries."

She licked her lips. It was true. He'd done that, she thought. She liked it.

"Do you remember us talking about what to do in here? How you can shape things if you try?" She gestured and the forest faded, putting them in a gray fog that would make it easier for him to imprint the Ephemeros with his own desire.

"Yes." Kent nodded, his hands still resting lightly on her hips. "Like this."

Slowly and imperfectly, walls formed around them. Some were made of bars, others concrete. The floor that appeared was of smooth black slate. Lighting overhead came from recessed receptacles glowing bright white.

"It's a vault," he told her with a grin. "With lots of money in it. Where else do you think we're going to find a thief?"

She laughed and went to her tiptoes to kiss him. "Good thinking."

"Now what?" He looked around them as the small details filled in.

He was getting better at this as she watched, and Stephanie added her shaping skills to his, anticipating what he meant to do. Stacks of cash. Boxes spilling with gold coin and jewels. It was the stereotype of every bank vault she'd ever seen in any movie. The question was, would it work?

"We call him," she said. "Concentrate. Think of what he looked like. Push it out there into the dream world. Tempt him in."

Others showed up first. Money was powerful motivation for many people, even those who wouldn't have

stolen anything, ever. She saw more than one cat bur-
glar in black masks, striped shirts. Some she didn't see
at all, only their shadows as they slipped into the cells
of the vault and carried away whatever they felt was
important enough to steal.

"I didn't realize it would be so…boring," Kent said.
"Or that it would take so long."

Time passed differently, so it could've been hours or
only minutes since they'd fallen asleep. Still, Stephanie
had to agree. "Yeah. Well…it's a job, you know? Like
any kind of job."

Kent looked past her at a couple of women who were
casually rifling through a box of tiaras and slipping
them into their oversize handbags. "Do you ever get
to just dream?"

"Sure. Of course. It's not like there are so many
dream crimes being committed all the time, at least
not ones serious enough to call attention to themselves."
She stretched, thinking that while this had been a good
idea, it wasn't going to work.

That was when she saw him, Mr. Slick, complete
with black leather trench coat and everything else. He
wasn't taking money from the vault, but he was whispering lasciviously in the ear of one of the handbag
ladies. It was so blatant she could hardly believe it.
She took a step forward, but Kent's hand on her arm
stopped her.

"I shielded us," he said.

Surprised, she paused to look at the shadows surrounding them. "You did? Wow. How did you…?"

"I thought it." Kent sounded as surprised as she had
been, and he shot her a grin. "I figured we wouldn't
want him seeing us, right? At least not until we got
close enough to grab him."

"You're so smart," she told him with a kiss that lingered, though she knew better than to mingle work with pleasure. "Let's get this dill hole."

Chapter 14

Kent was dreaming, and he knew it. More than that, he could control what happened in the dream, not only to himself but to his surroundings. It was like working out, though, when you'd never lifted before, never run a mile. He was tired.

Still, how fucking cool was this?

Distracted, he listened while Stephanie laid out what had to happen in order for them to catch the thief—they could bind him and try to get the information out of him for only so long before it would become dangerous.

"Not only to him, because keeping someone held here when they're trying to get out can lead to real-world problems, but to us, too. I'm used to dealing with people in here, but you're not," she explained while they both watched the guy move through the crowd of women who apparently liked to dream about shop-lifting. "You've got some measure of innate talent—"

"Thanks," he said.

"Focus, Kent," Stephanie said seriously, then paused to take him by the shoulders and turn him to face her. "You know what, I think maybe you should bow out."

He looked at her. "What? No! That asshole stole from my mother. I owe her this."

"You're so new to it." Stephanie shook her head. "I don't want you to end up getting hurt. And this is my job, not yours."

"And you haven't exactly done a great job at it, have you?" He couldn't believe the words had shot out of his mouth, but once out, they couldn't be taken back.

Stephanie moved away from him a step or two. She didn't seem mad. More wary than anything. "That's fair, and true, but what you don't understand is how easy it is to get caught up in here, and how hard it can be to get out. You feel a little drunk now, don't you?"

It was more like stoned, which he'd only ever experienced a couple times a few years ago when a back injury had kept him laid up on the couch dosing with pain meds. "I'm fine. C'mon, he's going to get away."

The tattered shadows he'd pulled around them tugged at his fingers, a physical pull. It hurt a little, keeping up that shield. He hadn't expected it to hurt. As the shield fell away, the thief turned, focusing on them both.

"Oh, you. I should've known." The thief took a second look, stepping closer, zeroing in on Kent. "Hey. I know you! You're that guy from…"

The thief cut off his own words, but in the next second, the overpowering stench of evil assaulted Kent so fiercely he staggered back. Okay, not evil, but the closest thing to it that he could think of. The reek of coconut. It flooded him, his eyes, nose, ears, mouth, tongue, coating it, the taste of it thick in his mouth no matter how he spat to get it out. He went to his knees.

He was aware, as though from far away, of the sound

of Stephanie's shouts, but he couldn't do anything but try to close himself off to the torture of coconut. It made him want to die. In the back of his mind, Kent knew there was no way real coconut, no matter how vile, could do this to him. It was the dream world. He was being manipulated. Knowing it didn't help. If anything, it made him feel worse, because as he watched Stephanie run toward the thief, he knew he'd failed her.

She'd had enough. More than, as a matter of fact. This punk was going to be very, very sorry he'd messed with her man.

That she'd started thinking of Kent as her man was a thought for a different time, because right now Stephanie was hell-bent on grabbing hold of Mr. Slick and shaking the shit out of him. Her fingers skidded on the leather, catching his sleeve. She yanked him forward, making herself taller as she did. Stronger. Faster. Tougher.

"If you don't stop this right now," she hissed, growing fangs, spitting venom, "I'm going to fuck you up so hard you will never get out of here. You'll spend the rest of your life drooling into your pillow while other people wipe your ass for you, because you will never wake up!"

Mr. Slick had been looking beyond her at Kent, who was still on his hands and knees. Now he looked startled. Almost as though he was going to…cry?

"Okay, okay! God, I just wanted to see if I could get away with it, and I used the money for shit I needed!"

Mr. Slick's features were fading and blending again. This time, though, Stephanie kept her grip tight. She dug deep. She held on, even when Mr. Slick started sending out arcing electric shocks, sizzling and burning.

"Who are you?" Stephanie shouted louder than she'd ever yelled before.

The Ephemeros didn't shake—she had nowhere near

that sort of power. It did rumble, though, with a hum and buzz like a hundred thousand angry wasps, stingers poised to attack. It surprised her as much as it did Mr. Slick, at least until Kent got to his feet and strode toward them without so much as a single stumble. His eyes looked red rimmed, his brow creased with pain, but he pushed forward with both his hands in a single shoving gesture that knocked Mr. Slick backward into one of the vaults, where the barred door swung closed and clicked.

Locked.

"You can't do this!" Mr. Slick's panicked voice echoed throughout the vault, which Kent was shaping to look less like a bank and more like a prison. The sound of metal on metal rang out through the vault—Mr. Slick had made his hands into iron bars.

Stephanie had gone against talented and powerful shapers before. This kid was strong, talented but untrained. And he *was* a kid, she realized as a wave of high school–era anxiety washed over her. He was projecting, and hard. She stepped up to the bars, looking in.

"We *can* do this," she said. "You knew there'd be consequences, didn't you?"

Mr. Slick shrank before her eyes, features blurring. He was having trouble holding on to his representation. "I didn't think I'd get caught."

"Well, you did," Kent said.

The entire vault faded around them. So did Mr. Slick. The rush of anxiety that had reminded her of all those times in high school that she'd forgotten her gym clothes or had been ignored by the cute boy she'd had a crush on faded abruptly.

"Shit, he got away," Kent said.

Stephanie shook her head, sagging in the aftermath. Putting the pieces together. She looked at him. "Yeah. But I know who it is."

Chapter 15

Of course the kid tried to run as soon as she saw Stephanie entering the coffee shop. They were ready for that, though. Kent was waiting outside the door, and he snagged the girl by her hoodie and kept her still. She squirmed but didn't scream.

"I didn't do anything. You can't prove anything," she said.

Stephanie glanced behind her into the shop to see if anyone was watching, but as she'd guessed, nobody ever seemed to notice this kid at all. "How do you do it?"

The girl stopped wriggling and gave Stephanie a narrow look. "Do what?"

Stephanie gestured for Kent to take the girl down the street toward the riverfront. They found a park bench, and Kent sat the girl on it. Stephanie stood in front of her, hands on her hips.

"Make yourself hard to see," she said.

"Nobody wants to pay attention to some raggedy

kid," the girl said. She clutched her laptop bag against her chest.

Kent shrugged. "That must suck."

The girl gave him a startled look. "What?"

"It must suck," he repeated conversationally.

Stephanie sat next to her. The girl shrank away. "What did you do with the money? Did you spend it all?"

"Not all. I just used some to eat. Pay for a hotel room. I needed it," the girl said with a lift of her chin, defensive. "Believe me, I could've done a lot worse, you know. I could've taken lots more."

"It was still stealing, even if you only took a little bit," Stephanie told her. "You're going to have to stop."

"Or what?"

"Or I'll make sure the police find you," Stephanie said quietly. "Or worse."

"What's worse than the police?" The girl sneered.

Stephanie's smile tightened. "People who can do the sorts of things you can do, only better."

"I'm not scared." But her voice trembled a little.

"Look, kid. What's your name?"

"Destiny."

Stephanie nodded. "Destiny. What if I told you I could send you to a place where people would notice you. And teach you, too. How to use the talents you have. Here and in the dream world, too."

"What, like some sort of high school for mutants? No thanks!" The girl got up, but Kent was there to stop her. She sat again, her fierce gaze going back and forth between them before she looked defeated. "Fine. I'm listening."

"The money you took will go back to the account

holders," Stephanie said. "And I'm going to send you to talk to a friend of mine. His name is Vadim, and he lives in Florida. He'll be able to help you with a lot of things. And in a few years, when you're ready, he'll probably give you a job."

"Why are you being so nice? Why not just call the cops? Or whoever else you said you'd call."

Kent sighed. "Because, and you know it, we can't prove it was you. There's no real-world tie. Nothing to trace."

The girl laughed. "I know, right? Fucking awesome."

"And because I think you have potential to be something more than a petty thief," Stephanie said.

The girl's laughter faded, and she looked at Stephanie warily. "You don't even know me."

"I know you have good taste in music," Stephanie said lightly and touched the laptop bag.

The girl's face fell. "That was my mom's. She left it behind when she ran off. It's all I have of hers. I don't even like Bangtastic Frogmen. I think they suck. Their songs make no sense and they sound like pissed-off cats in a bathtub."

"See? Excellent taste in music," Stephanie said. She leaned forward a little. "Let us help you, Destiny."

At last, the girl nodded. She still looked wary and defensive, but at least she was listening when Stephanie told her all about the Crew and what sorts of jobs they took. About Vadim, how he could help her and how Destiny could get herself to him.

"Think she'll actually go?" Kent asked as they watched the girl walk away from them without looking back. "She might take that train ticket and vanish."

"She'll go. I remember what it was like to find out I wasn't as weird as I'd thought I was," Stephanie told him.

Kent tugged her by the wrist until she was pressed against him. "Are you about to reveal to me that you had a lifetime of crime before I met you?"

She laughed and kissed him. "No. I was a huge nerd. A real Goody Two-Shoes. I never even kissed a guy until I was in my early twenties."

"You got really good at it," he said against her mouth.

The kiss lingered, getting deeper. Breathless after a minute, she pulled away to look up at him and felt the creep of heat in her cheeks. "Kent…"

"Yes," he said. "It's real."

"I didn't even ask…"

He kissed her again. Then once more. His hands on her hips anchored her against him. His mouth moved from her lips to her throat to press against the pulse beating there.

"Yes," he said again. "It's real."

* * * * *

DARK FANTASY

Megan Hart

Chapter 1

Jason Davis did not want to look inside the closet. Something disgusting was inside it—he could tell that already by the smell. The odor, a toxic mix of garbage and unwashed human body, was strong enough outside the closed door to make his eyes water.

"Think he's alive?" his partner asked. Reg Bamford had drawn his gun, ready at Jase's back.

"Hope so, or else this case just escalated." In the past month they'd been covering a spate of freakish attacks and injuries that seemed to be related, but none yet had resulted in a death. Jase pulled his knife, ready for whatever happened.

Reg shot him a grin. "On three?"

"I don't think we need to kick it down, Reg. Maybe just open it slowly." Jase gave his partner a raised eyebrow, knowing how much Reg wanted to go in full force.

"Fine." Reg didn't holster his gun. He gave Jase a nod. "Go."

"Hey, buddy?" Jase eased open the closet door, bracing himself for the stink. Shit, it was bad. Worse even than he'd anticipated. He put up a hand to cover his mouth and nose. "Hey, guy. You in here?"

Nothing.

Reg moved a step closer. "Careful, Jase. He could—"

Something launched itself out of the closet. Hulking, reeking, arms flailing. Fortunately, it wasn't very strong, and a double one-two attack from Jase and Reg got it on the ground with Reg's gun pressed to the back of its head.

"Please," the thing said. "Please, don't hurt me any more."

Chapter 2

He'd stalked her for days. Weeks. Watching her through the windows. Following her to the bus and then to the train, where he sat several seats behind her and counted the number of pages she read in the book she carried with her everywhere. He wanted to touch her hair.

He wanted to cut off her hair and keep it in his pocket, where he could touch it whenever he wanted.

But when he came up behind her and tried to touch her, the woman turned. Fists clenched. Teeth bared. She fought him, hard, in a way none of the others ever had, and he found himself on the ground with a mouthful of blood before he knew what had happened.

Chelle Monroe paused, her fingers lightly resting on the computer keyboard. This book wanted to be dark and fierce, edging toward the gory side. The problem was, she hadn't started out to write a serial-killer novel. She wanted to write a romance.

Shit.

There was a satisfaction in writing this, though. The guy at the bus stop *had* been a creep. She didn't think he wanted to keep her hair in his pocket, but you never knew.

It figured the only male attention she'd had in the past few months had been from some wild-eyed dude who'd thought flirting meant standing too close and breathing on her neck while she waited to catch a ride to the bookstore. Or in the form of the random dick pics she got every so often in her inbox, though she hadn't updated her profile on the LuvFinder site in forever. Dating had started to seem like so much freaking…work.

Yet here she was, trying to write a romance novel, and why, when her heart seemed more inclined to come up with stories about serial killers or creepy clowns or natural disasters? She had bunches of those stored away in her files, unfinished, as all the other pieces were at this point. It had been a long time since she'd gone on a date but longer since she'd actually finished writing something she felt was good enough to submit to a publisher. Grant would've pushed her, probably until she got annoyed, to stop screwing around and just finish something already. But Grant had left her behind a long time ago.

"C'mon, Chelle, get to it," she said aloud, working her fingers open and closed before settling them back on the keyboard. "Write the damned book."

With a sigh, she opened a fresh GOLEM file. The usual prompts came up—character, plot, research. There were places for her to add photos for inspiration. A word-count calculator. The program had been designed to make plotting and brainstorming a story as easy as possible. The only thing it couldn't do was actually write the damned book for her.

She tried again, typing a few words, but they came out sounding like a really awful late-1980s soft-core porn movie. She erased them. Tried again. Nothing.

The problem could be that she'd been suffering a distinct lack of romance in her own life for the past couple years and, in fact, had probably stopped believing in it. At least the hearts-and-flowers kind of romance you were supposed to read about in novels. Nope, for Chelle, love had come with a lot of baggage. She knew she wasn't alone in that, obviously. The world didn't go around without a whole lot of heartbreak along the way. It made writing about falling in love difficult, though.

Then again, she didn't believe in monsters or aliens, and she'd written horror and science-fiction stories that had gotten critical acclaim, if not a lot of money. Romance shouldn't be so hard, right? At least at the end you could be guaranteed a happy-ever-after, and that was something to aim for. Bringing a little joy into the world, even if it lasted only as long as it took to read four hundred pages or so.

It took staring at the blank computer screen for five solid minutes without typing a word before she gave up and opened the Works in Progress folder where she'd been keeping all her false starts. She'd tried a murder mystery, a comedy of errors, an experimental novel written entirely in iambic pentameter—that one she was proud of, actually. She'd made it to five whole pages before giving up on it. Not because the idea sucked, but because honestly, who the hell would sit through an entire novel written in iambic pentameter?

Chelle sighed, then clicked out of the folder and toodled around a bit online, but it was a lost cause and after a few minutes of being sucked into reading click-bait articles, she thought maybe the future lay in writing deliberately misleading headlines attached to lists that tried hard and usually failed to be clever. Oh, and stock photos, she thought. You had to have a sort-of-appropriate stock picture to go along with the list.

"C'mon," she said aloud again. "You got this. You can do it. You've done it before—you can do it again."

Except what if she couldn't?

With a frown, Chelle put her computer to sleep and pushed away from her desk. She wanted chocolate but would settle for a seltzer water and some grapes. She'd been spending more time in her chair than running, and it was going to show up on her ass if she wasn't careful.

Come to think of it, a good run might clear her head, inspire her and tire her out enough to get a good night's sleep. She changed into her running gear, grabbed her tiny iPod that strapped to her arm and tucked a twenty in her pocket. She'd head for the coffee shop, and if the universe meant for her to have a cinnamon bun, there'd be one left just before they closed. Usually Derek gave her a discount if she was the last customer of the night, but it had been a few weeks since she'd made one of these late-night trips. The weather had been too bad for running.

Outside now, though, Chelle breathed in the faint scent of spring. Snow and ice still collected in piles from the hard winter, but the steady sound of dripping off every roof proved the weather was warming.

She couldn't wait, frankly. Winter in Delaware, with its early darkness and chill temperatures, always took something out of her soul. She and Grant had often talked about moving permanently to where it was warmer, but he'd gone off to Arizona alone.

Veering to the left as she exited her quiet neighborhood, all the houses mostly dark even though it wasn't yet nine o'clock because this was the off-season, she ran for a half mile along the highway. In the summer, traffic on this road would make it impossible to run along here, so she usually ran along the beach instead. But then there wouldn't be coffee and a cinnamon bun as a reward, only the chilly ocean spray and sand in her socks.

She hadn't always liked running. It had been Grant's thing first. He spent so much time in front of the computer that he'd made it a point to take up a hobby that would keep him fit. He'd never pressured her to join him—that wasn't his style. She'd merely found herself picking up the habit because it meant spending more time with him. When their relationship had unraveled, she'd kept up running, not because it was any sort of tie to him, but because she'd ended up craving the mindless rush of pushing herself to the point where all she could think about was one foot in front of the other.

Her sneakers slapped the pavement. She dodged a puddle. She ducked into one of the side streets to take a turn around another neighborhood, this one almost completely dark, as well. She pushed herself a little harder to make the turn through the cul-de-sac. She still wanted to get to the coffee shop before it closed.

The bike came up out of nowhere, no lights, not even a glimmer from a reflector. Chelle screamed, breathless, and dodged, but the bike clipped her on the hip and sent her tumbling forward. She landed on her hands and knees, her running tights torn and her palms a stinging mess of scrapes.

The guy on the bike ended up in a tangle of limbs and spinning wheels. He let out a string of curses, all directed at her, including an incredibly offensive insult about her gender. And her weight. And her ancestry.

Chelle got to her feet, feeling for anything broken. She was going to ache later, for sure, but nothing seemed out of place. "Are you all right?"

"Watch where the fuck you're going!"

"You were riding on the wrong side of the street," she said and weathered the next barrage of insults before saying, "and I'm wearing a reflective vest!"

"Fucking moron," the guy said as he got up and lifted his bike. "You'd better hope nothing's wrong with my bike. I should get your name and number, make you pay for it."

"Sure, let's do that. Let's trade information," Chelle shot back. "I'll send you the doctor bill."

That shut him up anyway. Still muttering curses, he got back on his bike and rode it toward one of the condos at the end of the block, where he went inside. Chelle had paused to catch her breath and make sure she was really okay before she started running again, this time at a much slower pace. She was closer to the coffee shop than to home by this point, or she'd have turned around.

By the time she got to Waves, she was really hurting. Both knees, both palms, something in the small of her back. She limped into the coffee shop five minutes before closing, already apologizing.

"What the hell happened to you?" It was a surprise to see Bess there, since as the owner, she didn't often take the closing shifts. The older woman, brow furrowed, came around the counter to pull out a chair for Chelle. "Sit. Wow. Are you okay?"

"Some jerk hit me with his bike." Chelle winced as she sat. "Then tried to say it was my fault!"

Bess shook her head. "Wow. Thank God it wasn't a car."

"I think he was drunk," Chelle said. "He smelled like it anyway."

"Let me grab you a coffee. You want something else? I have some scones left. A piece of coffee cake." Bess frowned again, looking her over. "How about some ice packs?"

"Yeah. That would be great." Chelle pulled apart the torn edges of her running tights to look at the damage. No blood, but she'd bruise plenty.

Bess brought her a hot mocha latte and a plate of coffee cake, as well as two ice packs from the back. She sat at the table across from Chelle with her own mug of coffee. She asked for a few more details about the crash, though Chelle didn't have many.

"I couldn't tell if he was a local or a renter," Chelle said. "It's early in the season, but I don't want to think someone local would be such an asshole."

Bess nodded. "Yeah. That sucks. I'm sorry. Hey, can we give you a ride home? Eddie's going to be here soon to take me. You shouldn't try to run back."

"Oh. Yeah. That would be great, thanks." Chelle had met Bess's husband a few times. He owned Sugarland, the Bethany Beach fudge shop downtown. She tested out her legs, one at a time. Both hurt.

Bess excused herself to finish closing up while Chelle finished her drink and the coffee cake. Eddie came through the door with a greeting for his wife, stopping to double-take at the sight of Chelle. Bess explained the situation.

"Are you going to file a report or anything?" he asked, concerned.

Chelle shook her head and got to her feet. Everything still worked, but she was definitely grateful for the ride home. "Nah. I'm all right. Anyway, he'll get what's coming to him, I'm sure."

"Let's hope so," Eddie said.

Chapter 3

"He said it was King Kong." Reg craned his neck for a moment to look into the next room at the victim. "Big fucking gorilla."

Three days ago, Stan George had allegedly been attacked in his own living room. That he'd suffered some kind of attack wasn't in question, although the manner of it was suspicious. Not that everything they ever dealt with wasn't in some way weird. That was their job, after all.

Jase looked at the notes in front of him. Reg had done the interviewing while Jase checked out the rest of the house for signs of forced entry. None. Signs of paranormal activity. None of the usual. It was the same as the other four cases they'd been investigating, some dating back about six months without a clue as to what had caused them.

"Guy was online, surfing for…appliances?" Jase looked up. "So, porn."

Reg laughed low, dark eyes sparkling. "That's what the browser history shows, yeah. But then, whose wouldn't."

"So he's online, surfing for wank material. King Kong comes in, tosses the laptop, wrecks the room, beats the guy up." Jase shook his head. "How'd Vadim find out about this guy?"

Vadim, Jase and Reg's boss in the Crew, had a network of people around the world dedicated to reporting in on the strange and fantastic. Sightings of strange creatures, hauntings, that sort of thing. Jase didn't usually ask how Vadim found out about the cases; he went where the boss told him to go and did what the boss told him to do. In the last case, they hadn't even known there'd be a guy in the closet until they got to the house. They'd been called in to investigate what someone had claimed were flying monkeys. So far, they hadn't found any evidence of winged apes, but now here was this guy talking about a giant gorilla.

"I'm seeing a simian similarity," Jase said.

Reg laughed. From the other room came the sound of angry shouting at the television. "Dude's got anger problems," Reg said in a low voice.

Jase leaned back in his chair to take a peek into the living room, then looked back to his partner. "He filed a police report? Or did it come from the hospital?"

"We've got one of the EMTs with us," Reg explained. "He's the one who called it in. Said the guy's injuries weren't that severe but that he kept ranting about King Kong."

"Think the cases are related?"

Weird things often were.

"Let me go talk to this guy. You look around, see

if you can find anything we can use." Jase went into the living room, where the guy had propped his casted ankle on a footstool. He was nursing a glass of what appeared to be a very fine whiskey, though he hadn't offered Jase or Reg so much as a shitty light beer.

Jase helped himself from the decanter.

"Hey…"

"So, did the big monkey do that to you?" Jase gestured with the glass toward the guy's ankle.

His name was Stan, Jase recalled. Stan scowled.

"Nah, that happened because some dumb bitch ran into me while I was on my bike."

Jase sipped. Not as fine a whiskey as he'd thought, actually. The guy had money, that was obvious, but his taste left a lot to be desired. He put the glass back on the table.

"So tell me again when King Kong decided to show up."

"I know you think I'm making this up," Stan said. "So fuck off and leave me alone."

"You sure the booze didn't have anything to do with this?"

For a moment, Stan looked guilty. Then angry again. "A giant fucking ape came into my fucking house and fucked me up—you think I just imagined it?"

Jase did not, in fact, think the guy was making it up. He did, however, think Stan George was an asshole. "So, this woman ran into you while you were on your bike. She was in a car?"

"No, man, she was just jogging along!"

Jase paused. "So really, you ran into her."

"No! She was… It was dark. She was…" Stan

scowled again. "Look, I gave that other guy this whole story already. I know it sounds crazy. But it's the truth."

"Jase," Reg said from the doorway. "C'mere."

"Let yourselves out," Stan called after Jase as he left. "Close the door behind you."

On the front porch, Reg showed Jase the last glittering remnants of something glowing beneath the blacklight wand Reg had been using. It disappeared as they watched. Reg shrugged and slipped the wand back into his bag as the glow faded. "Same as the other case."

"Not ectoplasm."

"No. I don't know what it is. Lots of stuff glows under the black light," Reg said with another shrug. "But it stays glowing—it doesn't fade away."

"Did you send it to the team?" Jase ran a finger along the wooden porch railing, expecting to feel something. Sticky, gooey. Something gross. All he felt was softly splintered wood.

"Yeah, I took some videos and a few pictures. So far, nothing. Eggy and Burt are working on it, but Eggy said she'd never seen anything like it, either. And if Eggy hasn't seen it—"

Jase nodded. "Yeah, it's not in the database."

"So it's something new," Reg added. He grinned. "Great!"

Jase laughed at his partner's enthusiasm and clapped him on the shoulder. "Yeah. Great. Let's go grab a drink and something to eat. Did you get any info on the woman he says ran into him?"

In the car, Reg read off what Stan had told him. "Says she was about five-six, dark hair, he didn't know her. Referred to her as 'dumb bitch' several times."

Jase put the Challenger in gear and pulled out of

the cul-de-sac, heading for the Cottage Cafe. It was one of the only places open in the off-season down here at this time of night, unless they wanted to head into Ocean City. Since they were staying in one of the Crew's condos in North Bethany, he didn't want to make the twenty-minute trip in the opposite direction.

"Yeah, he's a real winner. Any police reports? Anything from the EMT about a woman with matching injuries?"

"Nope. If she got hurt, she hasn't sought treatment. From how it sounds, though, that asshole really bowled her over." Reg tucked his notebook away. "Maybe he'll get another visit from an angry giant gorilla, teach him a lesson about riding drunk. He lost his license, you know. That's why he was on his bike in the first place. Asshole. But I still haven't figured out the tie between him and the guy in the closet, or any of the other cases reported in the past six months. Other than they both seemed kind of like dicks who deserved to get the crap beat out of them by imaginary monkeys."

"Arguably," Jase said, "nobody really deserves that."

"No," Reg answered with another grin. "Some people deserve worse."

At the Cottage Cafe, they grabbed seats at the bar, ordered a couple drinks. Talked about the latest case a bit, though there wasn't much to say about it, since nobody from the home office had gotten back to them with any idea what the glowing stuff was. Reg ordered some wings and rings, and Jase got a burger to go.

"They have great burgers," said the woman to his left at the bar. She hadn't taken a seat but stood waiting for her own take-out order. "I should've ordered one of those instead of a salad."

"It's never too late," Jase said, taking in the fall of her dark hair and a flash of greenish-blue eyes. She had a great smile, though it was hard to tell what the rest of her looked like under the baggy sweatshirt and matching sweatpants.

Her smile widened. "You know what? You're right. Hey, Mitch. I'll also take a Cottage burger to go. Fries and slaw."

"Much better than a salad," Jase said as he grabbed his to-go bag and started to follow Reg out of the bar.

"Yeah, thanks!" She gave him a little wave.

Jase gave her one more look over his shoulder as he went out the front doors. Yeah, she was checking him out. For a moment, he considered heading back in to chat her up, but then Reg said something to catch his attention. When he looked back again, she'd turned away. Opportunity lost.

Not that he had time for it anyway, Jase told himself as he headed out to the car. Not while working a case. And in a month or so, less if he and Reg got themselves together and figured it all out, he'd be gone anyway.

Still, he looked back again before driving away, hoping maybe she'd be coming through the front doors, but all he saw was glass.

Chapter 4

Chelle woke from a dream about Grant, her heart pounding. Breath catching. She'd made a tangled mess of the sheets. Sticky with sweat, she pushed the blankets off and swung her legs over the edge of the bed. For a moment, the world tilted, and she closed her eyes, although the room was so dark it didn't matter if she had them open or not.

She was sure she'd stumble on her way to the kitchen. End up on her knees, still stinging from her run-in with the bike. She made it into the kitchen without turning on a light, so when she opened the fridge to pull out the jug of filtered water, the brightness made her wince and shield her eyes. She poured a glass and sipped at it, hoping to settle her stomach.

She hadn't dreamed of Grant in months, though she still thought of him almost every day. Almost. It was an accomplishment, she thought as she leaned against the counter in her dark kitchen and let the night soothe her. Making it to almost. In the beginning, she'd thought of him every second. Then minute. After a time, she'd managed to break it down to hour by hour, then day by day.

One day, she would not think of him at all; the thought of this broke her more than anything ever had and was what made her stumble more than any walk in the dark ever could. The glass slipped from her hand into the sink, where, fortunately, it did not shatter the way her heart had already done, over and over again.

Too many times she'd allowed herself to succumb to this sort of grief, but it had been a long enough time since the last that she was no longer used to how fiercely it could sting. There were choices to be made here. She could give in to it, let the sorrow sweep her away like the undertow in a storm-tossed ocean. Or she could force away the pain and refuse to let it drown her.

She could write.

Of course, this reminded her of Grant, too. After all, he'd been the one to code and design the GOLEM writing program, just for her. He'd never made more than the single copy locked into her laptop, and which she'd discovered only a short time ago while cleaning out some old folders. His big plans of making money hand over fist had never been realized. He'd gone to Arizona without her or the program. There'd been many times when she thought of erasing GOLEM—which stood for Genre Originating Laptop Entertainment Machine and had nothing to do with the famous *Lord of the Rings* character. Although she did think of her laptop as "the precious" sometimes, Chelle thought as she slipped into the chair at her kitchen table and opened the computer lid.

Her fingers rested on the keys as she closed her eyes,

letting her mind open up to the possibilities of new words. A story. A…man?

A face flashed through her mind. The guy from the bar. He'd been pretty cute. He'd do, for inspiration.

She opened a GOLEM file.

She started typing.

The man in front of her kneels, head bowed, to accept the garland of flowers his regent is placing around his neck. Roses in shades of ivory and crimson, her colors. She has sometimes wished to dress in gold and violet, in shades of night or summer sky, but no. She wears red and white, because that is what is expected of her.

The scout has been gone for some long turnings; that's what is expected of him. To go away and then come back. They both have their places in this world. He has returned to her with the treasures of a far-off planet, precious metals and gems to fill her coffers.

More important, he has brought her himself.

"Lady," he says and looks up at her with a longing that should not be there in his eyes.

It's not appropriate. Forbidden, in fact. She is meant for another. The fate of their two empires rests upon the union, upon the children who will issue forth to bind the warring regencies. Her wedding to Darten is set for only two turnings from now. She will wear red and white.

It's expected of her.

She cannot think of that now. Not with her scout on his knees in front of her with that look on his face and the soft touch of her fingers on his bristled cheeks. She needs to stop touching him, now, before all she can manage to do is keep touching him. She allows herself one last brush against his face before she sits back in her chair.

"You've done well," she says. "What price have you set as your reward?"

He's entitled to a portion of what he brings her. That is custom. What he asks of her, though, is not.

"A night with you."

A collective gasp reverberates through the greeting room. Anadais, the regent's companion, steps forward with her sword drawn. The scout has done more than overstep.

"You've insulted the regent," Anadais says in her clear, calm voice. "Punishment commencing."

The scout does not move. He has no weapon to draw—nobody can enter the greeting room armed. Still, he could rise and go hand to hand with Anadais, who will surely still slaughter him easily. But he does not move, does not flinch.

He looks into his regent's eyes.

"Wait!" She stands, hand raised.

Another gasp circles the room. She dares not look to see the source of the tittering, the sly glances of her ladies and lords. Those who would see her tumbled from power. She doesn't want to see the sympathetic looks, either, from those few who do not agree with her binding to Darten.

Anadais does not wait. Her sword already raised, it is on its downward slice, primed to take the scout's head from his shoulders. At the regent's shout, the companion barely falters. She would've amputated the regent's arm if the scout had not thrust himself between them and rolled with her onto the dais.

There is no gasp this time. No behind-the-teeth laughter. Silence, thick and severe, covers them all.

"You have touched the regent," Anadais says in that same calm voice. She raises her sword again.

"No!"

The weight of her ceremonial gown makes it almost impossible for her to get up on her own, so the regent doesn't struggle, doesn't make a fool of herself. She holds up a hand for Anadais to take, and the companion lifts her to her feet as easily as if the regent were made of air. The scout gets up, too.

"Regent, he must pay for the insult he's made upon your person."

The regent smooths the front of her gown. "Should I not decide what the insult is, and if he's made one?"

A rippling murmur travels the room. She looks out to her audience, but none will meet her gaze. She knows the rumors, the stories about her, the opinions that she is too headstrong for the role into which she was born.

"There are those in this room who have spoken of removing me from my place," the regent says aloud. "I would think that far more of an insult to my person than anything this scout could ask. This man has brought more wealth to this regency than any other scout. His price is not too high."

The regent lifts her chin, daring anyone to speak out. None will, of course. Not to her face, not here. As regent she has ultimate power. There will be whispers, rumors. Her advisors will meet and tut. She supposes she could be taken to task by her future spouse's representatives. Perhaps there will be repercussions. Maybe the war that has been threatening since her father's time will at last become reality, and she will be written in the histories as the most foolish regent to ever lead. She will risk it, she thinks as the scout takes her gloved hand. She will risk it all, for the chance to spend a night with him.

Chapter 5

The rush of a breeze swept past Jase's face and he rolled instinctively, then landed on the balls of his feet beside the bed, already pulling his knife.

There was nothing there.

He touched the back of his neck and felt the sting there. His fingers came away sticky. Blood? But he'd been on his back, sleeping, though in the dream he'd been on his knees with a blade pressed to his skin.

And then...other things.

"You okay?" Reg asked from the doorway.

Jase stood. "Yeah. Weird freaking dream, though. I was some kind of..."

Not a knight. Something else. An explorer or something like that. There'd been a journey of some kind, he'd felt that. He'd gotten into trouble, though the reasons for it were fading, hazy, back into dreamland. There'd been a woman with beautiful, sad eyes. He'd wanted to serve her. He'd have given his life for her.

That *had* to be a dream, because so far in his whole life, Jase had never met a woman who'd made him feel that way. The feeling lingered even now, that sensation of wanting to protect someone so much he'd have done anything to keep her safe. Sure, he'd worked cases where he had to keep people safe, but nothing like he'd just dreamed. Nothing like...love.

He shook it off.

"Some kind of what?"

Jase shook his head. "I don't know. It was just a dream, man."

"Think someone was fucking with you in the Ephemeros?"

"Nah. Just a regular dream." Though there had been a familiar face in it. The woman from the bar. That could've been his mind shaping her, or maybe she'd simply been dreaming in the same space he'd been.

It didn't mean anything, really, other than maybe he'd left an impression on her, the way she had on him. He should've gone back, chatted her up...but then, what was the point? He'd learned the hard way that a one- or three- or six-night stand always ended up being more work than it was worth.

"You sure?" Reg gave him a curious look. "It must've been some dream. You hollered like you were being murdered."

Jase laughed, stretching his arms and legs, trying to feel if there was any other damage than the now-fading scratchy feeling at the back of his neck. "Just a dream. Sorry I woke you, man."

"Nah, I was already awake. I've been online, working some data. Got a few more leads on some interesting shit that's gone down around here, things that might help us. Bunch of weird sightings, stuff like that, but I just can't quite pinpoint a connection. There has to be one." Reg, with all his banter and fooling around, liked to play at being the stupid one of the pair, the muscle and not the brains. It wasn't really true. Reg, when he got hold of an idea, was apt to hold on to it until he figured out whatever puzzle needed solving.

"Any updates from home base?"

"Nah. Been feeding them data, but..." Reg shrugged. "It could take a while, you know? I'm heading to bed now, though, unless you need me to tuck you back in. Maybe sing you a lullaby?"

Reg shot him a cocky grin, then laughed at the double bird Jase flipped him. "Yeah, yeah, whatever. See you in the morning."

Reg closed the door behind him, and Jase got back into bed. He couldn't fall back to sleep, though. He was suddenly hard as a rock, with no real reason other than it had been kind of a dry spell over the past few months. He tried to ignore it but should've known better. He hadn't been able to pretend away a hard-on since sometime in early junior high. He could wait it out or take care of it, and waiting it out wasn't going to get him back to sleep any faster.

Sliding a hand inside his boxers, he took his cock in his fist. Slow, up and down, he stroked. Lifting his hips, he tugged off the boxers and kicked back the covers. He'd left the window open a bit so he could hear the ocean, and he used the steady rush of the waves to time his strokes. Slick precome leaked, smoothing his grip. He thrust a little, closing his eyes.

Pleasure built, rising until it consumed him. Nothing much to it other than the steady throb of desire tightening in his balls. There'd been times in the past when Jase had edged himself to draw out ecstasy, but tonight he was intent on filling a need, nothing more. Faster, gripping for a second behind the head, then palming it. Fuck, it felt good.

Yet also, somehow, empty.

His grip faltered, until he heard the whisper of a feminine voice in his ear. The soft scent of perfume. The touch of a woman replaced his.

He went with it.

She's had lovers, of course. Mostly courtesans, paid to give her pleasure in the absence of a partner. The regent knows well how to please a man—but she also knows exactly how she likes to be pleased.

"You risked much to be here." She raises her glass of wine. They both drink.

The scout puts his glass aside and takes her in his arms. The suddenness of the embrace causes her to spill sweet red liquid down the front of her, but she doesn't care if her gown is ruined. Not when his lips are on her skin, licking away the crimson fluid.

"Lady, I have loved you since the moment I entered your service," the scout says against her throat. "You're worth every risk."

Her fingers thread through his hair, and she tugs until he looks into her eyes. "You entered my service when you were fourteen and I was ten. Surely you don't mean to say you've—"

"I have. Every second of my apprenticeship and every moment after that. I've loved you." The scout does not smile or make light with his words, though she wants to laugh and push him away.

She doesn't want to believe him. If she does, it might kill her. She's pledged to another, after all.

"Every raid I've made, every world I've plundered, every bit of treasure I have ever brought to you is a measure of my devotion." He has not yet kissed her mouth, but oh, how she longs for him there.

As she has always done, the regent thinks as she pushes her scout away and walks to the window to look outside at the night. Since she was old enough to understand desire, she has wanted this man. Never admitting it, never allowing herself to believe he could be hers. Because of course he cannot be.

At least not for longer than this single night. Turning, she loosens the ties at the front of her gown and allows it to fall away. Naked, she draws in a breath, lifting her chin, refusing to let herself look away from his face.

"You are beautiful," her scout says, and in that moment, the regent has no doubt that she is.

He's across the room in the time it takes for her to breathe in and out. Then at last he is kissing her, mouth on mouth. Her gasp draws him into her. His tongue strokes hers.

The marble windowsill is cool on her bare skin as he pushes her back to sit, her thighs parted. He kneels between them. With a reverent sound of worship, her scout kisses her again. Not her mouth this time. The pleasure of it, the heat and warmth of his lips against her most private flesh, tips her head back so the fall of her hair tickles her back.

His mouth moves on her. Tongue stroking. Lips tugging the tender pearl of her body, until she cannot stop herself from crying out. When his fingers slide inside her, stretching, she is sent shuddering over the edge.

Without time for the pleasure to fade, her scout

stands. He's pulled himself free of his trousers and is inside her, so deep the sweet sting of his entry sends another shiver of pleasure through her. Her body clutches him; he groans, thrusting, lifting her legs to wrap around his lean hips.

He kisses her again, harder this time. There's the tangy taste of blood on her tongue, and she loves it, she loves him, she is toppling again into the maelstrom of desire. No holding back.

They might have only this one night, this one time, but it will have to be enough to last for the rest of her life.

Sweet feminine flavor flooded Jase's tongue. He groaned aloud, blinking into the darkness as his orgasm rushed through him. He came so hard he bit his tongue, tasting blood. Shuddering, he let his stroking hand slow until, panting, he let it rest on the sticky heat puddling on his belly.

"Fuck," he whispered aloud. "What the…"

Still blinking, he shook himself and pushed up on one elbow. He'd been back in the dream, only this time, he'd been awake, he was sure of it. He'd been between her legs, lapping her sweetness, making her come. Even now, the memory made his cock twitch, though he was nowhere near capable of getting hard again, not after that explosion.

Something glittered in the air around him.

He sat up so fast his head spun. The edges of his vision sparkled, sort of like if he'd pressed his thumbs to his closed eyelids. Only, this faded and renewed when he tried to focus. Jase hopped out of bed, grabbing a stray T-shirt and swiping at his belly as he did. His black-light wand was in his bag, and he fumbled for it as the glittering lights faded again.

He flashed it around the room and let out a long, slow breath of wonder. The entire room lit up like the night sky. The glow faded even as he watched, leaving behind a few traces here and there, identical to what he and Reg had found on the gorilla guy's front porch.

Shit.

Whatever had happened to those other guys had just happened to him.

Chapter 6

With a short, sharp breath, Chelle lifted her fingers from the keys. Blinking, she sipped in another breath, this one slower. Every part of her still pulsed from the pleasure that had rocked through her while she wrote.

Whoa.

It usually felt good to write…but it had never felt *that* good. Yes, she'd been turned on in the past by something she'd written, but never to the point of an actual orgasm. Chelle sat back in her chair. The first hint of sunlight had started pinking the window over her kitchen sink. She'd been writing for hours. Pages of words…not a full story, but definitely the good start to one, she thought with a rueful shake of her head. Way better than that stupid one about the giant gorilla.

Making sure to save her file, Chelle stared at her computer screen for a few more seconds. GOLEM was more than a word processing program. Grant had designed it as a true writer's dream. She took the time to type a few notes for future plot points. Then she saved again and closed her laptop.

On still-trembling legs, she went to the sink to get herself another glass of water. This one she gulped down, refilled and drank again. She should've been exhausted, but every nerve still jangled. She'd never get to sleep.

Still, she had to try. Not having a day job to go to had to be good for something, even if it meant working all night and sleeping until noon. She took a hot shower first, letting the water beat away some of the stress and tension she still carried with her from being hit by the bike and from the hours she'd spent hunched over the computer.

Cupping her breasts, she let her thumbs pass over her still-sensitive nipples. They tightened at once, and there was an answering pull of arousal between her legs. Chelle laughed a little and tipped her face into the shower's spray, taking in a mouthful of water she spit out in a stream in an attempt at getting her mind off the slickness in her pussy.

She'd had an orgasm while writing.

She wanted to have another one now.

She was no stranger to self-pleasure—that was part of not having a lover, taking care of her own needs. Lately it had seemed her self-gratification had become fairly utilitarian, though. Fast, steady, she got off within minutes as a way to ease the buildup of arousal, though she hadn't found herself particularly turned on. When you were bored fucking yourself, she thought as she turned to let the hot water pound her back, that was bad.

She was turned on now, though. The story. It had filled her head as if she were watching a movie. She'd been immersed. The words, flowing the way her blood pumped now, swift and fierce.

Chelle let out a small groan as she slipped a hand between her legs to stroke her clit. Despite the water from the showerhead, she still found herself so wet that her fingers slipped easily against her folds. Then inside. One, then two. She put her other hand on the shower wall to keep herself steady as she fucked into herself, slowly. Her thumb pressed her clit.

God, it felt good.

How long had it been since she'd really felt this way? Months? Shit, had it been years?

Nipples tight, pussy clenching, breath coming fast. Her belly muscles leaped and jumped as her hips pumped forward. She circled her clit, then tweaked it. Her entire body convulsed with the first twinges of pleasure, building, unbelievable and delightful and yet also somehow desperate.

Her mind filled with the images from the story. The stoic regent, yearning for the touch of the man she loved. The steadfast and inappropriate lover who risked everything for a night with her.

She thought of the man she'd seen in the bar, the one whose face she'd appropriated for her hero. With another small groan, Chelle tried to turn her thoughts to someone else. A celebrity, a mishmash of features, something, anything but that real man who had turned back to look at her. It was useless. Her body had already started the inevitable journey to climax, and she couldn't hold it back any more than she could've stood up against a tsunami.

She gave in, letting the pleasure take her. So good, so fucking good, maybe even better because of that twisted twinge of guilt. Her fingers slipped on the wet tile as she pressed her forehead to the wall. Her body shook, racked with desire. Her pussy throbbed against her fingers and she gave her clit another slow circling tweak before cupping herself.

The water was starting to get cold, but Chelle stayed under the spray for another minute or so, relishing the chilly sting on her overheated skin. When she started shivering, she turned off the water and got out, toweling off and wrapping the towel around her hair to walk naked from the bathroom into her bedroom, where she fell down onto the bed and spread out her arms and legs to stare up at the ceiling fan taking its slow and inevitable journey round and round. Hypnotic.

She let it seduce her into sleep, which was jumbled and fraught with strange dreams, but when she woke, the sun hadn't yet angled into afternoon, and she was ravenous. Over a sandwich and iced tea, she typed some more notes into GOLEM. Nothing seemed as if it would spill into a full-length novel, but she thought she had the kernel for a few short stories, maybe.

On her front deck, she stretched out in the sunshine and let herself drift for a bit. Part of the creative process was refilling the well. Downtime. Grant had teased her that most people couldn't write off napping or daydreaming as part of their job, but he'd never been the sort to take a break. Grant had two speeds: on and off.

She didn't want to think about Grant now. It never led to anyplace good. She supposed one day she'd be able to just put all the memories of him aside, or at least face them with more dignity, but for now, it required a lot of wrestling with herself not to dissolve into grief at the thought of him.

So, she put it away.

She scribbled a few more notes, mostly junk, then went inside to grab her phone. She dialed her best friend, Angie. "Hey, you. What's up?"

"Ugh. Just finishing up this stupid database. What's going on?"

"Trying to write."

Angie was silent for a second. "How's it going?"

"Bad." Chelle laughed. "Not sure what made me think I could do this."

"You can do it. You've been writing stories since you could write. You'll get it. Anything from the editor?"

They talked for a while about work, family, television, shoes, gossip about a couple former classmates. Best-friend talk. It ended with an agreement to meet for drinks and dinner.

"I need this like you wouldn't believe," Angie said. "I want to make out with some random cute guy and just…ugh."

"Ugh, indeed," Chelle said with a laugh, already looking in her wardrobe. "It's the off-season. We'll be lucky to find a cute guy."

"It's the big sports-show weekend. There will be guys there. Cute, I don't know about. That's what vodka's for!"

Chelle paused. "Oh Lord. That kind of night?"

"If you're lucky," her friend said. "I'll pay for the cab, too. Don't argue with me about it."

Chelle wasn't going to argue. There wasn't any use in it—her friend would simply refuse to take any cash. Besides, it all worked out in the end between picking up the tab for drinks or dinner or any of the other things they did together—they'd been friends for so long that neither of them was ever going to be up on the other.

She spent the rest of the afternoon cleaning her house and taking care of some errands. Another few hours… yes, hours…getting ready for what was not promising to be a particularly "lucky" night out. She'd shaved her legs, after all. That was almost a guarantee that she wasn't going to hook up with someone.

Oh, the thought of it, though. A small shiver sent a tickling tremor up and down her spine when she remembered the new project she'd started. Her time in the shower. The guy from the bar… He'd been cute, Chelle admitted to herself as she pulled out dress after dress and put them all away before taking them out again. And if there was one cute guy around, she supposed there'd be more at Oceanside, especially, as Angie had said, since the sports show was going on in Ocean City.

The two of them hadn't gone out in forever, so it was more than past time, but damn if her wardrobe wasn't reflecting just how long it had been. Chelle held up a dress, finally, with a shake of her head. It would have to do.

"Pretty as a peach."

The voice, warm and sugary, nudged her ear and sent her a step toward the mirror. Eyes wide. Mouth open.

She turned, but of course there was nobody behind her. She was alone, the way she'd been since moving into this house, nobody to share this space. This bed. Her bedroom, all her own, decorated to her style and nobody else's.

Chelle closed her eyes for a moment, taking a long, deep breath. She'd imagined the voice. Grant's words, the compliment he'd always paid her. When she opened them, she lifted her chin and gave her reflection a long, hard look.

"You're going out tonight," she told herself. "You're going to have fun. And you're going to make out with a cute guy, if it kills you."

Chapter 7

"Why so...cereal?" Reg pointed at the bowl of frosted wheats in front of Jase.

Jase dug his spoon into the mess of milk and soggy mush. "Nice one."

"Seriously, man. You've been in a shitty mood all day." Reg pulled up one of the bar stools and gave Jase a long, steady look that wasn't going to be easy to ignore.

Jase shrugged, not wanting to admit that he'd had a... Well, shit. What had happened anyway? A weird kind of dream? An out-of-body experience? Whatever it had been, it might be tied to the rest of this case or it might not, but either way, it had happened to *him*, damn it, not some random asshole who probably deserved a little roughing up from an imaginary monkey. He didn't want to compare himself to guys like that, but the truth was, that weirdly fantastic dream and the aftershocks of glittering color had made him more than an investigator in this case. They had made him a victim.

Jase had not been a victim for a long damned time.

"The dream I had last night," he began and stopped.

Reg looked curious. "Yeah? What about it?"

"I don't think it was a dream. It was something else. Like a hallucination. But with physical results." Jase grimaced, remembering the exact nature of those results. He'd had to put the evidence in the laundry this morning.

"Like a giant gorilla beating on some douche bag?"

Jase nodded. "Yeah, but…"

"Not a gorilla," Reg said. "Please tell me you didn't have sex with a gorilla, dude. I mean, you've been with some ugly girls, but…"

Jase snorted. "Fuck you."

Reg crowed a little more about it, teasing him. That was his way, to make light of serious things. It was why they made such good partners. Jase took everything too seriously, Reg sometimes not enough.

"But seriously. It was like a sex…thing?"

"Yeah. But hard to describe. I mean, it was so real, but it wasn't." Jase shook his head. "Messed up, man."

"Too long between lays?" Reg offered, not even joking. "And you're sure it wasn't something in the Ephemeros? Dreams can feel really real."

"It wasn't. And there was all that glittery sort of…"

"Spooge," offered Reg.

Jase grimaced again. "Gross."

"So, we're definitely dealing with something related to the other cases. Spiritual, maybe? It's not ectoplasm. Something like it, maybe."

Jase got up to put his dishes in the dishwasher, then leaned on the counter. "No. But it felt like something close to that. Like…while it was going on, I couldn't have told you for sure it wasn't real, but when I came out of it, I could remember everything that happened but almost like it happened to someone else. Like I'd been watching it in a movie. Or maybe...more like reading it in a book."

"I don't read books," Reg said.

Jase hadn't read a book in a long time, though not because he didn't like to. "When you read a really good one, you sort of get immersed in it. Like whatever's happening to the characters is happening to you. You're still aware that you're, say, sitting in your chair, but you're in it, whatever it is. That's what it was like."

"Freaky. Remind me not to read a book."

"Like playing a really great video game," Jase said.

Reg grinned. "Okay, now I got it. So I guess the question is, why you and not me? And can we make it happen again?"

"I don't want it to happen again," Jase said at once.

"Sounds like it was a good time..." Reg began, then stopped himself at Jase's look. "Okay, sorry. I get it."

He didn't, really. Jase wasn't sure he did, either. Except that he worked cases. He didn't want to become one. Jase never again wanted to experience something like what had happened that long-ago summer when he'd nearly lost his mind and his life.

Not ever.

Chapter 8

Okay, so finding a cute guy to make out with wasn't going to kill her, Chelle thought with a look around the crowded dance club. But it very well might break something. She sipped her vodka Collins so she didn't have to make conversation with the guy who'd been trying hard to catch her attention for the past five minutes.

"C'mon," Angie said and put her empty glass on the bar. She glanced over Chelle's shoulder at the would-be paramour. "No."

Chelle didn't dare look behind her to see his reaction, just set her glass down next to Angie's and let her friend pull her onto the dance floor. The music was thumping, the entire floor shaking, and for a weekend in the off-season, the place was full to overflowing.

"Sausage party," Angie shouted into Chelle's ear with a grin. "We're outnumbered four to one!"

Chelle, being rump-humped from behind by a guy

in a pink polo shirt, could only laugh. "May the odds be ever in your favor!"

Boy, were they ever. Angie's goal had been to make out with a random cute guy? Before another hour had passed, she'd successfully been smooched up on by three guys who appeared to be in a bachelor party. The fourth guy in their group, a little shorter, a little less drunk, though that was relative at this point in the night, hung back laughing. He caught Chelle's eye.

Before he could say anything, though, one of the other guys took a break from twirling Angie to duck close to them. "Hey. This is Steve. He hasn't been laid in a year."

With that introduction, he turned back around to leave an embarrassed-looking Steve to face Chelle, who covered a laugh with her hand. Steve coughed. Chelle smiled.

"Why haven't you been laid in a year?" Vodka asked that question, not her.

Steve leaned a little closer so she could hear him. "I've been…busy? I guess?"

"Don't worry," Chelle said as they both danced a little closer, letting the crowd push them. "I haven't been laid in longer than that."

He put his hands on her hips to keep her from being jostled too much. They moved together easily enough. He was a good dancer.

"How come?"

Chelle leaned in to let her lips brush the curve of his ear. Vodka again, and more than that. The music. The crowd. The idea that the man in front of her hadn't been in bed with someone else in a long time.

"I lost my boyfriend," came out of her mouth instead

of something sexy and carefree, something casual. The truth slipped out of her, followed immediately by regret.

Lost him. As if they'd gone to the park and he'd slipped his leash. Lost, as though he could ever be found.

Steve didn't seem fazed by her admission. He pulled her closer and nuzzled her cheek. He had nice hands, flat and warm on her hips, his fingers curling against her. "His loss."

Chelle wasn't drunk, but when he kissed her, she did feel unsteady and uncertain. He tasted of dollar beers. He kissed too hard, too fast, but softened when she tried to draw back. Over his shoulder, Chelle saw Angie deep in conversation with one of the guys from the bachelor party, not the bachelor himself. The best man, the one who'd told Chelle that Steve hadn't been laid in a year.

She was going to do this, Chelle thought with sudden determination. Make out with a cute random. Have fun. Dance.

Forget the past.

She kissed him this time, and it was better. He laughed when she pulled away. His glasses were a little askew. She straightened them.

"Buy me a drink," Chelle said.

He did. They kissed some more, in a dark corner with black light turning the flecks in his black T-shirt brilliant white. The kissing got better. Steve got handsy, and it felt good to be wanted. To be touched. Dirty, in the good way. The music played on. They danced.

Chelle did not want to go home with him. Home being a room in the hotel attached to the club, a room he was sharing with two other guys. Definitely not her own house, which would require a twenty-minute cab ride and then breakfast in the morning.

"They want us to eat hot dogs with them," Angie said, bright eyes, lipstick worn off, her hair tousled. "Girl, I can't eat any hot dogs at this hour."

"You want to go home?" They'd ducked into the bathroom together, leaving the "boys" behind. Chelle washed her hands and used a damp paper towel to blot away the sweat. She turned to her friend. "We can totally slip out the side. They'll never know. Did you give him your name? Your number?"

"I said my name was Amy, and hell no." Angie laughed. "I wanted to make out, not get married. Let's run. Oh… Don't… You want to go upstairs? Sorry, I should've asked."

Chelle stepped aside to let someone else use the sink. "No. I mean, he's nice and all, but I don't want to go with him."

Angie took her by the shoulders gently and looked closely at her face. "Honey, if you want to go upstairs and kiss up on Steve a little bit more, I'm good with that. I just didn't want you to feel…"

"No." Chelle shook her head, refusing to give in to melancholy. It was that time of night, when the buzz from the drinks and the kissing was wearing off. "Let's get out of here."

In the surge of people exiting the club, Chelle and Angie managed to duck away from Steve and his buddy, whose name Chelle still didn't know. She caught a glimpse of him, looking for her, and guilt prickled through her. Not so much that she turned back, though. All she wanted now was her bed.

In the parking lot, something ugly was happening.

Too many drunks, not enough cabs. A fistfight. She and Angie held back.

"God, it's like a pack of zombies," Angie said as they waved over a cab at last. "You should write that story, Chelle. Two friends go out dancing and get caught up in the end of the world."

"Sexy," Chelle said with a laugh as the cab pulled out of the parking lot.

At home, though, with a couple glasses of cold water in her but a still-unsettled stomach, she wasn't ready for bed yet. She didn't want to think too much about Steve or why she'd ended up passing up the chance for what might've been a few more hours of fun. It wasn't the idea of hooking up—she'd had a few one-nighters, a long time ago.

It had been the way he'd looked at her as the night wore on. Hungry, but something else, too. Something soft and hopeful, which was not what you were supposed to find in the gaze of the random cute guy you wanted to make out with in a dark corner. At least, that wasn't what Chelle had wanted to find.

She opened her laptop, thinking to browse her emails, but instead, she pulled up GOLEM and a fresh file.

Hungry, she typed. Steve had never been so hungry.

Chapter 9

"You have to be fucking kidding me!" Jase pulled his knife from the back of his belt as Reg unholstered his weapon. "That's not... Is it?"

Reg spat to the side. "Sure looks like it to me, man."

The thing in question was a rotting, stinking corpse in tattered clothes. Half its jaw swung, gaping, but it still managed to burble a gargling refrain of complaint. Jase would bitch, too, if he were the walking undead trapped under a Dumpster with a beady-eyed gull aiming to pluck out his tongue.

The call had come in from a couple of drunks who'd gone into the alley to fuck but who'd found this thing instead. Whoever scanned the 911 calls had been quick to alert Vadim, who'd sent them out on this. The cops apparently hadn't done anything about it, and who could blame them? Ocean City at four in the morning had enough other shit going on without responding to a call about a zombie in an alley.

"You want to kill it?" Reg asked. "Splat, punch that effer in the brain?"

Jase was well out of reach of the thing's clutching fingers. "Dude, you know this isn't a real zombie."

"It looks real enough that you could kill it," Reg said mildly. "And shit, it stinks bad enough that you should."

"It's like the flying monkeys, or King Kong," Jase said in a low voice, easing closer. God, the thing did reek. Puddles of goo leaked out of it, so freaking gross. And it wasn't as if he wanted to take a chance on it getting its teeth into him, even if virus zombies had never been proven to be real. The kind raised up from voodoo, yeah, but this guy on the ground was clearly the product of someone's movie imagination. "Shine the light."

Glowing sparkles everywhere. The entire alley lit up with them. Not phosphorescence, and nothing actually present.

"What the hell is going on?" Jase murmured, going to one knee to look the zombie in its desiccated face.

Reg spat to the side. "Just off it."

That would've been easy enough to do. Knife to the head. Would it fade away, the thing, or would it remain as proof of what had happened?

It snapped its teeth at him. Jase studied it. "Trying to find the link between this and the others."

Reg stood behind him. "Same glowing stuff under the black light. That's about it."

"Did it attack anyone?"

"No." Reg scuffed at the garbage spilling out of the Dumpster. "Looks like it wants to."

Another thing shambled around the corner. Identical to the first, but this one upright and moving. It let out one of those disgusting gargles and reached for Reg, who rolled with a shout to escape. Jase, stuck between the Dumpster, the zombie on the ground and this new arrival, ducked its lunge and ended up with his back to the metal.

The one on the ground sank its teeth into his boot; a quick kick thoroughly crunched its face into mush, but it kept going. The walker lunged at him again, and over its shoulder, Jase saw Reg draw.

"No!" he shouted.

Gunfire would attract attention. It would also splatter zombie gunk all over Jase, and he didn't want to get a face full of guts. Instead, he kicked the looming monster in the knees, one at a time, sending it tumbling forward as he rolled out of the way. The thunk of its head connecting with the metal Dumpster was the sound of a watermelon hitting pavement.

"Cool," Reg said.

Jase got to his feet, waiting to see if the thing was going to get up again, but it didn't stir. He waved a hand in front of his face. "God, that smell."

"The smell's kind of the same as that guy in the closet," Reg said conversationally, turning as a couple of drunks stumbled into the alley. "Hey. You. Get the fuck out of here!"

"You didn't need to pull your piece on them," Jase said. "What if they call the cops?"

Reg grinned, but before he could answer, two more zombies rose up from behind the Dumpster. These were faster. Stronger. They didn't fall apart at the first punch or kick. Still, it took only about a minute's effort from both Reg and Jase to send them into a heap with the others.

Barely panting, Reg gave Jase a look. "Okay, so…

where are they coming from? Hole in the wall, like rats? What? Did you see them manifest or anything?"

"No." Jase nudged the pile with his foot. "And they're physical, for sure. I don't—"

Four more zombies rose up from the shadows, though it was impossible to tell if they'd manifested from the darkness or had been merely lying in silent wait all this time. Four against two was still odds Jase and Reg could handle, especially against rotten corpses unsteady on their feet. It took more effort this time, and Jase had to use his knife, but they downed all four of the things in a splash of goo.

"Okay, man," Reg said. "This is getting freaky."

Eight zombies.

No more conversation. He and Reg went into battle mode without words, without effort. They slipped as easily into the fight as if they were on the practice field. Fists and knives, still no guns because just around the corner, they could hear the laughter of a few more late-night revelers. The hint of a red-blue light drifted into the alley but faded along with the warning whoop of a police siren.

Sweating, Jase dropped the last zombie and stood over it, watching it writhe for a moment before it went still. Swiping at his face with a grimace of disgust at the goop and stench, he shot Reg a look. The other man was in a similar pose.

"The fuck," Reg said.

Jase shook his head. "Whatever's going on, it's got to be—"

Sixteen zombies. The alley swarmed with them, and they backed Jase and Reg against the Dumpster, ankle deep in dead, rotting flesh. They'd come from nowhere.

Slavering, lunging, jaws snapping. A bite wasn't going to turn either of them into the risen dead, but it was going to hurt like hell and might still get infected.

Reg waded in, knife slashing. Jase was right beside him, both pushing, slicing, kicking, punching. Jase brought his knife down, then up. Gore spattered. The zombie in front of him fell apart.

They all fell apart.

They were all gone.

Reg looked at him. "Dude."

The only thing left in the alley was a swiftly fluttering bunch of trash on the ground and the gull, and that flew away with a startled squawk.

Chapter 10

She didn't have to be up at any certain time, but Chelle set her alarm anyway because if she didn't, she'd end up sleeping until ten or so, and then it felt as though she'd wasted too much of the day. Writing wasn't a nine-to-five job, of course. The good thing was that she could do it anytime she liked. It was just that she liked to get a start on her day like a normal person, not like some slug who didn't have the wherewithal to get out of bed.

Even if she *had* been up until four in the morning, she thought as she groaned and turned off the alarm. Maybe if she'd been working on something new and fantastic until that time, she'd have felt more justified about not getting up, but instead, she'd spent a lot of her time fiddling around with stuff she'd already written, cutting and pasting and revising, cobbling together bits and bobs of old things without really creating anything new. GOLEM was an awesome program, but it was also a huge time waster once you fell into the pit of character work sheets and plotting tools.

The zombie story had been promising, she thought as she considered a shower but couldn't quite rouse herself enough to get out of the warm blankets. If only because it had been so darned fun to write. A raging orgy of fluids and flying limbs. Basically the same thing as what she'd seen on Friday night at the club, she thought with a giggle, then felt another small pang of guilt about ducking out on the guy she'd been kissing.

Stretching, Chelle snuggled back into her pillow for a few more seconds. Her eyes felt gritty. The residual aches and pains from getting hit by the bike were always worse in the morning, although her bruises had faded. There was just some remaining soreness in her shoulder and neck, and that could be attributed as much to her terrible posture when she was on her laptop as anything else.

"Get up," she told herself out loud, as though scolding were going to work. "Lazy ass."

When her phone pinged, she twisted to check the message, which turned out to be a reminder that her meter was going to be read. Excitement, she thought and gave herself permission to also check her email while she was there.

"Holy…" Chelle sat straight up in bed, phone clutched in suddenly sweaty hands.

Someone wanted to buy her short story. It was for an anthology, small print press, but there was a nominal advance. Far from what she'd been earning with her nonfiction work, but…it was a sale.

An honest-to-goodness sale.

She was already turning in bed to tell him the good news when she remembered she was alone. Still. Always.

Chelle slid a fingertip across the phone's screen to close her mail and let her hands rest in her lap. She was not going to cry, she told herself. Grant would've been happy for her no matter what had happened between them, and she would remember that, not any of the other stuff. She closed her eyes, breathing in. Breathing out. She was not going to cry.

She'd go for a run instead.

She would run and run and work this out, and when she got back, she'd answer the editor's email, and then she would write more words and maybe even put together something for another submission. She was going to do this, make it happen. She was going to do this.

Up and dressed, she decided against running through the streets. It was light out, but that didn't mean she couldn't get hit by another drunk dude on a bike. Besides, she needed the ocean today. She needed the rush and crash of the salt and sea.

She needed a lot of things, Chelle thought, but she'd have to settle for this.

Chapter 11

Jase had grown up so far from the ocean it had seemed like a myth. He'd been nearly thirty before he'd ever tasted that particular grit of salt water and sand you could get in your mouth only after being tumbled by a wave. Since then, he'd made it a point to get himself into the sea as often as he could.

He'd been up early this morning for a swim. The encounter behind the dance club had left him and Reg working overtime trying to put the pieces together, but though they'd interviewed a half dozen of the people who'd been in the parking lot that night, the ones they could find anyway, nobody else had seen anything except that first couple.

They'd been lucky, he thought as he stretched, bare chested, in the brisk early-morning air. Getting beaten up by King Kong would probably have been a walk in the park compared to fending off a pack of zombies, even if they'd turned out not to be real.

"I get it now," Reg had told him after it happened, on the long, quiet and stinking car ride back to the condo. "I totally understand what you meant, about being inside it but looking back as though it had happened to someone else. We really need to figure this out and stop it, Jase. Someone's going to get more than banged up. Someone's going to get killed."

Reg, for all his joking around, took his job with the Crew really seriously. Jase had never asked his partner what had brought him to the job, but whatever had happened to Reg had left a scar as deep as anything could.

They'd both been working all night but still hadn't been able to draw any lines. Eggy had been researching all kinds of explanations, including solar storms, which she said could cause insomnia and headaches but had never been known to lead to hallucinations with physical manifestations.

"Shit," Jase muttered and scrubbed at his eyes.

He stretched again, feeling ill at ease and with nothing to do about it. This morning he'd already swum farther, ran faster than usual. The cup of joe he normally needed first thing in the morning to even consider feeling like a normal person? Nope. The mug on the railing in front of him had gone cold from lack of interest. He tossed it over the edge now.

And heard a scream.

Shit—Jase looked over the edge to see a woman on the small path that led from the access road toward the beach. He'd completely drenched her, top to toe, with lukewarm coffee. At least it hadn't been boiling, he had time to think before she tipped her face up to see who'd done such an egregious thing to her.

It was the woman from the Cottage Cafe. The woman

from the other night. Her dark hair had pressed down over her forehead, coffee running in rivulets over her cheeks. It had stained her white T-shirt and made the fabric cling to her in ways his libido definitely sat up and noticed.

"Sorry," Jase called down to her. "Hey, c'mon up here—let me at least get you a towel."

The woman hesitated, looking wary. "I'm okay."

"If you're sure? Damn, I feel bad. Some paper towels, something. A napkin?" He paused, considering the situation. "You can stay out here on the deck if you're… worried."

That she'd even have to take one second to fear for her safety pissed him off, but he understood it. You didn't need to believe in things that went bump in the night to understand the world was full of monsters. He watched her doubt cross her face, but then she nodded.

"Sure, okay. I could use something to dry off." In half a minute, she'd made it up the wooden stairs to the deck.

Jase had grabbed one of the beach towels he'd hung over the railing to dry. Too late realizing it was still damp and cold from the late-spring air, he first handed it to her, then pulled it back before she could get a grip on it. He looked like an asshole.

The woman laughed. "Um?"

"Sorry, this one, it's… I used it earlier. Let me get you a dry one. You want to stay out here or…?" Now he sounded even more like an asshole.

At that moment, Reg took the opportunity to slide open the glass door and shake his naked ass all over the place.

"Looks like I'm not the only one who needs a towel," the woman said.

* * *

The cute blond guy with the amazing green eyes was Jason. Jase, the other guy called him. Reg, he of the bare-booty shaking and wicked sense of humor. Also Jase's partner, which just figured, didn't it? Chelle thought with an internal sigh. Two superhot guys, of course they'd be together.

"Here, drink this." Reg passed her a mug of blessedly hot coffee. "You sure you're all right?"

"It was cold, I told you that." Jase sounded annoyed. "I already told her I was sorry."

Chelle sipped the coffee with a sigh. "I'm fine. Really. I was more surprised than anything."

Her shirt still clung to her, and the run she'd been looking forward to now seemed more of a chore. The coffee would help with the creeping exhaustion she'd known was going to hit her, but it wasn't going to be enough to get her motivated for a run any longer than it took to get her back home. She wrapped her hands around the mug, warming them.

She watched the two men move around the kitchen with an easy compatibility that made her envious. "I should get going. Thanks for the towel, and the coffee."

Standing, she realized her mistake in sitting. She'd gone stiff and sore again. At the sight of her wincing, Jase moved forward.

"You're hurt?"

"Not from the coffee shower," she assured him as she rotated her shoulder. "Just sore muscles. I'll be okay."

"Let me give you a ride, at least. Shit, I feel like the biggest ass." He shook his head. "At least let me drive you."

She didn't want to say yes. It felt like too much of an

imposition, especially after she'd needed to bum a ride from Eddie the other night. But Reg looked her over with a practiced eye and nodded.

"Yeah, let Jase give you a ride. You look like you feel like shit."

She had to laugh at that, then again at Jase's expression. "Wow. Thank you."

"Reg!"

"No, it's fine." She waved a hand. "But I will take you up on the ride. Sure."

"So...you're local?" Jase asked as she gave him directions to her house. The twenty-minute run was going to be a five-minute car ride.

Chelle nodded. "Yep. Grew up in Millville, then moved away for a while. Moved back down here from Wilmington about four years ago, after... Well, I quit my job to focus on some other things, and I figured the beach would be a great place to do that."

"Other things?" He shot her a curious glance as he made the turn at the square.

"Yeah. I'm... Well, I'm trying to be a writer. I mean, I am a writer. I just am trying to be a different kind of writer." It felt awkward to say it out loud, like admitting something shameful.

Jase looked impressed. "Yeah? What kind of writing?"

"I used to be a journalist. Now I'm focusing on fiction." She pointed. "Turn here. Then the next left."

"Wow. I don't think I've ever met a writer before. Have you had anything published?"

She smiled. "You know, that's the first thing anyone ever asks."

"Yeah. I bet. Sorry."

"No, it's a legit question. The answer is yes, tons of

stuff in my old career. I wrote a lot of articles for different newspapers, a bunch of web content, stuff like that. My fiction has been taking a while to get off the ground, but…actually…" She paused. She hadn't told anyone else this, not her parents or sister, not Angie. The closest she'd come was that moment this morning in bed when she'd turned to a man who was no longer there. Taking in a breath, she blurted, "I just sold a story."

Jase twisted a bit to look at her. "No kidding? Really?"

"Just a short story, nothing big. The money's not that great, but it's for a good small press, they're respected and…" She stopped herself from babbling more. "It feels good. Like maybe I'm going to make something of it."

"Doing what you love—that's a real blessing," he told her.

She smiled. "What do you do, Jase?"

"I'm a private investigator. Mostly insurance-fraud stuff," he said casually. "Down here working on a couple different cases. I've never been to Bethany Beach before. It's a great little town."

"Very quiet," she said with a laugh. "If you want any kind of excitement, you really need to go to Ocean City or Rehoboth. Even Dewey."

"Oh, I don't know about that." He pulled smoothly into her driveway. "This the place?"

"Yep. Home, sweet home. Thanks for the ride." Chelle put her hand on the door handle, then glanced at him over her shoulder. He was the guy from a few nights ago at the Cottage Cafe, she was sure of it. Which meant she'd written something sexy about him. And he'd dumped cold coffee on her over a balcony. "Do you believe in coincidence?"

"No," Jase said firmly.

Fair enough. She did. There was proof of it, right there in the driver's seat. She didn't argue, though, just smiled and thanked him again. Right before she got out of the car, he stopped her with a question.

"Do you run up my way often? I mean, I like to get in a run in the mornings, do a few miles. Reg doesn't run. Sometimes it's good to have someone pushing you, though."

She paused, then nodded. "Yeah. I run up that way, along the beach. I know some great trails through the parkland, too, and you can get to them really easily from your neighborhood. If you want to grab my number, you can text me if you—"

"I'd like that," Jase said immediately.

They exchanged numbers. She got out of the car and watched him drive away with a small wave. It didn't mean…anything, she told herself. Just a running partner. Right? It wasn't more than that?

She didn't have much time to contemplate it further, though, because at that moment, her neighbors' pack of obnoxious dogs began their furious cacophony of barking. There were at least five of the tiny terrors, though sometimes in the summer, when the neighbors had guests, there'd been seven or more rowdy dogs creating havoc. They were supposed to stay in their fenced yard but often escaped to leave presents for her in her…

"Damn it," Chelle muttered. She'd stepped in a pile of poo. She let out a long string of other curses as she scraped the bottom of her sneaker on the driveway stones, then toed off her shoes on the front deck and went inside.

The noise was barely quieter—her house was in the

popular windjammer style, with sliding glass at the front and rear. Great for sunlight. Bad for soundproofing.

She'd spoken to the neighbors a few times, but Linda and Fred were the sorts of pet owners who referred to the dogs as their "fur babies" and who didn't seem to think letting the animals run wild and tear up the neighborhood, creating a noise disturbance in the process, was anything to worry about. She could've called the police. Made a complaint. That would lead to awkward interactions at the annual neighborhood picnic, of course, not to mention having to deal with them across the tiny backyards all summer long. Anytime she tried to cook out or use the outdoor shower or take a nap in her hammock. It wasn't worth it.

She could manage some kind of revenge, however, she thought as she went inside, stripping out of her dirty clothes and tossing them in the hamper. After a quick shower and some breakfast, she thought of her bed, but something else was more compelling.

She sat down at her computer and started to write.

Chapter 12

"A pterodactyl," Jase said. "Really."

"Swear to God," said the woman in front of her. Linda Rogers wore her teased blond hair like a helmet, her matching blue eye shadow like goggles. She was shaking.

Reg, to give him credit, did not laugh. Jase wanted to, but more at the inside decor of the woman's house than the fate of her dog. Four of the remaining pooches were huddled around her feet, all of them shaking, too.

He looked around the kitschy room before focusing on her. "Describe it again, please."

"I told you both already. I'd let the kids out in the backyard to do their doodles, as you do..."

"As you do," Reg murmured.

Jase shot him a look. "And?"

"And I heard them all barking, which they never do, and I looked out the back window, and there was this... giant... Well, it was a flying dinosaur. That's all!" She moaned, rocking, and one of the smaller dogs hopped onto her lap. "It carried off Pipsy!"

It wasn't funny at all. A third case, more of that glowing stuff and, this time, an actual death. Or presumed death anyway. They hadn't actually found the dog's body. Things were escalating, though. That was clear.

They got more information from Mrs. Rogers and left her with assurances that they'd be in touch. Out in the driveway, Reg avoided a few piles of dog crap, all glowing with the black-light wand, even in the late-afternoon sunshine. Jase looked across the gravel toward the house next door.

Chelle's house.

"Hey, go on and take the car," he said, pressing his keys into Reg's hand. "I'm going to say hi."

Reg grinned. "Uh-huh. I'll leave the light on for you."

"It's not like that," Jase said, though of course his protests did no good. Reg was already getting in the driver's seat and giving him two fingerguns of approval. Jase shook his head. "It's just part of the investigation. Maybe she saw something."

"Maybe she'll see a giant anaconda," Reg said with a straight face.

Jase didn't dignify that with an answer. He didn't wait for Reg to leave, either, before heading over to rap on Chelle's sliding-glass front door. He caught sight of her through the sheer curtains and hoped he wasn't overstepping.

Investigation, he told himself. That was all this was. It had nothing to do with that dark curly hair or the bright green-blue eyes or the lush body. It had nothing to do with how easily she'd laughed with him.

Nothing to do with the dream he'd had of being her guard, her champion. Her lover.

"Hi," she said, surprised. "Jase! What a surprise."

"I was next door." He jerked a thumb in that direction. "Um…investigating."

Too late, he realized he was going to have to backtrack to a lie, since he'd already told her he dealt with insurance stuff. What was he going to say now? That he was checking into tales about real-life flying dinosaurs making off with yappy little dogs?

"Linda and Fred? Are they in trouble?"

He wasn't imagining the swiftest glimmer of smug satisfaction rippling over her expression before neighborly concern replaced it. "No. I was just asking them some questions about something else going on."

Shit, what if she asked the Rogers about it? Linda wasn't going to lie about losing her dog or about the two guys who'd come around asking about it. She might not admit to seeing a long-extinct reptile, but you never knew.

He was getting sloppy, which wasn't like him. And for what? A pretty face? Stupid, he told himself as she stepped aside to let him in.

"Can I get you a drink? Coffee, cola?" She'd pulled her hair on top of her head, but a few tendrils had escaped to frame her face. She looked down at her clinging yoga pants and T-shirt, then at him with a twist of a smile. "I was working. I'd apologize for being a mess, but hey, at least I'm not covered in coffee."

"If it makes you feel better, you can dump it all over my head."

She tilted hers to look at him. "There might be a certain satisfaction in it, I'll admit. But nah, I think I'm okay. Do you want to sit, or...?"

"Yeah, sure. I'll take some coffee." He settled into one of the stools lined up along the bar separating the galley kitchen from the living-and-dining area. "Nice place."

She handed him the mug along with a shaker of sugar and some creamers in plastic tubs. "Thanks. It's more of a cottage, really. It wasn't meant for year-round living. But I had it winterized and stuff, so it's all right. And it's just me, so I don't need a lot of room."

He sipped. Perfect. "How long have you lived here?"

"Four years." She leaned her hip on the counter and looked around the space. "I love it down here. How about you? Where are you from?"

"Kansas, originally. Now, wherever I need to go. So, have you seen anything strange around here lately?" Smooth, Jase, he thought. So smooth.

Chelle frowned. "Like what?"

"Just anything."

"They're not supposed to have a shed," she said quietly after a moment. "It's against the homeowners' association. Fred and Linda, I mean. Their shed. It doesn't bother me or anything, if that's what you want to know. Are they getting in trouble for it?"

"No. It's not that."

She hesitated. "I'm pretty sure they have too many dogs."

"You don't like dogs?" Jase asked.

"I like dogs," Chelle answered after a second. "But theirs are very loud."

He decided to come clean, at least a little. "Yeah. They are. And they have one less."

"What?" She looked startled and put her mug down hard enough to splash coffee on the counter.

"Yeah. Something happened to one of their dogs." He watched her carefully, noting her reaction. "Know anything about it?"

"No," she said too quickly, with a cut of her gaze from his. "Did they have insurance for them or something?"

"Um…sure, homeowners' covers it," he lied easily. "But there's been a few weird things happening around here lately, so. If you've seen anything strange…"

Chelle, biting her lower lip, shook her head, then looked at him with a small, strained smile. "I'll let you know."

Something was off here, that was for sure, but he couldn't figure out what it was. Maybe, Jase thought, something had happened to her, something offbeat that she didn't want to share. That could be one of the hardest parts of his job, getting people to admit to something they didn't want to believe happened.

He drank more coffee. They made small talk. She relaxed visibly as the conversation steered away from the neighbors' dogs and weird things. It turned to her writing.

"My mom and dad aren't thrilled," she admitted. She'd curled up on the couch with another mug of coffee and a plate of cookies on the coffee table between them. "They didn't love that I went to college for journalism, but at least I had a job and was making money. They don't like that I'm living in Bethany Beach, which isn't that far from them at all, but they think I'm… Well, they think I'm kind of destitute."

She laughed, shaking her head, and gave him a slow smile that sent warmth all through him that had nothing to do with the fresh cup of coffee. Jase looked around the house. Small, cozy, but in prime real estate.

"Not many people would think that of someone who lives in this neighborhood. What are you, a mile from the ocean?"

"About that." She shrugged. "They want to see me settled, that's all. And they don't think I'll be able to maintain myself writing fiction. Truth is, the only reason I…"

She stopped with another small shake of her head and looked away. Jase waited. One thing he'd learned from his work—sometimes the best question to get the answer you wanted was asked with silence.

"The only reason I could afford to buy this house and put this effort into writing this way, without a job, is because I inherited a decent sum of money. They thought I should put it away for the future. But they didn't realize he left it to me so I could make *writing* my future." She cleared her throat, her gaze bright.

"He?" Shit, there was a he.

She nodded. "My boyfriend. We'd been together for eight years. They also thought he should've married me. It didn't matter in the end, though, except to them."

"He…died?" Jase held his mug in both hands, then put it down to take a cookie he suddenly didn't really want to eat.

"Yeah. Sorry, this is a terrible conversation." She put down her mug, too. "What a downer."

Jase shook his head. "No. It's all right. In my line of work, I meet a lot of people who've lost someone special."

"His name was Grant. What we had wasn't perfect, but really, what is? Unless it's in a story," Chelle said with a laugh that broke a bit in the middle. "We'd been talking about moving to Arizona. We talked about a lot of things. And then, suddenly, he broke it off with me. Took his stuff, moved to Arizona without me. He broke my heart. I mean, he shattered it, Jase. Have you ever had your heart broken?"

"No," he said without hesitation.

"Never been in love, huh?" Chelle laughed again, without much more humor than the first time.

He smiled, though the truth was he hadn't been, and that was pretty damned sad. "No. Not that lucky, I guess."

"I don't know about luck. To be honest, I'm not sure what is worse, the fact he broke me apart when he left me, or the fact he did it because he wanted, somehow, to protect me." She took up a cookie and put it on the small plate in her lap. She broke the treat into pieces, but she didn't eat any of them.

"Was he sick?"

"Yes. He had cancer. Fast acting, pancreatic. By the time he found out, I guess it had spread so far they told him he had only a few months." She wiped her fingers free of crumbs and shrugged, then winced, rubbing her shoulder.

"Still hurts?"

She hesitated, then nodded. "One of those things, you think it's going to go away and then all of a sudden you're in agony again."

"Kind of like a broken heart, I guess."

He'd meant it lightly, but boy had he overstepped. He saw that as soon as her eyes welled with tears, and then he felt like shit, all right. He'd had his share of women who used tears to manipulate him, and often the easiest way to get him to turn and run was to start crying, but now at the sight of Chelle's crumpling expression, all he could think about was how he hated that he'd been the one to make that happen.

She pressed her fingertips to her closed eyelids, visibly struggling. When she opened them, she shot him another stiff smile. "Sorry. God. So lame. But you know, this shoulder will heal. My heart did, too. Or it will. I have to think so, or else what's the use in going on?"

"Not sure I can do anything about the heart," he told her, "but I could try a little something with the shoulder, if you want."

Again he'd overstepped. The startled look she gave him was enough to make him curse himself. He stood.

"Sorry. That was… I'll just go."

She shook her head. "No. Really, if you can get this knot worked out, I'll be so grateful. Honestly."

"Sure. I know a few trigger points." That was true, not just a line he used. That the trigger points were more often the sort to send someone into unconsciousness was a little fact he was going to keep to himself.

Chelle slid around the edge of the L-shaped couch to expose her neck to him, lifting away the weight of her hair to let it fall over the other shoulder. He stopped himself from touching the soft hair at the nape of her neck only because doing that would make him a world-class creep who took advantage of a grieving woman. Yet he couldn't stop himself from thinking about that dream or hallucination or whatever it was.

The one in which he'd been her protector.

He found the spot at once, the knot of muscles tight beneath his trained fingertips. He dug in a little, encouraged by her soft sigh and the way she relaxed under his touch even though it obviously hurt her. Just a massage, he told himself as her low groan of pleasure/pain sent a ripple of desire through him.

Nothing more than that.

Chapter 13

"How's this?" Jase dug a little deeper.

Chelle moaned, softly at first. Then a little louder. He was finding all the right spots. "God. That's perfect."

The soft hairs at the nape of her neck tingled under the gust of his breath as he leaned closer. He wasn't going to kiss her there, but her body responded as though he had. Tight nipples. Parted lips. She held back another moan by sheer force of will. The guy behind her was a real person, not something she'd made up in a story. And he had a partner.

Jase rubbed another minute or so, then let his big warm hands rest on her shoulders. "Better?"

She turned to give him a smile over her shoulder. "Much."

They stared at each other for a long, long moment in silence. Chelle's smile faded, her brow furrowing. She tilted her head to look at him, curious about why he looked so awkward.

"Jase...?"

"So...when you write," he said abruptly, "how do you do it?"

Surprised, Chelle scooted forward on the couch away from him and gestured toward the kitchen table. "I use my laptop. I don't have a desk, so I sit there or out on the deck if the weather's nice."

"No pen and paper?"

She laughed. "Not usually. I have a program, actually. Grant wrote it for me. He was going to try to market it, but he never had the chance. It's called GOLEM."

"Like the clay monster?"

More than surprised this time. Startled. "Yes! Usually people would say like from *Lord of the Rings*, but yes, like the clay monster. You put the words—"

"You put the words in his mouth and he does your bidding," Jase said.

"Wow." Chelle smiled at him. "I can't believe you know what a golem is. Are you Jewish?"

"No. Just full of trivia."

"Do you want to see it?" she asked after another of those strange pauses. "The computer program."

"Sure. Yeah. That would be cool. I barely know how to use a computer," Jase said.

"You're kidding, right?" she asked as she got up and grabbed the laptop to bring over to the couch. She opened the lid and poised her fingers on the keys.

Jase laughed, leaning closer. "Nope. Reg is the one who handles all the computer stuff."

Reg. Right. His partner. It was a good reminder about getting all fluttery about him, Chelle thought as she tapped to open GOLEM.

Too late she remembered that the program automati-

cally opened up the last document she'd been working on.
And that had been more of the science-fiction romance
story. The sexy one.

The one that was kind of about Jase.

He has knelt before few, and even when protocol
required it, the scout bent out of respect and not obei-
sance. In front of his regent, his woman, his heart, he
kneels to serve her in all ways.

Right now he serves her with his tongue. Her sweet,
hot flesh beneath his lips is better than anything he's
ever dreamed. When he slides his hands beneath the
softness of her rear to lift her to his mouth, she moans.
His cock, thick already with wanting her, aches.

He has feasted on her forever and will continue until
the suns turn to ash, if only to hear her make that sound
again. He flicks his tongue along her folds, dipping inside to taste her honey. Then up to circle the tight knot
of flesh that is the center of her pleasure. She bucks
under that attention, her fingers finding his hair and
tugging, hard, though not to pull him away. She rocks
beneath him.

When she says his name, he pauses in his worship
of her to press a single soft kiss between her legs. He
looks up at her to see her staring down at him. Her fingers loosen so she can pass a hand over his hair, then
to cup his cheek.

"You are the true treasure," she murmurs.

Everything inside him squeezes. He has loved the
woman in front of him for as long as he's understood
what love is supposed to be. The scout never dreamed
he might have the chance to make her his, and he's
not such a fool as to think that making love proclaims

anything more than simple physical pleasure. She is promised to another. She is regent.

"I want you inside me," his love whispers. "Again, again, again."

It's everything he wants in that moment, especially if it's all he's meant to have. They are already naked, and all he needs to do is slide up her body and push himself into her heat. The regent moves upward on the bed, crooking a finger for him to follow. He does, as he always will, her servant, her slave.

But he does not push inside her. Instead, he teases her with the tip of his cock, using the slickness leaking from the head of him to lubricate her. She already glistens from the attentions of his tongue and her own sweetness. There's no resistance as he thrusts against her, only the most delicious friction of his throbbing cock against her swollen flesh.

When she arches, opening herself to him, the scout wants to slide into her so deep they will never be separated again. Yet he wants to tease her, too, until she writhes and cries his name and begs him to enter her. He gives her the tip, pressing just inside her. Not moving. His muscles tense and tighten, and he shakes from the effort of keeping himself from fucking into her fast and hard, pumping until they both shatter.

He gives her only this small part of him, because he wants to give her everything.

When her hands go above her head to clutch at the spindles of the headboard, he can no longer control himself. She is regent and he is meant to serve her, but the sight of her in such submission to him drives him mad with longing. They both cry out when he enters her.

Their eyes meet. She draws him to her, a hand at the nape of his neck to hold him close as she kisses him.

She bites lightly at his lips and takes his tongue into her mouth to suck it gently. The pleasure of that intimacy echoes in his cock, equally embraced by her body.

They move together. Slow, slow, then faster. Harder. Deeper. His body slams against hers. They will break this bed with the force of their passion.

They will break the world with it.

Chelle let out a low, embarrassed cough and closed the laptop with a snap. She couldn't look him in the face, not after that. Bad enough to share her unpolished work with a near stranger, but that particular piece…

More than that, how easily she'd lost herself in reading it. Only a few minutes could've passed, but it had felt like hours. She was used to getting lost inside the world she created when she was writing, but this had been different. Almost as though it had been really happening to them.

"What the hell," Jase said, "was that?"

"I'm sorry. It was inspiration. I don't know if you remember, but we passed each other at the Cottage Cafe, and I guess you got stuck in my brain—" she babbled, mortified, only to realize in a second or so that there was no way he could've known by reading that short section of her work in progress that she'd been imagining him as the hero and herself in the heroine's role.

He couldn't know that, but the way he was looking at her said he did.

"It's only a story," Chelle whispered. "It's not real."

"It felt real," he said. "I felt every word."

She swallowed against a strange tightness in her throat and shook her head. "No. That's not possible."

"You felt it, too? It happened to us. That room. Those

people," he said. "They were us, weren't they? Tell me I'm not crazy."

"That is crazy," she said sharply. Beyond embarrassed. This was fucking with her head, and she was not about to go there.

Jase kissed her. Hard, deep, his fingers gripping her shoulders so she couldn't pull away. Not that she wanted to. At the first touch of his lips on hers, she was lost. Caught up in a whirlwind of lust and passion, exactly what she'd been imagining and writing about and hadn't found in any random make-out session in a dark corner of a dance club.

Breathless, Chelle pulled away and put a hand over her mouth. Her lips felt swollen. Bruised.

"Shit," Jase said. "I'm sorry—"

She kissed him. Not as hard as he'd done. Hers was softer, exploring. She moved onto his lap, straddling, her knees pressing the couch's back cushions. She rocked against him. When he opened his mouth wider, she took his tongue and sucked gently. She'd written that but couldn't recall ever actually trying it.

Damn, that was hot.

Hotter was the way his hands gripped her hips, pulling her down against him. His moan in her ear when she broke the kiss to slide her mouth along his jaw. The way he thrust upward, grinding his hardness against her when she nibbled.

The rush of it left her trembling, but Chelle forced herself to pull away and cup his face in her hands. "Jase, this is crazy. What about Reg?"

"What about him?" His hands roamed over her back, nudging her closer.

"Won't he care?"

Jase paused, looking confused. The way he ran his tongue along his lower lip drove her crazy. She wanted to kiss him again so much it was like fire, but she held herself back.

"Why would he care?"

"He's your partner," she said.

"Yeah, but he doesn't usually get involved with my… erm…who I…" Jase blinked. "Oh. You think he's my 'partner' partner?"

This was all going wrong. Really wrong. Embarrassed, she tried to pull away, but the way her body had bent in order to fit on his lap made it impossible for her to gracefully extricate herself, at least not without a lot of wriggling. With his erection still pushing against her, wriggling was the last thing she wanted to do. Well, it was everything she wanted to do, she thought with a small, helpless giggle. She was just going to have to stop herself from doing it.

"No," Jase said in a low voice. His gaze burned into hers. He pulled her closer, inch by inch, until their mouths brushed with every word he said. "No, it's not like that at all."

His kiss plundered her again, and she loved every second of it. This was better than anything she ever could've written. She let her head fall back so he could get at her throat, and that was perfect, the press of his teeth and the swipe of his tongue.

He pulled her T-shirt off over her head, exposing her breasts to the heat and wetness of his mouth. Jase tugged a nipple between his lips, and Chelle let out a long, low and grinding moan of pleasure. It had been so long. Too long.

"I want you," she said.

* * *

Chelle slammed the laptop lid closed.

Jase blinked. His cock pressed uncomfortably at the front of his jeans. Heat had flooded him. He could still taste her mouth.

She stared at him. "I didn't... Did I write that...?"

He kissed her. She moved onto his lap, not straddling but twisted to half face him. She fell onto the cushions, but her arms were around his neck, pulling him down to her. He was on top of her, between her legs. He was so hard his dick ached, but he couldn't stop himself from pushing against her, dry-humping like teenagers—it didn't matter. He could only think about touching her. Tasting her.

He moved down her body, pushing up her T-shirt to get at her magnificent breasts. Her nipples were already hard, poking through the sheer lace of her bra. Jase covered one with his mouth, wetting the lace, nibbling her as he slid a hand beneath her ass to lift her against him.

Chelle moaned his name. She moved to let him get her shirt off over her head, then tugged at his to get him bare, too. Skin to skin, they moved on the couch until the cushions flew off. He was still on top of her. Moving. Thrusting.

She got a hand between them, cupping his cock through the denim, and fuck, it was not enough—he needed her to unzip and get inside there, to take him in her hand. Her mouth. Her pussy. He'd never wanted anything so much in his life.

"Fuck me," Chelle said and looked surprised. "Yeah, that is what I want."

He wanted it, too. But their clothes were still a barrier and he couldn't manage to get his pants unbuttoned, and she was moving, pushing at him, sitting up and letting him kiss and bite at her neck, but what he wanted was to dive between her thighs and eat her until she screamed.

"Yes, I want that," Chelle told him, though he hadn't said a word out loud. "Get your mouth on me, Jase. Get your mouth on every part of me."

Chelle closed the laptop, this time for real, and jumped up from the couch to take a few steps back from Jase, who was blinking, stunned. Not moving. She put a hand to her fast-beating heart, her pulse throbbing as though she'd run a marathon.

"What the hell is going on?" she cried.

Everything inside her was molten, melting, though she couldn't tell if it was from humiliation or arousal or some sickening combination of both. She drew in a breath and then another, waiting to see if he would stand up and kiss her again. Or if she'd kiss him. If they would end up half-naked or all-the-way bare, fucking on her couch like animals.

"Are you all right?" he asked her in a low voice.

She took a second to make sure she was answering honestly before nodding. Still wary, she took another step back until the L of the couch hit her behind the calves. She had no place to run. She didn't want to run. She wanted to tear off her clothes and have passionate sex with this guy.

"I have some things to tell you," Jase said. "About things that have been going on around town. I think you might be part of them."

"What kinds of things?" Her heartbeat had slowed, as had her breathing. When she shifted, she still felt tingly and slick between her legs, but she could see a bulge in his pants even from here, so she guessed he was feeling the same.

"We haven't been able to figure it out yet, but it's what we were sent here to do. Reg and I aren't insurance investigators," Jase told her.

"Reg. Your partner. Who's not your 'partner' partner." Chelle let out a small, strangely gleeful laugh. "Oh my God. This is madness. What is this?"

"I don't know, but I'm sorry I…" Jase coughed and looked away from her. "I shouldn't have touched you that way."

If there was any part of this that she regretted, it was definitely not that he'd touched her in "that" way or any way. "I'm not."

He looked back at her, and the blaze of desire in his eyes glittered a little brighter. Neither of them moved. She licked her lips and watched him follow the tracing of her tongue along them.

"I haven't had a lover in about a year and a half," she told him. "I tried a couple one-night stands, but they never were more than that. I tried going out with my friend the other night, tried to pick up a guy in Ocean City, but I only kissed him. When it came time to go upstairs with him, I wasn't into it. Not like this. Nothing like what just happened."

"You were in Ocean City on Friday night?" Jase ran a hand through his blond hair until it stood on end.

It only made him more attractive, that rumpled look. Chelle ran a hand along her chin, feeling the burn from his stubble there. Her nipples, too, she realized, though she didn't dare cup her breasts to feel the sting he'd left behind.

"Yes."

Jase stood so suddenly his knee hit the coffee table. Cold coffee sloshed, but he ignored it as he moved away from the couch to pace. He ran both hands through his hair this time before turning to face her with a grim look.

"Did you go home and write after? Like two or three in the morning?"

The heat was fading, leaving behind a seminauseated ache in the pit of her stomach. She nodded. "Yes?"

"Shit." Jase shook his head. "I think it's you. It's not just happening to you. You're doing this."

Chelle flinched. "Doing this? Look, I know I wrote that sci-fi story, and yes, I definitely used you as a model for the hero, but it really was just fiction. I had no idea—"

"Not just this thing with us. Damn, I wanted you from the minute I saw you," Jase cut in. "All the other stuff that's been going on around here. Flying monkeys and zombies and shit."

"You did?" She grinned, not sure what the hell he was going on about but not really caring. "That night at the Cottage Cafe, I saw you turn around to look back at me, but I didn't think much of it. Wait. What? Zombies? What?"

"Yeah. I saw you. Yeah, I turned around." His small smile turned tight in a second. "You started writing about me right after that. Didn't you?"

She blushed, more heat, not nearly as pleasant as the sort that had come from his hands on her. "Yes."

"I know. I felt it. The same as what just happened. Only, I was alone. I was that guy, that scout guy."

"And I was the regent?" Chelle asked in a whisper. She had to sit, or she was going to fall. She shook her head, not understanding. By the look on his face, Jase had only a little more clue.

"Yes. You were the regent and I was in love with you. And when I came out of it, there was all this stuff, this glowing remnant of something. It was the same as the other cases. I knew they were connected. I just didn't see the connection until now."

Chelle twisted her hands together in her lap to keep them from shaking. Chills had replaced the heat, though she was still sweating. She swallowed another rush of nausea. Her head was starting to hurt.

"I don't understand, Jase."

He moved toward her so fast that she let out a yelp and retreated against the couch. That stopped him. He moved slower then to sit beside her without touching her.

"Don't be scared," he said.

She was a little scared, though not of him. She ought to be, Chelle thought at the sight of his expression, which had gone dark and stern. She knew nothing about him except that everything he'd told her had been lies.

"Do you know what's going on?" she asked him.

Jase shook his head, pulling out his phone from his pocket and tapping a quick text. "No. But Reg might be able to put it together. If he can't, someone on the team should be able to figure it out."

"The team?"

He looked at her, then put away his phone. "Yeah. I belong to a team called the Crew."

"And you don't investigate insurance fraud," Chelle said.

Jase's smile shouldn't have sent another glittery slice of heat through her, not with all this other weird stuff surrounding them. But it did. The slight brush of his hand on hers did, too, when he moved a smidgen closer.

"No," he said. "Let me tell you what we do."

"When I was seventeen, my family and I went camping in Yellowstone Park. We'd gone every year for as long as I could remember. Sometimes we had an RV. Sometimes we stayed at one of the lodges. This year was the first time we'd gotten passes to go far back, off the marked trails. Me, my dad, my sister. My mom had stayed home with my younger brother, Corey, who'd broken his leg playing soccer.

"The three of us carried only what could fit in packs on our backs. My dad had camped like this plenty of times. He even served as a guide sometimes during the summer. He was a schoolteacher. Geometry. But he loved being outdoors more than anything else.

"We knew to watch for bears, of course. And there are wolves in Yellowstone, too. But my dad knew how to be careful, how to keep our food locked up in scent-proof containers so we didn't attract anything. We spent the first night hiking as far back off the trail as we could. We made camp right near a waterfall. There was a hot spring there, too, one of the small ones, but still pretty amazing to see. Every so often, it would bubble up a little higher, then settle down. Nothing like Old Faithful, but enough to make the evening entertaining without much else to do but play checkers.

"I beat my sister every time. She was laughing about that when the thing came after us. They would tell us later it was a bear, but I can tell you, Chelle, I saw that thing and it was not a bear. It was about nine feet tall and had teeth like swords. Claws to match. If it was anything, it was something out of the Stone Age, some kind of saber-toothed tiger hybrid that had been hiding out in the wilds forever. Like the Loch Ness monster, like Sasquatch.

"It killed my father and my sister. It left me for dead, and I wasn't faking—I was as close to death as I've ever been, and I've been hurt pretty damned bad since then.

"I lay in the backwoods of Yellowstone for three days before a ranger found us. By then the thing had taken my father's and sister's bodies. They were never found. It ate them. Everything, even the bones. I don't know why it left me behind. Maybe it was full.

"What I do know is that when I got out of the hospital, a man named Vadim came to see me. He told my mom he was a grief counselor. That's one of those things we learn to do, see. Tell lies in order to get where we need to be so we can figure out what the hell is happening.

"I knew he wasn't any sort of counselor. I didn't want to tell him anything. Nobody would've believed my story, I knew that from the start. If the rangers said a bear or bears had taken my dad and Karen, then that's what I was going to say, too. The nightmares were bad enough without anyone trying to also psychoanalyze me.

"Vadim, though, had a photo of something that looked a helluva lot like what had come out of the trees that night. Blurry—maybe it could've been faked—but as soon as I saw it, I turned and puked into the trash can by my bed. It didn't faze him. He's an unshakable bastard, Vadim. One of the bravest men I've ever known, and that's saying a lot.

"He told me others had seen this thing, close to where

it had killed my family. The picture had been found on the phone of someone who'd gone missing, leaving behind that as the only evidence they'd come to harm. He never told me how he got hold of it, but it didn't matter. Once I saw it, I knew I had to help him find it.

"My mother thinks I joined an elite branch of the marines, and I aim to keep her thinking that. She worries about me, but at least I never had to convince her I wasn't insane, not with the sorts of cases I've taken on. Most people can't wrap their heads around it. Hell, there are times I can't even figure it out.

"But I'll tell you this, Chelle. I found that thing that killed my dad and Karen, and I followed it to its lair, where it had a litter of kits, still sucking. No sign of a mate, and we never found out how it breeds, but we know there are more of them out there than we thought. They are real.

"So are a lot of other things you never believed were true."

Chelle had listened, her stomach twisting, to Jase's story. He'd told it without so much as a break in his voice, and it was somehow all the more awful for that lack of emotion. She wanted to hug him. She wanted to run away.

"So...you killed it?"

He shook his head. "No. Seeing it with its young, I couldn't do it. Yes, it had killed my family, but we were in its territory. A bear might've done the same. Wolves. My dad always taught us that entering into nature's realm meant taking risks. That we were the interlopers. I could've killed it, for sure, and its babies. But it was an animal, not some kind of monstrosity bent on slaughtering for the fun of it. Believe me, I've met those kinds of monsters, and they deserve to die. This thing was only trying to feed its children."

It was a more fantastic story than any she'd written, that was for sure. She shouldn't have believed it. Crazy talk, or at the very least, simple lies told for a purpose she couldn't comprehend.

"I've always believed in Nessie and Bigfoot," she told him, not quite sure why she was admitting it.

"They're real."

She bit her lower lip for a second. "I'm sorry about your family."

"Thanks."

They stared at each other again. She reached for his hand and he let her take it. She squeezed his fingers.

His phone buzzed, and he withdrew his hand with an apologetic smile to look at the text. He read it, then looked up at her with narrowed eyes. He looked at the computer.

"This writing program. GOLEM. You say your boyfriend wrote it for you?"

"Yes." She gestured at the laptop, wondering if suddenly she was going to find herself naked on his lap. To her regret and relief, nothing like that happened.

"The night after you went dancing, you wrote about zombies."

"Yes," she said, startled. "How did—"

"You wrote about the neighbors' yappy dogs. A dinosaur? And the woman that jerk ran over on his bike, that was you, too. You came home and wrote out a little revenge on him. King Kong?"

Sickened, Chelle fell back against the couch. "Yes, yes. Oh my God, Jase, what are you saying?"

"Everything you've been writing has come true," he said. "At least some of the things have. And I think it's because of GOLEM."

This was too much. Chelle got off the couch and pushed past him to go to the fridge for some cold seltzer. No, screw that—she needed something stronger. She pulled the bottle of vodka from the freezer and poured two shots, holding up one for him before setting it on the bar so she could toss the other. It went down like fire, making her cough and her eyes water, but she shook it off.

"That's crazy," she said. "I write fiction."

Jase leaned on the bar to take the shot of vodka. "Two years ago, Reg and I worked a case with a real golem, one made of clay. It had been made by a rabbinical student who wasn't happy with some of the things his rabbi was doing. It killed four people before we stopped it."

"I haven't killed anyone. Oh my God, I haven't, have I?" Chelle put the vodka back in the freezer, though she wanted another shot. She clenched her shaking hands into fists at her sides. "The dog. Oh, no."

"We don't know for sure that it's dead," Jase told her.

It wasn't much comfort. In the story she'd written, the pterodactyl had definitely eaten the dog. There'd been no gore in the story—she'd written it tongue in cheek—but even so. The dog was definitely a goner.

She took a deep breath and forced herself to meet his gaze. "The stuff with us. That wasn't real, then? Or did it really happen?"

"I think it really happened." He touched his mouth, which looked a little swollen, the way hers still felt. "Not the part on that other planet. But at least some of the stuff on the couch."

"Oh God," she whispered and put her face in her hands. "I'm so embarrassed!"

"Hey, hey. Don't." He came around the bar as though he meant to take her in his arms, but Chelle stepped back before he could.

She didn't need his pity, that was for sure.

"Would it be all right if I took a look at the program?" Jase asked after a minute. "Reg's text said he was sending some updates to the data team."

"Yeah. Of course you can look at it. It's not like you haven't already seen the most mortifying stuff already."

Jase shot her a look. "Chelle, don't. I meant what I said about seeing you for the first time. Whatever is happening has nothing to do with how attracted I am to you."

This time when he moved to take her in his arms, she didn't pull away. He didn't kiss her. He hugged her instead, and this simple comfort was enough to burn her eyes with tears she was helpless to keep from sliding down her cheeks. She pressed her face to his shirt. His hands rubbed her back in slow circles until she got herself under control.

"Let's take a look at that program," she told him. "Because if I'm really what's causing this stuff to go on, I want to stop."

Chapter 14

He hadn't been lying when he'd told Chelle he wasn't really that great with technology. Jase wasn't afraid of much anymore, not after facing down the things he'd seen. Comparatively, nothing on this case so far should've frightened him. Yet he hesitated before opening the laptop.

His fingertips tingled as they hovered over the metal. He glanced at Chelle, who'd been watching intently. Her brows went up.

"You want me to do it?" she asked.

"I'm not sure what's going to happen," he said honestly. "Twenty minutes ago, you and I were…"

"Yeah," she said. "I remember."

"If that happens again, we'll have to stop it," Jase told her.

She laughed lightly, a pink tinge climbing into her cheeks. "Yes. I know."

"But first," he said, "I'd like to kiss you again."

Chelle looked surprised. "Why?"

"Because right now we can be sure it's something we both really want."

She ducked her head, smiling. The blush spread across her face, sending a flush down her throat and into the V of her T-shirt. "Just a kiss, then."

"Yeah," he said, sliding closer. "Just a kiss."

He half expected to be taken over by that mad rush of lust again the way he had before, but this time, the kiss was truly just a kiss. If anything that sweet and tempting could be called "just" anything anyway. Her mouth was lush and delicious and everything he'd dreamed of it being, yet nothing like it had been while they were swept up in that previous madness.

"This," she whispered against his mouth, "this is real."

It was, which was more terrifying than anything he'd ever had to face with a knife. He kissed her again, softer this time. It lingered. When he pulled away, she was smiling.

"Are you ready?" Jase asked.

Chelle looked uncertain but then nodded firmly. "Yes. Bring it on."

He lifted the lid of the laptop, tensing. Nothing happened except for the whir of a fan inside the computer's workings. She laughed in relief and he joined her.

"Show me how this works." He leaned to the side so she could get her fingertips on the keyboard. He couldn't stop himself from breathing her in.

She gave him a sideways glance and a secret sort of smile but didn't shift away from him as she drew a finger over the trackpad to move the cursor to an icon in her task bar. She let it hover there for a moment, then clicked to open a small menu that closed the program down.

"It's set to automatically open the last-used document," she explained. "I just closed it totally, so when we start it up again, we should be able to choose which project to open."

He nodded and watched her double-click the icon again. A menu appeared with a list of document names and folders. "Don't open any just yet. Tell me how this works."

"Grant built it to not just help me write and make word count, but to really plot and do character development. Stuff like that." She gave him another sideways glance as her fingertips tapped across the keys. "See, you can start a new document like this."

She showed him, along with the tabs and functions that brought up different databases. All blank in this case, as was the document she'd started.

"He's the one who called it GOLEM," she said quietly as they both stared at the computer. "Grant had a fondness for myths and fairy tales. And he told me more than once, before the end, that he wanted to make all my dreams come true. Do you think that's what he was trying to do, Jase?"

He hated that she sounded so sad. "I don't know. Maybe. I've been on a few cases where someone who passed away had left unfinished business behind. Sometimes people linger long after they should've gone on. How long have you been using this program?"

Chelle hesitated. "Honestly, he gave it to me before he left for Arizona, but it was hidden. I didn't find it until about six months ago. How long ago did these odd things start happening?"

"Six months ago," Jase said.

Chelle looked stricken. "It *is* me. It has to be."

"Well, there's one way to find out." He tilted the laptop toward her. "Write something."

The room was filled with helium balloons.

Chelle sat back and looked around the room. Nothing had happened. They both looked at the screen.

"Do you do anything else?" Jase leaned forward to look at it.

"Well, I usually write more than that." She frowned, looking at the document. "But otherwise, no. Not really."

She laughed. Then a bit louder. She shook her head. Jase gave her a curious look.

"All of this is a little hard to take in, that's all." She nudged him with her knee. "Right? I'm sure you're used to it. But I'm not."

Jase grinned. "Trust me, every time I start a new case, there's something I'm not used to."

She couldn't stop herself from touching his face, tracing the line of his jaw and then letting her thumb run across his lower lip for a second before she leaned to brush a kiss against his mouth. "Just making sure this is all still real."

"Write a little more, maybe," he suggested when she pulled away.

She did, spinning a little tale about balloons and rainbows and pots of gold. Nothing happened. With a sigh, she saved the file into the Works in Progress folder.

The room filled with balloons. Hundreds of them, multicolored, bouncing and bobbing. Every time one popped, a rainbow shot out, covering them with glitter. Chelle laughed, hands out to catch it, watching as the colored and sparkling bits of light cascaded through her fingers.

"Boom," Jase said.

She looked at his face, cast in rainbow-shaded shadows. Glitter had settled in his fair hair. She brushed it off his shoulders.

"Now we know," she said. "The default setting to save files is the drafts folder. But if I put it in that one, it happens. I just don't know how."

He shook himself to let the glitter fall away. "We don't need to know. We just need to know how to stop it from happening anymore."

She thought about writing good things. Winning the lottery, finding a cure for cancer, world peace. A roomful of balloons had been fun and easy and hadn't hurt anyone. What if she used whatever this was, as crazy as it seemed, to make a better difference in the world?

"Jase..."

"Do you want that responsibility?" he asked quietly, though she hadn't said anything aloud. "Think about it, Chelle. You don't know the limits of this. Do you want to be in charge of the entire world?"

She definitely did not. More than that, she suspected she wouldn't have been allowed to be. Jase might've kissed her breathless no matter what she'd written, but he was here to do a job, and that job was to stop all this stuff that had been going on.

"I'm going to delete it," she said.

"The story?"

She shook her head. "No. The program. I know Grant wrote it for me because he wanted me to reach my dreams, but he couldn't have meant for it to hurt people. That's why he didn't give it to me outright—he was still working on it. He must've known it had issues. And he's gone and will never be able to fix it. I'm going to trash it."

Jase looked solemn. "I think that's a good idea. But all your work…"

"None of it was much good," she told him. "Besides, you do your best work in the revisions. I'll be okay."

"Trash it, then," he told her.

Her fingers nudged the trackpad to position the cursor, then dragged and dropped the program's icon into the trash. She waiting, expecting a warning or something to pop up, but nothing happened except that small crinkling sound that always occurred when she deleted something.

"Well," she said. "That's that, I guess."

"How do you feel?"

She'd expected a sense of loss. Months of work, tossed aside. Sorrow, certainly, at deleting something Grant had left her. Yet all she felt was unburdened. A weight, lifted. She twisted in her chair to look at him.

"I feel…inspired." She grinned and put her hands on the keyboard, fingers resting lightly on the keys but not typing anything yet. "I feel free, Jase. Is that weird?"

"What isn't weird in this world?" he replied with a laugh and sat back in his chair.

Chelle laughed, too. "Maybe you can tell me all about it sometime."

"So you can write a book?"

She pressed her lips together on another laugh. "You never know. Might be a huge bestseller. Romance sells, you know. Especially when it has a happy ending."

"Would you say this has a happy ending, then?"

She leaned forward in her chair to offer him her mouth, hoping he would kiss her. "You tell me."

He did. Sweet and slow and smooth, exactly what she'd been wishing for. His hand slipped beneath her hair, cupping the back of her neck.

"I think it's a good possibility," he said against her lips.

His phone buzzed, not a normal text tone but something harder. Jase pulled away, leaving Chelle confused, eyes half-closed, mouth half-open. He pulled his phone from his pocket with a muffled curse.

"What's wrong?" she asked.

"It's Reg. He says we should get our asses over to the beach. Now."

Chapter 15

"I was on the phone with Eggy, seeing if she'd had anything she could put together about this thing you said about the computer program," Reg said from his place on the condo's deck. "She hasn't, by the way, though there were a couple cases of computers being possessed by former owners and stuff like that. Nothing about a program that makes hallucinations with physical manifestations, though. And then... Shit. That."

He pointed. This time of year, there weren't many people on the beach, not like if it had been the height of summer, but you still had a few dog walkers and joggers and shell seekers strung out along the sand. All staring out at the way the ocean had retreated, not a normal low tide but much, much farther than that. Several sandbars had been exposed. Some flopping fish.

"Is it what I think it is?" Jase asked around the tightness in his throat. "Shit, Reg. It is, isn't it?"

Chelle, face drawn, touched his arm to turn him to face her. "What's going on?"

"It's what happens before a tsunami," Reg said. "The water pulls back, way back, because the wave is gathering."

"We don't get tsunamis in Delaware," Chelle said.

Jase took her gently by the upper arms and looked into her face. "Chelle. Did you write about a tsunami?"

She let out a choked gasp. "Oh my God, Jase, I never wrote about it, but I did make some notes about it in one of the plotting folders. I never researched it or anything. It was a ridiculous plot point I was thinking of using to beef up word count. It never went anywhere—"

"But you put it in the program." His stomach twisted, dropping.

She nodded and looked out again to the vast expanse of sand the retreating sea had left behind. "Yes. It was in there."

"What did you do with the program?" Reg asked.

"I deleted it," Chelle said.

Reg shook his head with a frown. "Right to the trash? You didn't run an uninstaller?"

"No. I didn't know I had to," Chelle said with a look at Jase.

"Yeah, he wouldn't, either," Reg said. "Shit. We have to do something about this. And fast."

"We'll take my car. C'mon." Jase grabbed his keys and headed for the steps, Chelle and Reg on his heels.

The gorilla stopped him at the bottom of the stairs with a single punch to the gut that sent Jase to his knees. With a roar, the ape then grabbed him by the back of the shirt and shook him until his teeth rattled. When his head connected with the wooden railing, everything went dark for a moment, though he could hear Reg and Chelle both shouting.

When he came to, it was under a stinking, sweating pile of fur. He couldn't move. His head hurt like a sonofabitch. He blinked, catching sight of Reg to one side and Chelle to the other. Together the two of them rolled the gorilla off Jase and got him to his feet.

"I think we're in some trouble," Reg said. "Girl, you'd better start remembering every story you ever wrote."

Watching Reg take down the gorilla with a single shot to the head had been awful. And it was all her fault, Chelle thought as she helped Jase take a seat on the bottom step. She'd done this.

"We have to get to my laptop," she said. "Before anything else starts."

"It's already started," Reg said with a jerk of his chin toward the shadows coalescing at the end of the street. "More zombies. Shit."

Chelle recoiled. "What? Oh. No. God."

"At least they're the slow kind," Jase said as he got to his feet with a wince.

"Of course they're the slow kind," Chelle said. "That's the only kind of true zombie. The kind that can run fast, they're not zombies."

Reg snorted and holstered his gun to grab up the car keys from the sandy grass where Jase had dropped them. "I'd love to debate this with you, but right now I think we'd better get our asses in gear."

She hadn't thought about the mess a pack of shambling undead would make when a car ran through them, and she'd certainly never written about it in any great detail, but it was a giant, disgusting mess. Chelle watched them scatter in a spray of guts and teeth and rotten flesh, then waved away the sudden rainfall of glittering light that lit up the inside of the car and faded as they drove away.

"It's the same thing," Jase said from the passenger seat. He'd argued with Reg about driving, but only for half a minute. He still looked as though he was hurting, and no wonder. An eight-hundred-pound gorilla had knocked him around like a rag doll. "If we shone the black light, we'd still see that glow. All the cases. Definitely from the program."

"We'll get there in time," Chelle said with more confidence than she felt.

She screamed, though, when the shrieking pterodactyl scraped its claws along the car roof, tearing open the moonroof to peer inside. Its long beak snapped, missing her by inches. Then it dropped a dog onto her lap.

The dog peed.

But at least it was alive.

Chelle was losing her mind. All of this, everything she'd ever written or researched or used in a possible plotline in the multitude of files and folders in that program—all of it was coming true. Right here and now as they drove through the streets of Bethany Beach.

Civil War soldiers fought robots in the town square. The totem in front of the police station had been toppled by a dead-eyed pack of dolls in lacy dresses that swarmed like a school of fish, devouring whatever lay in their path. A carousel horse galloped past, kicking up stones.

And the water, she thought. The water was coming.

"Drive over it!" she cried at the sight of an enormous

snake stretched out along the street. It was consuming its own tail. She didn't remember ever writing about such a thing or even researching it, but there it was.

She was never going to write again.

By the time they got to the house, she'd broken out in a chill sweat. Hands shaking. Yet determined, she followed Jase and Reg out of the car and into her house, where she flipped open the laptop to find a black screen.

"Shit, shit, shit," she breathed, dragging a finger along the trackpad. "Battery's dead. The program must've been sucking up power while we were gone. The charger's there on the chair—"

Reg found it and brought it over, plugged it in. The computer beeped, slowly coming to life. Chelle moved over so Reg could get at the keyboard, pulling up her trash can to get a look at the file.

"Where was it saved originally?"

"I found it when I was deleting some old letters and emails," she said. "It was in my archives folder."

"Got it." His fingers flew over the keyboard.

At the front door, a dragon hissed, staring in at Jase, who let fly with a string of curses and jerked the curtains closed. He turned to them. "Guys, hurry it up."

"No uninstall file," Reg said. "But there's a bunch of junk left behind from when you deleted it. Do you have a cleaner program or something like that?"

"I don't think so!"

From far away came a rumble. The ground trembled. Chelle and Jase looked at each other.

"Hurry, Reg," Jase said, too calm considering they were listening to the sound of the impending wave. "Hurry the fuck up."

Reg slammed his fingers on the keyboard, then let

out a triumphant shout. "Got it. Shit, yeah. Should've known from the start. It's a GOLEM, yeah? And how do you kill a golem?"

Chelle had no idea. She knew vaguely of the legendary monster but few details. Jase knew, though.

"Erase the first letter written on its forehead," he said. "*Emet* becomes *met*."

"Truth becomes death," Reg said. "And...done!"

The front glass door exploded into a myriad of splinters. The dragon roared. Flame flooded the room.

But only for a moment, and then all that was left was that glittering light that slowly settled and faded, leaving the three of them staring at each other.

Reg held out the flash drive. "I changed the file name, which basically rendered the program inoperable. Crashed it. Then I saved it to this drive and uninstalled all of it from your laptop. But I'd wipe the hard drive if I were you. Do a complete reinstall."

Chelle nodded. She still felt as though the world were tipping and sliding away beneath her feet, but at least they weren't being swept away by a wall of water.

"What are you going to do with the program?" she asked.

"Vadim will probably get Eggy to study it. And then destroy it," Reg said. "Either way, it's going to be safe and can't cause any trouble."

He caught sight of Jase's look and tucked the flash drive into his pocket. "Look, I'm going to go outside and grab a smoke while you two say your goodbyes."

"You don't smoke," Jase said.

Reg dropped a wink at Chelle. "Take your time."

When he'd gone through the front door, she stood.

Her palms felt sweaty, so she wiped them on the butt of her jeans. She cleared her throat.

"So. You're done, heading out of town right away, then?"

"I'll have to get to Florida and make my report," Jase said.

Silence.

"And then?" Chelle asked, kind of hating herself for being the one to pose the question.

She was in his arms before she knew it. His big hands warm on the small of her back. His mouth, kissing her. Oh, how he kissed her.

"And then," Jase said into the kiss, "I thought maybe I'd swing back up this way."

Her fingers linked behind his neck as she tipped her face to his, smiling against his mouth. "Yeah? And then what?"

"I figured we could see about that happy-ever-after," he told her. "Isn't that how this story is supposed to end?"

It was the best way a story could end, she thought and kissed him again and again and again.

* * * * *

Jen Christie is a writer who has a passion for reading and writing gothic romances. Jen lives in St. Augustine, Florida, with her husband and three daughters. She has a love of history, and her secret desire is to stop and read every roadside historical marker she drives by.

Books by Jen Christie

Harlequin Nocturne

House of Shadows

Harlequin E Shivers

House of Glass
Queen of Stone

Visit the Author Profile page
at Harlequin.com for more titles.

HOUSE OF SHADOWS

Jen Christie

I dedicate this book to my sister Penny,
who taught me that life is full of second chances,
and they are always worth taking.

Prologue

The grandfather clock tolled, echoing on and on. The sound reverberated in the tunnel until Penrose fell to the floor, covered her ears and buried her head in her skirts. The chimes came from everywhere at once, from all around her and even from within her own mind.

She couldn't think, couldn't move. She could only endure. Dust and plaster rained down and pelted her body. *Please,* she wished, *let it be a dream.* But she knew it wasn't. A dream doesn't hit you with plaster hard enough to hurt. Long, agonizing moments passed. It was as if time ceased.

Quietness returned slowly. The rumbling grew less ferocious until finally the ground was still, and the clock fell silent. Only then did she lift her head and take a breath. Dust filled her nostrils. Coughing, wiping her eyes and face, she called out in a panicked voice, "C.J.?"

He didn't answer. The only sound was a lone splatter of plaster falling to the floor somewhere in the darkness. She must find C.J. and see if he was okay, but it was too dangerous to crawl around without light.

Remembering that there were candles in the hallway, she began inching toward the door. She planned to grab a candle and hopefully find Carrick so that they could hunt for C.J. together. When she reached the door, she fumbled with the latch until it opened. The house was dark and quiet. Still on all fours, she took a deep, shaky breath and called, "C.J.? Carrick, are you here?"

No answer. She crawled out, stood up and brushed herself off, making sure she wasn't injured. Her hands traveled the length of her torso, but the lack of pain did nothing to reassure her that she was all right. She was not all right.

The air in the foyer was cold—too cold for August in Charleston. The house felt different. It smelled odd, of lemons and lavender. Something was wrong. She knew it in her bones.

"C.J.?" Desperation turned her voice harsh. "Carrick? Please! Answer me."

Still nothing.

Her eyes adjusted to the light, and she saw the grandfather clock standing against the wall. Standing. Not toppled over as she'd witnessed moments before. She looked around wildly. The table that normally held the candles wasn't there anymore. The chandelier hung still and straight as if it hadn't even moved, let alone swung wildly while the earth shook.

But what took the breath right from her lungs were the paintings. They were different—with odd, angular images in them. The more she looked around, the more uneasy she became. Yes, something was very, very wrong.

"Carrick?" she called again, taking minute, untrusting steps toward the great room, her hands pressing the air in disbelief. "Carrick! C.J.? Please?" she kept repeating in a whiny, almost begging manner. She held a last bit of hope that the world would right itself, and she'd see the familiar features of Arundell. Her Arundell. Not this twisted imitation.

When she entered the large parlor, she saw moonlight and shadows dancing around the room, revealing a dark doppelgänger of the room she knew and loved. The cold air around her made it scarier and even less familiar.

Yes, the bones of the room were the same. The same lofty ceiling, the same shape of the windows, even the familiar gouges in the doorway that marked the heights of the Arundell boys. But the essence had changed.

Everything had changed. She tried to reconcile the two different versions of her home—one familiar and one not—but she couldn't. It simply wasn't Arundell Manor.

Yet it was.

She went to the window and looked out. The world outside glimmered bright and white beneath the moon.

Bright and white. Snow.

No peaceful pond with a lazy oak tree beside it. No familiar road winding through the Charleston countryside straight to the front doors of her home. Only bare land covered in white stretched all the way to the horizon. Stepping away from the window as if it burned her, she found herself gasping for breath. She wanted to scream, to wail and cry for help, but she had no voice.

She took fast, short steps and went from room to room on the first floor, seeing unbelievable and frightening items everywhere she turned. The house had always been extravagant, but now it seemed garish. Every room was crammed with shiny and bizarre objects, things she didn't understand and was afraid to touch.

A huge mirror hung on the wall by the kitchen and her own shadowy form reflected back at her. Even she looked different. It was as if a ghost stared at her, coated in dust, hair wild and tumbling, the whites of its eyes glowing brightly. She had a horrible thought as she looked at herself. She'd died.

"I'm not dead," she said loudly, voicing that horrible thought. A worse thought sprang up behind it. Perhaps she'd been trapped in a kind of purgatory. A place between life and death.

"No." She shook her head wildly. So did the shadowy figure in the mirror. Leaning forward, she insisted to the image, "I'm alive. Alive." But her image seemed to stare back at her with accusing eyes and Penrose backed away, shaking.

The kitchen was unrecognizable, with silver equipment that had blue flashing lights on the different pieces. She knew it was a kitchen because of the sink, the knives that hung from the wall and the bowl of fresh fruit sitting atop the counter. A piece of paper lay beside the bowl, and by the dim blue light she read:

Dear Keat,
Welcome back to Arundell. Everything should be in order. The kitchen is stocked. The robots have been delivered and set up. If you need anything,

just call. Enjoy your time by yourself. Please, try to relax. Stop worrying. You do your best work that way.
—V

The note called this home Arundell, but unless the world had changed overnight, this was not Arundell. Not the Arundell she knew.

Part One

All in the dark we grope along,
And if we go amiss
We learn at least which path is wrong,
And there is gain in this.

—Ella Wheeler Wilcox

Chapter 1

Charleston, South Carolina
August 18, 1886

Penrose Heatherton stood at the window, her face lifted to the night sky, hoping for wind. But there was no wind to speak of. The skies were speckled with stars. The moon hung lazy and bright. It was a perfect Charleston summer evening and gave no hint of the troubles that lay ahead of her.

It was hot enough to boil water that night, and she wore her underthings in a futile effort to stay cool. The clothes clung to her damp skin and her black hair hung in sweaty strands. She fanned herself listlessly with the want ads from the newspaper. The effort only made her hotter. It didn't help that she'd just returned from the kitchen downstairs where she'd washed dishes for hours to help reduce the amount of rent she had to pay.

Rent. A knot of worry twisted in her chest and she rested her head against the window frame. Rent was due in the morning, and, even at a reduced rate, she had no way of paying. Renting her room at The Winding Stair Inn & Pub had already taken all of her funds.

She turned her face to the moon, pleading for wind. Tattered clouds sailed across it, scattering silvery light on the ground. None reached her. "Please," she whispered, hoping, waiting, for a gust to come and cool her down.

It seemed that, lately, she was always waiting. For a cool breeze or a hot meal, for a permanent job, for any sliver of relief, no matter how small, that would help fix the mess her life had become. She was tired, so very tired of waiting.

She tossed the want ads out of the window and watched as they fluttered to the ground. Worthless. If she'd learned one thing since her mother died six months earlier, it was that relief didn't come easy. If it came at all. No, she was beginning to understand the bitter truth—that if you wanted relief you had to grab it for yourself.

But you can't grab the wind, so she stood there sweating. Sighing, she went to the cot and lay down. If it got any hotter, even one degree, she would melt into a puddle. But right when she thought that was about to happen, there came a change.

A gust of wind slipped through the window and eddied in the small space. It was a strange wind. Wintery, cool and dry, with a touch of wildness to it. The breeze tossed about the room and swirled around Penrose like a cool promise. She sat up, feeling it slip and slide over her skin, and she had the sense that something, anything could happen.

Right at that exact moment, she heard the sound of boots walking down the hall. The footsteps belonged to Mrs. Capshaw, the landlady of The Winding Stair Inn & Pub. Her walk was distinctive. When it came your way you knew she wanted something, and sure enough, it was coming Penrose's way.

Not a moment later, the door flew open as the landlady swept into the tiny room. There was barely space for her, but she didn't seem to care. Mrs. Capshaw was an ample woman with frizzy red hair and a bosom that sat like a shelf over her stomach. She had sharp, assessing brown eyes, which right then took in the sight of Penrose lounging on the bed. She said in her tough-as-nails voice, "Look sharp, Penny. There's an opportunity for you downstairs."

Instantly, she had Penrose's attention. "What opportunity?"

Mrs. Capshaw was an enterprising woman, always on the lookout for any venture that would be advantageous. Coming from her, an opportunity could mean a million different things, most of them dubious. But opportunities were rare, and Penrose was desperate.

Another cool gust of wind blasted into the room, slamming the door shut. The older woman yanked it open again and held it in her meaty fist. "If you're clever," she said, leaning over Penrose and staring at her hard, "and I know you are, you'll listen carefully."

"I'm listening," said Penrose. She rubbed her arms as she listened. The temperature in the room must have dropped twenty degrees.

Mrs. Capshaw continued, "Right at this moment, there's a woman sitting at a table downstairs. She reminds me of you so very much, young and full of distress. Another sad story, I'm sure. Except unlike you, she's downright foolish. I think you might have a chance to secure a well-paying—" she looked at Penrose meaningfully "—and respectable job."

Penrose jumped up. "Tell me. Is it a teaching position?"

"No. Better." Mrs. Capshaw's sharp brown eyes narrowed and she lowered her voice to a whisper. "The lady is on her way to a post that her agency secured for her. She needs a room while she travels." She smiled, a small twist of the lips. "But she is sitting there downstairs right now, blabbing for all the world to hear about her doubts and fears over the position."

That *was* interesting news. "Go on," said Penrose.

"She's to report the day after tomorrow. Seven a.m. sharp. But, she's reluctant. In fact, she's more than reluctant."

"More than reluctant?"

"She's terrified," Mrs. Capshaw blurted out. "I'm telling you straight off to get it out of the way." She shrugged as if it were of little consequence. "She's heard rumors. It seems her agency was less than forthcoming about the post. Her employer is a troubled individual and the house might be haunted."

For the first time, Penrose felt wary, but just a bit. It was a job, after all. She hedged. "How troubled? And what kind of hauntings? The rumors must be awful for her to reconsider."

"Awful?" Mrs. Capshaw threw her hands into the air. "What can be awful about regular income and a roof over your head?" Her voice lowered an octave as she said, "And wages that would make your eyes pop right out of your head. And, truthfully, do you believe in ghosts?"

"No, I don't." Penrose felt breathy. For decent wages, she'd be blind to a lot of things. Including ghosts. And regular pay? Something she could barely imagine. But she wasn't a babe in the woods. She was twenty-one. Old enough to know a thing or two. Something was wrong. "Still…why such high wages? Something doesn't ring true. Maybe there's truth to the rumors."

Mrs. Capshaw huffed. "'Still' nothing. You've been here six months already. Six months since your mother died and no position to speak of. No prospects, either! I've watched your purse dwindle, your belongings dwindle. You're all boiled down like soup left too long on the stove. Only scrapings left." She wagged her hands in the air. "Penrose Heatherton, you are in debt to me. Not a small amount, either. And if you ask me, that's what awful is." She pursed her lips. "And, yes, the post seems…suspicious. But, if you listen closely, it also sounds like an opportunity." She lifted a pearl comb from the nightstand. "This is the only thing of value you have left, isn't it? And rent's due tomorrow? Do you think I'd take a comb in payment? You're a sweet girl, but you're fooling yourself if you think you'll find work as a schoolteacher. Not in this town. Not with your name."

"But my mother had such a respectable finishing school—"

"No offense, but you are not your mother. She was a Northerner. Sent to the finest schools and from a well-regarded family. She had credentials, Penny. Credentials. The big families in this town adored her because she attended those fine finishing schools. Yes, she fell from grace, there was always that."

"You don't need to remind me that I was her downfall," she snapped. Penrose always had trouble concealing her anger when the subject was brought to her attention.

"I'm not. A baby is a baby to the likes of me. But not to them. Not to those fancy folks. They never minded you as an assistant to her. But an illegitimate child as an assistant is one thing. As a teacher, it's quite another. Plus, your name. Penrose." She sighed. "Your mother did you such a disservice giving you your father's surname as a first name. She thought she was clever giving you that name! Calling him out and exposing him as the father. Those were passionate times, I'll give her that. But she was ignorant. The South doesn't work that way and she was foolish to think she'd change it. Oh, those abolitionists had such grand ideas, didn't they? No bigger name around here. Like a splinter in the eye of the most powerful family. You'll have a tough road around here. Surely my words are no surprise to you."

No, they weren't a surprise. Penrose shook her head. "Just painful."

"The truth hurts, Penny. It hurts." Mrs. Capshaw leaned down and put her hand on the bed. It creaked under her weight. "Just like when that young man stopped calling on you and I told you he wasn't coming back. I say it plain. You'll never find work on your own here. No education other—"

"My mother educated me." Heat burned her cheeks.

Mrs. Capshaw pushed down on the bed. "Let me finish, girl. I said no education other than from your mother. It may be a fine education, but there's no stamp of a finishing school on your papers. In fact, you have no papers. Even worse, you're now living in a pub by the wharf. Your stock is dropping by the minute…what's left for a girl like you? Hmm?" She loomed over Penrose, her shadow falling across her.

Penrose stared out of the window. A sliver of the moon was visible and she focused on that. Her chest felt tight, as if a belt were strapped around it and someone was tugging. Was it anxiety? Or something more? She remembered the strange breeze from earlier and felt the odd, prickly sensation spread over her once again. Change was in the air. Perhaps she should welcome it. "I deserve a break, don't I?" Her words came hot and fast. "Don't I?" She looked at Mrs. Capshaw with a pleading, angry gaze.

"You said it, Penny. Right from your own mouth. You deserve a break. But if you think a break is going to waltz in here and lay itself in your lap, you're mistaken." She shook her head, her frizzy hair barely moving on her head. "Listen, some girls are tough to their bones. Others are soft. Those are the ones that wilt. Still others, and I think you're one of these—are malleable, able to bend and sway. Adapt to changing conditions. You need to adapt. And I'm giving you an opportunity to do just that. What better than to work for a man who doesn't give two shakes what society thinks?"

Mrs. Capshaw was right. Penrose nodded.

"Get off that bed. Stand up and listen to me. Listen to what the post entails and then make your choice." She lifted her hand and stood straight.

Penrose slid from the bed and stood beside her landlady. "I'm listening."

Mrs. Capshaw seemed to soften then. She blinked and nodded, and gave a halfhearted attempt at a smile. "I'm sorry, dear. Life did you wrong. But I'm not a charity. You have to act fast."

"The post," Penrose reminded her. "I need more details."

"It's a single man, a bachelor, and he needs someone to help him in his scientific studies. Someone who can write, who has a bright intellect and one who doesn't mind…"

Everything sounded fine until Penrose heard those words. "Doesn't mind what?"

Mrs. Capshaw spoke in a rush. "Working nights. He works at night, from sunset to sunrise. Though don't worry, because it's respectable. The little miss downstairs told me that the three ladies that walked off before her have never accused him of wrongdoing. He has an affliction, she says. It makes him unsightly, very unsightly, and causes trouble with his eyesight. The sun hurts his eyes and the night is the only time he can see untroubled. But it's the strange rumors of the manor that scare her so. The hauntings. They whisper that he does odd things. Practices dark arts." Then she added pointedly. "But those wages…" She named the sum, a figure so high that Penrose coughed.

No, she choked. An amount like that, well, it seemed almost sinful. Penrose floated in an odd place, willing to be tempted, letting her mind imagine the riches of such a sum but knowing that she should be suspicious. *Those wages, though.* Finally, she said. "Very well, I'm interested. Not committing, but interested. What is your plan?"

"Smart of you to consider it. Just hear me out. I always say don't let the future toss you about. Sometimes you have to grab it." She smoothed her frizzy hair down, a useless habit because it just popped right back up again. "My idea is that we'll help the girl, make the decision easy for her. You'll steal her post." She watched Penrose.

"Steal it? Are you serious?"

Mrs. Capshaw nodded. "The girl doesn't want the job. One look at her face and I knew the truth of it. She let the name of the manor slip…" Her voice trailed off in an odd way.

"I can't steal her post!"

"Now you think to be ethical? Right now, when your whole future is blank—a black hole—and your present is nothing but hunger. Yes, life did you wrong. But you don't even have money for the rent! I'll have to move your room again, to the porch this time. And after that, who knows?" The threat hung in the room.

It would be easier to stand up and grab a future than to sit around The Winding Stair wallowing in the slim pickings that came her way. "I'll do it." She didn't feel entirely convinced, but somehow the words came out sure and strong.

"Very well," said the landlady. "The plan is simple enough. You only have to show up a day early. Let them know the agency sent you instead of her. Plead prudence on your early arrival. Better to be early than late. I'll let the young lady downstairs know the bad news. Let her down easy, let her know it was for the best. By arriving early, there's no mistaking the job is yours. I'll break the news to the young lady." Mrs. Capshaw looked away as she spoke.

"Ah, I get it now. I wondered why you were so generous with an opportunity," Penrose said spitefully. "And once you tell the poor girl she's been wronged, you'll give her the good news that you have a room to rent her. That, strangely, one was just vacated…"

The woman laughed, short and bitter, and her belly heaved. "You're a smart one, aren't you? Yes, I've seen her purse, and it's heavier than yours. Don't judge me. I have to survive. Just like you."

The tight feeling in Penrose's chest constricted even further. It became hard to breathe. "Mrs. Capshaw, I don't know… It seems like such a scheme."

"Well, you only have to listen to the girl to know I'm right. She's downstairs right now, blabbing away to Charlie, telling my husband all her woes." She plucked the heavy black gown from the peg on the wall and tossed it in Penrose's direction. It sailed across the room like a dark ghost and covered Penrose in an embrace.

Mrs. Capshaw continued, "At the very least, come and hear her for yourself."

The dress hung limply over Penrose. She felt small and uncertain all of a sudden.

"Don't dally," said Mrs. Capshaw, coming over and grabbing the dress, then holding open the bodice so that Penrose could step into it. "Here. Time's wasting, always wasting. We have to hurry."

Penrose stepped into the dress. The gown swallowed her. She had always been petite, but now she was thin— too thin.

Mrs. Capshaw didn't seem to notice and she stood back, admiring Penrose. "That's more like it. You'll see. It will all work out. Turn around, dear," she said.

Penrose turned, and the woman drew the gown tight and began buttoning it up. "This is your only dress?"

she asked with concern. "The one you wore to your mother's funeral?"

"I'm sorry. It's all I have." The rich black fabric had faded to gray at the elbows and the hem had turned to fringe. "I sold the others," she whispered, hating the need to confess the small, shameful adjustments she'd had to make in the past few months.

Mrs. Capshaw sighed. "It's so morose. I can only hope a somber look will work in your favor." She tightened the final button and cinched the ribbon into a bow. "Now, where's your bonnet?"

"I'll get it. It's at the window. I need to comb my hair, too." In her heart she was still reluctant, her decision not yet made. But she went through the motions, fighting the comb through her inky hair. While she wrestled her hair into a tight bun, Mrs. Capshaw explained what she was to do.

"Charlie can drive you to the manor," she said, referring to her husband and bartender. Even though Charlie was married to Mrs. Capshaw, he was no Mr. Capshaw. Simply Charlie. She continued, "You'll have to sleep the night outside. We can't risk you leaving tomorrow. She might catch on in the light of day. Anyhow, it shouldn't be too hard. The gentleman's name is Mr. Carrick Arundell. Remember, seven sharp. Very specific about that. Don't worry about the little miss here, it's all for the best." She took Penrose by the hand. "Come now, let's go down the stairs."

When they reached the landing, Mrs. Capshaw put a hand on her shoulder. "Hold it," she said. "Hmm. Can't do to arrive without any belongings. It will make you look wanting. Needful." She twisted her lips as she thought and then lifted a finger. "I've got it. Just a moment." She left Penrose on the stairs.

Penrose heard her then. A breathy, feminine voice wafting up the stairwell. She couldn't help herself and crept lower, down the winding staircase until she could see her—with the benefit of a wall that partially hid Penrose from view. The woman sat at the corner table. Even though the late crowd had begun to arrive, Penrose could still see her clearly.

No, this woman hadn't sunk to the level that she had. Oh, certainly she oozed that refined look of genteel suffering, a bit worn at the edges. No doubt, there was even a small, graciously suffering smile on her lips. The kind of smile that Penrose couldn't quite muster anymore.

The little blond head bobbed as she spoke. "It might not be worth the fear, the fright of living with such a man," she drawled.

What could be so frightening about a mere man? Nothing, that's what. But to make matters worse she continued, "I'm not so hungry that I will endure fright and intimidation. Not me. I can always stay with my sister. Perhaps another might endure such a thing, but I'm hesitant. Are things so bad that I must suffer for employment?"

Penrose's eyes burned, and her fingers itched with the urge to strike out. *Yes, they are, you silly woman. Yes, they are.*

"But what about those wages?" Charlie asked.

The woman named the amount of pay, and a small choking noise escaped from Penrose's lips. Both the woman and Charlie turned in her direction and she slunk back into the shadows.

"They say," the woman continued in a grave voice,

"that he must pay such a wild sum because of all the awful things that go on in that house. I've heard he's wicked. I've heard he's…dark."

"The men talk, you know. I've heard the same." Charlie stood leaning over the counter and wiping a whiskey glass with his rag. "And worse, too. Still, those wages. Any man would be proud to earn such a sum for a year's labor."

"Oh, that's not a year of wages. That's for a month."

The shrill clink of the glass slipping from Charlie's hand and hitting the counter rang out. Or maybe it was the sound of her conscience turning to ice. But whatever decency was left inside her hungry soul fled when she heard that sum. Right then and there, her mind turned rock-solid certain. The risks be damned. Dark arts meant nothing to her. That job would be hers. All she needed was one paycheck, just one, and she could recover. She could start again in a new city. She could open her own school with a new identity.

Distinctive footfalls came down the stairs. Penrose turned and saw Mrs. Capshaw standing on the rise above her. "Well?" she asked in a hearty whisper. "Heard enough?"

Penrose nodded. "Have you the bag?" she asked pointedly.

"Of course." Mrs. Capshaw held it out. "I stuffed it with newspapers to look full."

"It's perfect," said Penrose, taking the bag. It was dusty black and light as air. "I'll go and wait outside for Charlie."

"Of course. I'll let him know." The woman grabbed Penrose by the arm. "Penrose, you won't regret this. Trust me."

Trust was not a word she associated with Mrs. Capshaw, but the woman seemed sincere, and she nodded in reply. They descended the rest of the stairs together. Once on the ground floor, Penrose moved through the pub area swiftly, Mrs. Capshaw right behind her. Charlie looked up and smiled from behind the bar, but before he could say a single word to her, Penrose opened the door and stepped outside. Not once did she look at the woman. She couldn't bear to. She didn't want to risk developing a conscience and changing her mind.

Outside, she leaned against the wall of the inn and took deep breaths. What exactly was she doing? Mrs. Capshaw stood stoically beside her.

Penrose breathed a sigh of relief when Charlie emerged from the pub. "Are you okay, Penny?" he asked, taking a long look at her before turning to his wife. "What's going on? Why did you pull me outside?"

"I need you to ready the buggy. There's something you need to do."

"Oh, no," he said with a sigh. "What are you up to?" He shook his head. "I should've known—you had that look about you." Turning to Penrose, he said, "Has she pulled you into some plan?"

"Well…" began Penrose.

Mrs. Capshaw practically pounced on the man. "Charlie," she muttered, "leave be and don't intrude. This is for the best. You'll see. Don't say another word of protest. Go and ready that buggy. Take Penny to the river road that leads to the mansions. Drop her off and come right back. She's lucky enough to have a position waiting."

He looked dubious, his white, bushy eyebrows drawing together. "All of a sudden like this?" Suddenly he leaned toward his wife and his voice grew accusing. "This wouldn't have anything to do with our new guest, would it?"

A little huff of anger escaped the woman. "Of course it does. It has everything to do with our guest. But don't say a word, Charlie. Not a word. My plans will work out this time." Mrs. Capshaw spoke with authority. "You drive her to the river and return to me. Straightaway."

"Answer me this first, wife. Where's her position?"

"Arundell Manor."

It was the first time Penrose heard the name. Arundell Manor. The words hung in the air like an echo from a bell. It pleased Penrose and a strange sense of calmness swelled within her.

Charlie did not have the same reaction, however. "Arundell Manor! You're snatching that woman's job! That's no coup! Are you cruel? You're sending her there?"

"Charlie," said Mrs. Capshaw in something close to a growl.

"Arundell Manor? You must be three sheets to the wind! That man will kill her as surely as we stand here now. There's something very wrong with that man, and all of Charleston knows it. He's dangerous and wicked…and downright frightening. The stories I hear about that…that monster."

Beneath the lamplight, Mrs. Capshaw looked at Charlie with a gaze of iron. "Charlie Capshaw, you will keep your mouth shut if you know what's good for you."

"I can't in good conscience—" he sputtered.

"Stop," said Penrose. She was strangely settled in her mind with the decision. The name of the manor struck a chord inside her as if fate had been summoned and there was no stopping it. She put her hand on Charlie's arm. "Charlie, I've already accepted it, whatever may come," she said with resolve.

Charlie looked at her a moment before shaking his head. "You don't understand, child. I hear things in the pub. He's trying to create a man. Think on that. It's said that no woman will ever go near him. Ever. Some have even whispered dark magic is afoot in that house."

"Charles Edgar Capshaw. There you go again! I've told you before…" Her voice trailed away to nothing. Mrs. Capshaw had never spoken quite so harshly before and they all turned quiet. She looked to Penrose. "Don't listen, dear. Go, go to the position and see for yourself." Then she turned to Charlie. "Get the buggy! And be quick about it!"

He backed away in small steps, shaking his head. "Mark my words," he said in a low voice before turning and stomping off into the darkness.

"Don't let Charlie scare you."

"He doesn't," she replied, which was the truth. A future with no income scared her more than men's tales when they were deep in their cups.

Charlie returned with the buggy and, after she was settled, he drove her through Charleston, past the harbor with its ships bobbing in the water and the fat moon flying high above them. Penrose smelled the sweet perfume of gladiolas heavy in the air. She felt oddly happy. Dark magic or no, the pay would take care of everything. She laughed.

"I wouldn't take it so lightly," said Charlie, glancing over at her, flicking the whip above the head of the horse. They passed through the gates of Charleston and traveled through the thick woods before reaching the stone gates of the manor. The iron gates were thrown wide open, heedless of any intruders. Charlie slowed the carriage to a stop, then turned to look at her. "Penny," he said, patting her on the shoulder, "promise me you'll be careful."

"I will. I promise. Everything will be fine, don't worry."

"I always worry when Mrs. Capshaw is scheming."

She picked up the valise and climbed down. "This time, it will work out grand. You'll see."

"I hope so, dear. I hope so," he said, snapping the whip in the air. With a neigh, the horse came to life and the carriage pulled away. It had gone a few paces when he called out to her. "Remember, Penny, you can always come back and start again if you'd like. Don't think you're trapped. You're never trapped."

"Thank you, Charlie," she said, and watched as the carriage rode out of sight.

She set off down the manor road with nervous steps, unsure exactly what she had gotten herself into. Only one thing was certain. The choice had been her own, so she deserved whatever the future held for her.

Oak trees lined the bone-white road like sentinels, and she walked beneath them until the road spilled out onto a wide clearing of land. Some distance away, the house floated, eerie and ghostly white under the moonlight. She settled under one of the large oaks at the end of the path, her eyes trained on the ghostly house. Two windows were illuminated. They glowed like orange eyes and she saw the dark figure of a man cross in front of them. Her heart beat wildly. Was that him? Was that Carrick Arundell?

Once more the figure passed by the window, except this time he stopped and stood in front of it. Her skin pulled tight in gooseflesh. It seemed that he stared through the darkness and looked right at her. Her heart beat wildly, and her thoughts ran unchecked. Perhaps right now he was practicing his dark magic. *Stop it*, she chided herself. He was only a man. He couldn't be that bad.

The light of day would bring answers. Tomorrow she would know everything. Tomorrow her future would become the present. In the meantime, she must sleep. But she couldn't stop herself from watching the dark figure pace back and forth in the window. Back and forth, again and again. Endlessly.

Chapter 2

Penrose opened her eyes, her body stiff, the dew from the evening before settled on her skin and hair. Arundell Manor stood before her, no longer ghostly, but regal, and she couldn't stop staring at the sight. The early sun poured pink rays of light over the white stone walls. The windows—and there were dozens of them—all glistened in a gold sheen. The rich green grasses that stretched before her were silvered in morning dew. A pond, invisible to her in the night, lay under a blanket of mist. The home slept in quiet splendor.

Her gown was damp. She stood, brushing away the pine needles and drops of dew before straightening her hair and bonnet and pinching her cheeks for color. Lifting the valise, she walked along the bone-white gravel path, each step of her boots a loud crunch in the still morning air. There were forty-four steps leading to the massive front doors, she thought as she climbed and counted each one. She was aware of every move as if someone was already watching her from behind the glittering windows. Penrose couldn't shake the sensation.

Standing in front of the brass knocker, she took a deep, steadying breath. *You can do this*, she told herself. The rising sun warmed her backside and seemed almost to agree. Lifting the heavy knocker, she let it fall and listened as the hammer strike echoed on and on behind the door. She waited, then waited some more, but there was no answer, so she tried again.

Finally, there came a fumbling noise; a latch turned and the door swung open. Sunlight streamed past her and into the house, striking a crystal chandelier that hung low in the foyer. Glass orbs and shards grabbed the light and tossed about a brilliant rainbow of colors, blinding her. She flinched and stepped backward, her boot heel catching on the fabric of her skirt. Down she went, limbs akimbo, the piazza floor rising up fast to greet her. But as she fell, she caught a glimpse of a man—a dark outline of his tall frame. His features were invisible against the white stone of the house.

Then the ground slapped her hard enough to rattle her teeth. So much for a good first impression. The sunlight poured relentlessly on her. She shielded her eyes and looked up.

"You find me that offensive?" His voice was low and sleep-filled, tainted with anger. No, she realized, the voice wasn't tainted with mere anger—it was laced with something close to rage. Or worse.

From beneath her hand, her eyes darted left and right, searching for the man who spoke with such venom. "I can't see you," she said, feeling foolish.

A face swung into view, inches from her own. "I'm easy to miss," he said. Eyes the color of a thousand sunsets swept over her face in a harsh gaze. Reds and purples and blues shifted and swirled within the irises. She shrank from him and sucked air into her lungs like a dying woman. Her hand fell away from her brow, revealing the man in his entirety. Stupidly, she sat there, blinking, trying to fathom exactly what she was seeing.

He stood there in the bright sunlight, white as snow, clad in black sleeping trousers and a robe that lay open to his waist. His skin was powder white—white beyond fathoming—as if milk had been added to an already pale skin tone, bringing forth an unnatural brightness. To look at him was to look upon the facets of a diamond; it hurt the eye to take him in. His muscles were etched into hard lines on his torso and he had a winter's blaze of white hair that crowned a youthful, vigorous-looking face. All that white hair and he couldn't be more than thirty-five. She stared, openmouthed.

"At least have the courtesy to shut your mouth while you stare at me," he said, each word scraping out exactly as her boots had on the walkway moments before. He held out a hand.

She hesitated, swallowed hard and then finally slipped her hand into his. His hand was warm and she couldn't help but be surprised by this. She had half expected his touch to have the cold chill of death on it. He pulled her to her feet, yanked her right up, and she stood in his shadow—for he was very tall, indeed—panting, trying to collect her thoughts.

"Well?" he said, a sneer twisting his features. Was he handsome?

"I'm sorry," she said, her brain scrambling for words.

"The agency sent me, sir. I'm here for the position." She chanced one more look—she couldn't help it. His face was too young, too beautiful and too strong for that white hair. And those eyes. God help her, those eyes.

He said nothing, merely watched her as she watched him. He seemed determined to shock her, unconcerned as he was with his half-dressed state. "Have you seen enough?" he finally asked. A touch of sleep lingered in the drawl of his voice, giving him an almost casual arrogance.

"I apologize," she said, busying herself by leaning down to pick up her valise. "I was surprised, and all the lights startled me."

He sniffed and shook his head. "The agency sent you? And who exactly are you and why did you come to my door at this ungodly hour?"

"Heatherton." She extended her hand. "Penrose Heatherton."

He didn't take it. His eyes held hers. She thought of the crystal rainbow from the chandelier; the colors shifting, changing. Finally, he said, "Tell me, Miss Heatherton—"

"Yes?" She held her hand extended for another moment, a bit too long, before pulling it back and wringing both hands together awkwardly.

"Miss Heatherton," he repeated, his Southern drawl low and conspiratorial. "Why in the world are you knocking on my door at the break of dawn?"

"The agency told me to arrive at seven a.m." This wasn't going well, she realized. Not at all as she had imagined it. For a lot of different reasons.

"*P.M.,*" he said harshly. "*Post meridiem.* Or generally speaking…in the evening. I told the agency specifically that I needed the applicant to show up at seven p.m."

"Oh," she said foolishly, feeling the blush rise in her cheeks.

His gaze skipped over hers, lowered to her lips and returned once again to her eyes. "That's right—p.m.," he said slowly. "So, not only are you a full day early, you reported at the wrong time. I was asleep, and now you've woken me."

"I'm so sorry." The blush in her cheeks must be red as fire, because her face burned.

"I'm certain you've noticed my affliction. I am cursed with paleness. A lack of pigment. Albinism." His chin jutted into the air defiantly. "It does not lend itself to sunlight. I keep night hours, and I'm very protective of them." He sighed, and those unapologetic eyes didn't look away from her. "But you're here. Though I specifically requested someone who wasn't attractive. Makes it easier." Those eyes still rested on her. The heat on her face grew to volcanic levels. "I take it you can read and write?"

"Of course."

"How's your eyesight?"

"Perfect."

He nodded. "And your hands? Can you can handle fine tools and small mechanical parts? Smaller than a fingernail?

"I'm very sure-handed."

"You can work the night through? Adjust to my schedule?"

"Certainly."

"Good. It's what I value most. That, and discretion." He stepped aside the slightest bit to make room for her, forcing her to brush against him as she entered. "Come in."

She took in the interior of the house with a few quick glances: white marble floors, a high ceiling—two floors high—stairs that curled in an elegant arc to the second floor, archways that led to other rooms. A huge grandfather clock began to chime. Sheets covered the furniture and paintings as if the house were bedded down while its owners were away. Splatters of rainbow light still spun over everything.

He shut the door and the blinding rainbows disappeared. When she turned around, he was beside her, almost too close. Shocked at his willingness to invade her independent space, she pulled away from him. Her reaction was an odd mix of aversion and excitement. He seemed dangerous.

He stilled. "Forgive me. My eyesight is very poor, and I am used to stepping close in order to see something." Then, with a lingering glance, he turned around, and she knew that a moment where they might have established a cordialness between them was lost. When he spoke, it was with a firm and cold voice. "I won't give you a tour as you've already interrupted my sleep. I'm heading to bed. You will start tonight." He turned and began to climb the stairs.

She followed, taking small, anxious steps. "I'm to work your hours, then?"

"How else do you expect to be my assistant?" His voice boomed in the open space. The stairs creaked under his weight as he climbed, his black robe swirling in the air behind him.

"Of course, Mr. Arundell."

Without turning around, he waved his hand angrily.

"Don't call me Mr. Arundell. My father was Mr. Arundell, and he's dead now. Call me Carrick. You'll be ready to work at dusk and you'll be with me until dawn. The work is intense, requires a steady hand and a sharp mind. Are you certain that you're up for the task?"

"I am." She peered down the hall. "Is there anything you want me to accomplish before we start tonight?"

"The day is yours, Miss. Heatherton. But if I were you, I would sleep, for the night will be a long one."

"Yes. Of course."

"You have the run of the house, except for the doors in the kitchen that lead down to the cellar. That is my workroom, and you only enter with me. The house has no staff. You'll have to see to your own needs." He was standing on the landing by then. "I'm sure your agency has warned you of my…disposition."

"Yes. I've been warned." Not enough, though, not enough, she thought. Or perhaps she should have listened to Charlie more closely. But, still, the pay would be worth it. She hoped.

"Good. Then I can dispense with pleasantries. You'll find a small stairway in the second-floor hall that leads straight up to your room."

"Fine, yes, then I'll see you tonight."

"Yes. Tonight." As he walked away, she was unable to tear her eyes away from his retreating form.

Then he was gone, and she stood alone in the entry hall. Or so she thought.

It was a testament to Penrose's desperation that she stayed the day in that strange mansion. Forty-one rooms and she had walked through fourteen of them before her fear got the better of her and she went and sat in the front parlor, which was so large it was more of a great room. Not a person or servant had shown themselves, and yet the house looked well maintained and orderly. One thing drove her crazy—no matter where she went in the mansion, she could hear the grandfather clock ticking.

The front parlor had a large picture window that looked out over the front lawn. The view was like a fancy oil painting, with a serene pond and a large oak tree standing watch over it. It was easy to imagine a family gathering in this very room every evening, playing games and enjoying the twilight hours. But the eerie quiet of the house belied that image. It was a tomb. And even though the house was dead quiet, save for the clock, something else unsettled her even more. She was standing, staring out of the window and wondering exactly what it was, when the realization hit her.

It felt as if someone was watching her.

The sensation was similar to what she'd felt when she first arrived. But it didn't seem like nonsense this time. It was very real, and she spun around, eyes darting left and right, skimming the room. What did she expect to find? This was silly. She had the sudden urge to be free of the house, to stand outside in the sun, where everything made sense. There was nothing scary with the wind in your hair and the sunshine on your cheeks.

Her mind was made up. She would go outside. As she walked from the room, she glanced at the door frame and something caught her eye. A growth chart had been carved into the frame. Names and dates were scratched into the wood, noting the heights of children as they grew. All the scratchings were muted and dulled with age.

The tallest carving was dated 1865 and inscribed with the name Carrick. Twenty-one years ago; the same year she was born. She guessed Carrick's age at thirty-seven or so. Penrose ran her finger over the mark. He would have been too young to head off to war. She noticed other names, Carville and Sampson, that were almost as high as Carrick's. Older brothers, she reasoned, though the last dates etched for them were 1861 and 1862.

Penrose almost missed the last marking. It was so very low on the frame. She had started to walk away when her gaze caught the raw color of the newly scratched wood. There was no date, but the scar was so fresh that it had to be recent. Only the initials *C.J.* were visible, carved crudely, angular and far too large.

On the other side of the door frame, there were other odd markings. Tally marks—single lines gouged in the wood, with a slash running diagonally through them. Someone was counting in blocks of five, and there were dozens and dozens of blocks. She didn't know what to make of it and ran her fingers over the gouges, wondering.

She went outside the double doors at the rear of the house. There was a small flight of stairs that ended on a gravel path. Pecan trees dotted the rear lawn before they gave way to marshy grasses. The Ashley River flowed in the distance, dark as mud and slow as honey. Immediately, she felt better, walking along with the sweet aromas of the summer flowers perfuming the air. Honeybees flew lazy arcs around her head. She walked until the heat got the better of her.

It was getting late. She wanted to be well rested for work. When she turned around to head back inside the manor, what she saw stopped her cold. There was a stone cellar beneath the house, and in the window she saw two figures bent over as if working at a desk. For a long time, she stood there, hand on her hip, staring at the window.

They didn't move. She walked forward, slow as molasses in winter, her eyes trained on the window. She was half expecting one of them to jump up and scare her silly just for their own amusement. But, no, they were dark and still shadows in the dull shine of the windows. Standing and staring at them, she almost wished they would jump out and scare her. At least she'd know they were real people, then.

They definitely weren't real, or if they were, they were fantastic at posing perfectly still. There wasn't anything human about them. The way their bodies slumped looked awkward, a position that no one could hold for very long. Resting her hand on the wall of the house, she bent over the railing and tried to get a better look.

She had to lean out quite a ways before the shine on the window disappeared and she saw them clearly. They were faceless and formless wooden beings, slumped over in their chairs. The wood was perfectly cut and shaped to form odd, rounded limbs, hands like paddles and oval-shaped heads. They had no features on their faces, only smooth, dark wood.

Much as she tried to muffle her thoughts, Charlie's words about Carrick and voodoo spells kept popping up. What kind of man was he?

After backing away from the window, she turned and ran back into the house. She may have been desperate and the pay might have been high, but it might not be high enough to make her stay here.

She went to find her room, her skirts sweeping the floor as she walked. She climbed the stairs to the second floor, gripping the balustrade with one hand and her air-light valise in the other. A stretch of red carpet covered the hallway. Dust bunnies gathered at the edges of the baseboards.

There were so many doors. Which one was his? She slowed, listening at each door, goose bumps on her skin, afraid he would somehow know and yank open the door. But all was quiet. Finally, she found the small stairwell at the end of the hall. Grim narrow steps rose in a tight spiral, and she had to focus on her feet as she climbed. A single door welcomed her at the landing and she stepped inside a large and airy attic that had been converted into a room. Though sparsely appointed, it pleased her.

Certainly it was a huge improvement over the storage closet she'd slept in for the past six months. A bed and dresser were tucked in a corner and there was a closet against one wall. A circular window, the biggest she'd ever seen, looked out across the front lawn. She ran her hands over the sill. The ledge was big enough that she could crawl up onto the sill, curl up and survey at the grounds.

She undressed and stretched out on the bed, relaxing against the pillow. But that creeping sensation returned again, the feeling that someone was watching her. She crawled under the covers and pulled them to her chin. It helped a little bit. Dimly, she heard the grandfather clock toll eleven mellow chimes. It was still morning. It felt like a lifetime since she'd first arrived at the manor.

The lids of her eyes felt heavy. She gave in to the urge and closed them.

A few moments later, a strange shuffling noise grabbed her attention. It was an odd, sliding, shifting sound, like a cotton sack being dragged along a floor. Rising and wiping the sleep from her eyes, she went to the door and looked down the stairs. They were empty. But the sound persisted. She went completely still to pay attention.

The walls. The sound was coming from within the walls. A tight wave of icy fear swept her body as she listened. What a fool she'd been to race over here and hop on the easy-money bandwagon. That scraping, swooshing noise just wouldn't stop.

Penrose sighed. Better to know. It was always better to know.

In her white cotton underthings and with her dark hair spilled around her shoulders, she tiptoed to the wall. She pressed her ear to the wooden panels. Silence. But something or someone was there. Taking shallow breaths, she walked along slowly, swallowing often to keep the bile from her throat. Again. A scratching. Scraping. Following the noise, she traced her finger over the plaster, drawing closer to the source. When the sound increased suddenly, she knew she'd located it. The sound was low to the ground. Dropping to her knees, she pressed her head to the wall and closed her eyes. The noise was quite distinct and just on the other side.

"Who's there?" she whispered, surprised by the sharpness in her voice.

Complete silence. Then, distantly, the sound dimmed, more scratching. Still as stone, she stood, her whole being focused on the sound as it drifted farther away until there was only the sharp, quick hiss of her own breathing. She returned to her bed shaken, convinced she'd never sleep again, let alone take an afternoon nap. But she was wrong and fell quickly asleep.

Carrick Arundell parted the thick curtains and looked out at the unfamiliar sight of the afternoon sun. He hated the day, hated that aching yellow ball inching its way across the sky. It did nothing but bruise his eyes and burn his skin. It was the night he lived for— for the long, dark hours when the world was asleep and he emerged to create his inventions.

On most mornings, the rising sun was easy to ignore. Except for today. He'd twisted and turned in bed, reluctantly watching a streak of sunlight stretch across the floor. Finally, he'd given in. There would be no sleep today.

It didn't sit well with him. He needed his energy. A thousand small setbacks plagued his project, and every single one had to fall into place before the mechanical man took his first step.

Now he could add one more setback. An image that he couldn't get out of his mind. His new assistant standing in the doorway, pure midnight from head to toe. Black dress, black bonnet, black hair and a winterwhite face peering out at the world. Any man would be tempted. But he wasn't any man. He couldn't afford to be.

No, it was more than that. It wasn't just the project. It was the sight of her stepping back, her lips curling in disdain. The poor girl could barely talk. Dropping the curtain, he went to his wardrobe and began to dress for the evening.

Maintaining focus was crucial. Every day, his eyesight grew even weaker.

There was no choice but to control his thoughts about her. It wasn't that he didn't like women. Quite the opposite. It was that women didn't like him. They stepped away, turned away, or looked down at their shoes when he approached. The only companionship he'd ever known, he'd paid for. Even then, the women turned their faces away from him.

Penrose had turned away, as well, but not before he caught a glimpse of her expression in the bright flash of the lightning. She'd looked up at him in a mixture of fear and horror. He'd grown immune to such looks. But coming from her it angered him.

Long ago, his heart had turned to iron. If he had his way, he would shun everyone. Keep the whole damn world out. But he needed the help of a steady hand and a good pair of eyes. Pretty blue eyes, a voice inside him added.

He went and looked for her, and when she couldn't be found, he went up the small flight of stairs to the servant's bedroom. The door to her room was ajar a few inches and he peered in and saw her sleeping on the bed. Toeing the door open, he stepped inside. Maybe he should have just knocked, but it happened before he knew his foot was moving, and then he was inside the room.

He watched her sleep. It seemed wicked, an indulgence more sinful than the women he paid to lift their skirts for him. Here he was, a man of thirty-six, and he'd never once seen the serene, soft expression of a woman lost in her dreams. Her features were soft now, not guarded like when he'd first met her.

The attic was warm that afternoon. She had two high spots of color on her cheeks. Her beauty was unusual, angular even. A sharp prettiness. The kind that could cut a man. But those two spots of color flaming away against all that tumbling black hair softened her looks. She sighed, and flung an arm out, revealing bare skin all the way to the strap of her undergarment. It was damn tempting.

He heard the clock chime the half hour. A half hour of prime working time lost just watching her sleep. Like a fool.

When he reached out to wake her, he shook her much harder than he intended to. Her eyes snapped open and met his gaze. For a brief second, she looked at him openly, her expression unafraid. He wanted to stop time, to linger in that tiny moment. But then the moment was gone.

Penrose's eyes widened and her hands clutched at the covers, instinctively pulling them higher. She was like all the rest, he realized, as he felt the shutters on his heart slam shut.

Chapter 3

Penrose came to alertness from sleep in an odd rush, as if rising from a fog. Images still swirled in her brain—of Carrick looming above her, the chandelier spinning and spinning out of control, and the glittery windows of the manor watching her with their golden gaze. She knew if she opened her eyes, it would all prove true. So she lingered, stubbornly refusing to be roused. The grip turned harder still and shook her shoulders just firmly enough that she couldn't ignore it anymore. Finally, she looked up and right into the kaleidoscope eyes of her new employer.

"You overslept." It sounded like an accusation coming from him. The shadowy light of the afternoon made him appear deathly pale. Anger or some other emotion etched his face in a deep scowl.

"I'm sorry," she said, voice heavy with sleep. She

was disoriented, staring hard at him before rubbing her eyes. It was difficult to know if she still slept and he was just a dream. "I must have been very tired," she managed to say.

He nodded. "Well, then, I'll leave you to get dressed. Meet me downstairs in the cellar."

"Fine. I'll hurry."

He left. She jumped up and dressed quickly, blood pounding in her veins. She wasn't sure if it was fear of him or guilt at oversleeping, but she ignored it and moved quickly. She went to the kitchen to take the stairs that led down to the cellar and was surprised to see Carrick standing at the counter, eating.

"Come. Eat," he said, barely turning to look at her. She went and stood next to him. He held out a steaming cup of coffee for her and she grabbed it greedily and took a sip. He was eating johnnycakes. She lifted one from the basket, smeared it with butter and took a bite. It was warm and buttery.

"Tell me, Miss Heatherton," he said, between bites, "how it is you came to the agency?"

Her stomach dropped when he mentioned the agency and she spoke quickly, trying to change the subject. "Please, my name is Penrose. But everyone calls me Penny. If you want me to call you Carrick, I'd like the same."

"Penny it is, then," he said, and took a swig of his coffee. "Penrose. A prominent name around here. How did you come by that as a given name?"

She froze, johnnycake in midair. She wanted to lie. It was right at the tip of her tongue, yet when she opened her mouth, the truth came tumbling out. "My father was a Penrose."

"I see. Skeletons in the proverbial closet, then? Since the family name is your first name and not your last, I'll ask how come he tossed over your mother?"

For some reason, his harsh tone didn't bother her. Nobody spoke plainly about this subject. It was a refreshing change and she found that more truths came forward. "My mother was an abolitionist."

He made a strange noise and spit coffee out of his mouth. He laughed, hunched over next to the counter. Finally he regained his composure. "A Penrose and an abolitionist? Now that's funny. They are the most painfully backward family on God's good planet Earth. So, was your mother able to sway him to her point of view?"

"No. Then he died in battle right before the end of the Civil War. Just before I was born."

"Hearts and beliefs are the two hardest things to change. You were born at an interesting time. You were born before or after the Civil War ended?"

"More than that, I was born on the very last day of the war. At midnight, in fact. My mother said that they had to choose what day to pick as my birthday. Obviously, my mother chose after the war."

He went completely still. "My, my, my. A midnight baby, and on the last day of the war? The very last minute? You're doubly cursed, Penny. Can't you see it? One foot on the bright side of freedom and one foot in the shameful past. A suspicious mind might say you're destined to live two lives."

There was something sinister about him standing there—easy as you please—talking about curses. "I wouldn't dare believe in such nonsense. I'm a practical sort." But her words sounded forced, a bit too high.

"Are you, now?"

She nodded and took a bite of the corn bread. Silence fell over the room.

A few minutes later, he spoke up. "Ready to work?"

They walked down the stairs. This house had so many stairways, she thought to herself. The foyer. The attic. The kitchen. It was as if the house intended for people to get lost in it. Cool air rising from the cellar swirled around her as she followed him the last few steps into the workshop, looked around and struggled to keep her chin from dropping to the floor.

She couldn't take even one more step. Not one. The room was simply too much to absorb. She could only stand and stare dumbly. It wasn't so much the space. Oh, it was impressive—cavernous, cool and dark, with high ceilings and a fireplace big enough to stand it. It was more the feel of the room. Expectation hung in the air, with the sharp smells of woodsmoke and oil. Every inch of the floor was crammed with odds and ends, books, piles of gleaming metal bits, cords, tubes, wires and tools. She felt as though she'd entered a deep and secret mine where magical things could be wrenched free.

Her entire life had been orderly. Downtrodden, perhaps, but orderly. Their little home had been converted to a humble finishing school, the kind the middle-class folks sent their daughters to. She grew up amid books that were neatly shelved and papers that were always stacked neatly. There was the feeling of possibility in the school, too—and it felt wonderfully familiar. But the school had provided an orderly process of discoveries. This room was chaos. She wasn't sure what to make of it.

"It used to be the kitchen," Carrick said, walking to the fireplace and tossing a handful of tinder into it. He struck a match and threw it onto the wood. A flame blazed to life. He fanned it, sending a hiss and spray of sparks into the air. "When my project outgrew the library, I moved the kitchen upstairs and took over this room." He gathered some logs and fed them to the growing blaze. Even though it was high summer, the cellar was chilly, so she welcomed the heat.

Carrick walked about the room lighting lamps and candles. He handed a candle to Penrose, and she helped him with the rest. He continued, "The problem with this room is the lack of light. I have lamps on all the walls, but the large open space where I do my work needs even more light."

A schematic of the human body hung on one wall. Another had a large calendar. And then she saw what had scared her silly earlier—the wooden beings slumped in their chairs. Her heart stopped, she swore it did, and she brought her hand to her chest to feel its beat before relaxing a bit. What did he do with them?

"Are you coming?" he asked.

"Of course."

He continued, "Though lamplight is fine, the direct brightness affects my eyes. I prefer candles close by. You'll be making candles for me. I require special ones."

"I see," she said, making a mental note to arrive early and have the workroom lit and ready for him.

He gestured toward the center of the room, where a huge work area made up of many tables pushed together formed a half circle. In the center of the tables, something large bulged from underneath a blanket. Whatever it was, it was larger than a man and twice as wide.

Approaching, she held the candle in the air. "What is it?" she asked, unable to hide the wonder in her voice.

Carrick stood behind her. She neither heard his approach nor felt his presence, so when he spoke, it startled her. He stood inches away. "That is the future. A mechanical man." He held up his candle. "Go ahead, pull the blanket off."

. She bent down, yanked the blanket away, and the mechanical man stood before her. She blinked and looked up. He was tall, taller than Carrick, taller than any man she'd ever seen. He had a barrel chest, a boxy head and two small lanterns that served as eyes. Wide shoulders sat atop his torso and rivets ran up and down his body like buttons. He resembled a metallic boxer, stout and strong, his skin glistening silver-orange in the firelight.

"What does he do?" she asked in awe. "Can he even move?"

"Anything you want," Carrick said with pride. "Within reason, of course."

He seemed to burst with life. He seemed solid. Dependable. But there was something threatening about a heap of metal sculpted into the shape of a human. Some inner part of her recoiled. Not a big part, but enough of a part to steal her words for a few moments as she took in the sight of him. *Him*. Funny that she thought of it in such familiar terms already.

"Just like in those paperback novels," she said. She'd once read a scary story about a man who built a steam-powered person and then attached him to a buggy. The man walked across the entire country step by step. When they reached Kansas, the steam-powered man went haywire and killed the man who had created him. That was fiction. She now stood before the real thing, and she wasn't sure if that made her feel better or worse about it.

"Yes. Just like in those fanciful stories. Except this one is real." She'd almost forgotten about Carrick. Almost. But the he stood close enough behind her that when he spoke she could feel the air from his breath on the back of her neck.

"How do you give him life?" she asked. "How do you do that?" It was the thousand-dollar question in her mind. She whispered the next word. "Magic?"

He laughed harshly. "Is that what you heard?"

"Perhaps."

"And what do you think of the things you've heard?"

"You're not paying me to think about what I've heard." She turned, forcing her eyes to meet his and hold his gaze. "That's what I think."

"You're either very clever or very hungry."

"Or both."

"Are you as prim and proper as you look?" The tone of his voice changed in that instant. It grew deep and mellow, almost dreamy. But not soothing. Not by a Georgia mile.

She stood stiff, aware of the length of his body right behind hers. He didn't touch her. He didn't need to. She could feel the heat from his body as surely as she could from the fire in front of her. "Now, you tell me. Do you like to be judged by the way you look?"

"Touché, Miss Heatherton."

"Penny. Call me Penny."

His lips graced the tender spot behind her ear. "Penny," he whispered, saying the name so low that it came not as a sound but as a rumble against her skin. Then he was gone, the hard strike of his boots ringing out on the stone. She was left with a wave of cool air.

He strode in front of her to the mechanical man. "Does he scare you?"

"Yes. He makes me nervous. It's a feeling I can't describe. But I'm drawn to him," she answered, unsure if she was referring to the mechanical man or to him.

He was quiet. "Some quake in their shoes when they see him," he finally said.

"What's his name?"

"Name?" He laughed, a mellow, rolling, velvety sound. "He doesn't have one, of course."

"But he has to have a name. How can you create something that looks so, well, humanlike—and not give it a name?"

"You can name him. It makes no difference to me."

"Harris." The name came to her instantly and once she spoke it, it fit nicely. "We'll call him Harris."

"Harris," he said thoughtfully, walking to Harris and running a finger along his steely arm. "That sounds fine. And yes, to answer your question, he can move. When he's functioning. But that's part of the problem. Somewhere inside of him, a gear is tooled wrong. The timing is off, so he can't walk. I've altered the design a million times. It seems there's always a fatal flaw, and I always discover the flaw too late to correct it. Then I'm forced to destroy my creation and start again. I'm hoping that I've discovered the flaw in time."

She looked up. "How do you know that all flaws are fatal? Perhaps you shouldn't design them with one goal in mind but rather an open idea of their potential."

He turned. "You're sharper than I gave you credit for, Penny."

"Thank you." She felt a rush of pleasure at his compliment.

The heat from the fire filled the room, making sweat break out on her forehead.

"You grasp the fundamental concept. One that I'm aware of. The earlier types I created were simply too crude. It's been an agony just to get to this most basic creation. And even though I love doing it, I rue the day I first got the idea." He sighed and went to the windows, opening them first before going to the doors and propping them open, too.

"My apologies. I get too wrapped up in it." Sweet night air filled the room. A pleasant, earthy smell filled the room, carried up from the river by the wind.

He walked over to a wall where a poster of the human anatomy hung. Pencil marks and notes covered the simple drawing of the human being. "I have a question for you. What do you think is more important, form or function?"

Penrose thought for a moment about whether beauty or purpose should be held in higher regard. "Well, I think the function should be the guiding principle."

"Agreed."

"Whenever possible, the form should be pleasing, as well."

His eyes moved from the picture to Penrose. "Very good. I'm pleased. Ideally there would be a balance between the two."

He went to the wall and placed his hand over the image of the human hand. He was a big man, tall, and his hands eclipsed the one on the diagram. "The real key to designing a mechanical man is to decide where form and function join. Where they come together."

"I don't understand."

"I need to reduce form to its barest minimum. Man

will never be able to reproduce the complexity of the human body. It's up to me to decide what's essential and what I can leave out to save on engineering costs and time." He looked back to the poster. "What is the most basic element of being human? If you can answer that, then my instinct says you'll also have perfect form."

He saw the confused look on her face and approached her. "Here, I'll show you. Hold out your arm."

She lifted her arm and held it straight out to the side. He put one hand on her waist. "May I?" he asked.

Nodding, she felt strangely giddy.

He lifted his other hand to her shoulder. Using two fingers, he traced a path down her extended arm. Fire followed his touch. She wrenched her lips closed to contain a gasp.

He whispered, "I need to decide what part of this arm is inconsequential. Of course, it's all perfect in the flesh, but I eliminate what's not necessary, and decide what is essential."

His hand stretched out to grasp hers. He lifted her arm high above her head and stepped closer, bringing the scent of pinewood shavings with him. "The question is, what is it that allows you to raise your arm like this?"

"Muscles," she replied in a whisper.

"Of course. And tendons, too. The delicate interplay between them, when to pull and when to push, that's what matters most. That's what fascinates me." He leaned forward and looked into her eyes. "The real question, the one we're not asking, is what gives the signal to these muscles, what tells them to move?"

He let go of her arm and tapped her temple. "This does. Right in here. That is something we'll never, ever be able to replicate. But I want to."

He was so close she could count his eyelashes. He kept speaking, but she heard nothing save for the pounding in her heart. Her nipples tightened, and the sensation unnerved her. Her cheeks burned, and she tried to step back to gather her wits. She felt fear and excitement, a potent combination. He was unlike any man she'd ever known and she wasn't sure what to say.

He pulled away, a cold look settling over his features. "Did the agency tell you what your duties would be?"

"A little bit," she said, turning away, trying to hide the flash of shame because there was no agency. Mrs. Capshaw would be the end of her, she just knew it.

He pointed out a simple desk, off to the side. "Part of the time, you'll work there. Taking notes. Sketching for me. The rest of your time will be spent helping me tool the components. I struggle to see those small details, which is what caused the problem I have to begin with."

"That sounds fine," she said. She looked again at the wooden figures, remembering how mysterious and lifelike they looked from outside the window. There was no life in them now. They looked defeated, slumped. Ropes bound them to the chairs and held them upright. They had no faces, no features. The wood had been whittled and etched away to reveal the essence of a human body. Arms, legs, hands.

Yet they were beautiful. It was as if whittling them down hadn't made them less—it made them more. It brought out their essence. She walked toward them and gingerly touched one on the shoulder, half expecting it to turn and look at her. "What are they?" she asked in a hushed tone, afraid of his answer, knowing full well how silly she was being. But there was definitely something curious about this man.

"Mannequins. My earliest attempts. I keep them because I have a fondness for them. They remind me that progress is possible. Why? Did you think I used them for another purpose?"

"I wasn't sure."

It was too hot. Carrick stood at the door, lingering and scraping his boot absentmindedly back and forth over the gravel. Her hands didn't flutter. That was the first thing he noticed. Some of the others that came here stood trembling, their hands fluttering like trapped butterflies as they stared up at the mechanical man—Harris. Hell, even he thought of him as Harris now.

But her? He saw it. Interest. She looked afraid, yes. But for one brief instant, he saw the spark of wonder. Plus, she named him. That had to be a good sign. She might be the one to help him for the long, hard haul that he knew lay ahead.

Her gasp when she first saw the mechanical man was the single most heavenly sound he'd ever heard. They both saw the same thing in his invention—potential—he knew it in his bones. Of course, he'd become too excited, got too close and scared her. Scared her. Scaring people was something he was far too good at.

Even with that painful disappointment, his spirits were still riding high because she just might work out. Her intellect was apparent. Other assistants worked methodically but without vigor, and he felt the burden of constantly explaining task after task to someone who didn't care to learn the concepts or take leaps of initiative. He held out hope that she might work out just fine.

"How long have you been designing the mechanical man?" she asked, turning to look at him with those blue, blue eyes, and he found himself struggling to pay attention to her words.

"Six years."

"Six years?" Her perfect lips made an O of surprise. "That's a long time to remain committed to something that still hasn't born results."

"The results? The end?" He laughed. "What's that? Every morning when I go to bed, I have to restrain my mind from dwelling on my project. I would think of it all day, every single moment, if I could."

Penrose returned to her desk and began working again, but the uneasy, flighty feeling in her chest lingered. The feeling was strange, excitement and fear mingled together. He was exciting to be around, but he was a volatile person. And mysterious. Her stomach twisted at the memory of his hand on her shoulder.

He paced the room while he spoke. She took notes. Scribbling furiously, she did her best to keep up with him. His ideas were explosions of brilliance, and as he spoke, she slipped into a kind of trance, channeling his words directly onto the paper.

He spoke of the function of the mechanical man, of ways to solve the dilemma with the gears, of the possible need to retool some of them and the supreme need for flexibility of design.

It was revealing to hear his thoughts aloud and easy to take measure of his mind. He had an organized way of thinking, linear and clear. His ideas were concise and simple to understand, and her pen flew across the paper. At times, he paced the floor or hesitated before speaking. She waited, pen in the air, and as soon as his words began to flow once again her scratchings on the paper renewed.

He came and stood behind her. After discussing the particularly difficult redesign of a gear, he put his hand on her shoulder and asked, "Did that make sense? I think if we change the ratio, the output will be stronger."

A twist of nervousness tightened within her. She looked up at him, her eyes wide. The sight of him—tall and regal, with his white hair framing his handsome face—affected her, making her breath heavy.

"Yes," she said, nodding as if she understood perfectly. But the only thing she understood was his hand and those long elegant fingers resting on her shoulder.

She couldn't breathe. More than anything she wanted to rest her cheek on that hand, to feel it caress her skin. Never before had she reacted in such a way. Something strange was happening.

Somehow, her pen kept moving, danced across the paper and finished the last sentence. The realization that she wanted more of that touch made her hand shake and her script wobbly.

He had such passion. A singular-minded obsession. She wondered what it would it be like if he lavished that passion on her.

The thought flamed her cheeks, and she pulled away from him, turning her head. Instantly, his hand disappeared from her shoulder. She wanted to face him and say something, but what could she say? Nothing at all.

Stepping away, he continued speaking, pacing the floor. And she continued writing as if nothing had passed between them.

She wrote so much her fingers hurt, and the tips of

them became stained with ink. It felt like an instant later the grandfather clock tolled the midnight hour. Time seemed to speed up when she was with him.

She stretched her tired, achy fingers, waiting for the chimes to stop and Carrick to start lecturing again. But as soon as the clock fell silent, another sound rang out.

It was the sound of crashing noises coming from outside, and the second she heard them, a terrible sense of foreboding settled over her.

As soon as Carrick heard the crashing sounds coming from outside the workshop he was up and out the door. He didn't know what he was expecting—C.J. maybe, up to some antics—but when he went outside only the summer breeze greeted him. He looked around. Nothing.

He heard the faint sound of a woman's gasp. It was light and breathy with an air of surprise and something else, something he couldn't name.

He looked in the direction of the sound and saw a woman standing just outside the circle of light that came from the window. She wore all white and had a sheen of yellow hair that trailed just below her shoulders.

An angel. That was his first thought. She floated out there in the darkness, hovering with a strange look of fear and longing on her face. Such longing.

She couldn't be a ghost. No such thing. "Hey," said Carrick sharply. "What are you doing out here?"

Instead of replying, she shook her head slowly and began to back away.

"Hey!" he called again, louder now.

The woman began backing away, the shadows swallowing her. "Stop!" he said, "Don't go. Tell me who you are."

Penrose came and stood right behind him, her body pressed against his.

"What is it?" she asked, craning to see outside. "No!" she shouted, surprising him so much that he startled. "Go away!" The tone of her voice was frightened. More than frightened.

"Do you know that woman?" Carrick asked.

The woman turned to Penrose, and something passed between them. He felt it like a bolt of lightning.

The woman outside looked angry, beyond angry. Her posture was rigid. She lifted her hand and pointed at Penrose. For a moment, it looked as if the blonde were about to speak, but she shook her head again and, in a swirl of white skirts, turned and fled.

Some primal instinct flared inside of him, and he took off running after her. No one should be on the property. He didn't know what she was up to, but he fully intended to find out.

"No, Carrick!" screamed Penrose. "Don't follow her!"

He paid Penrose no attention. "Stop!" he shouted to the woman. It was dark. He had trouble enough seeing at night, let alone running through the trees.

He heard her crashing through the woods, and this made her easier to follow. He loped along behind her, his long legs closing the distance between them. Her crashing sounds were getting louder by the second. Once he caught her, he would get to the bottom of this little mystery.

* * *

A heavy, oppressive feeling settled in Penrose's chest. As soon as she saw the woman, she knew her ruse was up. Her breath died in her chest at that moment. So did the little feeling of hope that finally she had started to feel. She should've known the scheme would end badly.

Anytime she tried to get ahead, something came along and set her back. Now Carrick was out there, chasing that woman, that beautiful, perfect woman who by all rights should be standing right where Penrose stood.

Now alone in the quiet workshop, feeling numb, Penrose looked around her. The budding hope that had begun to grow inside of her was already dying. She looked around, trying to memorize everything in the room because she knew she would be leaving. Carrick would show up any minute, yell at her and kick her out. She'd never see the workshop or Harris again. Or Carrick. Her reaction surprised her.

In one quick fix, she had thought she could solve her problems. But she'd only made them worse.

She noticed that her fingers were stained with ink, and she went to the table, picked up a rag and began wiping the stains away. Minutes dragged by, and when the clock gonged again—one in the morning—the door swung open.

Carrick filled the doorway. He looked wild. His white hair stood on edge.

Penrose's hands stilled and fell to her side. The rag dropped to the floor.

He stared at her long and hard, his shoulders squared, and he took great, heaving breaths.

She wasn't sure how to react. She was too afraid to say anything, to reveal anything at all. Perhaps he hadn't caught up with her.

But one look at his face told her he had, indeed. More than caught up with her, she realized, noticing the angry set of his lips. He'd spoken with her.

In three strides, he crossed the room. She barely had time to gather her breath before he loomed over her, his beautiful, angry features hovering right above her face. "What trickery are you up to, Penny?"

He knew. It was over. A horrid wrenching twisted in her gut, but something else was there, too, some wild, fluttery, panicked sensation. A painful feeling of loss and shame. She didn't want him to think badly of her. "I'm sorry," she blurted out. "I'm sorry," she repeated. "I never intended…"

He shook his head slowly. "The conversation I just had with that woman," he said, walking around her. "And the things I've learned about you." He stopped, leaned forward and took her chin in his hand, forcing her to look into his strange eyes. Angry eyes that seemed to swirl with dark colors. "It seems you weren't honest with me, were you?"

"No," she whispered, too flustered to come to any self-defense of her behavior. She felt the hole that she'd dug widening beneath her feet, and the blackness threatening to swallow her up. If only she could look away from his eyes, but his hand at her chin was no longer gentle. It held her tight.

"What game you play, I don't know," he said. "But you will not win it. This I guarantee you—you will not win it. You came and looked me in the eyes, and deceived me." He leaned close. She smelled the woods on him and the scent of summer blooms. "I know your secret. And I wager there are even more to find out, and, trust me, I'll find every single one."

Penrose knew what he was talking about. He was talking about her. About the blonde. "Please, you're scaring me," she said. Her words came out too soft, too weak. "Where did she go?" she asked him.

His chest pressed against hers, and he made no accommodation for her at all. She was forced to hold her breath. He said, "Do you care where she went? Do you really care as long as she's not here?" He stepped even closer, forcing her tighter against the table. "And why is she here, Penny? Do you know that?"

"I needed a job," she whispered her confession. Her eyes met his, imploring him to have sympathy. "I was hungry. I didn't know…" Her voice trailed off.

"She gave me the impression you knew a great many things, Penny. And that you weren't so innocent, that you committed a crime against her, and now she suffers for it," he said. "Her words, not mine."

His demeanor was decidedly very, very different, and she didn't know what to make of it. Mrs. Capshaw be damned to hell. "I'll leave," she whispered.

He chuckled, and the threat behind it gave her shivers. "You'll do no such thing. You made your bed—now you'll lie in it." Lifting her chin higher, he leaned closer until his lips touched her ear. "Or you can lie in mine, if you prefer," he said. "In fact, she mentioned something of the sort."

Not one word came to her lips. Not one. She could only breathe, but even that was a struggle—little gasps that caused her breasts to push against his chest. "I'm sorry," she finally whispered.

"Are you?" With his other hand, he traced up the side of her torso. Higher and higher, skimming over her breast, her shoulders, until his long fingers caressed the back of her neck and edged into her upswept hair.

Yes, his demeanor had changed so very much. Whatever the woman had said, she unleashed a new man in Carrick.

Penrose closed her eyes, unsure if this was even real. But her body told her it was real, very real, for it throbbed with life and feeling.

With his other hand, he traced a thumb over her lips, and she whimpered.

"Perhaps she wasn't lying." His voice, now at her ear, smooth and cajoling, seemed to be speaking right into her soul. "Are you afraid of me?" His voice was so, so low.

With his thumb on her lips, she couldn't speak. She shook her head no. But she was trapped and could only stand there, enduring the feel of him.

He removed his thumb. "Let me repeat my question. Are you afraid?"

She couldn't keep lying to him. Oh, she wanted to, but her pounding heart wouldn't let her think of an excuse. "Yes," she said, nodding. It was everything about him. His sharp, strange beauty. His odd ways. The way he frightened her.

But it was too late to say anything. His fingers guided her to look at him and then his mouth descended onto hers, deceptively soft.

She stilled, hardly believing what was happening. But it was happening.

He drew her closer, enveloping her, holding her against him. His kiss turned hard and demanding.

Anger lurked underneath. She knew it from the way his lips slashed, hot and accusing, over hers.

It wasn't merely anger. It was more than that. Something almost dangerous. Seductive.

Sinking, melting, she surrendered to the feeling. He tugged at her lips, coaxing her mouth to open and then his tongue thrust inside, claiming her. Triumphant.

Heat spread between her legs. An odd sound escaped her mouth, and a shiver swept over her. Her whole body shook from it, surprising her.

Her reaction seemed to inflame Carrick. A rumble came from his throat, and his kiss grew bolder, hungrier. All night long, his touch had been measured and precise. Incremental. Now it turned wild. Uncontrolled. His hands swept up her skirt hungrily, grabbing fistfuls of fabric, digging for her body beneath. When he found it, he growled and pressed against her, and she felt his hardness through the folds of her skirt. It made a pulse of pleasure beat between her legs.

From deep inside, an unrestrained, breathy shudder swept over her body. She whimpered and pressed farther into his kiss, overwhelmed with wanting him.

He stilled. Through her dress, she felt his hands clench angrily. "Dammit," he said harshly. "I can't do this." He stepped away from her. "I'm sorry," he said, avoiding her gaze, already turning away from her. "It's too damned complicated. More than that. God, it's so much more than that."

Reaching out and putting a hand on his chest, she leaned up and tried to kiss him. "Please." She didn't want it to stop.

"You are young and foolish," he said in a measured voice.

Taken aback, she stared at him hard before she said, "And you have no heart."

"Now you know the truth of it. My real affliction. Let's get back to work and forget this ever happened."

Chapter 4

Penrose went to bed agitated, filled with thoughts of his touch. Her lips were still numb from his kiss. Her body still betrayed her attraction to him. She lay on the bed, certain that she wouldn't be able to sleep and that images and memories of Carrick would haunt her. She snuggled deep under the covers, trying to block out the sun.

She had finally settled in and let out a long sigh, when a sound came from behind the walls. The noise continued for a moment, and then it stilled, too, almost as if whoever or whatever made the noise realized she was listening.

A sharp zing of terror shot up her spine. She held her breath, not breathing, waiting for the sound to begin again. It did. Slow, halting little noises. Self-aware noises, as if the need to be quiet was paramount.

No. This wouldn't do. She simply had to find out what caused the sounds.

She sighed in an exaggerated manner and made rustling noises from the bed. She slipped quietly from the bed, her feet hitting the floor softer than a mouse's, and then she padded with delicate footsteps to the wall. Leaning close, she pressed her ear to the wall. And that was when she saw it.

The morning sun slanted just right over the wood, illuminating all the imperfections and she saw a minute gap between two of the boards. Tracing her eyes along the gap, she saw hinges that were hidden so well in the pattern of the wood that she'd never have seen them if she weren't looking for them. They were painted white to match. Once she found the hinges, the outline of the secret door was easy to spot.

She dug her fingernails into the gap and pulled. Nothing. Following a hunch, she placed her palms on the wood, and pressed quick and hard. She was rewarded with the sound of a click, and the door sprung open.

The pale face of a child appeared. Violet eyes, big as dinner plates, stared into her very soul. She careened backward, struck by a shock stronger than lightning. Down she went, landing in an awkward, crab-like position, gasping, staring into the wide and shocked amethyst eyes of a child.

Three or four breaths passed before the child broke her gaze, spun around and began to scurry into the tunnel.

Her heart pounded so hard that she should have fainted, but anger rose up hard. Swiftly, she dived forward, plunged her arm into the hold and grabbed the child by the ear. A yowl came from the tunnel, and she pulled with all her might until the body of the child— a boy—came tumbling out and lay on the floor. Wide eyes—he looked just as shocked as she felt—stared into hers. The boy lay panting. Eight years old, she guessed. Pale like Carrick, white hair and bright skin.

"Who are you?" She sounded possessed, her words strangled.

No answer. She twisted her grip on his ear. "Tell me, child."

"C.J.," he spit out. His little face twisted in anger. "Now leave off."

"No. I'll not leave off." She said. "Who? What?" Her thoughts were tumbling as she struggled to understand exactly what she was seeing. "What in God's name are you doing crawling around in the walls?"

"I live in there." He threw the words out. Almost boastfully. "It's where I belong."

"No one belongs hidden in the walls. No one." She let go of his ear. Her hands were shaking. "Who are you?"

"I told you my name is C.J. For Carrick, Junior. Son of the great inventor." His tone was biting. "Only I'm not his son. No matter what my ma said."

"Don't be so hateful," she hissed. "And what do you mean by your ma said?"

"I mean when she was alive. That's what I mean. She died. Last summer. That's why I came here to live."

"I'm sorry she died. But this is madness! A child living in the walls!"

He looked away and slid his foot from side to side across the floor. "It happens. Life isn't all roses."

She agreed with him on that point. "No, C.J., it's not. But how come…" She struggled for words. "Why aren't you in a bedroom? In the house?" A horrible thought came to her. "Does he make you stay there?"

He laughed bitterly, a sound no child should ever make. "He didn't make me go in there. But he sure doesn't mind."

"You shouldn't be so hateful toward your father," she said. "Surely he must care for you." But she doubted her words even as she said them.

"That's what you think."

"Hey, now," she said, trying to be friendly. She put her hand on his shoulder, and she noticed with some relief that it had finally stopped shaking.

"Stop!" He pushed her hand away, his entire body curling from her touch.

"Okay, okay," she replied. "I'm sorry. Listen, it's strange to crawl about in the walls. Maybe I should talk to Carrick. You need to be out of the walls. For your safety."

His look turned sly and challenging. "Go right ahead. *Miss Penny.* Yes, I know your name." His chest puffed up. "I'm none of his concern. I'm no one's concern but my own. Least of all yours." He darted away, quicker than a rifle shot, diving right back into the tunnel.

Though the thought of entering the dark space made her shudder, she dropped to her knees and raced behind him through the little door. Light shone from behind her and lit the way ahead. Once she crawled in, the space opened up, and she was able to stand, though just barely. The walls were tight at her shoulders. The space unnerved her, and she considered turning around but didn't. "C.J?" she called out. "Come back. Please. I can help." She wasn't quite sure how, but she'd at least try. She crept forward until she saw a wall ahead, and just before the wall, the floor opened up into a hole.

Here she stopped, looked over and saw a wooden ladder fastened to the wall. Rough ridges were gouged into the floor. Markings, she realized, so that in the dark the child would know where the hole was, and he wouldn't fall through it. Peering down the hole, she was afraid and yet mesmerized by it. She wouldn't dare descend into those depths. Ever.

C.J. made rustling noises as he scooted around in the darkness.

"I'll know if you come up here again!" she called to him. The movements stopped, and she took it to mean that he was listening. "The next time you come to my room, announce yourself by knocking." She added, in a kinder tone, "And I'll invite you in. I could use a friend, you know!" Her voice echoed in the hollow space before dying away.

She made her way back through the tunnel and crawled from the hole. Then she climbed into bed and lay, panting and coated in dust, staring at the ceiling, thinking of the bizarre events of the day until, finally, she slept.

Penrose slept all day. In the late afternoon, a shaft of sunlight bathed her bed and woke her. She stood, went to the window and looked outside. Charleston was glorious. It always was in the summertime, but there was something special about the light in the last days of summer. The colors were bright and rich, almost dreamlike. But she barely enjoyed the sight because she was so very angry at Carrick. A child in the walls. Sickening.

The grandfather clock began to chime, a distant, dim

sound. It was time for work. Penrose tidied herself and went downstairs, her mind stewing.

He was waiting for her beneath the chandelier. The second she saw him, she flew down the stairs, rushed right up to him. "How come you didn't tell me you had a son?" she asked, and then her voice turned shrill and accusing. "A son who lives in the walls? The walls!"

"I didn't tell you because you didn't ask." His eyes were a maddening swirl of colors as a sneer cracked his lips apart. "You said it yourself. You're not paid to wonder or worry. So don't. It's none of your concern."

"None of my concern!" Her hands flew up in the air. "He's a child! Who is caring for him? He's lost his mother. He needs parenting. If you're letting him run loose in the walls, who feeds and clothes him? And why doesn't he go to school?"

"He cares for himself. And if you spend some time with him, you'll see that the last thing C.J. needs is schooling." He looked at her sharply.

"He's eight!"

"He's ten. And raising myself worked out just fine for me. I spent countless years in those walls. I survived, so I imagine he'll survive."

"You lived in the walls?" She couldn't hide the shock in her voice. "Why?"

His back grew rigid. "Sometimes it's easier not to be seen. Even in your own family." The last words came in almost a whisper. "Especially in your own family."

She kept thinking of the little boy's eyes. Those eyes that looked right into her soul. "But he's your son!" she said passionately, following him through the hallway.

"I don't even know if he's my child. One day, right out of the blue, he just showed up. I found him inside the house. In the hallway. He told me the sheriff dropped him off and left him because he was my son." A muscle by his eye twitched. "Clara—his mother and a…a woman of the evening—died of consumption. Because of his coloring they assumed he was mine."

He turned suddenly and began to walk away, heading toward the kitchen. She followed hot on his heels as he sped through the kitchen, lit a candle and then disappeared into the stairwell that led to the workshop. "I don't even know if these things are passed father to son. My father certainly didn't have my coloring. And my mother sure as hell wouldn't lie with a man who had even a single flaw, let alone a grand one like mine.

"Let's go start our work, shall we?" He began descending the tight spiral staircase, holding the candle for light.

Her steps were quick and fervent as she followed him. "Why didn't you just deny it?"

He stopped. She bumped into his back.

Slowly, he turned around. They were mere inches apart. Even though he stood a step beneath her, he still towered over her. His gaze roamed freely over her face. "Because I couldn't deny it," he said. "But I couldn't confirm it, either."

It took a moment for the implication to sink in. She sucked in her breath. "Oh."

"Yes," he said, "Oh. Take a good look at me, Penrose. It'll be no shock to you that upstanding women don't seek out my company."

There was some truth in his words. She was ashamed to admit it, but before today, she might have felt the same. She looked at him with fresh eyes—the uncertainty over his coloring and features was welling up once more. She still feared him. But there was no denying his strong features and wide shoulders. Or that intense, driven gaze. There was something else, too. Something she couldn't quite name. Even now, she wanted to reach out and touch him. But her fear of him held her back.

But all she could do was say quietly, "Just because you were raised like that doesn't mean he has to be. I wager that you are his father. He favors you in more than coloring and looks. He favors you in attitude, and that is not exactly a compliment. Now he'll walk in your footsteps for sure and learn to squirrel himself away from the world." She didn't mean for her last words to sound sharp, but they did, and there was no taking it back. Trying to make it better, she said, "You're merely pale. It's no reason to hide."

"No," he said in a steely voice. His gaze swept over her face before announcing, "*You* are 'merely pale.' *I* am colorless." His face contorted in anger. "You would have me teach him the world is a kind place for people like us? You want me to send him out there?" He jabbed his finger in the direction of Charleston and ground out the next words. "I've been out there. And even if he weren't my son, I wouldn't torture the child like that." He shook his head, turned around and kept moving down the stairs. Over his shoulder, he said, "You can't understand what it's like to not fit in. To stick out in a painful manner. We do okay by ourselves." His sigh echoed in the stairwell. "Now, are you planning on working or not?"

"Of course," she said, immediately chastised and regretting her boldness. She needed this job. She'd better learn to keep her mouth shut. "I'm sorry if I spoke out of place."

He didn't answer her. The moment was gone, the discussion over.

Even though Carrick lit a fire in the workshop, the room remained cold. He was cold, too, like ice to her. He sat at his desk and spoke to her in a dispassionate, monotone voice, issuing orders without ever looking up from his task.

Penrose followed his directions almost as if she were a mechanical woman, but inside her a tempest of very human emotion roiled. Fear, anger, awe. Was there no end to the wild emotions this man caused in her?

The night dragged on and when dawn finally came, she was relieved to slip away and try to get some sleep. She said good-night to him and began walking up the stairs. When she was halfway up, she heard his low voice echo in the space. "Wait. Penny, wait."

She stopped. She felt every strike of his boots on the stairs somewhere deep in her soul, and she trembled, wanting but at the same time afraid of what might be coming. What she hoped was coming. He came into view like a ghost floating up toward her. Then he was right there, just in front of her, and she could feel the maleness of him like a potent force.

He looked like no man she'd ever seen. He was so wild looking as he towered over her, staring at her with an angry, set expression. "Penny," he said in a rough voice.

"Yes?" She was breathing hard, her chest rising to within a hairbreadth of his.

He kissed her, his hands swooping behind her back as his body pressed against hers, propelling them upward and forcing her to climb the stairs until she felt the wall at her back. Then his body came down hard, and his lips harder still. She felt his erection pushing against her, and she moaned.

"The fault is my own." He pulled away. "Christ Almighty, you make me break every promise to myself." He said. "You should stay away from me. I'm no good for you."

Angry, she wiped her mouth. "I agree completely," she said, then spun around and ran up the stairs.

Chapter 5

It was midafternoon when Penrose woke up, still angry at Carrick. He was so unpredictable. She dressed, yanking on her clothes and dragging the comb through her hair. A knock came at the little door that led to the tunnel. "Just a minute," she called out, finishing up and then pressing on the secret spot that opened the door. It opened, and there stood C.J. with a candle in his hand, backing up as if he'd changed his mind. He retreated even farther, almost disappearing, the flame of his candle flickering in the darkness.

"Don't go," she said, dropping to her knees and holding out a hand to him. "Please. I need a friend. You do, too."

There was only silence. She couldn't see him in the darkness but thought he was still nearby. She didn't want to enter the tunnel again. Not if she could help it. "I'm too afraid to follow after you, and I could use your help today."

"With what?" he asked in a small voice.

She smiled. "I need someone to show me around. To show me where the food is kept and the supplies, too. I need a washtub. I have a list of things I'd like to accomplish before work starts this evening. I don't want to bother Carrick."

Finally, there were shuffling noises, and the towheaded child popped out of the opening. Penrose scooted back to allow him to exit, and out he came, shyly until they both sat on the floor facing each other. She took his hand and held it in her own.

His hand was cold, and he didn't return her grip, but he didn't pull away, either.

"Thank you for agreeing to help me," she said.

He nodded.

They stood up and went down the stairs together, and she had her first real tour of the home. C.J. showed her the washroom, the new indoor bathroom that Carrick had installed. Then he took her to the kitchen and showed her a sideboard full of food, prepared and stored well. There was salted ham and pickled onions, breads and jams, and even a few jars of honey. C.J. sat at the kitchen table, and Penrose looked for something to eat.

"Who made these? Not Carrick." She knew him well enough already to know he didn't care about food. The man was too skinny by far.

"No. Twice a week Mr. and Mrs. Algood come. They help us around here. They bring provisions, and Mrs. Algood does the washing. Some cleaning, too, but Carrick gets grouchy if she stays in the house too much."

"Who keeps the grounds?" She dug around in the

pantry, lifting items and reading the tin cans. She settled on a couple of biscuits and some jam and sat down next to C.J.

"Mr. Algood. He brings goats and cows to eat the grass when it gets too high. The rest of the time, we are on our own."

Penrose looked at him pointedly and playfully pushed his shoulder. "You mean you are on your own."

C.J. shrugged. "It's fine. I like it this way. It's better than going to an orphanage."

"No school?"

"I don't need it."

"You can read?"

"Yes. Arithmetic, too. I'm smart. I don't need school. I'm through with that."

She raised her eyebrows at the ferocity of his words. "You haven't been to school for a whole year?" She opened the container and pulled out a biscuit, which she split, smeared with jam and then handed half of it to him.

He looked surprised but took the biscuit from her. Biting it, he said between chews, "No, ma'am. I haven't. I can show you that I don't need it. I'll be right back." He jumped down from the stool he sat on and ran toward the foyer of the house. He was gone a few minutes, and when he returned he carried a stack of papers in his hands. Spreading them on the counter, he said, "Have a look."

She leaned over the papers and saw that numbers, equations and drawings of body parts lined the sheets. They were so advanced that there was no possible way a child had created them. "You did this?" she asked.

"Yes."

She held the stiff papers close, trying to take in the sketchings and mathematical equations, but the meanings of them eluded her. The concepts were, quite simply, above her. "What are they?"

"When I first came here, I saw Carrick working. I've been thinking about his projects ever since. These are some of my ideas."

The sharp mind behind them was clearly evident. "Have you shown these to Carrick?" she asked, peering at him over a paper she held.

"Never." He was emphatic.

"Hmm," she said reflectively. Penrose had better sense than to press the issue. "Come on, let's finish eating."

After they had eaten, C.J. showed her around the grounds and took her to the river. The path led straight from the rear doors of the home, past the gardens, down the lawn and to the marshy banks of the water. The brown water ran slowly, obstinately, and the mayflies danced readily on the surface. The sun was beginning to arc downward.

It was a struggle to keep her mind away from Carrick, and she had such confusing thoughts, too. Anger and lust braided together. Sometimes it was hard to tell the two feelings apart. Well, there was nothing to be done about it, she reasoned.

Although it was still afternoon, Penrose wanted to open up the workroom before Carrick. "I have to go to work now," she said as they walked back to the house together, "but I hope we can spend more time together."

"Me, too," he said.

Penrose walked into the workshop early, as intended, while the space was still and quiet. She felt better, calmer, but still confused by Carrick. She watched the dying sun stream faint orange light into the dark room, lighting the dust motes that floated as fiery colors in the air. The wooden mechanical men stared expressionless out of the window.

The room was inert without Carrick. Whatever she thought of his personality, there was no denying his force in the workroom. She started the fire and lit the lamps and candles. The room still seemed empty. When Carrick was there, he brought motion and excitement, and something more…a wild possibility that at any moment a discovery might happen. She walked over to his workbench and ran her fingers over the many papers that covered it, taking in all the rushed drawings, evidence of a bright mind that was always thinking.

A noise came from behind her, and she turned to see C.J. standing by the mechanical man, looking up at it. "You know he's doing it wrong," he said with assurance and certainty. He was so young to possess such a confident intellect.

"How do you know he's doing it wrong?" she challenged him.

"He lacks vision. He has a purpose but no vision." The boy threw down the words as if they were laws. "This design is too heavy to work well. He's ignoring a better one."

She almost choked trying to hold back a laugh, not because what he said was funny, but because it was so succinct, so prescient, that it shocked her to hear it coming from a ten-year-old. She didn't doubt the truth of his words, because he was so very driven. Like his father.

"Well, you must be quite the inventor to have such knowledge."

"I am," he said proudly. "I already have mechanical things. Beings and such." He spoke in an offhand, boastful way. "You can come see it if you like." His purple eyes looked at her questioningly.

"I'm afraid I should stay here and wait for your father," she said, eyeing the door. "But how about tomorrow? And where is it? Is it upstairs in your room?" Penrose asked.

"No. I have to take you somewhere special." He lowered his voice and said, "Into the walls."

"C.J." She wasn't quite sure what to say to him, the thought horrified her so. "I can't go in there."

"You have to," he said. "It's the only way I can show you my experiment." He added, "You did promise, you know." Then he brightened. "Plus, you've already been inside of the tunnel. It's not very scary. My secret room is on the bottom floor, and it isn't near so scary down there."

How could she say no to such an eager request? "All right, I'll do it. But it'll have to be tomorrow. Your father will be here any second, and I need to work. I'll wake up early tomorrow, and you can show me everything then."

His eyes lit up. "Really?"

"Really," she said. "You better run along for now."

"Okay. Thanks, Penny," he said, his white hair bobbing up and down as he nodded. He turned and ran up the stairs.

Penrose tidied and cleaned the room, and then sat at her desk rereading her notes while she waited for Carrick.

"See something you like?" Carrick's voice surprised her, and she jumped.

"I was just…"

"Relax," he said, swooping past her, wearing his dark shirt and pants. "I was teasing." He was putting on a leather apron, tying the strings around his back, and he threw her one, as well. She put it on.

All of a sudden, he became serious. "Penny, I want to apologize," he said. "For my anger, and for making you feel bad." He dragged his fingers through his white hair. "It's just that…"

"Don't worry about it," she said.

He held up a hand, silencing her. "Penny, I'm not someone you want to be with. I can only focus on my project. I don't want complications or distractions, or pity."

"Pity?" she said. "I don't pity you at all."

"Enough. My decision is made, let's let the matter rest." He walked toward Harris, who stood gleaming in the glow of the fireplace. "Now, for tonight I think I'll have you work right beside me," he said. "We are to begin assembling some of the components that I've repaired."

So they began. He put on powerful eyeglasses with lenses thicker than her wrist, and as surgeon and nurse they operated on the mechanical man. One by one, he handed her gears and then gave her instructions on how to install them, peering over her shoulder to oversee.

"Can you check this?" she asked when one trouble-some gear wasn't falling into place.

He leaned over her shoulder. "Press that small part. Yes. That one." He guided her hand to the right place.

When he touched her, her body reacted.

Her mind split into two halves. One side followed along with his instructions. The other side of her could feel only his presence. The scent of him—a hint of pine—and his body pressed against hers swamped that side and threatened to swamp the other side, as well. He was too focused to notice anything other than his project, so she indulged her senses and absorbed all that she could.

"Here, now hold this piece," he said, touching a small knob.

She grabbed the piece he was referring to, and Carrick tightened another. The gear slid into place.

"That's it," he said. "This is what vexes me. One tine on a gear and my whole future swings in the balance. One little cog out of place and it can all be ruined."

On and on they worked in tandem, their hands constantly touching, meeting briefly. He was right beside her, and she grew to know his breathing and the catch of his breath before he uttered a curse in frustration when something didn't go the way he expected. His hands were beautiful. Long, tapered fingers that caressed the parts and coaxed stubborn pieces into place. Their bodies brushed against each other. Only once or twice did she lose her composure, but she covered it up and pulled away. Her reactions, no matter how small, seemed to make him angry, so she did her best to control them.

Carrick was lifting a small tool when it clattered down and landed behind the mechanical man.

"I'll get it," she said, and twisted around the mechanical man to pick up the tool. When she tried to rise, she found she was trapped. Threads from her underclothes had become snagged on a sharp weld. If she moved too quickly, she risked toppling the mechanical man, but she couldn't undo the snag herself and stood there with one leg raised into the air.

"I think I'm stuck," she said, trapped in her strange position.

"I'll help," he said, pressing his body against her as he dug into the folds of her skirt. "Your threads have come undone," he said.

"So they have," she answered in a breathy voice. His hands on her body were such an intimate, thrilling sensation that Penrose felt dizzy and worried she'd fall over. She steadied herself by putting a hand on his back, but that made her light-headedness worse.

He tugged on her shift, gently. "Your dress needs mending," he said softly. "All of these loose threads."

"Everything about me needs mending," she said.

"I wouldn't say that," he said, tugging again. "There, you're free," he said when the fabric suddenly came loose.

She stood up, strands of her hair escaping from her bun. Loose wisps floated around her face. "Thank you," she said. A touch of willful impulse filled her. She wanted him to kiss her again, to have his hands on her body. She'd never known anything like the hot and sudden rush of lust that overwhelmed her at his touch. She lingered, willing him to touch her.

He turned around and kept working. It was as if he had no desire to revisit their kiss of the night before. With a mask of indifference on her face, she focused again on the task at hand.

It took all his effort, but Carrick kept his face still as stone as he worked. He was a man, after all. A man in too close proximity to a woman he wanted to kiss. Once again. More than kiss. He shouldn't have touched her. Once was excusable. Twice was unforgivable. But unforgettable, too. Dammit, he had a goal. A singular goal that he'd woken up every day and worked toward for the past six years.

Here he was, almost at the finish line. His libido wasn't going to ruin it for him, not for a woman who didn't want him anyway. When she had shuddered so deliciously under his touch the night before, he wanted to believe.

He stared at the component that he held in his hands, turning it over, fiddling with it but not seeing it. His thoughts kept returning to her. Why was he so cruel, so dismissive of her?

He knew why. Of course he did. He was cruel for the same reason he had hidden in the walls as a child. Better to reject and push away than to be scorned and mocked. That was a pain he didn't care to visit again.

Besides, he had to keep his focus on his goal. His life might be lonely and painful, but he could accomplish this one thing. Leaving a legacy and making a difference was most important, and he needed to steel his desire. The last thing he needed was complications.

No, the last thing he needed was to put his heart, his tin heart into the hands of another person. He swore that would never happen and, so far, he'd kept his word. Christ, she tempted a man. Beyond reason and sanity. The boy liked her, too. It would be so simple to let her in.

Simple, yes, but impossible. Easy lives didn't come to tortured souls, and he damn well knew he was a damaged person. If he fooled himself into thinking that he could have an easy life, fate would laugh at him.

A part of him wanted to fire her and send her away. God knew, he had a good reason. But the glisten in her eye when she looked at his creations… She believed in him. The rest he could forgo. He could suffer through an erection. He could endure the soft feel of her skin when she touched him.

In just one day, he'd already become wickedly attached to her presence in the workshop. The way her whole body lit up from the most minor successes, something as simple as finding a screw that fit perfectly. Every other assistant that he'd hired either refused to enter the house or sat next to him every night and uttered sharp expressions of disdain. He was so linear, his thoughts mapped out and his daily routine planned. She was as wild as the summer wind. He'd been cold for so long. So very long.

After his mother died and he was finally able to live all alone, he'd rejoiced. *Forget the world*, he thought. He didn't need the hassle of lingering looks and snide remarks. No. Gladly he'd spent year after year squirreled away in his mansion. He was fine with it. Only now, he couldn't imagine being without her in the workshop, let alone the house. Or his bed. That scared him. Scared him more than anything.

He would keep his head down. And try like hell to keep everything under control.

Chapter 6

It was close to dawn, but Penrose was still bent over her desk cleaning the tines of a gear with a miniature wire brush. The past few days had sped by in a rush. She had worked hard, hard enough to be stressed. But the repetitive motion of the work at hand soothed her. There was a change in the air. Instead of the cool, unmoving chill of night, a breeze blew and played with the stray hairs that fell across her temples. Shades of sunrise would begin at any moment.

She looked up from her work and watched him as he hovered over a piece of metal. He wore his thick glasses and, with his wild white hair, one would think he'd look like an old man. Nothing was further from the truth. He looked vital and fierce and completely obsessed with the object he was holding. Over and over he ran his fingers along the surface, following the curve of the metal.

He closed his eyes as his fingers danced along it, as if he was listening to it. His eyesight may have been very poor, but his hands saw more than enough. She realized that Carrick was an artist as much as an inventor, coaxing life from the objects he created.

Those hands. She envied the metal. She wanted to know what those fingers would feel like running along her thighs, her stomach, her breasts. To see that concentrated look in his face as he listened to her body with his touch. The things she would say to him...without ever muttering a word. She sighed.

Carrick looked up at her, smiled and said, "Don't worry, Penny, we're almost done for the evening."

"I've cleaned the gear," she said, shaking the thoughts from her head. "The edges are sharp again. I think it will work now." She put down the magnifier glass and rubbed her hands together. Her fingertips hurt from using the small tools.

He gave her a nod, a simple thing. But, in the workshop, any approval from Carrick was hard fought and won, and she took it with great pride. It was, for him, a compliment. The quiet coo of mourning doves sounded through the windows.

Carrick said half-dreamily, "For countless generations my family has sat right here and listened to the mourning doves. It's a timeless sound."

She closed her eyes. He was right. It could be any time in history.

"Sometimes it bothers me to think I'm just a link in the chain," he said.

She looked up then and saw him blowing away dust that had collected in his workspace. He continued, "And sometimes it soothes me to be part of something bigger than myself."

His words and the wistful quality of the morning coaxed a small confession from her. "I wish I had a place that I belonged to. A home. I feel like a leaf in the wind, tossed about."

He said nothing. Only the sound of the doves filled the air. She'd revealed too much. She felt his eyes on her, but she didn't want to look up and meet his gaze. No, she didn't want him to see into her soul. Busying herself, she gathered the tools to put them away. Partly to change the subject, she said, "Carrick? Can you tell me about the tunnels in the house? They're so strange. Where did they come from?"

He stood up and stretched his arms high into the air, then wound them around in circles, loosening his muscles, and said, "The manor was built before the Revolutionary War. The rumor is that the tunnels served as a storage area for ammunition and to hide troops. My father once said that eighty men lived in the walls for a whole month once." He removed the thick glasses he'd been wearing, rubbed his eyes and laughed. "I'd hate to think of the smell that created. The mansion means a lot to my family. It's always been in the Arundell family. For good or bad, we are the manor, and it is us. We'd do anything to protect it."

Penrose brought him the piece she had been working on. "Here you are." Their fingers touched as he took it from her.

"That makes me curious," she said. "How is it that the manor survived the war? How did you save it from Sherman when every other plantation was razed to the ground?"

She should've noticed the bristle in his words. The pain. But she hadn't and pressed on. "What did you have to do?"

His eyes flicked in her direction, angrily, as if they were conceding something. Holding her gaze, he nodded. "All right, I'll tell you." Turning away, he walked toward a shelf and began to fiddle with the tools. "Sherman came through when I was about twelve or so. At the time, my gangliness as a young boy only added to my strange looks. Worst of all, I had embraced rebellion. I couldn't enlist like my pa and brothers. I was too young, and my affliction made it impossible. The slaves were all gone by then. I had a part in that, too, but that's a different story. Anyway, one of my brothers was already dead. We didn't know it, but at that moment, my pa was dying of fever in a camp. It was only my mother and I. We heard that Sherman was close, and my mother, clever woman that she was, came up with a solution that kept him far away from here." He snorted softly. "I must tip my hat to her because it worked."

It seemed that only a moment had passed, and yet the day was noticeably brighter. He was so complicated. Intense. She didn't so much fear the darkness in him anymore, but rather the depths of him. Or rather the depths of his pain.

They were both quiet, like a lull before a storm, and then he continued. "I was the solution. She put a sign about my neck, mussed my hair up fierce and then put faint streaks of mud beneath my eyes. On down the road, she put up another sign that read Warning, Yellow Fever. Then she brought me down to the gate along with the Persian carpet from the drawing room. She had me lay on the carpet and then rolled it up around my body, leaving my head and the sign exposed. I had to lie there, pretending to be dead for the entire day while the troops marched by. She made it clear, abundantly clear, that the entire future of the manor rested on my back."

It was so awful that she couldn't think of a word to say because anything she uttered would be an insult to him, so she walked over and put her hand on his arm. He pulled away sharply, almost meanly. But her touch seemed to trigger something deep within him because he began to speak so fast she could hardly follow his words.

"For more than an hour, I heard that army coming. You could hear the footfalls from miles away. A rumbling thunder headed straight toward me. I lay there with my eyes open, watching the birds flit about in the trees. When the troops drew close, I stilled and closed my eyes. When the harmonious thunder of an entire battalion's boots echoed loud and clear, I knew that they were just down the road. All of those soldiers walking in lock step." He shook his head. "They were a machine. The ground shook. I never looked. I didn't dare. Boot after boot stomped by my head and I lay there like a talisman warning them away."

He took a breath and continued on, "It was the officers that I hated most—those foulmouthed righteous men that called me the devil and many more names I won't say to you. I'm certain that if their troops weren't there, if they didn't have to keep up impressions, they would've abused my body just for sport. Though I was grateful they gave orders to pass by, I was more grateful that my mother was smart enough to keep my arms wrapped up tight because if I'd been able, I'd have smashed their faces to pulp."

A soft purr came from the doves outside. After his horrible story, she was surprised to hear that the doves still cooed. His festering wound of a memory had been lanced, the poison drained. In the lull after such an admission, she could see him stiffening, contorting his body the way he did when he was full of hate. When he spoke, it had a false brightness to it. A barely concealed bravado. "Well, Penny, now you know just how important Arundell Manor is to our family."

She was going to speak, and he must have sensed it, for he moved abruptly, nodding his head toward the stairs as he walked away. "Come on. The sun is up. It's time to quit."

C.J. woke her later that afternoon. "Are you ready?" he asked.

She rubbed the sleep from her eyes and leaned up from the pillow on one elbow. He was looking at her with a hopeful expression and an infectious smile, holding a lantern in his hand.

"Why do you have a lantern in the afternoon?" she asked, still confused by tendrils of sleep.

"Did you forget? We're going into the tunnel. So you can see my workshop. I have one, too, you know."

She had forgotten, and she was still exhausted. Another hour of sleep sounded wonderful. But how could she disappoint him? Forcing a smile on her face, she told a little white lie. "How could I forget?"

"Where we're going it's pitch-black. Don't worry, you won't be scared. You'll have me."

"Okay, let me get dressed first. But, C.J., I don't want to climb down that ladder."

"You don't have to. You can take the other entrance, the one right next to the grandfather clock."

"Okay, I'll meet you downstairs, then."

After he had shut the door, she dressed and readied herself for the day. She wished she had another gown instead of her dour black one. Perhaps after she'd been paid, she'd go to town and buy fabric to make one. By the time she made her way downstairs, she felt more awake and greeted him with a smile. He waited for her by the grandfather clock, a small, pale child next to the mammoth timekeeper. Looking at the clock, she was surprised to realize that she'd grown so used to it that she rarely noticed the chimes anymore.

"Are you ready?" he asked. "Hold this for a moment, will you?" he said, handing her the lantern.

She took it from him, and he went to the wall by the stairs. He pointed to the perfectly concealed doorway and pushed on the wood. It snapped open quickly, revealing a three-foot-high door. He crawled inside. Penrose dropped to her knees and handed him the light.

"Aren't you coming?" he asked.

Her stomach shouted a thousand protests, but her mouth said, "I'm coming. I promised you, so I'm coming in." It was hard to crawl with a skirt on. She was forced to push up the fabric so that her knees had purchase on the ground. With the hiss of her skirts scraping against the floor, she crawled into the space.

His angelic face was illuminated by the light, and she focused on that, ignoring the darkness that framed the boy. Darkness that seemed never-ending.

"You did great, Penny!" he said. His cheery voice echoing inside the tunnel sounded macabre.

"Thank you, C.J.," she said. "But we're still right at the entrance. Let's hope my courage holds out."

"It's not much farther, just a little bit and then the space opens up to a little room. My own workshop," he said with more than a touch of pride in his voice.

She crawled along a small stretch of tunnel. All of a sudden the space opened up and lamplight filled the emptiness, revealing a small room. A pile of blankets lay in one corner, and a few plates with crumbs on them sat beside it. In another corner stood a makeshift worktable piled with tools, candles and wood scraps.

Able to stand now, she walked over to the rough table made of wood scraps. She lifted a tool. "You stole this from your father?" she asked.

His chin went up. "He doesn't miss 'em."

Setting the tool down, she said, "No, I imagine he doesn't." She ran her touch over a box of candles and matches. Then something at the end of the table caught her eye. It was a strange box made of metal with wires protruding from the top of it. The wires ran to the floor into two containers that held some kind of liquid. She reached down to one of the containers.

"Don't touch it!" He ran over to her. "It's an acid compound made of zinc and carbon. It could burn you. It's called a battery. It provides power to my creation. Here, let me show you how it works."

From underneath the table, he pulled out another box. "Here," he said, holding it up to her. "You can open it."

He held the lantern while she bent over and lifted the lid. Yellow light spilled into the box and revealed a wooden bird. It was roughly hewn, its body still covered with chisel marks. The beak and eyes were merely suggested, not finely etched. Delicate wings made of paper unrolled in her hands. They'd been cut to shape, glued to the bird's body, and were decorated with pencil-drawn feathers. Two strings ran from the edge of the wings. "It's beautiful," she said. It was beautiful. Childlike, yes. But she couldn't help recalling his words from the other night—purpose and vision both. "You made this?" she asked.

C.J. unspooled the string as he spoke. "I did," he said proudly. "I carved it myself. Had to cut the block in two, scoop out the insides and then glue the two halves together. It's lighter with the insides scooped out." His shot her a look. "Weight is important, you know. Crucial." He threaded the string to a contraption that sat right next to the battery. It had gears and two loops that he tied the string to.

He pulled a wire from the battery and touched it to the contraption. The two prongs clicked to life and rotated. The strings drew taught, and the tension stretched to the bird. The wings lifted, and then as the prongs on the device swung in a circle, the string went slack, and the bird's wings dropped down again.

The motion was so simple… Slow, yes, but beautiful. The motions were repetitive, harmonious and fluid. It was like watching a primitive bird. One that couldn't yet take flight but was determined it would.

"It's amazing," she said to C.J. And it truly was. The child had a brilliant connection of ideas in his mind to bring about such a complex creation. The design was simple yet beautiful.

"Look," he said. He held the bird up in the air and mimicked flight. "One day…" he said meaningfully. "One day. I think the real trick of such movement is a simpler source of power. That and the external rope that mimics muscle movement." He no longer sounded like a child when speaking of his invention; he sounded focused and single-minded. C.J. looked up. "Well, to have true, free range of movement you need an almost portable power source. Think of the mechanical man. He's practically a locomotive with all the steam he requires in order to run."

"Does your father know what you're doing in here? He should if he doesn't."

"He won't care."

"I assure you, he will care, C.J. He needs to know how smart you are. You and he are so much alike. I know you could help him. More than I can." She had no doubt about that. How had Carrick missed the boy's genius up until this point? It seemed an impossibility. Carrick must be so far into his own world that he was blind to what was right in front of him.

C.J. huffed. "I don't care if he does know. He could care less about me, and I care even less about him."

She put her hand on his arm. "I'm sorry. You don't have to live in the tunnels, you know. There's nothing to be afraid of out there."

He yanked away and looked up at her with anger. "I love it in here," he said passionately. "Everything about it. And even more, I can travel the length of the tunnel. It's safer for me in here, rather than out there. I feel... I don't need to be afraid in here."

"You don't need to be afraid out there, either. You belong here. It's your home."

He shook his head somberly. "No. You don't understand. It's his home. This—" he looked around "—this is my home."

Standing next to the peculiar child, and buried in

the dark, dank place as they were, she wondered what her place was in the whole bizarre situation. A beautiful but frightening house, a beautiful but frightening man, a ghost of a child, and more secrets and mysteries than she knew what to do with.

Suddenly chilled, she rubbed her arms for warmth. "Come on, C.J.," she said in a hollow sounding voice that echoed around them. "Let's get out of here."

Chapter 7

August drew to a close. Penrose felt herself unwinding, settling in and growing roots. She adored everything about Arundell Manor, from the peaceful pond and the graceful oaks to the crickets that sang outside the windows every evening. Sometimes she wondered if the house had a soul. It was a strange thought, even to her, but it was as if the house welcomed her, made room for her and enjoyed her presence. Every afternoon, summer storms rolled in, and after waking to the sounds of thunder, she went downstairs to sit on the veranda and watch the spears of lightning in the growing clouds, waiting for the pelting rain to begin. Her mother had always told her that with rainstorms came invitations for second chances, and it seemed she was right.

More often than not, C.J. came and sat beside her. Twice he brought his marbles, and they used chalk to sketch a wide circle onto the floor. While the persistent rain fell, they played marbles with Penrose on her knees, analyzing each shot and trying desperately to win. To no avail. C.J. was a tough player and both times trounced her soundly.

Work on the mechanical man progressed, though Carrick still seemed unsettled. He regarded her with a frozen indifference—always polite and encouraging, but never more than that. Their two, brief encounters seemed more like a dream than a memory. She ached to feel his touch again though she hid it as best she could.

Just after a thunderstorm ended late one afternoon, Penrose and C.J. were shooting marbles when they heard Carrick coming down the stairs. C.J. made himself scarce, running down the steps of the veranda and across the lawn. "C.J.!" Penrose shouted. "Please stay!" But the boy was long gone, and when she turned around, Carrick stood in the doorway. His expression was like stone. Lately, it was always like stone. "Are you ready to work?" he asked.

She nodded but felt far from ready. Had they really kissed? She'd thought of it so many times, yet it seemed like a thousand years ago. But her skin still burned with the memory of his touch. Her body felt alive when she looked at him.

She pressed her lips together and tried to maintain composure. She wanted that bliss…the sweet bliss that carried her away when he touched her.

On that night, all of her propriety had slid away so quickly, so easily, and she would gladly forgo it again. With his stern looks and cold coloring, he was so visually arresting. She'd seen the essence of him, his heart of fire.

The look he gave her burned right through her. She stood up, smoothed her skirts, blushed and stammered, "I'm...ready."

"Is everything okay?"

"It's fine," she insisted. "Let's go."

Carrick stepped aside, and she squeezed past him. In the center of the foyer, she looked at the family portrait that hung in such a place of prominence. "Are you in that picture?" she asked.

He stood behind her, not touching her, but his presence was a wall of strength at her back. "What do you see in that picture?"

Ignoring the surge of butterflies that fluttered in her stomach, she answered, "I'm looking at a perfect family picture." It was idyllic, three young Arundell boys were frolicking on the grass while their parents sat on a blanket looking over the scene. Arundell Manor appeared behind them, looking serene and stately on the hill. The oak by the pond was there, though younger and with less stately branches.

"Look closer. It's far from perfect," he whispered in her ear. From behind her, he reached over and traced a finger along the canvas until he reached a brown-haired boy, younger than the others, with cherub cheeks and a wild look to him. The boy was running down a hill, laughing, with his brothers in pursuit. His finger tapping the boy, Carrick said in a low, harsh tone, "That's me."

"How can that possibly be you?" Confused, she turned and looked at him.

"It is me." His jaw clenched. "Or I should say, it's the me my parents wished for. The one they pretended they had."

She looked at the child in the picture once more. If he was anything like he was now, it was cruel to paint him so carefree and happy. Crueler still to erase his coloration. He'd been completely eradicated and a fictional character painted in his place. She put her hand on his arm.

He pulled away. Ignoring that, she continued. "It's a shame they did that to you. I'm sure you were a beautiful child. It must have hurt."

"Hurt?" he said with a laugh. "It didn't hurt me." His next words pierced her soul. "It destroyed me. Now, for all time, whichever Arundell descendant looks at this picture will think me to be that child. A happy little boy living a happy life. When I was someone else entirely."

He pointed to the parents. "Look at them. Look. The perfect couple. One would never know that they made their child hide in the tunnels whenever they threw a ball or guests visited. You'd never know that man…my father…looked me in the face and told me I should have died rather than bear the Arundell name."

Carrick was right. It was such an injustice. If Penrose were the artist, she would have painted him off in the distance, always in the distance, beautiful but cold, like an icy angel. "They did you an injustice," she said. Anger flared in her. "Now you do it to your own son."

"You're mocking me," he said.

"It's the truth and you know it." She reached out to him again, but he shook her off. "Please."

"It's not all bad. I wouldn't have the mechanical man if they hadn't treated me with such disdain."

"Why is that?"

"I hate pity," he said simply. "I don't want people to think of me with pity. I have plans. I want to change the world. So don't pity me. God, the irony. My family fought to keep their slaves, and all died in the effort. They told me that a person's dark skin color made them inferior. Yet, every single one of them treated me as if I was the most inferior of all." His words tumbled out fast and harsh. "Me! Me. I'm the palest of them all, and yet I should hide? They're all hypocrites! Every single one of them. Every man on earth. I reject them all."

"There are many who wouldn't judge you…" Her words faded as she spoke them because she doubted the truth of them. No, he would be judged, and harshly. The world was cruel. It judged a woman for being poor. It judged a man for being dark, and it judged a child for being too pale. People had such a narrow idea of perfection.

He took a deep breath and said, "Now that we've belabored a part of my life I'd rather skip over, would you care to work?"

"Of course, I would. Let's get the mechanical man up and running right away. We're so close." She followed him down the stairs and into the workshop. Right away, Penrose noticed the empty chairs by the window. The wooden mannequins were missing.

It was shameful, but immediately her mind went right to C.J. She looked at Carrick. His attention was focused on the mechanical man, and he didn't notice the chairs were empty. She had the urge to ask him about it, but she also knew that if it was C.J. who had stolen them, he would be in serious trouble, and she wanted to talk to him first.

Penrose went to her desk and busied herself, and soon enough Carrick was hard at work on the mechanical man. As he moved about, he muttered under his breath.

A few hours later, he said, "Penny, come take a look at this."

Carrick stood next to Harris, who towered over him. Carrick turned and looked at her with barely contained excitement. "I think we're there. I think it's a go. Every dowel, every rod, every gear fits perfectly. Let's fire him up."

His excitement overtook her. She wanted to hug him, and the urge was so strong she gave in to it. She threw her arms around him, pulling him tight and kissing him on the cheek. "Let's do it!" she cried.

Stepping back, he thoughtfully rubbed his cheek where her lips had been. But he didn't look upset. Not at all. "Yes," he said. "Let's do it." He stoked the fire and pulled the vats into the enormous fireplace, and while the water heated, he paced the room excitedly.

"I'll be right back," she said. C.J. should be with them to watch Harris brought to life.

Carrick paid her no mind. He was too busy preparing the mechanical man.

She grabbed a candle and ran up the stairs to check C.J.'s bedroom, but, of course, the boy wasn't there. There was one other place the child could be. In the walls. Gathering up her courage, she went to the little door by the staircase, opened it and peered into the dark tunnel.

"C.J.!" she called out. She heard a rustling noise and held up the candle. "C.J., wake up! Something exciting is about to happen! Carrick is about to fire up Harris. The mechanical man!"

"What?" he said in a sleepy voice that echoed down the tunnel to her. "He's going to start him?"

"He is! Come on…hurry!" she urged. Penrose backed out and waited for him in the hall. At that moment, the grandfather clock began to toll. Twelve mellow strokes of the bell rang out. "Perfect," she said to the empty hall. "A new day. A new beginning."

The boy emerged from the tunnel with sleepy eyes and mussed clothes. Day clothes. The child should be on a schedule, she thought. He needed tending to— and badly.

She hoped that once Harris fired up, the excitement would spill over between father and son and that they would bond. A fragile hope, but still there. If nothing else, they had the love of inventing in common. It would be something to build on. She dared not voice her secret hope. It was such a silly hope that she was even reluctant to wish for it, but she couldn't help it. The child needed his father, and the father needed his son. He was just blind to it.

She held C.J.'s hand and led him down the cellar stairs and into the workroom.

The room crackled with excitement. In the fireplace, the flame burned brightly as the sun and threw an orange gloss over Harris. The vats steamed and the vapor billowed out and filled the room with a thick haze. The mechanical man stood stout and proud, his tin skin shining bright, and his lantern eyes already lit and glowing with excitement. It was as if Harris knew something terrific was about to happen to him.

Wild-eyed with excitement, Carrick looked up at them as they approached. "It's all set up. We need to wait for the steam to build up enough pressure to bring him to life."

"Do you think it will work?" asked C.J. He had the same bright look of expectation on his face that his father did. If Penrose needed any further proof that they were father and son, it was right there.

"I think it will work," she announced confidently. C.J. and Penrose stood side by side and waited.

Suddenly, the tubes that fed the steam into Harris stiffened. A grinding noise and a series of rattles came from deep in the belly of the mechanical man. C.J. squeezed Penrose's hand, and she squeezed his back. Carrick came and stood next to them, completely still. Everyone waited.

With a puff of steam from the top of his boxy head, Harris came to life. His eyes burned bright, and his massive body shivered and clattered with the sounds of metal against metal, followed by a whirring noise, and with aching slowness and a loud clacking noise, the mechanical man lifted his arm.

Goose bumps crawled over her skin. "He's saying hello," she said in a breathy voice.

"Just wait," said Carrick. "He'll take a step." He stood eagerly, leaning forward, eyes riveted on the mechanical man.

With a series of rapid clicks, the mechanical man lifted his leg, cranked it higher, then higher still. With a sudden finality, the leg came down and he lurched forward.

They all shouted at once and threw their arms in the air. Everyone hugged. Penrose felt such joy. Of course, Harris was no different than a train or an engine, but somehow to her, he was so much more. He was the extension of their hopes and dreams and with this step, he gave them what they desperately needed.

"It's the second step that's always the problem," said Carrick in a worried voice.

More clicking noises came from Harris. He cranked forward on his foot, settling his weight on it, and then his other foot began to wind, to lift higher, and as the leg moved, a whiny squeal came from him. He began to lean, just a fraction at first. "Please," said Carrick with a voice bordering on desperate.

They waited with their breath held, watching that metal foot move higher and then swing forward.

With a loud groan, the mechanical man heaved forward, held itself upright for a moment, tottered, and then collapsed. Right to the ground in a riotous heap. His lantern eyes shattered. His limbs came apart. Tubes sprang from his backside and whipped wildly around the room, hissing and spewing steam. Harris crashed loudly as he broke apart and the pieces skidded across the floor.

Penrose gasped. C.J. screamed.

Carrick stood stock-still, staring straight ahead, his arms limp at his side.

Thinking fast, Penrose went and pulled the tubes from the kettles. The hissing and whipping lines slowed and then came to rest. The corpse of the mechanical man lay in pieces with steam rising from his broken body. He looked like a fallen soldier. A dead dream. It was the very worst thing that could ever happen. Ever.

Without saying a word, Carrick went to a chair, sat down, slumped over and rested his head in his hands.

C.J. looked shocked, crestfallen and scared, too. She took the child by the hand and reassured him. "It's okay," she said, wiping the sweat from her brow with her sleeve. "We'll try again. Maybe tomorrow," she said though in her heart she doubted the truth of her words. Harris was just too broken. "Why don't you run to bed and let me talk to your father?"

The boy nodded. All of the excitement had left his face, and he looked much as he had before. Sullen. Angry. "I knew it wouldn't work anyway," he said in a defiant tone.

"Go on back to bed now," she said, and turned him toward the stairs. "Go on."

He raced up the stairs without looking back.

Penrose walked over to Carrick. With the steam hanging in the air, she could barely see him.

"I can't get it to work," he said, not looking at her, not lifting his head from his hands. "No matter what I do, I can't get it to work."

At his feet lay an iron rod that had broken apart from Harris. Carrick reached down and picked it up, studying the piece. When he spoke, his voice was deathly quiet. "God, I can design a clock. I can design a mechanism to specifications so miniature that it boggles the mind. But I can't take this damn project to completion." He looked up at her with an anguished expression. "It vexes me. I've tried wires, but they catch on the internal mechanisms and corners. I've moved the central housing. Nothing has worked." He clenched his fingers. "Steam is too damn problematic. The components are a nightmare."

His eyes met hers and her heart broke to see their flat, dark color. "I've failed." He shook his head. "Ruined. Ruined before anyone even knows my name. Why did I think I could make a difference? That the world would even care?" He sighed, the most defeated sound Penrose had ever heard. "I'm just another fool with a dream."

Penrose went and knelt beside Carrick. Steam curled around them. "You can't give up," she said. The conviction resounded within her. "We're not giving up," she said, placing a hand on his leg. "I'm not."

"It's easy for you to say. You can walk right out that door and get yourself a new life. I don't have that luxury." He dragged his hands through his hair. "I wanted the world to know my name. To remember me." Carrick lifted the heavy rod and bounced it in his palm a few times. He drew a quick, sharp breath, lifted his arm and threw the rod across the room. It crashed into the wall and clanged onto the floor. "Is that too much to ask?" he shouted.

She tried to calm him. "It's not too much to ask, Carrick. You just haven't asked the question enough times. Let's try again."

"I'm done."

She scrambled for the right words, the exact right thing to say that would lift his spirits and renew him. "Even a misstep is a step forward," she said, knowing that those words were wrong. Any words would be wrong just then. But she had to try. She took his hand into hers. Heat flooded her skin.

Full force, the memory of their kiss swept over her. The way his lips had claimed hers, the sensation of his entire body pressed against hers. On impulse, she brought his hand to her lips and then ran it tenderly along the line of her jaw. "No effort is ever wasted," she whispered.

Carrick slumped forward, resting his forehead

against hers. He took fierce breaths. His hands wound into her bun, needy and demanding. He pressed his lips against her forehead and leaned onto her. He was heavy, but she held his weight. Still taking those angry breaths, he dragged his fingers deeper into her hair, loosening it from the bun. It spilled around her in a midnight fall of curls.

He moaned when her hair sprang free and grabbed handfuls of it, pulling forward and draping it around the two of them so that the whole world was distant. Her hair was a black river against the white ice of his skin.

When he spoke, his words were angry and biting. "Look at you. All soft and pliable. Soothing me." His grip was a vise holding her against him. "You think to lure me into revealing a tender heart beating in this chest? Well, you'll be disappointed, Penny, because I'm as empty as the mechanical man."

He wrenched her face upward, and she stared at him, inches from him. His nostrils flared, and his eyes glistened with unshed tears. She wanted to wipe them away, but she couldn't move. Suddenly, his lips came down fiercely on hers, revealing an anguished part of himself that knew no words, only pain.

She clung to him and kissed him back, desperately, achingly, her hands grabbing at him, trying to convey what words couldn't. He kissed her with a volatile mix of passion and need. Penrose, who for so long had focused on how little she had in life, realized how much she had to give.

She pulled away from him, but her hands had somehow wound into his hair, and she gripped him tightly. "Carrick Arundell," she said. "You will change the world. Mark my words. Mark my words." She began to stand, pulling him up from the chair as she did.

"What?" he asked her, "Do you have plans for me? Are you going to fix me and bring me to life like the mechanical man?"

"No, Carrick." She took his hand, kissed it and then ran it over her breasts, past her waist, before pushing it deep between the folds of her skirt. "I'm going to bring you to life in an entirely different manner." The boldness of her actions surprised her.

A low, guttural sound came from his throat. His hands wrapped around her, pulled her tight against him, and through her skirt she felt his hardness.

"Is that what you want?" he asked, still a trace of anger in his voice.

She didn't answer right away, simply stared up at his troubled eyes. Finally, she spoke. "Yes. That's what I want. And more."

"God, you drive me crazy," he said in a hoarse voice.

Kissing, bodies entwined, they moved across the room, with Carrick guiding her toward a table. With one fell swoop, he wiped the table clean, sending parts and pieces clattering to the floor. He pushed her against the table, his hands at her back as he unbuttoned her gown. Jerking the dress down, he shoved it impatiently to the floor.

She wore her shift, and it stuck to her damp skin, revealing every contour and shadow. The air chilled her skin. Her nipples tightened, and she saw his gaze move to her chest. It made her hotter for him, and her chest rose and fell as her breath grew fast.

He slipped a finger under the fabric and peeled it away from her skin. He unwrapped her body slowly, dragging the cotton down her body. When he bent to lower the shift past her waist, she gasped, knowing that he was right there, right next to the spot that ached for his touch. He tossed aside the clothing. She stood nude before him.

Stepping back, his gaze traveled the length of her body. "I promised myself I wouldn't do this," he said. "And every day I struggled to keep my promise. But dammit, looking at you now, I was a complete fool to do so. You are mine, Penny. Remember that."

"I am yours." The words had come out before she realized what she said. But they felt right to say and, listening to them, they felt right to hear.

She stepped forward and began to unbutton his shirt, and when it was off, she ran her fingers over the ridges of his muscles. Goose bumps rose on his skin as she touched him. There was so much power underneath his skin, but that's not what drew her to him. No, what drew her to him was his mind. His fierce passion for creating. But those muscles under her fingertips were heaven.

He placed his hand on her chest and gently pushed her down until she sat on the table, legs dangling. He nestled between her legs. The feel of him, right there, shocked her. It was so intimate, almost a promise of what was to come.

He kissed her, leaning forward, forcing her to lie back on the table, and she peered up at him, nervous. He towered above her and ran his hands along the length of her legs. She closed her eyes, shutting out every sensation except for his touch, which left a trail of heat along her skin.

"You are perfection," he said.

She opened her eyes. "You are, too," she whispered.

And he *was* perfection. But he looked dangerous just then, almost feral, his eyes darkened by an intensity she'd never seen before. They were gray streaked with purple, the color of early night. She squirmed against him. "Please," she begged, not certain what she was begging him for.

He stilled. "Please what?" he said, lifting his hands from her body, a wicked tilt to his lips. "What exactly do you want?"

Her hips bumped against him. She tried to speak with her body, but his hands didn't respond, remaining a fingertip above her skin.

"No." He shook his head. "No. Please, what? Tell me, my little Penny. I want to hear you ask for it. I need to hear it."

She whimpered, reluctant to say the words. Unsure of what she even wanted.

But he was insistent. "Say it," he ordered her.

"Please," she whispered in a low voice. "Touch me."

"Louder." He spoke fiercely, as if hearing her words were the most important thing to him.

She spoke full and loud, but her words came out in a rush. "Please, please, Carrick. Touch me. Take me. Please."

He made a deep growling sound and raked his hands across her body, over her breasts, fanning out over her stomach before pausing above the cleft between her legs. "So beautiful," he said, feathering a touch over the center of her. "Black as night." His hand dipped between her legs, and with two fingers he spread her lips, looked down, and then he hissed. "Hiding a pink rose."

She cried out as he touched her. With his fingers on her body, he became an artist once again, tracing over her most secret part, exploring her, bringing breathy whimpers from her lips. Instinctively, she spread her legs wider, wanting more. Needing more. "Please, Carrick," she said again, no longer whispering.

"Not yet," he replied. She saw his pale skin lit by the firelight, his large shoulders throwing her into shadow. He unbuttoned his pants, and she heard them fall to the floor. She closed her eyes again, waiting.

But then she felt his breath between her legs and then his hot tongue slid between her folds. She made a choking noise and lifted herself up, leaning on her elbows. She took in the sight of his head buried between her legs.

His eyes were closed. His hands held her buttocks, and his mouth was wild. Demanding.

She cared about nothing except that tongue—hot and private, and so wicked. She began thrusting against him, lifting one hand and lacing her fingers through his hair. Directing him.

She began to moan his name over and over again and fell back against the table. Suddenly, his mouth was gone.

He stood above her. "I need you right now," he said.

Climbing onto the table, he covered her. Their bodies were slick with sweat and slid against each other. She opened her legs wide and felt his hardness pressing against her center, sliding up and down against her wetness but never entering her. It was torture.

And it was really happening.

"Please," she said.

In response, he kissed her deeply, and she tasted the tang of her own arousal. He pressed against her open-

ing and then pushed. She cried out from the sharpness
of the pain and dug her fingers into his back.

He froze. "Are you okay?" he whispered into her ear.

Nodding, she said, "Just move. Please, just move."

He did, but gently, in a long, slow thrust that opened
her farther. Every sensation faded away, and she was
aware of a sharp feeling of fullness. An exquisite ache.
He pushed even deeper, so slowly that she cried out in
frustration.

"I'm holding back," he said with his mouth against.

"Don't hold back. Go." She needed him.

"You don't know what you're asking for."

"Maybe I don't. But I want to find out."

"You drive me wild," he said, sliding his hands beneath her shoulders, lifting her torso and pressing her
breasts against his chest. He began to move.

She felt herself yielding, opening up to him. The
pain was completely gone, replaced by a delicious, tingling numbness. Lost to the feeling, she grabbed him,
urging him on. That feeling ruled her. It was all she
could focus on.

The tingling spread, deepened and turned to hot little
pulses of pleasure every time he buried himself deep
inside her. She lived for that moment, that brief colli-
sion of their bodies. Every thrust pushed her higher, and
soon she found herself whimpering and crying out in
time to his movements.

The feeling gathered force and built inside of her,
and Carrick was insistent, plunging into her, forcing
her closer and closer to an abyss that she didn't understand. She teetered on the edge, resisting until the very
last moment when she couldn't fight it anymore.

She gave in to it completely, to the rush of pleasure

that exploded inside her. It felt as if she were flying and falling at the same time, and she called his name over and over again. Almost from a distance she was aware of his cries, his hands at her as he found his own ecstasy.

And there, in the steamy workshop, amidst the wreckage of his dreams, they clung to each other until the world slowly returned.

He sat up, and she wanted to cry out from the loss of his body next to hers. "Come to bed," he said. "My bed." Taking her hand, they walked up the stairs together.

Chapter 8

It was not yet dawn, and Penrose sat upright in Carrick's bed, her knees tucked beneath her chin as she studied Carrick. He lay dead to the world, sprawled out and tangled in the covers, his hand possessively thrown over her hip.

In sleep, the mask he showed the world was removed and his features had smoothed out to reveal a classically handsome face with lips that looked as if they might curl into a smile at any moment.

She had a confusing mix of emotions. Her body felt chafed and raw and alive. Her were lips swollen, her heart full. But worry plagued her. He couldn't give up on his dream.

She couldn't sleep. It was useless. She closed her eyes for a moment, just to rest them. When she opened them, a pink aura glowed on the horizon. Dawn had arrived.

Energy coursed through her body as soon as the thought came to her. She wouldn't give up. Very carefully, she disentangled herself from his hand, slipped from the bed, and began to dress herself. If she cleaned the workroom and restored order, if she organized the parts of the mechanical man, that might clear the slate for Carrick. It might inspire him again. Winding her hair into a tight bun, she vowed to herself that she wouldn't let him walk away from his dream. Not if she had anything to say about it. Especially not if she enlisted his brilliant son.

Her plan set, her hopes renewed, she flew down the stairs and went to the hidden door to the tunnel. With a quick knock, she pushed open the door and poked her head in. "C.J.?" she called out. Looking down the passageway, she saw his little room ablaze with light. He appeared, first his feet, but then he ducked down, and she saw his face. "Hi," he said to her. "How come you're not sleeping?"

"Because I need your help," she replied. "Can I come in?"

The darkness of the tunnel closed around her as she crawled along it. C.J. waited, holding up the lantern for her to see. When she emerged into the little room, she was surprised by the sight of the wooden couple sitting on his desk. She'd forgotten about them. She said in a sharp voice, "You did take them!"

"What of it?" he replied defiantly.

It made her so angry. Hadn't Carrick endured enough? She was about to chastise him—and harshly, too—when she noticed something. One of the mannequins was propped up into a sitting position. His wooden skin had fresh scrapings on it. He had wires running from his limbs. Wires that extended to the alkaline battery on the floor. "C.J.! What did you do?"

He shrugged. "I fixed him. Or I'm in the process of it. Watch." He went to the alkaline battery and started it, and as Penrose watched, the wooden man began to move. Only his arm. The man lifted it easily and gracefully if not a little slowly. Yet there was a simple beauty in the movement that spoke of a real step forward in design. "I hollowed out the limbs," he said. "Scraped all of the wood out. The shavings are in the corner. That eased the burden on the battery. It works like a charm." He scratched his temple. "It's still limited. I have to reconfigure the whole mannequin, but it's a start."

"C.J. Do you know what you just did?"

"Yes. I'm redesigning the mechanical man the correct way."

She laughed at his childish boldness, nodding through the film of tears that gathered in her eyes. "I knew it! I was coming here to talk to you, and look! Look what you've done!" She pulled him into her arms and hugged him. "C.J." All she could manage to say was, "Please, explain it to me."

He did, telling her about his plans for the wooden mannequins. Based on his explanations, Penrose knew in her heart that the boy spent a lot of time in his workroom while his father slept. By the time he finished explaining, she couldn't contain her smile, which stretched from ear to ear. "We have to tell Carrick!" she said.

C.J.'s face twisted in anger. "No!"

"Why not?"

"I hate him. That's why not."

"You don't hate him. You're mad at him, and you're

scared, too. You have a right to be, but you don't hate him." Her words were matter-of-fact.

His whole demeanor changed, and his body stiffened. "I don't care what you call it. I still don't want to share it with him."

Penrose knelt and took his small hands into hers. "Will you do it for me? Please? I have this feeling in my heart that it might change everything."

His teeth gnashed together.

Clearly it was not an easy decision for him, but she waited, hoping that he would agree to her plan.

"Oh, I suppose so," he said, letting out a big, dramatic sigh. A look of pride flitted across his eyes.

"Thank you!" she said, "I'm going to the workshop to tidy it up a bit. Can you gather up all of this safely and bring it to me? After we set up, we'll have a grand reveal to Carrick."

"I can do that," he said. "But do you promise I won't get in trouble for stealing the mannequins?"

"I promise," she said, tousling his hair, leaning down and giving him a kiss. "Thank you, C.J."

He pushed her away, but halfheartedly, and a smile tugged at his lips.

The workshop looked as if a crime had been committed there. Penrose supposed that, in a way, one had. Harris resembled a murder victim who'd been cruelly dismembered. Fragments of tin and iron lay everywhere and she busied herself stacking the broken parts of the mechanical man in an orderly fashion. She swept the floors and arranged the tables so that the room recovered some of its organized look.

"I'm here," said C.J. He carried two boxes, one in each arm. "But I'm not sure what you want me to do."

She smiled at him. "Just set it up, and then we'll go and wake Carrick. Do you need any help?"

"A little," he said.

After clearing a table, she helped C.J. unpack the boxes and position the mechanical man. He went and retrieved the battery, walking stiffly down the stairs so as not to spill any acid. "I'm going to have to enclose this acid," he said, thinking aloud to himself. "It'll be safer and more portable that way."

Listening to the child, Penrose felt like singing. "You'll have to explain it to your father."

"I'm not sure he'll be happy." He looked very doubtful all at this thought.

"Well, there's one way to find out, isn't there?" she said. "Let's go upstairs and wake him up."

Penrose barged into Carrick's bedroom, full of ideas and hope, but as soon as she entered the room she stopped in her tracks. The room was dark, with only a tiny ray of sunshine sneaking under the drapes. The ray of light fell on the bed and illuminated Carrick's half-naked torso. Hot memories flooded her, but she put them aside. There was no time for that now.

"Carrick?" she said.

He stirred in bed but didn't wake.

Her resolve notched back a few rungs, and her excitement turned to a flighty nervousness. What if he got mad or didn't like the idea? But C.J. looked at her so hopefully that she couldn't back out.

Coughing first, she said, "Carrick." Her voice was far too quiet for the task of waking a sleeping man.

C.J. tugged on her hand and said, "Louder."

Carrick stirred. "Who's there?"

"Us," she replied.

He lifted his head at the sound of her voice. He twisted around and squinted his eyes. "What do you want?"

Her stomach tightened to hear his husky, sleep-laden voice. Her own voice sounded too high, too excited as she said, "Get up! Something big has happened."

He popped straight up in bed. "Is there a fire?" he asked. The sheets had slipped farther, revealing a fine trail of hair sliding down from his navel.

"No, nothing like that." She rested her hand on C.J.'s shoulder. "C.J. has made a breakthrough for the mechanical man."

Carrick made a face. "C.J.?" He sounded incredulous.

She inwardly cringed at the tone of his voice. Next to Penrose, C.J. shifted his weight from foot to foot. "Yes, C.J." Her voice was sharp with rebuke. "Is it so inconceivable that your son would have ideas just like you did? That he'd be as smart as you." Oh, he made her angry. "Or even smarter than you?"

The more she spoke, the angrier she became. She tossed her arms in the air and almost yelled, "We're going downstairs to wait for you. Get dressed and meet us down there." She took a few steps, saw C.J. lingering and went back to take him by the shoulders. "Trust me, Carrick. It's worth it."

He rolled to the edge of the bed and rubbed his eyes. "Let's do it, then."

Penny and C.J. waited for Carrick in the workshop. He sailed into the room, dressed haphazardly, his white hair tangled from sleep, and greeted them with a nod.

"C.J., go on and show him," she said, urging the boy toward Carrick.

C.J. shifted from foot to foot nervously. He began to speak, "Well...I got the idea from this toy I made." He picked up the bird and held it out. "I made it all by myself."

Carrick looked at Penrose briefly, his eyes accusing her of wasting his time.

"Carrick," she warned him.

The boy continued, "Sometimes during the day I come in here and look around." He looked very sheepish.

Carrick said, "Go on."

C.J. said, "You have a few good ideas."

Carrick raised an eyebrow but remained quiet.

"Well, anyway. I programmed the toy to move."

Carrick held it in his hand, turning it from side to side. He lifted the paper wings, ran his fingers along the strings. "How did you do that?" he asked.

"I made a battery."

"Humph." Carrick's expression was unreadable. He was still analyzing the bird. "So, it's a decent design, but I don't know if it was worth getting out of bed for."

"Wait." Penrose held up her hand. "Just listen. C.J., tell him about the mannequins."

The boy said excitedly, "I thought to myself, if we hook up a mannequin to the battery, I can make it move, too."

Carrick stilled for a moment. "Say that again."

"If we hook the mannequin up to the battery, I can make him move, too. With some work. He's too heavy right now. But I got his arm moving, at least."

Carrick turned and looked at the mannequin, which

was propped up on the table. He took a breath as if he was planning on speaking, but then he closed his mouth and stared again at the mannequin.

Penrose saw his brain fire to life. Now he was looking at the bird. He pulled on the wing and it went up and down. His fingers danced over the bird as if absorbing some essence from it. Then his eyes darted to the mannequin.

"C.J.," she said, "go start the battery."

C.J. sprang up, ran over to the battery and then, a moment later, the wooden man lifted his arm in a graceful salute. There was no steam, no clanking noises. Only a simple movement by a simple wooden creature. And it was marvelous to see. The arm kept moving in a circle, and C.J. excitedly explained all that had gone into the design. How he'd hollowed out the wood and adjusted the gears in the box to program that one simple movement.

Carrick watched all of this silently and then said in a near whisper, "Penrose."

Penrose shook her head. "No. Not me. C.J. Your son."

"C.J.," he said.

The boy stopped talking. He looked at the ground, his cheeks reds.

"Come here," he said gruffly.

C.J. went and stood next to his father, and Carrick did the most surprising thing of all. He leaned down and gave C.J. a hug. The hug was awkward, as if neither of them knew quite what to do, but then Carrick said, "I'm proud of you. Proud. God Almighty, you just changed everything."

Penrose smiled, and C.J. beamed.

Chapter 9

The next day, even though the sun came up hot and fast, Carrick never returned to his bedroom. Rather, he and C.J. stayed in the workshop, side by side, each talking quickly, eager to share their ideas. Within a few hours, the mechanical man had a new life and a new vision. C.J. proudly announced that the man would be called Harris prototype number two, which made Penrose happy.

The morning passed in a blur with Penrose bringing them food while they toiled, heads bent over sketches, arguing over the merits of this or that feature. Whatever happened from here, whether the mechanical man failed or succeeded, at least there was a connection between father and son. A smile lingered on her lips, and she had a quiet happiness within her.

It would have been impossible to sleep, so she

stayed up and kept busy working around the house. She brought in more firewood for the workshop, tidied the kitchen and made beeswax candles. They were wide, so they'd burn longer and Carrick could use them without a candleholder. As the day came to a close, she thought to herself that she felt truly at home and, additionally, that there was so much promise in the air.

She went downstairs. The workshop seemed brighter than before. Perhaps it was the fresh candles she lit and arranged around the room, but it seemed just as likely that C.J.'s enthusiasm and ideas lifted everyone's spirits.

Penrose approached Carrick and C.J. They were huddled around their project and she cleared her throat. When they turned around, she saw what they'd accomplished. A new mechanical man had risen from the ashes of the previous one. He was a mixture of wood and metal, with thin, spindly limbs and a stout metal torso. His gas-lamp eyes were enormous on his new wooden head. He looked otherworldly with his spindly limbs and futuristic body.

"What do you think?" asked Carrick with an excited expression. "It's good, isn't it?"

"I can't believe it!" she said. "Look at him! I never would've thought to blend the two men together." She wanted to remember this moment forever.

Carrick had taken C.J.'s suggestion of the alkaline battery as a source of power, and C.J. had listened to Carrick's belief that metal was necessary for the design. But perhaps the biggest breakthrough was that C.J. had talked Carrick out of making the robot walk. Instead, they had used the wooden legs and put rollers on the bottom. Carrick explained to her, "It's simpler. Such a simple solution that I couldn't see it. But there it was right in plain sight." The joy of discovery seemed to outweigh the pain of previous disappointments.

"You should see it work. It's not finished yet. Only the two arms are functioning, but when we attach the gears to the rollers in the feet, it'll be in operation. What gears we put in the power box will dictate his movements. Everything is falling right into place." He smiled. "As if it was meant to be."

C.J. tugged at her sleeve. "We put the entire housing of the gearbox inside the tin torso. It's perfect. I knew it would be. I just knew it."

"You did know it," said Carrick approvingly.

At his words, C.J. looked down awkwardly and shuffled his feet, but the corners of his mouth tilted up in a smile.

Penrose helped them until ten o'clock, when C.J. started to nod off.

"Off to bed with you," she said to him and walked him down the hall. When they reached the tunnel entrance, she said to C.J., "Are you sure you don't want to sleep upstairs in a real bedroom?"

Shaking his head, he said, "No, I still feel safest in the wall. Maybe one day…" His voice trailed off. He looked up at her. "Would you mind tucking me in?"

"Sure," she answered, a bit reluctantly.

They crawled into the tunnel together, C.J. in the lead holding the candle. He crawled into his little bed on the floor and she sat beside him.

"Today was the best day ever," he said.

"It was a great day," she agreed. "But I have a feeling there are many more to come."

"I hope so, Penny," he said.

She kissed him good-night and crawled out of the

tunnel. When she emerged, the front doors were wide open, and she saw Carrick by the pond. He stood there, his hair brilliant in the moonlight. A blanket lay spread out on the ground behind him, surrounded by a dozen lit candles, all twinkling like stars. He looked like the king of midnight holding court, made to rule the darkness.

He motioned to her, and she stepped outside.

A mellow moon hung in the sky. Fireflies swirled in lazy arcs above the lawn. Carrick held a candle in his hand and stood staring out at the water as she approached.

Without turning, he spoke. His voice was low. "Have you ever wanted something so badly that it was all you lived for?" he said, handing her a candle. Their fingers touched.

"I don't have those kinds of passions. I wish I did." Penrose looked at the flame. She'd never burned bright for anything.

"No, you don't. It's a desperate feeling. A compulsion. Sometimes you don't know why you're doing it, you just can't stop." He sighed, and it was a lonely sound.

They'd worked so hard and still he wasn't pleased. She walked closer to the water's edge, leaned down and placed her candle in the water. It bobbed but remained lit and began to move away from the shore, directed by some unseen current. It seemed a hopeful omen.

She turned around and was surprised by Carrick's expression as he looked at her. In all her days, she would never forget the sight of that look. It was a look of pain but also one of surprise. His eyes were wide and almost appeared shocked. His mouth was drawn down at the corners. "What's the matter?" she asked.

"I just realized something." He seemed faraway and lost in thought as he spoke. "We are like that candle floating on the water. We have one brief moment to shine before we're doomed to the dark mercy of the fate. One little moment. Think on that, Penny." He shook his head. "And I was chasing the wrong thing the entire time."

She went and put her hands over his. "No, you weren't. Of course, you weren't."

Almost as if the universe disagreed with her, the candle on the water bobbed and, with a hiss, the flame disappeared.

A cynical, half laugh came from Carrick. "Penny," he said. "Fire has no choice but to grab its moment, whatever moment it's given, and burn. I know this now, and I burn for the wrong thing, don't I?" He bent down and picked up another candle and went to the water.

"Don't," she said, suddenly afraid of another flame disappearing. Suddenly it seemed so hopeless.

He turned away from her, leaned down and placed the candle on the water. "Even if its fate is doomed, it still has to burn. It can't miss its moment. Even if it's the wrong one."

The night sky seemed big and vast and dark above them. It frightened her. Her voice was too sharp when she spoke. "It's not dark mercy, Carrick. It's indifference. The water doesn't care if the candle sinks."

Turning around, he looked at her and said, "Whatever we call it, the truth is that we have such a short amount of time." His brows drew together, his eyes dark. "It's so easy to get lost."

She stepped closer to him, and he wrapped his arms around her. His touch soothed her. Looking at him, she asked, "So this moment right here, you think this could be our one chance at happiness?"

He placed a finger beneath her chin and lifted her gaze to his. "I hope there are many more. But let's treat it as it is. As if this is all we have." He took her hand. "Come, lie on the blanket with me. Let's look at the sky."

They went to the blanket and lay down. Carrick propped himself up on one elbow, and she lay beside him, tilting her head back to look at him. He was so handsome in the moonlight. Behind him stretched the night sky, dotted with stars, petulant and flickering.

She bit her lip and looked at him, knowing what was coming but nervous just the same.

Leaning forward, his lips came down, gentle but insistent.

She lifted up, meeting his kiss eagerly.

He responded by kissing her harder, guiding her to the blanket and pushing her down upon it. Never in her whole life would she tire of the feel or the smell of him. He stole the thoughts from her mind, and she was left with only reactions. Reactions to his touch and the need for more.

Then he hugged her and whispered in her ear, "If there were only one day left and this were it…if this were all I had, I would be a happy man, because this…" His lips touched hers. "This is heaven."

With a will of their own, her hands crossed his chest as she pushed the shirt from his shoulders. Running her hands over his warm skin, she drank in the feel of all that strength bound beneath his skin. How could his skin look so fragile and his body be so strong? He was like lightning, beautiful and bright. And scary.

A wild need overwhelmed her. She wanted the lightning. She wanted all of him, everywhere at once. Lifting her skirt, she tried to shove his hand beneath it, but it got tangled in the fabric.

"Here," he said, lifting her to sitting. She faced away from him while he traced a finger along the row of buttons that ran down her back. "Patience," he murmured. "If this is our one night, let's linger."

Unlike the night before, he moved with aching slowness unbuttoning her dress. His fingers trailed from button to button, his lips kissing each section of exposed flesh. Finally, he shrugged the dress and undershirt from her shoulders. Night air swept over her bare skin, and she turned cool, with only his hot touch to anchor her.

Those hands, hot as sin, slipped around her waist to her breasts and traced rings of fire around her nipples. Her whimper sounded out into the night and turned the crickets silent.

He took a sharp breath and his fingers dug into her flesh. Roughly, he rubbed his palms back and forth over her nipples before cupping each breast fully and squeezing them greedily.

"Yes. Yes," she said in a dreamy voice, lost to the sensations and craving more.

He grabbed again at her, fully yanking her dress from her body. She helped, grabbing at her undergarments and pulling them off. Then she was nude and helping him shed his clothes.

He pulled her on top of him with her back against his chest. They both looked up at the night sky and saw above them a universe of lights, scattered stars, long ago locked into their positions, petulant and flickering. She felt so exposed. To him. To the night air. To the universe above.

His hands ran down her torso, right to the center of her. When he touched that spot, that one little spot, she cried out, spread her legs and raised her hips into the air, opening herself more fully to touch. He seized the opportunity, and, with one hand, he cupped her buttocks while the other moved deeper, pushing two fingers inside her. She arced her shoulders against his chest. His touch was exquisite, and she couldn't help writhing about and bucking against him.

It didn't take long. Swiftly, Carrick lifted her and placed her beneath him on the blanket. He loomed above her, and she stared at him in wonder. Never breaking eye contact, he parted her legs and pushed himself inside of her. She felt a slow piercing that filled her and made her moan.

A long, drawn-out groan came from his throat. He lifted her hands above her head and pinned them to the ground. Then, he thrust fully into her, hard. Letting her know who was in charge. She was aware of an exquisite, full sensation. Again and again, he entered her with slow, powerful, deep thrusts until she experienced that delicious feeling between her legs and she met him thrust for thrust. Until she begged him, "Faster, please." He obliged until once more her cries silenced the crickets.

Afterward, their bodies lay knotted together on the blanket. Hours passed until fragile dawn gathered in the east. Half the sky was the inky color of night, and the other half was the peachy hue of the morning.

Light and dark were evenly balanced. The world held its breath. For a moment, it looked as if the light might change its mind and flee. But then, a crescent sliver of the sun appeared over the trees and night shrank away, defeated. She smiled.

Her clothes lay in the dewy grass, and she stood up and gathered them, shaking the moisture from them before dressing. Waking up Carrick, she said, "Let's go to bed." She blushed to hear her words. Because after just two nights, they already felt natural to say.

Once in his bedroom, Penrose opened the windows. She lay beside him and listened to the sounds of the morning settling in. In her heart, she knew everything was changing. The world would soon see his brilliant creation and learn his name. She fell asleep with a smile on her face, certain that the future was bright.

Chapter 10

When Carrick woke up in the morning, he announced that they would formally unveil the mechanical man that evening and attempt to power him up. His enthusiasm was contagious, and spirits ran high. Even C.J. was excited. Carrick surprised everyone by announcing he wanted to set Harris Two up in the great room. "A place of prominence." He smiled at Penrose. "Don't worry, Penny, I know it will work. Even if it doesn't, I'm not discouraged. Not one bit."

Carrick and C.J. fiddled with Harris for most of the early evening. They wouldn't let Penrose downstairs into the workshop, telling her, "It's going to be a surprise." When the clock struck nine, they brought the new Harris up from the workshop but made Penrose go into the other room until they had him set up and covered with the sheet. He sat in a place of prominence in the great room, right in the center, looking almost like a ghost with the sheet covering him.

Penrose had prepared a small spread of food—grapes, cheeses, cookies and bread with jam. On an impulse, she grabbed a bottle of wine she'd found in the kitchen. Since it was a celebration, she even made sure C.J. looked his best, telling him to go and change his shirt and wash his face.

While C.J. was gone, Carrick poured two glasses of wine.

The red wine was potent and stung her tongue. "Here's to second chances," she said, lifting her glass.

"Hear, hear," he replied with a smile as they clinked their glasses. "Penny," he said in a low, conspiratorial voice, running his hand around her waist. "After C.J. goes to bed, come outside with me. Let's lie under the stars again and turn one night of heaven into two."

"Yes," she said, smiling, her heart pounding in her chest.

Just then, C.J. came back downstairs, looking handsome in his dark trouser shorts and white shirt. They gathered around the mechanical man, staring at him in a quiet wonder. Then with a flourish, Carrick removed the covering, and Harris Two gleamed triumphantly in the candlelight, his wooden arms at his side, and his legs stiff as boards with rollers underneath him.

It was an amazing sight, and the three of them fell silent. "Should we start him?" asked Penrose.

Carrick nodded at C.J. "How about you start him up?" he asked.

C.J. stepped forward somberly as if it were a great honor. He went behind Harris, to the battery pack, touched the wires together, and everyone waited, eyes trained on Harris.

She heard the faintest buzzing noise. Harris shivered to life, jerked, hesitated and then began to move. He inched forward, rolling along, his stick legs straight and his barrel chest proud. His bright silver eyes gleamed with hope and promise as he slowly, gracefully, lifted one spindly arm. He waved.

Laughing with delight, she clapped her hands and said, "It looks like he's saluting the future." Raising her hand, she waved back at him.

Standing beside her, Carrick took Penrose's hand into his. "He is," he said.

C.J.'s head turned. He looked at them holding hands, and he smiled shyly at Penrose.

Harris continued to wave. It was such a simple movement, and anyone looking in might think it foolish. But Penrose knew better. Harris *was* the future. He was their hope and, better yet, he was their renewal. Two failed projects had come together to create a new vision. *Please let it last.*

They ate and drank, laughed a lot, and Carrick talked about his plans. It delighted Penrose to see him animated and happy.

Afterward, she cleared the food and dishes and carried them to the kitchen. Setting down the plates on the counter, she heard Carrick yelling in an angry tone and ran back to see what was happening.

C.J. stood in the doorway of the great room, a knife in hand, gouging a mark into the wood. Sawdust lay sprinkled around his feet. Carrick towered over him, a harsh look on his face. He yelled at the boy, "There are hundreds of marks here! How long have you been doing this?"

"Carrick," Penrose said, walking up to them.

C.J. looked from Penrose to Carrick and back again. "I… I can't explain it," he began to say, when suddenly he threw the knife down and ran from the room.

Penrose chased him into the foyer. "C.J.!" she shouted. But he ignored her, opening the front door, running outside and down the steps without looking back or closing the door. She was standing there wondering what to do, when Carrick called to her.

"Come back, Penny. It's okay, he'll be back."

Sighing, she went back to the great room and found Carrick standing and looking at the door frame. "Look at these marks," he said. "I can't believe I haven't noticed it before now. Some marks look old. Others are new." He shook his head. "He must have been doing this a long time."

"There has to be a reason for it," said Penrose, looking closely. She saw the marks that she'd noticed on the first day. The vertical hash marks in groups of five. She shrugged. "I don't know. I saw them on my first day here. But, because he's your son, there's a genius in his reasoning."

Carrick laughed. "You're probably right. I didn't mean to be so hard on him." He sighed. "I still have a lot to learn."

"Do you want to go outside and get him, or should I?" she asked.

Carrick slipped his hands around Penrose's waist and pulled her tight. "Let the boy go," he said. "I didn't mean to scare him. And, look, he ran outside, not into the tunnel. It's a step in the right direction. He has a lot to learn, too."

Pressing his cheek against hers, he whispered into her ear, "Plus, it gives us a moment alone. A stolen moment with your lips."

He leaned down and kissed her. He was warm, and his hands were strong at her back. She loved the scent of him, the feel of his stubble against her cheek, but nothing compared to his lips against hers. The second he kissed her, the world fell away, leaving the two of them, which was just fine by her. The kiss deepened. He pulled her closer, his hands all business.

She pushed back gently and whispered in a soft voice, "Later, Carrick."

"Promise?" he said.

Nodding, she laughed. "Of course."

He gave an exaggerated sigh. "Well, that leaves me with the chore of putting Harris away."

"I'll finish the dishes." She kissed him on the cheek. "We'll meet later," she promised. Returning to the kitchen, she began stacking the dishes, listening to the sounds of crickets as she worked.

Suddenly, the crickets stopped chirping. The silence was booming, overwhelmingly louder than their songs. She stopped, an eerie fear creeping up her skin. From the distance, there came a low roar. How strange.

She set down the dish and listened. A throaty, rolling growl came from somewhere far away, out in the night. It sounded like a train approaching from a great distance. She peered out of the window, half expecting to see the light from a train splitting the darkness. But there was none, just the twinkle of stars. A pungent odor rose in the air, almost like sulfur.

The sound grew louder, angrier and closer.

The plates on the counter rattled. The chairs vibrated around the table. Unsteady, Penrose held out her hands as her eyes darted all around her, trying to figure out what was happening. A rumble surged beneath her feet. The house shuddered. The dish she'd set on the counter fell to the floor and shattered.

Carrick yelled to her from the workshop, "Earthquake! Get out, Penny! Get out!"

Earthquake! In Charleston? Impossible.

But the ground heaved again and she knew the truth of his words. Then the sound of crunching stone and shattering glass as the kitchen window burst drowned out Carrick's screams. Another surge exploded beneath her feet, bucking Penrose into the air, and she fell to the floor.

The gas lamp shattered, plunging her into darkness. Her thoughts fractured into a thousand worries, but she focused on Carrick's words. She needed to get out—and fast. She stood and tumbled forward.

The house made horrid, loud protests to the shaking as she lurched into the hallway. She was dimly aware of her surroundings. Pictures falling, walls cracking and windows shattering. Her world had frighteningly turned very wrong. The ground could not be trusted. A particularly big tremor came, and she fell hard to her knees. It took a moment before she recovered, and when she stood, she saw C.J. at the front doors.

He stood there holding on to the frame for dear life. She watched in horror as the grandfather clock rocked from side to side, tilted, and then came crashing down.

C.J. was shouting at her, screaming, but the chaos

and wild noises drowned him out. He looked so afraid, in a panic.

She knew where he was going. The tunnel. The most dangerous place in an earthquake. Stumbling forward, she raised her hand to him. "Stop!" she shouted. "Don't go inside! It's dangerous!"

His face, contorted in shock and fear, seemed not to register her words. He let go of the door frame, and the shaking earth pitched him forward. He landed right in front of the door of the tunnel, which swung open and shut with the shaking earth. An eerie blue-and-white light flicked from within the tunnel, and above him the chandelier swung wildly.

A primitive scream tore from deep within her. She kept her gaze on C.J., willing him to turn back. Time slowed as she raced toward him, trying to stop him from going to the one place he considered safe. Horrified, she watched as he dropped to his knees and disappeared into the opening. She had to get him out. In a wild leap, she dove headfirst and slid across the floor, following him into the open door. The darkness swallowed her whole.

Part Two

Out of the night that covers me,
Black as the pit from pole to pole,
I thank whatever gods may be
For my unconquerable soul.

—William Ernest Henley

Chapter 11

The earthquake seemed unbelievable. But this, Penrose realized, looking around the kitchen and rereading the note, this was unreal. She held out a last, thin thread of hope that Carrick might be in the workshop, and she ran down the stairs that led to his space. The smells that greeted her in the stairwell were familiar and even comforting, and she breathed in the scent of metal, wood and grease. Finally, one thing that gave her hope.

When she reached the floor, the workshop was dark, and it was hard to see. After taking a few steps, she looked up and stopped cold. Shadows stretched across the walls, revealing a handful of dark shapes that loomed in front of her. Shapes that looked like people.

The forms stood stoic and motionless, like ghost soldiers standing at attention.

She stood still, her hands half raised, her legs paused midstride. Her gaze darted around the room.

She watched and waited for one of the mannequins to move, half hoping they would move, half hoping they wouldn't. But not a single one flinched.

After what felt like a million years, she crept forward, ready to bolt. When nothing moved in response, she burst into a run and fled up the stairs. Running without thinking, she sped down the foyer and up the grand staircase, heading straight to the one place she felt safe—her bedroom.

Barging into the attic bedroom, she saw that it too had changed. Her bed was gone. Tables crowded the space and were piled high with the chaotic look of junk. Even the safest place she knew petrified her. Leaning against the wall, she slid to the floor sobbing, not willing to get up, unable to take even one more step in that terrible house of shadows.

After an eternity of staring blankly at the still and strange room, she slept.

A dull gray light filtered through Penrose's eyelids. She opened her eyes. Dust motes flitted about her, glowing in the sunlight. Confused, she squinted and blinked, trying to understand what she was looking at. Her dress was filthy, coated with grime, and her hair hung in strands around shoulders. She looked at the strange sight that used to be her bedroom.

And then she remembered. Everything rushed back. She stood up, bones aching from sleeping on the floor, muscles sore, and looked, really looked, at the room.

The morning sun was harsh as it illuminated the room. Colorful metallic arms and legs lay strewn on tables and all over the floor. The limbs were very clearly fashioned after the human body but made of a shiny and hard-looking substance. Her nightmare was real.

Morbid curiosity drove her to walk over and touch a leg. A cool, hard surface greeted her finger, and she yanked her hand back. Why wouldn't this strange torture end? What had she done wrong to deserve it? She'd done one thing wrong. She'd stolen the destiny of another person. Perhaps this was penance.

Walking the room, she went to the closet and opened it. It was no longer a closet, but a washroom with a sink and a toilet. The toilet looked so very different, yet its purpose was immediately clear. She pressed a lever on the side of the toilet, and jumped back in shock when the water began to swirl and then disappear right before her eyes.

The sight and sounds of the water reminded her of the very real urge she had. A practical part of her urged her to go to the bathroom, and when her bladder agreed, she did so, making sure to press the lever afterward.

The very basic act soothed her. It reminded her that a person resided in the home. Not ghosts.

The sink impressed her as well, its steamy hot water shooting out from the faucet when she turned the handle. She washed her hands and face, brushed the dust from her hair and then smoothed it down. She tried to wind it back up into a bun, a task she abandoned when the house began to shake and she heard a thunderous roar.

Her first thought wasn't fear, but joy. The earthquake made loud unusual noises, perhaps another one was coming, she thought foolishly as she rushed from the washroom. Maybe it would bring her back to the home she knew. On shaky legs, hopping over limbs, lifting her skirts to do so, she made her way to the window. The sound intensified, became sharper, and the roar changed to an incessant thwacking noise.

She went to the large circular window, which was now covered by a drape. She craned forward but still couldn't reach the drape. The sound continued, loud and getting louder. Winds buffeted the window and rattled the panes. She had to find out what made that noise. Climbing onto the windowsill, she leaned forward, pulled back the curtain the tiniest bit and peered outside.

Charleston was gone.

The world had been scrubbed of life. Windblown grasses tumbled over a snow-covered prairie that held nothing at all to catch the eye except for shadowy mountains that lurked on the horizon. A huge swath of sky stretched in all directions, the bleak blue of a winter day. The green lawn, the duck pond, the ancient oak with its limbs dragging along the ground—they were all gone. In their place was a bonfire pit, and a road that snaked through the landscape—a black surface glistening in the sun, with clumps of snow clustered at the edges.

Clumps of snow. A sky of winter blue. Arundell Manor stood at the edge of the world.

The windows rattled again, and the roar grew so loud that the sound seemed to be inside the room with her. She looked up and saw a huge, metallic dragonfly speeding past her window. As she watched, it slowed, sounds chopping the air as it hovered over the ground before setting down gently.

* * *

Keat Carrick Arundell guided the helicopter low over the manor, visually inspecting his home. Everything was just fine, but then again, everything always was. That was how he liked it, how he demanded it. The home had been well cared for during his year-long absence. The swimming pool covered for winter, firewood freshly stacked beside the garage, the snow plowed from the driveway and landing pad. On the patio, the hot tub steamed invitingly. Inside, he knew that the house would be spotless and completely stocked for his arrival. Everything was in order—as it always was.

After all, his staff knew his habits, knew to have the house ready and to make themselves scarce for the month. Every December, he lived at Arundell. Like a programmed robot, his life operated on schedule, as it had since the day he was born. As heir to the Arundell fortune and CEO of Arundell Industries, he lived according to standard operating procedure. And the user manual dictated he spend every December at Arundell because it was what he'd always done, ever since he was a kid. He liked things that way, orderly and under his command. Control was vital.

He guided the chopper to the landing pad, passing the garages where he stored his toys, and the Range Rover waiting in the driveway for his use. His gaze swept over the house again. It was a major production to move the house, but it had been worth it. As Arundell Industries grew into the largest robotics company in the world, the family fame and fortune grew with it. Security became a real problem.

Thirty years ago, his father, Carrick Arundell IV,

who loved the family home as much as he did the family history, came up with a solution that kept their ancestral home intact while providing them space and privacy. As an added bonus, it gave them a shorter commute to Silicon Valley, which became a necessity when the robotics industry exploded.

Now, coming to Arundell was his annual retreat. In order to run the company, he had to live in the valley— and he loved all of the excitement it brought him. But he also loved to unwind and get away. To be Zen with his ideas. This month-long retreat to his beloved home would give him countless hours free of distractions to do what he did best. What every Arundell did best.

Create robots.

He now set the chopper down gently, listening to the engine as it spooled to silent. He removed his helmet, revealing a thick head of jet-black hair, clipped short. He looked out at the skies. Clouds towered behind the mountains. He'd beaten the storm, but not by much. Once the clouds made it over the ridge, they'd bring plenty of snow. Wouldn't bother him one bit. Hibernation sounded just fine.

Grabbing his bags, he jumped out of the chopper and walked around it, checking the landing gear, and once satisfied that everything was in order, he began to walk to the house.

A shrill cry split the cold winter air. A woman's cry. Looking up, he promptly stopped in his tracks, his gaze locked on the attic window. The bright sun fell on the window, illuminating the unmistakable outline of a woman. A pale hand held back the curtain, and a porcelain face peered out at him. A china doll with jet-black hair.

It couldn't be. It must be a trick of the light. Increasing his stride, he ripped the sunglasses from his face and watched a ghostly silhouette recede into the shadows.

"What in the hell?" he said, and stormed toward the house.

Penrose watched the jaw-dropping sight of a dark-haired twin to Carrick jumping down from the flying contraption and walking toward the manor. In this strange, mixed-up world, white had turned to black, summer warmth had turned to winter cold, and her hope now turned to despair. Still, she wanted to believe. They were almost the same height, with the same lanky, muscular body and, most disturbing of all, the same sharp features.

Perhaps it was Carrick, she thought, half convincing herself. She was too nervous and too scared to feel anything but relief at his familiar form. She couldn't stop herself from reaching out, touching the window in longing and yelling, "Carrick!"

Instantly, the man's head snapped in her direction, and he stared up at the window, wearing strange glasses that blackened his face.

He began walking in angry steps toward the house, looking right at her window as he did so. Incredibly, this man's hair was dark, raven-black just like her own. The hairs on her neck rose and dread filled her soul as she realized he was not Carrick. Where Carrick brooded in anger, this man striding toward her prowled, eating up the space between them.

The curtains fell from her fingers. She was in danger. He was coming to her, she felt it. She edged away from the window inch by inch, hoping her slow movements would conceal her. She'd never been so afraid and yet so drawn to a man before.

The front door opened, once a familiar, comforting sound. But now it now petrified her. A moment later, it slammed shut, hard enough that she felt vibrations under her feet. Footsteps pounded up the stairs.

She had to hide. Scrambling, she leaped from the windowsill and tumbled onto the floor, knowing she had only one place to turn: the dark tunnels that she swore she'd never enter again. Jumping up, her feet a blur of motion, she careened forward, arms outstretched, and dove for the tunnel door, scattered the strange limbs in all directions. Her hands slammed into the door, and she desperately grabbed at the seam, trying to open it, but a thick coat of paint sealed it shut.

Like a drum, his footsteps continued to beat up the stairs. She could tell by the sounds of his footfalls that she had only seconds to disappear. The door she pressed on was as stubborn as always. It refused to open.

"Please," she begged, slamming her fist into it again and again. It wouldn't budge. Desperate, she flew forward, shoulder first, ramming her body against the door, and heard the quiet click that she once feared. The tunnel door had opened.

The door to the attic rattled just as the darkness revealed itself to her, and without looking, without thinking, without pausing, she dove into the blackness, knowing it was her one hope. She yanked the door closed behind her and flung herself to the floor, panting, shaking and shivering. Waiting.

The bedroom door creaked as it opened, and she

heard footsteps. "Hello?" The voice was velvety. Deep. The rich timbre of it startled her. "Who's in here?"

Keat paced the attic. The room crackled with an energy that told him someone had just been there. No doubt about it. It angered him. He felt violated.

Raising his voice, he asked the question again. "Is anyone in here?" There had to be. He'd even heard noises as he came up the stairs. "I'm warning you to come out now."

There was no answer, but there was a presence. Christ, there was a presence.

He walked into the bathroom, looked at the sink and saw faint droplets of water around edge. He ran his fingers over the cold drops. Someone was here. Enraged, he stormed back into the attic, stood in the middle of the room and shouted, "Whoever you are, come out right now!"

But no one answered. Nothing moved.

He went to the window, lifted the curtain and looked outside, thinking through the possibility a person had actually been in the room. The way he saw it, the odds were somewhere between impossible and not a chance in hell. No one could slip past the perimeter. It was patrolled. It was digitally monitored and had a laser beam to detect anyone crossing over the boundary.

With such a fail-safe system guarding the perimeter, Keat never felt the need for a security system inside the house. The only technologies at Arundell Manor were Keat's robots and his cell phone. He liked it that way. It had never been an issue. Until just that moment.

He looked around the room again. Maybe he was wrong. It was possible that his assistant, Valerie, could have used the sink up here when she prepared the house for his arrival. It was entirely possible, now that he considered it. He dug in his pocket, whipped out his cell phone and called Valerie.

"Hello, Keat," she said, answering on the first ring in her no-nonsense voice. "Did you get my note in the kitchen? Is there a problem—"

He cut her off. "Did you use the attic bedroom upstairs?" He sounded harsher than he intended.

"No, of course not. No one was up there."

"You're certain?"

"Yes, of course. Why, what's the matter?"

"I'm trying to figure that out. I'll be in touch," he said, ending the call. He spoke out loud, not knowing exactly who or what lay hidden in the room and was listening to him speak. "Someone or something was here and I promise I'll get to the bottom of it."

He stormed from the room, trying to keep his emotions in check. Really, he should be reasonable. The chances were so very slim. He had a lot to accomplish and couldn't waste time chasing ghosts. Besides, what were the odds?

Chapter 12

Penrose heard him leave the room. Then the only sound was the beating of her heart. It was so very black in the tunnel. But the darkness was a blanket that comforted her, kept her hidden, and for the first time, she understood why C.J. hid in the walls. Better to hide in a secret place than to be in a world that was so very frightening.

She lay there, overwhelmed, wondering how two men could be nearly identical in features, and yet the difference was night and day. Try as she might, she couldn't forget the sight of that man or the deep timbre of his voice. But he sounded like a Northerner when he spoke.

Hidden, she waited uncountable minutes, thoughts tumbling as she crouched in the space. Every creak and groan in the house traveled to her in eerie waves. Scratching noises came from somewhere behind her, and she tried not to imagine what was causing them.

Minutes turned to hours. Dust and darkness were her only companions. She hardened her mind just as she'd done when her mother had died, shoving out feelings, coldly tallying needs and necessities. She shuddered at what she had to do. It was almost unthinkable, but it was her only hope. She had to get to C.J.'s little room in the tunnel where she could safely sit and think. She must go even deeper into the tunnel.

Taking a shaky breath, she began. She crawled blind, afraid to stand, moving along inch by agonizing inch, unsure if her eyes were open or closed. Sticky cobwebs grabbed on to her fingers as she swept her hands back and forth in front of her. More than anything she wanted to yank her hands away, but she couldn't. The ladder lay somewhere ahead of her, and she needed to find the notches in the floor so she wouldn't fall into the hole. It seemed that she crawled for hours, but finally she felt the rough grooves under her fingers. Turning around, she gathered her skirts about her waist and began to descend into the belly of the house.

Down, down, down she went until she was convinced that the ladder stretched straight into hell. Then her foot touched solid ground. She took a few steps, sliding her hands along the wall. The cold, damp stone scared her, but she needed to have something to guide her.

She pressed ahead until her breath didn't echo back as quickly and she didn't feel as contained. The space had opened up. Fairly certain that she was in C.J.'s room, she ran her hands along the wall again until she bumped into something.

Something wooden. Her fingers danced over the object figuring out what it was. C.J.'s desk.

She rummaged over it. She gave a tiny shout of joy

when her hand bumped into the familiar tin box that held the candles and matches. Nervous, she fumbled with the matches until she managed to strike one. It sputtered and went out. She tried again, and the flame arced to life.

For the first time since the earthquake, she smiled. Light. It was the sweetest thing she'd ever seen. Touching the flame to the candle, she looked around her. The space was exactly as she remembered it. Even the wooden mannequins were slumped against the wall in one corner, the mechanical bird placed almost lovingly between them.

C.J.'s makeshift bed lay in the other corner with the covers all bunched up. She rushed over to it, hoping he might be asleep under the covers. When she pulled them away, the fabric came apart in her hands. She was left holding nothing but shreds and looking at an empty bed.

"No!" she cried, the word echoing in the stony room. She thought of Carrick and C.J. In her heart, she knew with absolute certainty that they weren't here. Where were they? She didn't want to acknowledge the awful thought that swirled in the back of her mind. She had to believe that they were alive, that they had survived the earthquake and were right now comforting each other. It didn't seem very likely.

She sank to her knees while the candle beside her burned brightly. The last thing she wanted to do was cry, but she couldn't stop the hot tears that splashed onto the ground. She would rather rage than cry, but she didn't want that man to hear her. He wouldn't exactly come running to her aid. Wiping the tears from her cheeks, she resigned herself to the truth of her predicament. Something terrible had happened, and though she didn't understand it, she needed to accept it. Possibilities streamed through her mind, each one too frightening to consider.

Not long after that, she heard the man, Keat—he must be the man from the letter—thundering down the stairs. Since C.J.'s room was beneath the stairway his steps sent booming echoes into the space. The front door opened and then, a moment later, it banged shut. She listened keenly, waiting for another noise. Everything was silent, and she knew he'd left the house.

She huddled in the orange glow of the candle, her hands linked together over the flame, seeking a comfort the fire couldn't provide. She had to face some facts. She couldn't be dreaming, or even dead. Her body was still alive. Needful. Hunger gnawed at her, and her dry mouth tasted like chalk. Thank goodness, she'd used the strange washroom, but right now, she needed to find some way to eat.

The only real choice was to wait until the middle of the night and sneak out to find necessities, and hopefully gather some information about what exactly had happened to her. Maybe find a way home, a little voice inside of her whispered. That little voice felt very fragile and what it said seemed almost impossible to achieve.

The front door opened again. She heard his footsteps and the muffled noises of a house coming to life. Very normal sounds, ones that shouldn't scare a person. Yet they scared her senseless. She listened for every noise, trying to guess his whereabouts and what he was doing. Even though she was scared, she knew that she needed a plan and, at the very least, more information.

Convincing herself that she should know the layout of the tunnel, she grabbed an extra candle and some matches and made her way out of the room. Moving quietly, she explored, discovering that vents lined the walls. She didn't notice them at first because they were all closed, shut tight and hard to see. But little streaks of light coming through the slats drew her eye. She figured out that if she wriggled her fingers between the slats, she could force one open wide enough for her to peek out. The tiny opening provided slips of light that illuminated the crawlspace.

Using her candle, she spent the afternoon moving from vent to vent, peering into each room. The vents gave her a birds-eye view. Each room she saw was like looking at a perverse painting of the home she knew only yesterday. Except for the workshop. She found the vent to the workshop and approached it hesitantly, still nervous about the shadowy human forms she'd seen. She pressed her face against the vent, peered out and saw the men from the night before.

Lined up in straight rows, a half dozen men stood lifeless and still. They wore matching dark jumpsuits, were the same height, and their facial features were identical. The expressions on their faces were smooth, too smooth. The longer she stared, the more oddities she noticed. Their skin was too waxy, their hair looked painted on.

Instantly, Penrose knew what she was looking at. Mechanical men.

Her grip around the slats tightened. These mechanical men were fantastical, almost unbelievable. The thoughts in her brain whipped around like a tornado. Possibility after possibility leaped into her mind, and her hands shook with delight. She couldn't wait to tell Carrick.

Carrick. She couldn't tell Carrick anything. Just to think the name caused an ache in her soul.

Just then, the man—Keat—strode into the room wearing denim jeans and a black shirt. Her heart stopped at the sight of him.

He resembled Carrick with one profound difference beyond the jet-black hair. Carrick was driven, the need to create etched into tight expression that was always on his face. This man? He was driven, but he had the satisfied look of a man who had achieved his goals. He didn't have the burning look of need. He had achieved. There was no other way to describe the cool confidence he displayed. He looked fierce, yes, intense, yes, but this man had the easy, almost sated expression of a man at the height of his achievements. She couldn't tear her eyes away.

A five-o'clock shadow shaded his jaw and outlined his perfect lips. A longing swept over her, hot and needy, surprising her with its fierce intensity.

But there were too many similarities between Carrick and Keat to ignore. Face pressed against the vent, she studied him closer, looking for discrepancies. But the differences were minor. Keat's lips were a fraction thinner, his height an inch taller.

She shuddered as chills ran through her, which deepened to goose bumps as she considered what it all meant. So similar, yet different. Just like the strange and scary Arundell she now hid in compared to what she had left behind.

There was only one explanation for this similarity. It was hard for her to accept the impossible, but the resemblance between the men was so strong that she couldn't deny it. This man was related to Carrick. No doubt about it.

The incredibly complex mechanical men, the flying contraption. Keat. She must have come forward in time. Because she certainly hadn't gone back in time. Somehow, the earthquake must have propelled her forward—as unbelievable as that sounded. Yet the proof was all around her—she just didn't know how far ahead she'd come. But, staring at all the strange things in the room, she knew it was a significant amount of time.

It was hard to accept. It would be far easier to think herself gone mad—or dead—but the facts came together in support of one hard truth. She was witnessing the proof of it.

She watched as Keat sat down at a workbench, sipped a cup of coffee and stared at a small white device he held in his hand. He kept touching it, swiping his finger across it. Occasionally he'd frown at it and Penrose found herself wondering what captivated him so. Finally, he set it aside, stood up and went to a large chest against the wall by the fireplace. He opened the doors and pulled something out.

She saw a quick flash of blue before he turned his back and blocked her view. Whatever it was, he hovered over it for a few minutes and then he spoke out loud.

"Power up, Harris," said Keat.

Harris. He'd spoken the name *Harris*. She leaned forward intently, straining to hear every word. But all she heard was odd whirring noises. Keat stepped away, revealing another mechanical man. This one was different than the others. It was smaller, half the size of a person, with metallic blue skin and a helmet for a head.

A black screen covered the front of the helmet. He was like a shiny, miniature human. Childlike.

An image illuminated on the blank screen that covered the mechanical man's face. Its facial expressions sprang to life and looked like a painting in motion. Its eyes blinked, and its mouth moved, and the mechanical man—Harris—spoke. "Hello, Keat," it said in a droll, monotone voice that was unsettling to hear. "Good morning to you."

"Good Morning, Harris," said Keat. "Are you ready to begin work?"

"I'm always ready to work, Keat."

Harris. This was a newer version of Harris. She remembered the first Harris, her Harris, with his stout iron body and his lantern eyes. That Harris seemed childish compared to this version of Harris. But that didn't matter at all. What really mattered was the truth of what she was witnessing.

Carrick had done it.

He'd changed the world. He'd left a legacy. If only she could tell him. She hoped that he survived the earthquake to witness it. It pained her to have such a morbid thought, but that was the truth of it. The horrible reality.

She watched for hours as Keat worked with Harris and the other mechanical men. She learned a new word for them: robot. Again and again she heard Keat use the word. It was a thing of beauty to watch Keat in the workshop, and the afternoon sped by. It was a strange thing to assess a man so similar in looks and demeanor to her Carrick. It was stranger still to be attracted to both men.

She noticed other differences. Where Carrick was an artist at heart when he invented, this man was a conductor. The robots around him were like musicians in an orchestra, and he was constantly moving, jumping from table to table, pushing buttons and pulling levers. He had dozens of robots turned on at once, all of them performing different tasks, moving with elegance and grace. Like a colorful band, they performed their tasks.

Penrose was riveted. This man was impassioned, sexy and at ease with himself. She recognized another similarity between the two men. They were happiest when they were deep in thought, creating robots. He seemed to be focusing on Harris, the blue robot. Whenever Harris talked, the screen lit up on his helmet.

Every time she saw the familiar smile tug at Keat's lips, or the tight, intense expression on his face as he worked, she remembered the same expressions from Carrick. She couldn't help comparing the men. Keat was different. He didn't seem angry at the world.

After Keat had left the workshop, she made her way back to C.J.'s room. Once there, she ran her fingers over the wooden mannequins. The wood was dry and aged. They seemed so lifeless; dead.

She couldn't help remembering the conversation that she'd had with Carrick on her first night at Arundell. When she asked him how he gave the mechanical man life, he told her that he simply made them move.

Thinking of the bright-eyed, newest version of Harris, she realized that Keat had some essential element that Carrick didn't. For Keat didn't just make the mechanical men move, he gave them life.

Chapter 13

Keat loved the workshop. Maybe it was because it offered direct connection to his memories of his childhood and with his love of inventing. He'd spent countless hours next to his father in this very spot. The space soothed him. He could've built a bigger, modern workshop, but it wouldn't be the same. It wouldn't have the same scuff marks on the floor, the same smells and the same rusty tools.

Even though there was a massive, subzero storage facility beneath him, housing all the computing power he'd ever need and countless spare parts and previous prototypes, he preferred to work in this space.

He communicated via email and text to corporate every morning. After that, he turned his phone off to work on Harris. Harris #142, to be exact, the latest prototype in development.

Robots would soon be in every household, and Keat

intended to be the front-runner. He worked on it every moment he could and fell asleep thinking of it.

The project was a daunting one. The prototype had problems from day one. The newest trouble was with voltage regulation. It demanded his full attention because everything came to a halt if the battery pack wasn't working right.

Removing the plastic casing from the back of the robot, he grabbed a pair of needle-nose pliers and threw himself into solving the problem. For the first time since he'd arrived, he was able to wipe thoughts of the dark-haired woman from his mind. She'd haunted his thoughts.

Starving and thirsty beyond reason, every minute felt like an hour to Penrose as she waited for the house to quiet down. Finally, the velvety chimes of the grandfather clock struck two in the morning. She slipped her shoes and stockings off and opened the little door that led to the foyer. Slowly, cautiously, she crept out into the hallway. Keat could be around any corner or hiding in any shadow, waiting to pounce on her and…and what? She didn't even want to think about the answer to that question because every outcome seemed awful.

The marble felt cool and hard beneath her feet as she padded silently toward the kitchen. Once there, she grabbed a banana and three apples, careful to take what wouldn't be noticed. She used her skirt to hold the fruit. A closet door was open, and by the faint blue light that shone from one of the strange devices in the room, she saw a box with the word "cookies" on it. She impulsively grabbed that, too. Even though she was hungry

enough to take much more, she knew she shouldn't, and
began to walk back to the tunnel.

She stopped in front of the great room. The flickering light that shone from the room still called to her.
Needing to know what caused it, she entered the room
and looked around, ignoring the pit of dread in her
stomach that told her to run. But she couldn't run. She
had to know.

The light came from an enormous picture frame that
hung on the wall. There were images inside of it that
looked as real as the world she stood in. And the pho-
tographs moved. The images were in motion. Penrose
went closer and, when she saw what the images contained, her knees almost buckled.

A man carrying a gun chased a group of people on
the street. They screamed in horror, soundless. The
image faded, switched, and she saw a person sitting at a
desk, the words "evening news" spread out underneath.

A rustling noise startled her. She whipped around.
Keat lay sleeping on the couch. As she watched, he
rolled over and his hand slid to the floor with a thud.
His eyes fluttered open.

Penrose stood frozen, afraid to move, waiting for
him to close his eyes again. His unfocused gaze slid
over her body, and she felt undressed and exposed. For
one brief second, he looked into her eyes, and she saw
something register in them. His eyebrows lifted, and
he looked at her the way a man looked at a woman he
coveted, and her pulse raced in response.

Please, she willed him, *fall back asleep.* Finally, his
gaze moved away, and his lids shuttered closed.

Keat was having a dream. A very good dream.
Normally he dreamed about designing robots, but this

dream was a welcome change. It featured a beautiful woman. The dark-haired one that he had seen in the window. He dreamed that he could see all of her features clearly, down to her perfect pink lips and neon-blue eyes. The dream was so good he didn't want to wake up even though a warning came from deep inside him.

For the first time, in the dream, he was able to see all of her. She wore an old-fashioned dress, severe and tight in the bodice, and he wondered how a waist could be so small. And that hair, wild and free. He wanted to tangle his fingers in her hair, to grab it and pull her down on top of him. But something stopped him. An expression of fear—no, of horror—marred her features. In his dream, he realized that the woman was afraid of him. That he was the monster she so dreaded.

Something wasn't right. The feeling boomed in him, finally rousing him from sleep though he kept his eyes closed. He was aware of everything around him. He waited, his instincts sizzling with readiness.

There was a quick swishing noise, and a small gust of air rushed over him.

His eyes snapped open.

For a split second, he was certain he saw a woman, but when he looked again she was gone. And it was the woman from his dream. With the same sharp, classic features. The same dark hair and eyes so blue he could make out the color in the dimly lit room. There was nothing there. Damn, the dream felt so real.

Too real. He shot up from the couch and looked around the room. Everything was in perfect order. The news still played on the television. Nothing was out of place. From the coffee table, his iPhone blinked at him, reminding him of the hundreds of messages he had to respond to. He ignored it.

He must be going crazy. There was no way in hell he'd seen the woman just now. He must have dreamed it. An exceptionally lifelike dream. It was too bad because she was exquisite. She looked so very real and had a mysterious, chiseled beauty. Keat settled back into the leather couch and closed his eyes, trying to conjure up the dream again. Snippets of it came back, teasing him.

But now his lust burned hot for her. Part of him wished it wasn't a dream, because if it wasn't…oh, the things he would do to her. Unmentionable things.

Only a moment later he heard the distinct sound of footsteps running down the foyer. He jumped up instantly, grabbed his phone and bolted across the room. He flew down the hall to the foyer and looked up the staircase. Nothing. Christ, was he going crazy?

With a surge of fury, he shouted, "Wherever you are, I will find you! And you will regret it!" He yelled so loudly the crystals in the chandelier rattled. Wherever the woman was, she most definitely heard him. Even if she was still in his dream, she heard him.

A new possibility occurred to him, one that was so ridiculous he almost laughed it off. What if she was a ghost? The house was 250 years old, after all. The perfect age for a house to be haunted. Besides, he'd seen a ghost already in this house, long ago, when he was a child.

"Dammit," he mumbled to himself at the creepy absurdity of the whole situation.

Climbing the stairs, he whipped out his phone and texted his director of corporate security. He wrote, Can you do a sweep of the video from the cameras around the perimeter of my land? Worried about a breach.

There was only one road to the manor. One way in and one way out, and it was protected by a guard gate. If anyone came over the fence, it would be on those recordings. He'd know for certain how that woman got inside. Or if he had a ghost, instead.

He stood in the foyer, chest heaving, enraged. "You'll regret the day I find you," he roared into the dark and empty house. At least, he hoped it was empty.

Penrose crawled to the door and pressed her cheek against it, listening. The wall seemed paper-thin. His anger easily penetrated through it, and the heat of it rolled over her in waves.

It wasn't just his anger. She was coming undone. The sight of him lying on the couch had taken away her breath. Her entire being responded to the sight of him, and that scared her almost as much as the man did. How could she be desperately frightened of a man and still attracted to him?

She curled into a ball, right there by the door, holding back sobs that racked her, afraid that Keat would hear her.

Carrick. C.J. Keat. They all blended in her thoughts. The one thing that shone brightly as a beacon in her mind was Arundell Manor. Even though she couldn't make sense of what was happening, she knew to the depth of her soul that she could always count on Arundell. It might be the only thing she could ever rely on.

Her bones hurt when she finally made her way back to C.J.'s room. Without bothering to light the candle, she felt along until her hands bumped into the wooden mannequin. She lifted him gently and brought him over to the bed, sitting him upright next to her. Even though he was a wooden man, she felt safer with him beside her. It was a piece of the home, the man, and the little boy she missed so much.

She ate her fruit in silence. The food tasted like dust, but she forced it down anyway. Then she curled herself into the tattered blanket, and tossed and turned until sleep claimed her.

Chapter 14

A few days later, Keat carried a cup of coffee into the workshop and began his day by removing the mother-board from Harris #142 and checking it for defects. He felt a kinship with the robot. He understood its nature.

It felt good to get away from Silicon Valley and reconnect with the robots he loved. Plus, he avoided Christmas.

It sounded silly, but there it was. He hated the sight of the wreaths and trees, the holly, and even the Christmas songs. They were constant reminders of the life he didn't have. He could hole up and hide out without seeing one single Christmas decoration. Not one reminder.

For the rest of the day, he drank his coffee, fiddled with the motherboards and circuits, and played his music at full volume. On the surface, everything seemed normal. But he was unsettled. He couldn't shake the feeling that someone was watching him. It affected his concentration, and he found himself making foolish mistakes. What should have been an easy fix on Harris was now testing him to his limits.

All he could think of was that tiny waist of hers. His little ghost. He longed to wrap his fingers around that waist and pull her close to him. Ridiculous, he reminded himself, pushing the thought from his head. He needed to focus on Harris's electrical problem.

Over the next hour, Keat tried numerous things to fix Harris, but nothing worked.

Nothing was going right, and the least of his worries was that wreck of a robot.

Blood pounded in Penrose's temples, part in fear and part in anger at Keat. If this was a dream, then he was the monster of her nightmares. But, no, it was real. He was agitated yet again—hands darting in the air, shouting sharp words that vibrated straight through the walls. He was a sight to see, a dark-haired version of Carrick and in the bright light of day, no less. And his passion—the same intensity, the same brooding quality. And, yet, something truly sinister emanated from him.

He stood in front of the robot. Waves of anger emanated from him. "I'm done!" he yelled, "Why can't you operate the way I programmed you to? What the hell is wrong with you?"

The mechanical man's head turned and he opened his cartoon mouth and spoke. "I'm sorry, I do not understand your request."

"I'm tossing you right into the snow!" he said in a roar, yanking the robot up, pitching it over his shoulder and storming from the room. As soon as he left the room, she flew like a bird through the tunnel and emerged into the attic bedroom. Racing to the window she pulled back the curtain, not caring if he saw her.

Keat strode across the snow. Harris lay draped over his shoulder, his metallic legs sticking straight out, his small head bobbing with Keat's quick steps.

The distance and the falling snow blurred Keat's image. He stood like a shadow figure on the bleary landscape. With a rage-filled roar that she heard all the way in the attic, he hoisted the mannequin over his head and threw it in a huge arc. Harris landed with a thud on the ground.

"No!" she shouted, clutching the window helplessly. "Please, Keat! No!"

Without looking back at the house, Keat stormed toward that terrible vehicle of his, jumped inside, and with a roar of the engine he drove away.

Penrose looked at the helpless robot. He didn't move, just lay there like a doomed man resigned to his fate.

The thought of stepping outside struck pure fear into her, but she felt she had to. She must save Harris.

She fumbled at the latch before finally opening the door. "My God," she said, for it was so different than balmy Charleston. The cold was deep. The world was white and crisp, and even the blue sky looked brittle. This land of the future was cold. Very cold. She stepped out into a crusted pathway that led to the bonfire pit. But before she got very far she turned around and look back at the house. It was and it wasn't Arundell.

The manor sat on this blank land, oceans of it that stretched in all directions. She looked at where the pond should be, and yet there was nothing but flat white ground. She hurried her steps, dancing along an icy path until she knelt beside him, and with a gentle push turned him over. He stared lifelessly up at her, the strange lights in his eyes gone dark. His screen was slicked with icy mud, and she wiped it away gently.

She scooped him up. He was light in her arms. With quick but careful steps she walked back to the house and brought him into the tunnel with her. When she finally reached C.J.'s little room, she set him down, fumbled around in the darkness and lit a candle.

She felt wild, giddy from her crime. Her cheeks were hot, her hair and dress damp from the snow, her fingertips numb from the bitter cold. She studied the robot.

Her prize sat motionless. His presence in the room made for a strange party, with the wooden mannequins in the corner, the mechanical bird and now him, too. A giggle escaped her. She couldn't help it—it just felt too good to claim something from Keat.

And the robot looked magnificent. In the cloistered space with the flickering warmth of candlelight playing on his metallic blue skin, he seemed alive. There was a vibrancy to him. It warmed her to look at him, and all of a sudden she didn't feel nearly as hopeless.

She set about clearing him off, wiping the mud from his body and patting him dry as best she could with her skirts. Finally satisfied, she tried to wake him up. "Power up," she said.

Nothing happened. Turning him around, she ran her fingers over his back. There was a small door on it. Lifting it, she felt the cables and metal frame that lurked underneath. But she could feel no lever or buttons.

Perhaps if she lifted him, she might find something. Slipping her hands underneath his arms, she hoisted him. Then a sharp noise came, startling her.

It was the front door opening and shutting, followed

by a shout of hot anger from Keat. She dropped the man a second time, watching as the side of the wooden table thumped him hard, right on the side of his torso.

He landed loudly, faceup on the floor. Lights flashed numbers and letters across the black screen where his face should be. "Rebooting," he said.

"Hello?" she asked, confused.

A series of beeps and whirring noises continued. It was funny, watching the lights that played across the screen. And then a cartoonish version of his face appeared. He blinked.

Gently, she lifted him upright and leaned over him, studying him closely. "Hello?" she said.

"Hello," said Harris, blinking at her.

Tears pricked her eyes, and for the first time, she allowed herself a vulnerable moment. There'd been precious few in her life. Penrose wiped the tears from her eyes, leaving spiky black lashes in their wake. Her heart pounded in her chest. "Please," she said. "Talk to me."

"Harris responding," it replied in his strange voice. "Request?"

Keat drove wildly across the countryside, trying to cool down. His life was out of control. Of all the things he hated, this was top of the list. To make matters worse, a storm was coming. He saw the clouds building dark and high over the mountains. He had to get back to the house and take the robot inside.

He turned his Range Rover around. As he pulled into the driveway, his phone buzzed with a text message from his head of security. It read: After reviewing the recordings, there have been no breaches in the past six months. He sighed. There wasn't an easy answer.

He went and looked for the robot. It wasn't there. He'd thrown it down, right there, not thirty minutes before. Walking back and forth in disbelief, his boots crunched the snow. His lead robot was missing, and he wasn't even sure what to make of it. He couldn't shake the feeling, ridiculous as it was, that he knew who had taken the robot. With suspicion pounding in his veins, he went to the house. He could find out for certain in a few minutes.

Once inside the workshop, he sat down on a stool, pulled his phone out and launched Harris 142's interface app. Hoping, praying, that the robot's battery would still be functional, Keat connected to its internal receiver. He activated Harris and crossed his fingers that the battery still worked.

It did.

The black screen on his phone brightened as the image came into view. He saw movement, blurred images that appeared as white streaks on the screen. Then, a bright, glowing ball came into focus. He stared at the odd sight until he realized what he was looking at. A candle. How odd.

Not a moment later, a face appeared. The face he'd been dreaming about. His ghost. Except she wasn't a ghost. She was real. Real.

Rage pounded in his veins, but her beauty was undeniable. High cheekbones. Wide, scared eyes that glowed brightly in the light of the camera. "Tell me about Keat Arundell," she said. Her voice came to him scratchy and muffled, as if she was speaking from the moon, only she wasn't. She was speaking from somewhere inside of his house.

"Dammit," he whispered. He felt sick to his stomach as he stared at the woman on his screen. She wasn't a ghost. She was a living, breathing person inside the manor. Clenching the phone in hand, he vowed to catch her right away, and when he did, he'd make her pay. But first, he wanted to introduce himself. After all, she was a guest in his home.

She was so happy when the robot began to speak to her. A garbled squeal escaped her mouth. Harris. Her Harris. Her hands shook so violently that she had to hold them together. She said in a shaky voice, "Hello." Then she asked foolishly, "Who are you?"

"My name is Harris 142. I am an assistive device for humans. I was conceived and designed in 2015 by Arundell Industries as a personal project for Keat Arundell, CEO."

"Harris," she whispered.

"Yes," he replied. "Harris. Prototype number 142. May I ask who I am talking to?" His voice never rose or fell, rather he spoke in a monotone.

"My name is Penrose." She smiled at those strange eyes, unsure of herself, and she resisted the foolish urge to hold out her hand and offer it in greeting.

"Pen Rose," said the robot in a halting voice. "A pleasure to meet you, Pen Rose."

She smiled. Hearing her name, even incorrectly, made her feel more human. Safer somehow. The man's strange, picture eyes moved and then settled on her face.

"Tell me about Keat Arundell," she said impulsively, not even expecting him to answer.

His voice surprised her. "The following is a Wikipedia entry. Keat Carrick Arundell," said the assistive device. "Born October 18, 1984. Fifth generation Arundell, CEO of Arundell Industries. Known for his genius and his reclusiveness. He reportedly lives in Montana at a location so secret even his own company doesn't know the location."

Penrose grew quiet, trying to absorb what she was hearing. The creature stopped talking. Quietness settled in the room, except for her heavy breathing. The robot's words had flitted through her mind again and again when, suddenly, a different voice came from the robot. A familiar voice. Keat's.

"Hello, little ghost, did you know I can see you?"

Darkness blinded her. It had nothing to do with the tunnel, and everything to do with the fear that threatened to make her faint. Choking for breath, she leaned closer to the robot, trying to understand how it could speak with Keat's voice. Sudden realization hit her. Carrick was never a wicked man of magic. Keat was. She scurried away, deep into the tunnels, knowing that trouble lay ahead.

She was somewhere in the house, but where? Keat raced through the rooms, searching for her but coming up empty. He was missing something. Was there a passageway? God, he should have paid more attention to the relocation of the manor. He never bothered with details about such things, he only cared about his robots. But he remembered that he stored all of the architectural plans in the safe. Right in the workshop.

He raced to the workshop, passing a window and noticing that the snow was really coming down now. It would be a whiteout soon. Good. She'd be trapped for real. Only this time she'd have him to answer to. He opened the mammoth safe and dug through the family papers, journals, pictures, pulling them out and carelessly throwing them to the side. The fire blazed hot enough that beads of sweat ran down his face. Finally, he found the large, rolled-up architecture plans. Unraveling them as he walked to the kitchen, he spread them out on the table and studied the drawings. When he saw the tunnel and its two doors, a slow smile spread across his face.

"Showtime," he said softly, already anticipating the shocked look on her face as he caught her. He would win. He always won.

His plan was simple. He'd crawl into the tunnel, find her and bring her out. After that, he was undecided. Call the authorities, certainly. But he wanted to hear from her own mouth why she would do such a thing.

Keat gathered random tools, uncertain how the doors would open. He took a flashlight, an ax in case he had to break through the wood, and a rope. His plans for the rope involved her. His heart felt like ice, his soul blackened by the ire that someone would think to violate him like this. Screw his fantasies about her. Those were over. All of that paled next to the cold, hard and sickening truth about her.

Now that he knew there was a tunnel, it was surprisingly easy to find both entrances. He decided to enter the tunnel from the attic. Whoever had built the tunnel had been a talented craftsman and hidden the seam perfectly in the wainscoting. After giving the little door a hard shove, it opened.

The blackness was absolute, like a void in the universe. He feared nothing. Or thought so, but staring into the tunnel, knowing that woman hid somewhere inside of it, he felt uneasy. Every man had his limits.

He flipped on the flashlight. The white beam split the darkness and illuminated the rough stone walls. Dropping to his hands and knees, he paused just outside the door. It took a force of will for him to enter the tunnel, but he did, flashlight in one hand, the beam bobbing ahead of him.

Six foot three doesn't fit easily in such a tight space. His shoulders brushed against the wall, and his back scraped against the ceiling. His breathing was loud and too fast. The tunnel widened, surprising him, and he could stand.

At full height now, and feeling more confident, he swung the flashlight around the tunnel. The meager light was worthless. A thin beam against the hungry dark.

He moved deeper into the bowels of the house, and every step was a struggle. How had he lived and grown up in this house when it had a secret like this tunnel? He came to a hole in the floor and shone the light down into it. The beam illuminated halfway down the shaft. Beyond that, the bottom remained a mystery.

A sound echoed from deep within the innards of the house. A feminine gasp. Surprised, his grip slipped from the flashlight, and it fell, a ball of light sailing down until it hit the floor with a loud crack and then shut off. Blackness reigned again. Now the light came from behind him, weak sunlight streaming in from the attic window.

"Forget this," he said. There was no way he would crawl around in the dark. Cupping his hands together, he called out, "I'm coming for you, little ghost. I know you're in here. You're going to regret the day you started living in my walls. That's my promise to you." His voice traveled down the hole and echoed deep into the shaft.

Backing away from the hole, he turned around and crawled back out.

As he walked down the stairs, he devised a plan for getting her out. The cat-and-mouse game, only just begun, was over. He had to trap her inside so she couldn't escape from one door or the other. Or force her to pick one door while he lay in wait.

Coldly, calmly, he went outside to the garage and began gathering supplies. He grabbed an ax, electrical tape, another flashlight and a metal washtub. With a chilling look of determination on his face, he stormed back to the house. Dumping all of the items onto the floor of the foyer, he went to the workshop and grabbed thin, green pieces of wood, which he stacked in the washtub.

He knew the best way to get rid of rodents. By smoking them out.

Penrose listened to him retreating from the tunnel and couldn't help the tiny smile of satisfaction it brought her. When he'd shouted at her from inside the walls, it had turned her blood cold. Knowing the tunnel was intimidating enough to send him away gave her a sense of pride. He'd be back, of course, so she knew it was foolish. Still it was a victory, and that mattered to her.

But it didn't change the fact that he knew where she was hidden. The tunnel was now a trap. Her options had dwindled to nothing. Something bad was going to happen. *Run*, her instincts told her. But to where? Out the front door into the cold, featureless land that stretched on forever? She pushed her hands through her dark hair, wondering what to do, but every single option seemed hopeless. There would be no running. She had to fight.

A moment later, she heard the downstairs entrance to the tunnel open, and a dull gray light shone into the crawlspace. He was coming, just as he'd promised. She inched ahead, uneasy, and peered down the hall. Sunlight streamed into the space, illuminating the walls. All of a sudden, his arms appeared in the doorway pushing a metal tub piled with wood into the tunnel. Then once more as he dumped crumpled paper onto the pile of wood. She saw the small flame from a match as he tossed it onto the wood.

"No," she whispered to herself, "not that. Not fire."

As if he could hear her, he said, "Hello, my pretty little ghost. The game is over. It's time to come out. I'm smoking you out like a rodent. Your only escape route is up and into the attic, where I'll be waiting for you." The door slammed shut.

He was forcing her into his trap. Penrose stifled a scream that if started would never stop. She watched, horrified as the flame licked to life, bright and happy, unaware that it would bring about her doom. Tendrils of white smoke curled higher, hit the low roof, flattened, and spread along the ceiling.

It took a moment before the pungent trail reached her room. The acrid smell burned her lungs when she breathed. As she watched, the fire was growing and smoke billowing out thickly.

Panicked, she grabbed Harris and dragged him down the hall, deeper into the tunnel. No matter what, she wasn't leaving Harris behind. Ever. She came first to the kitchen vent. He had closed the vent. When she pressed against the slats, they didn't budge. He'd secured it shut.

Without a candle, and with the vents sealed tight, she couldn't see the smoke. But it hung thick as a cloud. A deep fit of coughing overtook her. Eyes burning, she pressed on. Every vent was tightly closed, and no matter how she clawed at them, they wouldn't open. He was right. Her time was up.

Panic came easily. It would be so much easier to give up and lie down, let the smoke suffocate her. But she wanted to live. The need beat within her. She knew that trying to escape might be futile—he could catch her, and if he did, he'd kill her. No, she had to try to escape.

Three thoughts repeated in her head. *Get to the attic, lock the door, and don't let him in, no matter what.* She had to lock him out and then she could escape through the window or perhaps compromise with him. Mind made up, she scurried, holding her breath, using both hands to pull her along to the attic.

She'd never moved so fast before. She determinedly refused to let go of Harris. He scraped the floor as she ran. She dropped him once and almost left him, but she couldn't stand the thought of abandoning him.

When she reached the ladder, she heard Keat on the stairs, pounding up them. It was a race. She had to reach the door before him. Awkwardly tucking Harris under one arm, she climbed as fast as she could. When she reached the attic door, she listened for a moment and heard nothing. Punching the door open, she fell sprawling onto the floor. Smoke poured from behind her.

Hacking, stumbling, taking deep gulps of air, she reached the front door to the attic bedroom. He was so close. She heard his breathing. Quickly, she threw the lock and leaned against the door, partially stopping the smoke from pouring in. A small win.

He was on the stairs, climbing closer. There was still so much smoke. She had to be quick. She darted to the window, grabbing a limb of the robot from the table, and she smashed the glass.

Cold air poured in and sucked the smoke outside, sending a plume of white into the gray cloud-covered afternoon sky. Brutal, unrelenting snow slashed sideways. Snowflakes and ashes swirled around the room and landed on her. The snow nipped at her and disappeared, but the ash clung to her, mottling her skin and dress.

She was numb, disconnected from the world. Every difficulty, every challenge in her life paled before this moment, and, yet, it didn't seem real. She heard his shouts coming closer. His voice sounded hollow. Distant.

She stood, turned and faced the door, tucked a stray hair behind her ear and smoothed her skirts. She felt wild and crazed as she waited for him. The moment she feared most was at hand.

The door handle rattled, followed by four vicious strikes of his fist against the door. Then, his soft voice called to her through the door frame. "Hello there, ghost. I know you're in there. Why don't you come and say hello to me? Are you shy?"

Words would not form on her lips. Her hands began to shake, and she stood foolishly, mute and dumb.

"Come now," he cajoled. "Won't you open the door for me? I just want to say hello. To meet my guest face-to-face."

Knowing the end was near, she spoke the first words she'd ever said directly to him, "I would rather be dead than meet you face-to-face."

Chapter 15

Keat's anger made him crazed. "So harsh!" he said. "Here you are, a guest in my home, and you throw insults at me?" His fingers rattled the door handle once more before he slapped the wood with his open palm. "An uninvited guest, I might add, and I'm getting impatient." His velvety voice barely concealed his rage.

She didn't answer him.

"Answer me this. How could you get inside my house? Forty miles to the nearest building and guards protecting the perimeter twenty-four hours a day? How did you manage that, ghost?"

His ghost was quiet. He hoped she was afraid. He leaned forward, his shoulder first, and barreled forward, smashing into the door. With a loud thump, it bounced against the frame, trying to break open. But the lock held fast.

She screamed. He heard her scurrying and, with

a thump, she pressed against the door. He heard her breathing. Trying to hold it shut.

Foolish.

He collided with the wood, and the force of his blow made her bounce off. He heard her fall to the floor. A moment later she was back at the door, pushing, panting. She took quick, feminine breaths. But he wouldn't be stopped.

He pressed his lips against the door and spoke. "Maybe you are really a ghost. Why don't you prove to me that you're not?"

Her soft voice surprised him. "I'm no ghost. I'm human."

"Then prove it. Let me see you. Give me proof that you are flesh and bone. Or if you prefer, I can use this ax I brought along, split this door in two and find out for myself whether you live and breathe. One way or another, you better prove it."

He lowered himself to the ground and slid his hand underneath the door. "Shake my hand, ghost. Introduce yourself."

Penrose leaned forward and watched as four fingertips appeared underneath the door and slid back and forth.

"Don't be rude," he said in a mocking voice. "Shake my hand."

She examined his fingers. The whorls in his fingertips were oval. He had the skin of a working man. Calloused. Nicked. Her face screwed tight, she reached out and light as a butterfly's wing, she ran her fingers over his. His touch was warm.

With a pounding heart she snatched her hand away.

* * *

As soon as he felt the warmth of her skin against his, he jumped back and stared at his hand as if he'd been burned. The tingling that lingered on his fingers was all the proof he needed. She was real. Flesh and blood. And it deepened his rage. "Open this door!" he demanded, banging against it loudly. "Open it right now!"

Penrose listened as he spoke in a low voice. "Please. Listen to reason. I will not hurt you. I promise. I need you to open the door."

Lies. She was close to breaking. She shook her head wildly, covered her ears and tried with all her might to wish her way back to the real Arundell. Through her covered ears, she could hear him, his anger rising in intensity.

"I suffered with you here. With you hiding in my home." His voice grew louder. "With you spying on me. With you stealing my food. Worst of all, you convinced me that I was crazy." He gave a low, maniacal laugh that sounded crazy to her. "Don't you have anything to say to me?" Then a moment later, he continued. "No? A cat has your tongue?"

She whimpered.

"What's that?" he said in a soft, lulling voice. "Do I hear a little bird in her cage? Or do I hear a criminal, someone doing things they shouldn't? I'm going to give you five minutes, little ghost, and then I'll break this door down. Your time is up. Though I do enjoy hearing your feminine whimpers that ring of fear."

"I am afraid," she said.

"I'm holding an ax," he said through the door. "I'll give you to the count of five. Then I'm splitting it wide open. If I were you, I'd back away."

She scooted back, all the way across the attic until she reached the little door to the tunnel. Even though the tunnel was closed, smoke streamed through the doorjamb. Harris lay in a heap. She grabbed him and propped him in front of her like a little soldier trying to protect her.

Keat began counting. "Five."

"Four."

"Three."

"Please."

It was quiet for a moment. "Open the door," he said.

"I can't."

"Two."

"One."

He heard a scream as his shattering blow hit the door, sending splinters flying through the air. The ghost made a last-ditch, foolish effort to save herself. Throwing open the door to the tunnel, ignoring the plume of smoke that poured from it, she dove into the crawl space, covering her mouth as she scrambled.

Again and again Keat swung the ax and struck the door—too hard and too wildly—but he didn't care. Each blow brought him one step closer to a resolution. When the ax finally split the wood, he reached inside the room and unlocked the door. He turned the handle, but the door wouldn't budge. It was jammed on the splintered wood. Stepping back, he lifted his leg and kicked it open. And he saw his ghost as she disappeared into the tunnel.

Penrose screamed and clawed the floor as strong hands grabbed her ankles. She was trying to dig in, to prevent him from pulling her out. He had the grip of an iron vise and wrenched her from the tunnel. "You won't get away from me," he said.

She emerged kicking and screaming before he dumped her onto the floor, his hand a shackle around her leg. She stole a peek into his rage-filled eyes. He seemed beyond anger, as if he had gone to some deep and awful place in his mind.

His gaze slid over her face. "I cannot believe there is a woman hiding in my walls!" he screamed. "A person! I knew I wasn't crazy!" His hand squeezed her hard as he spoke. "And look at you. Wild hair, wild clothes. Disgusting. What are you doing in my walls? My house?"

"I don't know," she whispered, her eyes wide, and shaking her head. "I really don't know." If only she knew what to do, how to respond to a monster like him. She could barely look up at the man.

"Don't mess with me," he replied, grabbing her by the wrist and yanking her to her feet. He spun her around, dug the rope from his pocket, and wrapped the cord around and around.

He pointed at her dress. "What are you doing, dressed like a creepy ghost? Are you a nutjob, or what? Crawling around in my walls? Are you spying on me? And the prototype? Why would you steal my prototype?"

She was afraid to look up at him, as if the mere challenge of eye contact would send him over the edge. That rage was so explosive. "I had no choice," she managed to whisper before her voice failed her.

He sounded deceptively smooth and gentle as he said, "Who are you and where are you from?"

"My name is Penrose Heatherton. I'm from Arundell Manor," she said in a wavering voice, her face contorted in fear. It almost hurt to tell the truth but, somehow, she couldn't stop herself. "I work for Carrick Arundell, helping him design a mechanical man."

"In what year?" he asked.

"Eighty-six," she whispered.

"You expect me to believe that you came forward some thirty years?" He laughed.

"You mean, it's 1916?" She shook her head slowly as the impossible sunk in. "Oh, my God," she whispered.

"No. It's 2016."

She saw it then. Something inside him snapped as the disbelief on his face etched in deep, and his features twisted down and hardened into uncontrolled fury.

Keat felt as if he had been kicked in the gut. There she was—living, breathing proof that a person hid inside of his home. There were no words to describe the level of anger he felt.

Temples pounding, chest heaving, he stood and took in the sight of her, for she was a sight. A sorry one. Her face and hair were smeared and grayed with ashes. Why did he ever think she was beautiful? He'd never seen an uglier creature in his life. She looked like an old woman. "You're coming with me," he said, his voice thick with disdain as he grabbed her by the arm.

Dragging her down the stairs, he took her to the workshop. It was the room he felt most in control, and right then, he needed to be in control. More than ever, he needed that control.

Careful not to let her fall but not showing any kindness, either, he led her down the stairs. Her dress felt foreign to his touch, the cloth too thick and the fabric rustled, heavy as a drape, as she walked. Together, they barreled into the workshop. He pushed her forward until she stood in front of a table.

"Down," he said, his iron grip forcing her to the floor.

The robots watched with disinterest as he tied her to the leg of the table with the cord. He made sure she was close enough to the fire to warm her and to dry her clothes. She sat in a crumpled heap, grayish hair hanging limp over her face, her eyes trained downward and her skirt a black bell around her.

"Look at me," he said. He wanted her to look him in the eye.

She shook her head.

"Look at me," he repeated.

She lifted her head and looked up at him through wild tufts of hair. She held his gaze with a tight expression of malice on her face. The blazing fire behind her gave her an evil, witchy look, and he was taken aback by the sight.

He dragged a chair across the floor, spun it around and sat in front of her. Staring at her with crossed arms, and close enough to reach out and touch her, he said, "Tell me who you are. And be honest."

She tossed her head, moving her hair aside, and he saw her bright blue eyes more clearly. "I told you my name. My name is Penrose Heatherton." She spoke harshly. "I already know yours."

"Aren't you cute?" he said. "Giving me attitude when you're tied up." He tilted the chair forward until he hovered right above her. "So, Penrose Heatherton. You said you worked here before?"

"I did." Her gaze swept over the room, and she said, "I created robots with Carrick in this very room."

He laughed outright. "You're entertaining, I'll give you that. A wild ride." When his laugh died away, he simply said, "Or you're crazy."

"You are mistaken on all accusations," she said, her eyes a blue flame. "I have no delusions about what happened. The last thing I am is crazy. Trust me, it would be a blessing if I were crazy, a far better fate than this."

"Penrose Heatherton, your fate is about to get a lot worse."

"Call me Penny," she said.

"Oh, you're no Penny. I'll stick to Penrose."

In the light of the fire, it looked to Penrose as if steam rose from Keat's skin. He looked so angry, staring at her with the darkest eyes she'd ever seen.

For the past week, she'd known him from afar. In that manner, it was easy to cast him as a monster. But standing there, shaking with rage and something more—something like fear—he looked like a man, a very powerful, very angry man. One pushed to the edge. By her. It was a thousand times scarier than a mere monster.

It wasn't her fault, however. At least that's what she wanted to believe.

"Why don't you just admit that for some sick reason, you chose this house to break into? Because who would head out into the middle of nowhere to live in the walls of a house?"

"I don't even know where this house is!" she screamed. "Or why we aren't in Charleston? Why are we in this strange winter land?"

An eyebrow lifted. "We moved it," he said. "But I think you already knew that. This home is not one a person would accidentally find, or even seek out. There's something wrong with you breaking in here to live. Don't you think you're laying on the Southern accent a bit thick? You sound like a *Gone with the Wind* rerun."

"I don't know what you're talking about!" she said in a shrill voice that couldn't be her own. Everything collided within her, all of her fear, panic and anger at the situation. She leaned forward, arms taut from the cord, until their noses almost touched. When she spoke, it was low and threatening. "How dare you," she spit the words out. "I am at my worst. Reduced to crawling about like a rodent in your walls, and you think I chose you? That I snuck in here of my own free will?" She took a ragged breath and continued, "I would shave my head to be free of you. Chop off my limbs. You frighten me more than any man."

"Don't tempt me," he said. "And I frighten you? You haunt my house and want to blame me for freaking out over it?"

Her eyes ticked back to his, saw the cold disdain in them. That was the worst of all, the disdain. For as she'd spied on him, she alternated between fearing him and desiring him, but never ever disdaining him. And she was surprised to discover that hurt her. "I don't haunt this house. I'm alive."

He snorted. "Yes, you're alive. It's not the nineteenth century, darling. Which means you're no ghost. You're merely crazy."

Impossible. Yet there she was. The woman, Penrose, lay in a heap on his floor, her black skirt billowed out like some bad dream. Insisting she was from the past. Insisting he listen. Worse, that he believe her. The sad thing was, she looked so earnest that he was actually tempted once or twice.

He needed to think. While she was tied up, he went and doused the fire and boarded up the tunnels, and while he worked, he thought about everything she'd told him. Her story was impossible. Utterly impossible. But he knew that she hadn't crossed the perimeter of the land. Yet, there she sat, on the floor of his workshop, in an old-fashioned dress. The whole damn situation was creepy and odd.

When he came back to the workshop, he asked her, "Why didn't you just come out of the walls and tell me?"

"Because I watched you. When you first chased me into the wall, I was scared to death. You're a horrid man. You don't know how frightening it is for me to be here. Until you suddenly appear in a different time, you won't know the fear I face."

"I don't believe you," he said. She was beautiful. No denying that. Once he looked beneath the grime, he saw the china-white skin, dark lashes, full pink lips. He knew there was some kind of body underneath that crazy gown. But she was a nut. Or a stalker. He'd already been there, done that with a stalker. No repeats, thank you. He'd find out for sure. It was a mission.

"Listen to me," she said. "Just listen. I don't know how I got here, only where I came from." She leaned back with a strangely pretty expression on her filthy face. "Hear me out. I am speaking the truth. I came from Arundell Manor. In Charleston."

She knew far too much about Arundell. "That's impossible."

"I know. It is impossible. Yet here I am." She looked

away with a pained expression. "There was an earthquake. A terrible earthquake that came out of nowhere. Everything shook. Everything. I was trying to save C.J. Carrick was there, too."

"An earthquake? Everyone knows that South Carolina doesn't have earthquakes. You've got your states mixed up. California is what you meant." But for the first time, the hairs rose on the back of his neck when she mentioned the name C.J.—Carrick, Junior, the founder of Arundell Industries. Carrick Arundell was the original inventor, but his son C.J. was the real genius, the one who founded Arundell Industries.

With all of his instincts on edge, he urged her on. "Continue."

"C.J.," she said. "He lived in the walls. He felt the safest there. When the quake came, he ran right into the tunnel. It was dangerous, and I had to get him out. That clock, that grandfather clock kept on ringing as the house shook, and I darted into the tunnel with him." Her tears were so thick he couldn't see her eyes through the glisten.

He asked warily, "Then where is C.J.?"

"I don't know! He could be dead! I just don't know!"

"He didn't die young."

Her head snapped up with such a look of joy that the creepy sensation returned full force.

"Okay, so let's assume that's true," he said, partly to appease her, but more to keep her talking until the truth finally came out. "When was this earthquake?" he asked.

"August. August 31, 1886."

He stared at her. "In 1886? You really expect me to

believe you came here from one hundred and thirty years ago?"

"If there were some way to prove it to you, I would."

"How convenient that there's no way to check."

"As I said, I'm not lying."

"Okay, I've had enough," he said. "I'm calling the police. They'll haul you away."

"No!" she shrieked with an urgency that made him jump. "I can't leave the manor! Please, it's the one thing I can trust. I need to stay here. I feel it in my bones."

There was something about her tone that struck a chord in him. He stared at her, hard. Finally, he nodded. "Okay, for now you can stay. It's a whiteout anyway. Lucky us, we can enjoy each other's company for a while longer."

Chapter 16

Penrose watched as Keat left the room. He returned a short time later and sat down on the chair right in front of her, holding a bowl in his hands. The smell of soup filled the air. Her mouth began to water. It'd been days since she had real food.

He lifted a steaming spoonful of the hot liquid and held it in front of her mouth. "Eat." It was an order. "You looked hungry."

His kindness surprised her. Wary but starving, she tilted forward and clumsily came down, mouth open, on the spoon. The hot liquid scorched her lips. She hissed and fell back on her heels, soup in her mouth, gasping for air to cool it down.

"Blow first."

"It's hard to get the motions right, tied up as I am," she answered once she was able to swallow the soup.

It felt so good sliding down her throat. Hot and filling. "More, please," she said greedily, her stomach practically forcing her to beg.

He held up another spoonful and she blew hard, making little waves on the surface before she took another bite.

"Right now, we're going to have a heart-to-heart. If you need help with something or if you're having personal problems, there are other options." He spoke slowly, always spooning more liquid into her mouth.

"The only problem I have is that you don't believe me."

"Penrose, people don't travel through time." He almost looked like an adult trying to reason with a child.

"I did."

He set down the half-empty bowl of soup and sighed. "Aren't you growing tired of this?"

"Yes, I am. I'd like nothing more than to be in my home. My real home. To wash up—"

"God, you need to wash up." She shot him an angry look and he lifted his hands in the air. "I'm just saying. Maybe it's not such a bad idea. Do you want to take a shower?"

"A shower." She said. "I'd love to," she blurted out.

"Okay." He nodded, his dark hair gleaming as the firelight played off it. "But no funny stuff, all right?"

She didn't know why he was suddenly a nice guy, but she wasn't about to turn down a shower. She felt like the world's dirtiest creature just then, and a clean body sounded heavenly.

"Do you have a change of clothes?"

"No. All I have I'm wearing on my body. And I'm not sure I know how to use your shower stall."

"I have to hand it to you. You're good." He came and untied the cord from her arms, then helped her to stand up. "So, I suppose I'll teach you how to use a shower, and get you something to wear." He stood beside her as she stretched her arms. "Let's call a truce. A temporary cease-fire."

He led her upstairs, one hand holding an elbow, the other rested on her waist. "Will I have to escort you everywhere? Or can I trust that you won't run away? You won't be going back into the tunnel, that's for sure."

She stopped abruptly. "I'll never run away from Arundell," she said fiercely.

He looked at her long and hard. "Why do I believe you?" he asked before urging her forward again.

They stopped in his bedroom along the way, and he gathered some clothes for her. Handing them over, he said, "I'm sorry, I only have men's clothes." Gesturing at her body, he continued, "I'm short on old-fashioned dresses at the moment. They're mine, so they'll be too large for you."

"Thank you," she whispered, taking the clothes from him. He was so imposing that she felt flustered next to him. Unsure of herself. "Whatever you can provide is welcome." She held up the pants. "What are these?"

He laughed harshly. "You're good. They are sweatpants, as if you didn't know. And feel free to drop the Southern drawl anytime now."

"I couldn't even if I wanted to, and I don't want to. It's who I am," she said stubbornly.

They entered the bathroom. He took a few towels from the closet and handed them to her. They stood side by side in the large, tiled space. The wide tub in front of her looked more appealing than the shower, but he seemed intent on her taking a shower, and she didn't want to cross him. He had just started to show a sliver of compassion.

The shower stall was huge with glass blocks all around and two nozzles. He stepped inside and guided her by the elbow until they stood side by side. He looked at her with those dark, thickly lashed eyes. Almost pretty, except for the gaze. Finally, he said, "Are you certain you need directions on how to use a shower? Don't you think the show has gone on long enough?"

"Please," she said, answering both of his questions with one single word.

"I take it you've been in here, too, right?" he asked.

"I have." It sounded like a confession, being in such an intimate room in his house without his knowledge. She hated the feeling.

"Did you watch me in here?" He stepped closer, merely an inch, but it was a step intended to intimidate her. She knew that. It infuriated her that it worked.

"No," she assured him. "I didn't. I tried not to invade your privacy."

"So you've never seen anything you shouldn't?"

"No."

"Too bad," he said, sending a hot thrill through her body.

He studied her. "Maybe you want to see something now?"

She stepped back from him, nervous.

"Never mind, I have my answer." Instantly, he was all business again.

No you don't, she wanted to say, but the words didn't leave her lips. It was too risky with a man like him. Too dangerous.

In a cool voice, he showed her how to turn the hot water on. He began to explain the shampoo and conditioner to her, but once she lifted the bottle to her nose and sniffed, the feminine part of her understood instinctively what these were for. She was a quick study in girlie indulgences.

"I'll leave you alone," he said, "I'll be just outside the door, waiting for you when you finish."

After he had left, she undressed, gladly letting the tattered black gown and underclothes drop to the floor. She stepped into the shower, turned the handles and felt the icy shards of cold water rain down on her. She screamed at the top of her lungs.

From the other room, she heard him bellow, "It takes time to heat up!"

She stood shivering as she followed his directions. When steam began to billow in the air, she stepped inside and fell instantly in love. Hot water on demand. What a glorious thing.

Needles of hot water pulsed over her skin. She turned slowly, letting the water burst over her skin from above, flooding her with heat and invigorating her all the way down to her soul. She had never imagined such decadence, a hot shower with soaps and lotions to slather over her body.

Time ceased to mean anything. Her skin turned bright red. She used the shampoo, the conditioner, the soap, and scrubbed her skin raw with the washcloth. She stayed until the water turned cold.

After the shower, wrapping herself in a thick, luxurious towel was a second treat for her. She brushed her hair, feeling cleaner than in God knows how long.

She went to the pile of clothes Keat had laid out for

her. They smelled so sweet, as if they'd been washed in perfume. The first was a man's soft cotton shirt, and she slipped it on, acutely aware that it belonged to Keat. Her stomach flipped at the knowledge his body had touched the same thing. And it was so soft. Her wet hair hung in strands down her back, but even that felt like a luxury.

How long had it been since she'd had wet hair? And she'd never had wet hair that smelled as good as this. She picked up the other article of clothing. Sweatpants. They reminded her more of soft pantaloons as she slid them on, but they too were heaven. She felt clean and pretty, with clothes as light as air on her body as she left the bathroom.

Keat waited for her in the sitting area of his bedroom, two overstuffed chairs on a thick rug in front of the fireplace. His iPhone in hand, he was using it to run searches. When he discovered that there really was an earthquake in Charleston, he'd gone cold. He planned on searching her name, but when he typed in Penrose, the autofill feature suggested something called a Penrose staircase. Intrigued, he clicked on it, and promptly wished he hadn't.

According to Wikipedia, a Penrose staircase was an impossible object, a staircase that looped around and around upon itself. A person could climb it forever and never even rise one flight. He sighed. He just wanted some answers. And all he got in return were riddles. Sickened, he set the phone down, tired of searching.

He went downstairs and grabbed two sodas for them. At least he could test her at every turn, to find some way to trip her up. Even the sodas were an attempt at that. It was almost midnight, but he wasn't ready to let go of his intention of forcing her to admit the truth. He wanted more information before calling it a night.

After the longest shower known to man, she finally emerged from the bathroom. "Come and dry yourself by the fire, little ghost," Keat said to her as she walked toward him.

His intentions were noble. Mostly. At least they weren't indecent. Until she stepped into view. As soon as he saw her walking toward him cautiously, looking shy, any nobility he had instantly disappeared. Her jet-black hair gleamed a long trail over her shoulder. Beneath it, the T-shirt was wet, and either she didn't know it was transparent or she was very clever at her game. He drank in the sight of her, and when he saw the dark outline of her nipples beneath the shirt, his cock responded immediately. Her breasts were small. The perfect shape. Her skin was red and shiny from being scrubbed, and she was the sexiest thing he'd ever seen.

The sweatpants were baggy on her and as she walked they fell down. She was fast about yanking them back up again, but that didn't stop him from seeing the curve of her hip.

The intensity of his reaction surprised him. How had he been so enraged at her before and now wanted her so fiercely? There was no easy answer, and, right then, he didn't care to analyze it. All he knew was that he wanted her. From the moment he first saw her as she haunted him, he couldn't get her out of his mind. Before he could stop himself, he made a vow. He would have her.

Handing her the can of soda, he said, "I brought you a drink. Have a seat."

"Thank you," she said, taking the can. She sat down,

crossed her legs formally and analyzed the can in her hand.

"Don't tell me you don't know how to open a soda can."

"I'm sure if I look at it a moment, I'll be able to. I just need to study it."

"Hand it over," he said, holding his arm out.

She gave it to him. He cracked it open and handed it back.

She took a sip and promptly spit the soda out everywhere. Wiping her mouth, she looked at him and said, "It burns."

"It's a good burn, though," he replied. Another test passed. Point in her column, he supposed.

Trying again, she took a small, dainty sip and stared straight ahead at the fire.

After a few minutes of silence, Keat asked, "What are you thinking of?"

"I was thinking of Carrick and C.J.—Carrick, Junior."

"Tell me about them." He wanted to hear what she had to say, and see if it lined up with the Wikipedia entry. Or the corporate website.

She began to talk. Her Southern accent was pronounced. It gave her voice a lilt that made it sound musical and very sexy. The soft orange light fell on her features. Her hair had dried wild and curly, and her lips were rosy pink and tempting.

"Carrick is an artist," she said. "He's an inventor, like you, and very intelligent. It's a family trait."

Christ, it bothered him that she spoke of a long-dead man in the present tense. What the hell could he do to shake her conviction?

"He has such a passion for inventing robots—I mean mechanical men," she said with a smile, and then laughed. "I get confused now. You say robot. We say mechanical men. I think Carrick coined the term," she said wistfully.

Suddenly he realized something. "You were with him." It was a statement, not a question.

She blinked, and the blue of her eyes disappeared underneath a fringe of dark lashes. She looked so pale that even the warm glow of the fire gave no color to her skin. "Yes," she said. One quiet little word. One big giveaway.

"You loved him."

The fire crackled and snapped as he waited for an answer.

Finally, she opened her eyes. "No," she said. "But oh, I don't know... I've known him for such a short time. It's more like I'm in awe of him and overwhelmed. He's almost a force. He's moody, and can have a sharp tongue. He's obsessed with his work, and anything that interferes sets him off. But when he talks about his ideas... oh, you should see him. He uses his hands, painting pictures in the air trying to get me to understand. I have this one memory of him standing over a table in the workshop, his white hair tousled, his clothes disheveled. Nothing else mattered but that mechanical man. If I had dropped a glass, he wouldn't even have looked up."

Keat was confused. "Wait. He's old? He had white hair?"

"No." She shook her head. Her brows came together, and she looked at him, confused. "Don't you know?"

"Know what?"

"Carrick has albinism, and so does his young son, C.J. They were incredibly pale skinned."

An uneasy feeling gripped him. A nagging sensation that something was right there at the edges of his memories. "I had no idea," he finally said, after struggling and failing to figure it out.

She gasped. "There's a reason you don't know," she said, looking at him with wide eyes. "I can show you," she said excitedly.

"How?"

"Follow me," she said, and jumped up from the chair. He was hit with the sight of the sweatpants falling down again, and this time he caught a glance of the downy hair between her legs before she yanked them back up. It was too damn late, though. He was instantly hard. Thankfully, she walked in front of him, and he followed her, trying to push that hot image from his mind.

Holding the sweatpants up with one hand, she led him down the hall to the row of portraits. He'd never noticed the pictures before. They'd always been there, and he'd stopped seeing them many years earlier. She walked up to a large painting with an ornate gold frame. It was a long-ago portrait of Arundell Manor, and judging by the bell skirt that the woman in the picture wore, it was painted around the time of the Civil War.

Two older boys chased their younger brother on the lawn. Not one of them had albinism.

"I don't see him," said Keat.

"Exactly," she said softly. "But he's there. In fact," she traced her finger along a mended tear in the middle of the youngest boy, "this is him. His parents wanted to portray him as having normal coloring." A sigh came from her. "I was with Carrick when he tore this. Jabbed his finger right through the fabric. It burned him—being rejected, hidden away, and colored over. Painted a different color for the world to see, and all by his own family. Imagine this wonderful child with bright white hair and pale white skin."

He stepped back in shock. The memory that had tugged at him but not risen to the surface only a few minutes earlier came on hard. It all happened so long ago, he'd long forgotten it. Though for years it haunted him. He was a boy himself when it happened. The house was still in Charleston, not yet moved, and he woke up one night to see a white-haired boy standing over his bed and staring at him. The boy looked so much like himself, a ghost version of himself, that he lay frozen in his bed, unable to move. Finally, the ghost ran—not floated—but ran from the room. Though Keat was petrified, he followed, running out into the hallway. But the child-ghost was gone.

He felt sick and angry. There was no way he'd ever mention that memory to her. Hell, with this woman standing in front of him saying those things, he never wanted to think about that again. He lashed out at her. "But all of this has nothing to do with you, does it? And it certainly means nothing to me."

She whipped around, her face pinched down with anger. "Nothing to you? I'll tell you what it means," she hissed at him. "What it should mean to you. Carrick's biggest fear was being remembered the wrong way." Her chest heaved. "But maybe his biggest fear should've been that he'd be forgotten completely and that nobody could trouble themselves to care."

Keat said, "He's dead anyway, Penrose. It doesn't matter anymore."

"It doesn't matter?" Her features fell. "Were you even listening to me?"

"Penrose," he began, "they're all dead. Gone!"

Tears shone in her eyes, but her cheeks blazed an angry red. "No, they're not! They live! I saw them not one week ago!"

He opened his mouth to speak, but she cut him off. "And maybe they are dead. Maybe you're right." Her voice hitched. "But they should live on. In your heart, at least. They certainly burn brightly in mine! And I'll tell you why it matters. His pain at the way the world treated him—that pain pushed him, drove him to create the first mechanical man. That one thing about him, his affliction, the thing everyone tried to hide…" She swept her hand in a wide arc, indicating all of Arundell Manor. "Well, it brought about every single thing you have today. He envisioned mechanical men, beings who would be judged by their abilities rather than their color. It was a blessing. Never a curse. I wish he knew that. I wish he could see with his own eyes what he accomplished."

Feet apart, shoulders thrown back, she leaned forward, and her ice-blue eyes stared hard at him. "Everything you are, you owe to him, and it makes me sick to hear you say those words. To deny the gifts your ancestor plopped right into your lap. The gifts that you so casually disregard." She spun around and walked away, somehow managing even in sweatpants to look proud as she strode back toward the bedroom.

He didn't know what to make of her. From the walls

of his house, he'd pulled out a strange woman with fierce blue eyes and strong convictions, and the strangest story ever. And against his better judgment, against every smart thought he'd had, she made his heart pound and his cock hard. Keat stood perfectly still and stared at the painting. The whole thing was pure insanity, and yet he couldn't take his eyes off the boy with the scar running across his body. Keat raked a hand through his hair and sighed. "What the hell is happening to me?" he asked the boy. But the child ran down the hill with that damned expression of glee on his face.

He walked along the hall with slow steps until he came to his bedroom. Closing the door behind him, Keat saw Penrose sitting in front of the fire. She looked gloomy and stared at the flames with a blank expression. He sat beside her, but she didn't look at him.

He cleared his throat and said, "I'm sorry. I didn't mean to be harsh. But you have to understand that this whole thing is nuts, and you...just plopped into my lap. I came here to get away, to go on my annual retreat. I do this every December."

Her gaze shifted warily from the fire to him.

"I came here expecting great things this year. And look what happens." He laughed, a hollow sound, and shook his head. "I can't help but think of my father. He died, you know."

"I'm sorry." Her voice sounded very small.

He shrugged. "I can't decide if my father would be delighted by you or scared to death of you. Both, I suppose. He did love family history. I never listened to him talk about it, though. It just wasn't important to me." He kept it to himself that he still wasn't sure if he believed her. But he couldn't ignore the feeling in his gut, or how she knew so much and how passionate she was about it all.

"I forgive you," she said. "Trust me, I'm just as shocked as you are. If I could wish it away and then return to my time, I would."

No. It was more than a word that popped into his head—it was a force. No, he didn't want her gone, which made everything even stranger. "Tell me about them," he urged.

She seemed hesitant.

"Please," he urged. "Help me understand."

She cleared her throat, a tiny sound, and then began to speak. At first her words were soft and shy and tinged with her Southern accent. As she spoke, the light of the fire danced with the shadows on the walls, and soon her words took on an almost dreamy quality. He stared into the flames as she spoke, and he saw her memories come to life.

She explained everything to him. Carrick and C.J. became real to him, not merely names listed on paper or a corporate feel-good story recited to shareholders. They were his family, trying and failing and trying again to succeed. Now, 130 years later, he was still part of the legacy. A rush of pride, sentiment and humble awe filled him. He couldn't remember ever having such feelings.

He knew she could be deluded or lying, or both. But the intensity of his response to her stories made him not care. She spoke words that his soul needed to hear. Fabrications they might be, but it felt too good listening to them to stop her. He often thought of his father, of the times they'd spent together here at Arundell creating robots. Much like Carrick and C.J.

The realization left him unsettled. His thoughts raced ahead of her words, recalling the stories his father had shared with him. He wished he'd paid better attention. When his father died, all was lost, and he'd never thought of those stories again. His entire focus became creating the next invention or reading the next profit report. The hollow reality of loss settled inside of him. Would his father be forgotten, too, one day? Would he?

It would've been easier if he'd never seen her and faced these emotions. His thoughts returned to the present, and he realized that she'd grown silent.

She slept. Sitting upright, leaning against the side of the chair, with her chin tucked into her chest, she looked soft and beautiful. He checked the clock. One in the morning. Quietly, trying not to wake her, he scooped her into his arms. She weighed nothing, and as soon as he felt her soft body against his, he realized his mistake.

Sighing, stirring slightly, she leaned against his chest and whispered, "Carrick."

He felt that familiar, hot rush of jealousy as he carried her to the bed. It drove him crazy, because the last thing he should be feeling was lust for her. He laid her down. Seeing her body sprawled out on his bed made him wicked hard, and it took a force of will to cover her with the blanket, but he did it. Then, with his lips set in a grim, disciplined line, he pulled down a few pillows and a blanket and lay on the floor in front of the fire, staring up at the ceiling.

He listened to her breathing. She took the most feminine little breaths, and it captivated him. Settling under the covers, she let out the softest sigh of pleasure.

Groaning, he rolled over and stared at the fire, and only when the flames turned to embers did he fall asleep.

Chapter 17

Last night hadn't been a dream, after all, Keat realized as he woke up with aching bones from sleeping on the floor. His ghost lay sleeping in the bed. She was buried so deeply under the covers, all that was visible was the dark waterfall of her hair. Her breathing was heavy and even, and he knew she would sleep a bit longer.

He didn't know exactly what to do with her. But he knew what he didn't want to do, and that was to call the authorities. Not yet. He wasn't about to hand her over to anyone else until he found out the truth. He had no fear that she'd try to escape. Unless she was going to walk countless miles on ice and snow from last night's storm, she was stuck.

Which, he realized as he stared at her, didn't bother him one bit.

But did she travel through time? Last night, listening to her talk it seemed not just possible, but definite. She knew so much about that era, subtle nuances that only someone who had lived during that time would know. He felt the strong emotions behind her words and stories. She had lived those experiences, or at least thought she did.

But, there, in the bright light of morning, without the seduction of the fire and her words, his doubts crept back again. The whole thing was insane, and yet he still wanted to believe her. And the strangest thing of all was that he felt connected, rooted in history and part of a legacy.

He padded downstairs, lit the fire in the workshop and made a pot of coffee in the kitchen. Using his phone, he checked his email and on impulse messaged his assistant, Valerie, to find out everything she could about a woman named Penrose Heatherton who lived in Charleston in the 1800s. He didn't want to look anymore. If there was anything to be found, Valerie would find it—she worked miracles every single day.

His stomach grumbled. He pulled a packet of bacon and a dozen eggs from the fridge and began to cook.

Penrose woke to the morning smells of coffee and bacon. In her whole life, she hadn't ever been as comfortable as she was at that moment lying in the big, fluffy bed. Opening her eyes to the sunlight, she blinked at the strange sight of it before quickly closing her eyes and snuggling under the covers to savor a few more minutes of heaven. The dark tunnel was behind her. That was one good thing at least.

For a moment, she felt she was at Arundell with Carrick, and he was downstairs making breakfast for her.

She indulged in the fantasy, enjoying the rush of happiness it brought her. It was such a sweet reprieve from the anguish she'd known since the earthquake. She let the minutes tick by, listening to the distant sounds of him banging around in the kitchen.

But the persistent sunlight shining in her face forced her back to reality. It was a reminder that this would never be the Arundell she knew. If this were her real home, she'd be sleeping right beside Carrick instead of waking up, bright eyed and ready to face the day.

Everything was the opposite of what it should be. There was nothing she could do about it, and she wasn't sure she minded, she realized as she lay there.

The smell of the coffee tempted her. Well, there was one thing she could do, she could get up and have some coffee. After so long without it, it sounded glorious.

She went to the bathroom and washed up. She brushed her hair until it glistened and the curls were no longer wild, but smooth. She wound her long hair in a bun and tucked a strand in deep to lock it in place. Checking herself in the mirror, she was glad to see her reflection in the light of day, not always in the shadows. She looked alive and felt better than she had since the night she'd arrived.

Her dress hung on the back of the door. She intended to put it on, but when she got close to it, the rank odor almost choked her. It reeked of smoke and filth. There was no choice for her but to leave Keat's clothes on until she washed the gown. Gathering the dress and her underthings, she went downstairs.

Keat stood in the kitchen wearing denim blue jeans and a white button-down shirt. He huddled over the stove tending to the bacon that sizzled in the pan. She took her time and watched him. He was surprisingly graceful and looked even more handsome this morning. Seeing him up close suddenly made her shy and nervous.

The look he gave her as she approached made her even more nervous. He stood still, and his eyes traveled the length of her body. "Good morning," he said, holding up the coffeepot. "Want a cup?"

"Please," she said, sounding almost desperate.

While she stood holding the cup, he poured the steaming coffee to just under the rim. "You look much better this morning."

She smiled. "I feel much better."

"Cream and sugar are over there," he said, nodding at the table.

"I like it black," she said. "I have a favor to ask of you. My dress is filthy, and I need to wash it so that I can have something to wear. Can I use your washtub?"

His lips tilted up in a smirk. "We use machines nowadays. Follow me. I'll show you. I have to be fast though because the bacon's almost done."

She followed him down the stairs to a little space in the back of the workshop where two square machines stood side by side.

"Here they are," he said, opening the door of one of the machines. "You simply put your clothes in here," he said, and then pulled open a little drawer near the top. Nodding at the bottles and boxes on the table, he said, "And you put the soap in there. Shut the door, hit the blue button, and easy as that you'll have a clean dress."

She nodded, looking at the machine in wonder. "I think I understand it," she said.

"Okay, let me run back upstairs. Bacon needs me."

After he had left, she pushed her dress and underthings into the opening, shut the door tight. Then she chose a bottle of soap and poured it in the cup right to the top. Pushing the blue button, she watched through the window as her dress began to tumble around, and water filled the tank.

Immediately, the water turned inky black. Her dress must have been filthy.

"Breakfast is ready!" called Keat from upstairs.

"Coming," replied Penrose. She patted the washing machine to thank it and then headed upstairs.

Keat sat drinking his coffee and watching her eat. She took a seat, politely asked for a napkin and calmly unfolded the paper over her lap. As she ate, she took small bites and chewed daintily. Watching those rosebud lips barely move as she chewed her food drove him crazy. He couldn't explain it, but damn, it was sexy.

She even cut her bacon with a knife and fork. *Who cuts their bacon?* he thought. She did. No doubt about it, she was a strange bird. Oddly, knowing these curious habits of hers pleased him. He could almost imagine the genteel Southern upbringing that would bring about such polite eating. But just because she had old-fashioned table manners didn't make her an old-fashioned woman.

He wasn't buying it. Oh, he wanted to believe her. More appropriately, a certain part of him already believed her. That part of him had bought into her story lock, stock and barrel from the moment she opened her rosebud mouth.

Watching her eat, it was easy to imagine her, sitting at a table 130 years ago, eating in the same manner. But if that were the case, she wouldn't be sitting there driving him wild with that mouth.

He was almost sad when she politely, delicately, placed her napkin on her plate and pushed the plate away.

"Your dress is probably clean by now," he said.

Her eyebrows lifted perfectly as if in total shock. "Really?" she replied. "That fast? That's amazing!" she said in what looked like real surprise. She could win an Oscar. "Is it dry, too?"

"No. It might be too delicate to put in the dryer." He decided to play along with her game of not knowing anything. "Let's go get it."

They went down into the cellar together, but when they reached the washing machine, she slowed and said, "Oh, no!"

"What?" he asked sharply, responding to the shock in her voice. "What is it?" Then he saw it.

She'd bleached her dress. "Why did you put bleach in?"

"I put in the soap that you pointed to." A sharp aroma came from the washer. "What did I do wrong? I didn't know it would take the color out."

"You put bleach in the washing machine. It whitens everything. All colors."

She pulled the dress from the machine and held it up. It was almost uniformly white. A couple of gray splotches. The aroma of bleach was unbearable.

"It's ruined," she said.

"Not necessarily," he said. "Let's wash it again and get the smell out. We can lay it over a chair in the kitchen to dry. It's warmer in there than the workshop.

Give it a few days. Then you can decide whether to toss it or not."

"But I have nothing to wear."

He smiled. "I bet women have been saying that for centuries. Never fear. We'll take a trip into town."

After making Penrose don a black winter coat that swam on her small frame, Keat led her outside and opened the door to the Range Rover. She looked a little odd wearing filthy boots and sweatpants that were too big on her, but she was still sexy. Her cheeks glowed rosy red in the bitter cold, and with her black hair long and free, she was unforgettable.

"Are you sure it's proper?" she'd asked him in a serious voice when he suggested she leave her hair down.

"It's more than proper," he said. "It's expected." Even if it weren't entirely proper, she looked too damn good with it down. It was so shiny and bouncy, like a dark, swirling halo around her beautiful face. Even without makeup, she aced out any woman he'd ever met.

Helping her into the front seat, he shut the door. She looked at him with a face of utter fear, and he smiled encouragingly at her as he walked around to the driver's side. He'd play her game and win.

He was determined to trip her up, to catch her making that one small mistake, one slip of familiarity that would prove he was right and she was lying. He knew it would happen. He just had to be patient.

The way he saw it, she deserved far worse. If he turned her in to the authorities, she'd be carted away, and besides, he might get in trouble himself for failing to report her right away.

Even though he still felt rage pounding in his blood,

he didn't quite want that for her. He was so used to winning, so used to being triumphant that her calm, sweet smile as she steadfastly refused to budge from her story drove him insane. He would win this battle. It might take time, but he would win it.

Sitting in the seat, he turned to her and said, "Are you ready to have fun?"

She looked flushed. Excited. "I think I am. You're sure this is safe?"

"Most of the time," he said with a wink. He fired up the engine, did a three-point turn and drove away on the snow-covered road.

Not five minutes later, he had to fend off her requests to go faster and faster.

"It's snowy, Penrose, we have to keep it pretty tame."

She looked around, eyes wide with amazement. "We have to go faster," she said passionately. "I love it! I cannot believe things can travel this fast!"

"Watch this," he said, as he pushed the button that lowered the windows. Cold air whipped into the car, making her hair fly all in all directions. She squealed in delight and for the first time in a long while, he laughed—a great big belly laugh.

How long had it been since he laughed? Too long by far.

Chapter 18

Penrose felt wild and out of control traveling so fast. Once, when she was eleven, she'd taken a train ride to Savannah with her mother. She had sat on the train, forehead pressed against the window, the world sliding like a backdrop screen behind a play. The images captivated her. Riding in a car, the images assaulted her. Demanded her attention. She gladly, willingly, gave it. "There's no feeling in the world like this!" she exclaimed. "It's amazing!"

"Oh, my dear Penrose," he said with a smug look, "you have no idea what fun this century can be." He gave her a wicked grin. "We're just getting started."

When she looked at him, her stomach flipped. Her black hair whipped around and stung her face, and she smiled at him.

When they came to town, she was surprised by some

things but unsurprised at how similar one town seemed
to another. Keat assured her that was because she was in
a small town. "You should see New York City," he said.

"Oh, I'd love to. My mother told me tales of the city.
She's from New York, you know."

"I didn't know," he said. "What was your mother's
name?"

Was. What a terrible word to hear. It reminded her
that not just her mother was dead, but everyone she
ever knew. "Her name was Diana Heatherton. She died
six months ago." She looked at him apologetically. "I
mean…you know…one hundred and thirty years ago."
It pained her to say those words and to think about her
poor mother, so very long in the grave by now. Forgotten by all.

Keat seemed to understand. He reached out and patted her arm. "You don't need to talk about it. I know
it's hard to lose someone."

She blinked away the sharp tear that poked at her
eye. "Your father?"

"Yes." He grew still and silent, and she felt his mood
turn dark. He didn't elaborate, and from the intensity
of his gaze she thought it best not to pry.

"I'm sorry," she said.

"Thank you," he said. "We're almost there. I'm taking you to the finest shopping establishment backwoods
Wyoming offers. The Supercenter."

"The Supercenter," she repeated after him. It sounded
as exciting as New York City.

Once in the store, Penrose had to recall a simple trick
from her childhood to cope with things that frightened
her. Just keep putting one foot in front of the other.
Stare at your feet, she commanded herself. She con-

centrated on doing that as Keat led her through the enormous store. When she first walked in, everything shouted at her. Lights brighter than a sun shone down from the ceiling. Goods and supplies were jammed on every shelf and stood in piles in the rows. People jostled against each other, pushing their carts.

"Get whatever you want," he told her when they got to the makeup and grooming section. "Get two if you like. It doesn't matter to me."

"I have no way to pay you back," she said.

"You were lucky enough to haunt the house of a very rich man. So trust me when I say get whatever you want."

"Thank you," she said.

"I'm going to get a salesclerk to help us buy some clothes for you. Stay in this section, and I'll be right back."

"I will."

With Keat gone, she indulged all of her urges, marveling at every single product. She put lipstick, hairbrushes, hairpins, ribbons, lotions, creams and body spray into the cart. Next came mascara and blush. In the hair-color aisle, she stood in front of the rainbow of available colors, hardly believing what she saw. She picked colors that appealed to her and tossed them into the cart. She read every package with awe, learning of all their unbelievable powers to make her beautiful and change her whole appearance.

Keat returned with a salesperson, and they went to buy clothes. Once they figured out her size, she was off and running. Jeans were a problem. She couldn't quite get the hang of walking in them, and strode up and down the dressing room in an odd, hitched gait.

But the rest she loved. From blouses to bras, skirts and panties, sandals and heels. Even a pair of sneakers. She adored them all, and when she left the dressing room, she thanked the clerk who had helped her.

"No biggie," said the woman in a bored tone, and shrugged. But to Penrose it was very much a biggie.

When they were paying for their items, Keat picked up the boxes of the hair coloring. "You can't buy these," he said.

"But I love the idea of changing how I look," she protested sadly. She really wanted to experiment.

"You can change how you look. I don't know too much about beauty routines, but I can tell you that your hair is too beautiful to risk on a box of color. I'll make an appointment to have it colored at a salon."

It sounded exciting to her. "Thanks," she said.

After shopping at the Supercenter, Keat said to Penrose, "How about a bite to eat?"

"Sure."

He took her to Trixie's Diner, a mom-and-pop establishment with silver siding and a neon sign. "Now you're in for a real treat," he said. "One of the many benefits of living in this century."

A waitress sat them at a booth near the door. The seats were red plastic, and the table white and full of dull gray scratches. They each slid into the seats, and Keat noticed that she smiled and bounced a little bit, testing the seat.

She was like a child in some ways. Not in the ways that counted, that was for sure. But this innocence, the willingness to explore the world and the sheer delight in doing so, amazed him.

He took a menu from the stand and handed it to her. She spent as much time running her fingers over the clear plastic as she did looking at the items on the menu.

"I'm not usually one to make decisions for another," he said, "but Trixie's diner is famous for their cheeseburgers." He smiled at her. "And will you split a chocolate shake with me?"

"A cheeseburger?" Her eyebrows drew together.

"You haven't heard of a cheeseburger?" he said, making a mental note to research it later. But he appeased her by saying, "I suppose they hadn't invented those yet. What about a milk shake?"

"I haven't heard of that, either."

"Well, then, you are in for a real treat."

An older lady in a yellow uniform came over to take their order. "What'll it be?" the waitress asked, holding a pad of paper and a pen.

"Two cheeseburgers with everything and a double chocolate milk shake. Extra thick. And two straws, please," he said.

A short time later, they sat sipping chocolate milk shakes and eating their meals. Penrose took extra delight in the French fries, swirling them in ketchup until they were dripping before popping the whole thing in her mouth. "These are the most delicious things," she said. "And, yes, I'm familiar with them."

She was adorable. She sniffed the cheeseburger and then tried to take it apart to eat it.

"No, no. Try it like this." He took a big bite, motioning at her to try it.

Raising it to her mouth, she opened wide and took a bite. She nodded to show him how much she liked it.

He took a sip of the shake. "Try this." Pushing the glass over to her, he held out her straw. "It's heaven."

She put her lips around the red straw, and his cock stirred at the sight. He could tell the moment the milk shake hit her mouth because her expression completely changed. Her eyes widened, and her mouth began to work overtime to suck up the sweet concoction. After a few moments, she said, "I think I've died and gone to heaven. This is the most delicious thing I've ever tasted." Pulling the straw from the glass, she ran it through her lips.

He hissed under his breath to see her red lips wrapped around the straw. "I'm glad you like it," he managed to say.

Later that evening, Keat sat at a table in the workshop, reading an email from his assistant, Valerie. There wasn't much new information on Penrose Heatherton, but what little facts Valerie found supported what he already knew, or rather, what Penrose already told him. She was born on May 10, 1865, in Charleston, South Carolina. Her mother was listed as unmarried on her birth certificate. Her father was listed as James Penrose. She appeared in both the 1870 and 1880 census, but there were no records of her after that, save for the listing of her name in the Charleston newspaper as one of the missing in the days after the earthquake.

Seeing her name as one of the missing was new, but beyond that there was frustratingly little to go on. His jaw twitched. That itch was rising up in him. Once he set his mind to something, he wouldn't let up until he got what he wanted. And what he wanted from her was the truth.

Was that all he wanted? An image of that perfect hip, of which he'd caught a glimpse when her sweatpants slipped off, came to mind. He thought of those blue eyes and the way they glittered fiercely at him and the way her face lit up when she laughed, which happened far too rarely.

Maybe it was something else entirely. When she spoke about his family, it made him feel whole again. He knew it was just an illusion, him believing her stories, but whatever the reason, he wasn't about to let her go. If it was an illusion, he wanted it to linger on just a little bit longer.

A sound drew his attention away from his cell phone, and he looked up to see Penrose standing in front of him.

God Almighty.

Her modern look completely surprised him. Her hair was a glossy black cloud. Wearing just a touch of lipstick, she looked hotter than most women looked with a full face of makeup. She wore a blue sweater and a long, formfitting skirt, and the way it clung to her body left no doubt as to the perfection he saw on the first night. She held her now-white dress in one arm and, remembering her in it, he had a definite preference. Modern. All the way. Standing there with those rose-colored lips, she was a temptation like none he'd known before.

"I just went to grab my dress. I'm going to dry it upstairs."

If she was really from another era, then she moved effortlessly between the two centuries. The only indication something wasn't quite right was the uncertain, almost apologetic expression on her face. As if she wasn't comfortable in her own skin.

"You look wonderful," he said, speaking the truth.

She visibly relaxed. "Thank you," she said in that Southern lilt of hers. Taking a few, maddeningly sexy steps forward, she came in front of his table and said, "What are you working on?"

He held up his phone and watched her expression.

"What does it do?" she asked with a curious expression on her face.

"Come now," he coaxed. "Isn't there anyone you'd like to call?"

"To call? No."

"Oh, you'd rather text."

"Please stop," she said. "I don't know what you're talking about."

He looked at her long and hard. "I'll stop for now," he said. "But what I was doing before you walked in was making an appointment at the salon for you to have your hair done."

"Really?" She looked suspicious. "But why are you so nice to me?"

"You're my guest, remember?" he said simply. The truth was, he wasn't entire sure why he wanted to indulge her. He had to run a few errands anyway, he told himself. It didn't hurt anything and, besides, he rather liked the modern Penrose that was blossoming before him.

"Thank you," she replied, tucking a strand of her black hair behind an ear. Her eyes darted around the room. "I was hoping that maybe I could help you with something. I'd like to feel useful." She bit her bottom lip.

That was enough to make a man crazy. She stood

there, looking so eager, so hopeful, that he couldn't say no. "I could use your help with a few things."

She blessed him with a million-dollar smile in return and damn if it didn't turn him into a lovesick teenager, his heart fluttering like mad. It was a smile to move mountains for.

He set her up at a workstation and had her organize the hardware—he was always messy when it came to those things—and she sat patiently, sorting through the nuts, bolts and screws. Her presence in the workshop pleased him, which was a surprise. He usually liked to work alone. After that, he had her clean up the lines on some of his drawings so that he could scan them in and upload them to the 3-D rendering program. When he handed her the bottle of white-out, she seemed fascinated by it.

"You mean, you can just paint white and erase these stray marks?" she asked.

"Yeah, no big deal, Penrose."

"Hmm," she said, reading the bottle with such a studious look he burst out laughing.

He found himself telling her about his ideas and plans. It surprised him. She sat there quietly, her small fingers sorting through the bits and pieces, and soon enough he began talking. She listened eagerly, asking smart and pointed questions that caused him to rethink more than a few things. Which, of course, brought about new ideas.

She inspired him. And maddened him. If only she would admit who she was. It didn't matter where she came from, he just wanted her to tell the truth. He could live with that.

They worked side by side until well past dinnertime

and then ate sandwiches in the kitchen. During dinner, Keat received an alert on his phone that a severe winter storm was headed their way and expected within hours.

It was late when they finished dinner. Penrose looked as if she could work all night, but Keat was tired. "Let's go to bed," he said.

Penrose wasn't sure exactly what she was expecting when he mentioned going to bed, but getting her own bedroom wasn't it. His face was stony as he led her up the stairs. "I've moved your belongings to a spare bedroom," he said. "I think you'll be more comfortable there, and you'll have privacy."

"That's fine," she said, trudging behind him, running her hand along the railing, trying to hide her disappointment. The knowledge that he didn't want her in his bedroom hurt. It was foolish, of course, but it still stung to hear it. Not that she wanted anything to happen. No, of course she did. After being alone in the tunnel and watching him from afar, his nearness only intensified her longing.

He brought her to a room a few doors down from his and opened the door for her. Doing her best to keep her face neutral, she thanked him. The room was fine, comfortable, with a twin bed and a dresser, and she'd be safe with him nearby. But she wanted to hear his breathing, his footsteps, and the muttered curses when he was frustrated. She craved his presence.

After he had left, she went to her pile of new belongings and pulled out a nightgown to wear. It was the lightest blue color and slipped over her body like silk. It was so thin she'd have to snuggle under the covers to stay warm.

After crawling into bed, she was restless and sleep wouldn't come. Images of Carrick and Keat kept popping into her mind and blending together, confusing her. And arousing her. Each of them held a different appeal. Finally, she gave up. She sat up, sweating and wiping her brow, wishing that they were the same man. A foolish wish, she knew, but her heart still desired it. She wanted both men and yet she could have neither. Keat distrusted her, seemed bent on proving her a fraud, and she would probably never see Carrick again.

Finally, she fell into a restless sleep.

The next afternoon, Keat drove her to town. They walked side by side along the main street until they came to The Spiral Curl Salon. Penrose stood in front of the window, staring at the pictures of the models that hung in the window.

"What are you staring at?" he asked her.

She couldn't believe how beautiful the women were. "I could never look like that," she said. "I can't believe how all the women are so perfect in the future."

"Penrose, you outshine them all."

Her blue eyes darted to meet his own. He changed the subject. "Come on, let's go inside and see what they can do for you."

The beauty parlor had a bell on the door that jingled loudly when they entered. It was at the end of the day, and the shop was quiet. It smelled of spice and perfumes and a stick of incense burned by the checkout counter. From the back of the shop came the clack-clack-clack of a pair of heels as a woman approached the counter.

"Can I help you?" she asked.

Looking at the woman, Penrose thought of a rainbow.

In her late forties, she had rich brown hair and wore a collage of colors, from her red vest to her black fancy shoes. Gold rings gleamed from her fingers. There was something so coiffed, so perfect about her. The woman took one look at Penrose and said, "My word. I have two things to say to you. Trim and eyebrow wax." She smiled warmly. "And I say that with love, darling."

Penrose looked at Keat for help. She was hopelessly lost.

"We have an appointment," Keat said, barely containing a smile.

"I've cleared the decks. A complete makeover. And my pleasure." She turned to Penrose. "And look at you. You're like a blank canvas." She walked around the counter and circled Penrose, analyzing her hair. "How long has it been since you had a haircut?" She spoke sharply before adding in a kinder tone, "My name is Ophelia, and I'm the owner. And, honey, what rock have you been hiding under that you've gotten this far in life without at least highlighting your hair?"

Penrose wasn't sure how to answer, and again Keat had to speak up. "She's been out of touch with modern times. That's the easiest explanation," he said.

Ophelia looked at Penrose. "You poor thing. You mean like a cult?"

"Something like that," said Keat.

"Come on back," she said to Penrose. "Let's sit you in the chair and find out what you're interested in." She pointed at Keat. "You can either make yourself comfortable or make yourself scarce. Your choice, mister."

"Scarce," he said, chuckling.

"Come on now, darling," Ophelia said to Penrose. "Have a seat."

Keat finished his errands and returned to the shop. He walked inside and then stopped. He stood there staring stupidly at her, trying to absorb the shock of seeing her as a hot, modern woman. Not just any hot modern woman, but the hottest one he'd ever seen. He had loved her black hair, but it didn't hold a candle to her as a blonde. God wasn't supposed to make mistakes, but he sure made one with her—she was meant to be a blonde.

"I told you," Ophelia said proudly. "He'll be eating from the palm of your hand." She beamed from behind the counter.

Penrose stood up. She looked anxious, standing with her hands in front of her, wringing them together. He knew he should say something, give her a compliment at least, but damn if he couldn't speak.

"Yep. That's the best compliment of all. The speechless kind."

Keat looked at Ophelia and then at Penrose. "She's right. You look amazing. Beyond any compliment I could give you."

A tiny smile pulled at her mouth. Her cheeks turned the faintest pink, and she stared at her hands. Keat looked at her hands. Eating from her palms sounded mighty fine to him.

Chapter 19

Penrose lay in bed later that night, marveling at her new hair color. The blow-dryer had impressed her, the magical hair color impressed her—everything did. Except for the dragging hollowness that she felt with Keat.

There were bright spots, like the rush she got when he looked at her a certain way. But he maintained the foolish insistence that she was putting on a ruse. Or worse. It made her angry, the way he played with her. Nice one minute but cruel the next. She wasn't crazy, as he accused her of being, but she would be soon if he kept it up.

The two centuries were so different; yet, there were things she loved about both of them. She thought of home—the scent of pine in the air, the green trees that crowded every piece of land they could. It was so lush, so beautiful that she longed for it. She looked out of the window. Another storm.

Snow never seemed to end here.

She wanted to go home. The longing came on strong. If only there were some way she could. But maybe…

After all, there were so many amazing technologies in the present. Maybe she was missing something, some kind of science that could send her back in time. Back to the Arundell she belonged in. The idea took hold. Of course, she wouldn't ask Keat. She knew the answer he'd give her. No, the only one she could ask was Harris.

She decided to try it. Slipping from her bed, she walked across the cold marble floor, quietly opened the door and made her way down the hall. The clock struck two in the morning, and she noticed the snow falling even heavier outside. No wind, just big, fat flakes dropping heavy and fast.

It was cold downstairs, and she regretted not putting on a robe, but she wasn't about to turn around and fetch it. She went through the kitchen and down the cellar stairs to the workshop.

In the workshop, it was colder still, and her skin puckered. The robots were lined up like soldiers. She saw Harris over by the fireplace. No fire burned. He seemed almost lonely, waiting there. She went and knelt in front of him, and the stone floor hurt her knees. She said, "Power up."

The black screen on his helmet flashed bright white before the image of two blinking eyes appeared. "Hello, Pen Rose," he said in a loud voice.

"Shh," she urged him, pressing her fingers to her lips. "Can you talk lower?"

"Yes, of course I can," he replied in a softer voice.

Penrose looked left and right as if she was about to commit a crime, and then whispered, "Harris, can you tell me how to travel back in time? I want to go home. I can't stay here anymore."

Keat opened his eyes with an uneasy feeling. He'd had lots of uneasy feelings lately, but this one had teeth and put him instantly on edge. Something wasn't right. Rolling from his bed, he threw on a pair of jeans and went to check on Penrose.

She wasn't there. His first thought, when he saw the empty bed, was that she'd gone back to the tunnel. He flew down the stairs two at a time, racing to the entry door of the tunnel. When he opened it, the lingering, offensive odor of smoke rose out of it, sharp enough to turn him away. The reek was too heavy in the air to tolerate. He was sure of it. Then, as he was shutting the entry door, he heard the faint monotone voice of Harris coming from the workshop, and he went straight there.

When he came to the stairs, he saw Penrose. The sight of her on her knees in a nightgown that was thin as paper stopped him in the doorway. He saw her in profile, saw the teardrop shape of her breasts, the swell of her backside and her hair trailing down her back. The look on her face, earnest and pleading as she whispered to Harris, should have brought about pity, but instead it angered him. Damn her. He stood there, breathing hard, emotions pushing and pulling at him, and he heard her ask, "Harris, can you tell me how to travel back in time? I want to go home. I can't stay here anymore."

The foolishness must stop, and it would stop right here, right now. He felt a tidal wave of sickening emotion. And worry for her. He had thought she stuck to her guns because she was lying, but that look on her face was too eager, too hopeful, to be lying. She truly believed that she lived in that era, and that angered him even further.

She was his little ghost. But she was disturbed, and he had to face that fact. He pawed his face in despair. He should have known better. He was a bit of a celebrity. Whenever he went out with a woman, her face appeared in the magazines, with some crazy title that the reclusive billionaire might have found his bride. His team had always cautioned him to have a security force around him. God, it made perfect sense. She had just hit him sideways with all of her passion and facts about his family.

She was a stalker. The knowledge hit him like a ton of bricks, and it didn't sit well. He stepped into the room and said in a cold voice, "Harris."

Penrose gasped and turned sharply. He should have empathy for her, with those big eyes and that scared expression, but he ignored the feeling. Once and for all, he would prove to her, and to him, that she was deluded.

"Hello, Keat," said Harris. "What can I do for you this morning?"

"Harris," said Keat, walking into the room. "Can you tell me everything you know about Penrose Heatherton, born in 1865?" he asked the robot, knowing the files had been uploaded to the server by his assistant.

"Of course, Keat," began the robot in a chillingly dispassionate voice. "Penrose Heatherton was born in Charleston, South Carolina, on May 10, 1865…"

With cold disinterest and a monotone voice, Penrose listened as the robot recited the facts of her life. The stone floor beneath her knees was softer than the truth. She watched the bright, happy eyes of Harris fade away

and pictures of Charleston in the aftermath of the earthquake began to flash across his screen. She felt numb
and almost sick to her stomach to see the images that
flashed across the screen. Her beautiful hometown destroyed. Lives lost. But whose lives? She choked back
a sob and looked at Keat, unable to hide her despair.
He was cruel.

Without a trace of passion or life in his voice, the
robot continued. "Penrose Heatherton is found in the
1870 and 1880 census as living with Diana Heatherton.
According to the *Charleston Observer*, she was listed as
a missing person in the aftermath of the Great Charleston Earthquake, and there are no further records of her."

"Enough," said Keat. He strode over to the pile of
firewood, picked up a few logs, tossed them into the
fireplace and lit a fire. His back was to her, and she had
the urge to push him into the flames.

"You're cruel." She leaned back and rested on her
heels. She felt crushed. Furious. Her voice shook as
she spoke. "If you think those facts will convince me
that I'm not her, you couldn't be more wrong." Tears
stung her eyes, and she pressed at her eyes hard, trying
to stop them. "It breaks my soul in two. Because my
life has been broken in two." *And now my heart*, said a
little voice deep inside of her. She'd only just begun to
realize the depths of her emotions for him.

"I can't decide if you're a schemer or if you're crazy,"
he replied, turning around slowly to face her. He looked
cold, dispassionate. Like a robot himself. "I'm still not
sure. But I'm sure of one thing, Penrose—if you are
who you say you are, and if you were born in 1865, then
you are a ghost. According to the newspaper, you were
never seen again. And the man you ask for is dead, as

well. Look at the calendar. Carrick is long dead. You are, too. Which makes you a ghost in my home." He sighed, deep and heavy, and strode forward until he stood above her. "But you know the real truth."

His words took a moment to sink in. Of course, looking at the calendar gave a simple truth, but one she never really dwelled on. The truth hurt, more than hurt. It destroyed her. Everyone she'd ever known and every person she'd ever seen was dead. C.J. was dead. Carrick was dead.

Carrick was dead. Of course he was, but still she found it hard to breathe. It was so strange, the way the fact kept pounding, swirling in her thoughts. She stood up slowly, her knees screaming in protest. "I know what you say is the truth. But, Keat, inside of me, I know what I say is also the truth. Nothing you can do to change it. Nothing. The truth stands alone, and it stands in my heart."

"There are only two possibilities. The first and factual one is that you are someone else, and that you suffer from a severe mental problem. The second is that you are dead and a ghost—"

Angry, she cut him off. "I'm not dead! And I'm not lying, either!" She was defensive, taking steps backward and shaking her head. "I'm right here, Keat. Alive. Not dead, and I'm telling you the truth." Something inside of her broke open. "You think that you have it all down, don't you?" Her hands shook as she ran them through her hair. "You have all the facts. You have robots. And fancy things. Machines. And now you're going to stand there and tell me what I am. So, tell me, do I look like a ghost to you?"

He didn't answer but stood there with a clamped-down expression on his face.

She was tired of trying to understand everything, to make the best of the mess she was in. "I'm not crazy. I'm not a ghost." But her voice wavered as a sick little thought came into her head. Suddenly, she needed to prove she was alive. She needed to feel. Taking a few more steps, she spun around and ran to the doors of the workshop, flung them open and ran out into the snowstorm wearing nothing but her nightgown.

The whiteness swallowed her up, and the cold was a million thorns on her skin. Flakes swirled around her, eddied and blew past her. She ran as far as she could, kicking up rooster tails of powder until she couldn't see the manor anymore and the world was merely a blur of white and gray. Breathing heavily, she stood letting the cold eat at her, bite her skin, trying to savor every sensation. Even the pain. "I'm alive," she said, and it felt right to say those words. It felt affirming. So she raised her voice, and over and over she repeated, "I am alive. I am alive. I feel this. I feel this," until her voice rose to a shout.

The wind whipped higher as if it agreed with him and she screamed in reply, "Aren't I alive? Doesn't my heart beat?"

There was no answer but the wind.

A shadowy figure appeared through the curtain of falling snowflakes.

"Penrose!" Keat called out, moving in her direction. "There you are," he said, coming to stand in front of her. He rubbed his arms over his bare chest. "Come back to the house."

The snow swirled around them. "No," she said,

angry. Everything hurt. Moving hurt. Shivering, she took one step forward, close enough that she reached out and jabbed him with her finger. "I've had enough," she whispered. "Enough of your taunting. Your jabs. Your eyes on me every second, waiting for me to slip up. I've spoken the truth since my first word to you."

Her chest heaved as she spoke. "You call me ghost. The newspaper calls me missing. The calendar calls me dead." She shook her head back and forth wildly. "But I live. I'm alive. Aren't I?" she asked in a hopeless voice. "How can I be dead and feeling all of this? I'm not dead, Keat. I'm alive, and I'm not lying."

Flakes of snow clung to his hair and his eyebrows. Looking up at his eerily familiar face and snow-white hair, for one brief moment she saw Carrick. An anguish filled her soul.

"Please, Keat, I want to go back. I want to go home. You can keep your lightbulbs and your helicopters and your washing machines. I want the Arundell I know and love." She stepped closer, close enough that their chests touched. "I want the duck pond and the oak tree," she whispered. "I want people around me who believe in me."

Carrick was a damaged soul, but he needed her. Keat was whole and strong, yet he rejected her. Life wasn't worth living unless you lived it in the company of those who valued you.

She shook so violently from the cold that she could barely speak, and her words came out in a pathetic whisper, "I want a man who looks at me and believes in me. You distrust me and look at me with disgust. So yes, I want to go home. Can you blame me?" She was numb and cold. Burned with cold. Burned with anger. But she reveled in the feeling because it was proof she lived.

She raised her finger and pointed at him accusingly. "You. Do you think that I came here to be with you? You're wrong. My body may want you, but my mind knows what you are. A monster. The sad truth is that I'm stuck with you, and I'm stuck in this damned new century."

She called him a monster. Keat didn't care. It was what she said before that that mattered. She wanted him. The second he heard those words it was as if an iron band that had constricted his chest for the past few days had been cut and he could breathe again. Hope again.

He hands slid behind her head, and he lifted her face to his. Her hair felt icy, but her skin hot. Hot and most definitely alive. Suddenly, nothing mattered but that one fact. "You are alive, Penrose," he said. "I promise you that and I can prove it."

"How?" she cried in a desperate voice. The snow-flakes on her hair created a white, lacy shawl around her face. Her cheeks were flushed pink, her lips even pinker. She looked up at him with anguished eyes, a desperation he'd never seen on a person before.

It was a fear so deep and a pain so real that any lingering doubts he had about her story disappeared. Facts and science no longer mattered. Only she did, and the sudden, booming certainty inside of him. He believed her. He felt it in his bones. He'd never been so angry, so scared, or so taken by a person before. From the moment he saw her, his emotions had been wild. Fear to lust, hate to longing, and now something deeper.

She looked up at him. She seemed so small, shivering

as she was in his hands. He felt a fierce need to protect
her and an even fiercer need to kiss her, to claim her in
some way, as if that might lock her into this century.
"I want you. I believe in you. Come inside and let me
prove it." He kissed her, his lips coming down hard, his
hands gripping her.

Chapter 20

Keat's lips took hers, descended on them and claimed them. A flame came to life within Penrose. If she weren't alive, his lips would've coaxed her back from the dead. She had ice on her fingers, her feet had turned to stone, and her body was frozen. But her soul burned with life. The sensation of his lips on hers was stronger than any snowstorm, any sting the world could give her.

The kiss traveled to the bottom of her soul and back again. She most certainly lived. The smallest whimper escaped her lips, and Keat seemed to understand what she said. Yes. She'd said yes. He scooped her into his arms, crushing her body to his for warmth, and carried her through the snow back to Arundell Manor.

"You need a bath," he said. "You need to warm up." Melting snow dripped onto the floor as he carried her up the stairs to his bathroom. It was all she could do to cling to him. Her thin nightgown was plastered to her body, and she felt the heat from his skin.

He didn't turn the bathroom light on as he entered. The dim light from the hallway spilled through the open door and made the bathroom shadowy. With his foot, he kicked the tub faucet and water streamed into the tub. They stood while the water filled the tub, and he held her in those strong arms of his.

It seemed that in an instant everything had changed. The way he looked at her was different. The way he held her was protective. It was hard to know how to react, and she felt a bit shy. Uncertain. Fluttery.

When the bath was almost full, he placed her, standing upright, into the tub. The warm water swirled around her shins. "Don't go," she said.

"Penrose, I'm not going anywhere." His voice was low. Standing right beside the tub, he put a hand on her shoulder and slipped a finger beneath her strap of her nightgown. She tilted her chin, the slightest nod, and his fingers worked their way down her shoulders, taking the wet fabric with them. Looking down, she saw her chest rising and falling rapidly. His hands were so warm and seemed to sear her cold, damp skin.

Her breasts were bared. He looked down and sucked in his breath, and a rush of pleasure flooded her at his reaction.

His fingers moved again, and, with aching slowness, he peeled the fabric away from her stomach. The nightgown dropped into the water at her feet.

He took a huge breath and exhaled in a soft whistle. "The sight of you," he whispered.

The mirror beside the tub reflected their image. The faint light illuminated every curve of her body. Her nipples were dark points jutting out, and a dark shadow was visible between her legs. Keat looked tall, imposing. Dark. His jeans were soaking wet. They revealed every muscle of his strong legs and the stiff tent that bulged at his crotch, and suddenly she shivered from head to toe.

"Water," he ordered her, putting his hand on her shoulder.

"It's not from the cold—"

He interrupted her. "I don't care. Down." Putting his hand gently on her, he pushed her down. She slid down, right in front of his jeans and saw his erection more clearly. Immediately, her eyes darted up to meet his dark gaze.

"You do that to me," he said in a low voice. "Even when I thought I'd imagined you."

A tiny thrill of sensation rushed between her legs as she slipped into the steaming water. Penrose wasn't embarrassed or shy lying down in front of him. Maybe in some way she invited his gaze. After all, she'd been hidden for so long, and spent her days secretly taking in the sight of him. It thrilled her to have him taking in the sight of her. She lay in front of him as if to say *here I am*.

He took a deep breath. "Sometimes I think you enjoy making me insane. You know I'm coming in that water with you."

"Yes," she said.

Suddenly there was a fierce gust of the wind that shook the house, and the lights went out. The room was plunged into darkness. The house, which hadn't seemed very loud before, was suddenly as quiet as a tomb.

"Keat?" she whispered. Her heart punched in her

chest, and all she could think of was the tunnel. "Keat?" she asked again, her voice rising to a whine.

"It's okay, Penrose." He moved. His voice came to her from a different place. "Stay there," he said in a calming voice. "It's just a blackout. A power outage where the lights go out. It's temporary. I'm going to get some candles. I'll be right back. Be calm."

He was gone. The room was too quiet. When she moved, the rippling water sounds seemed unbearably loud. Breathe, she reminded herself. Dim moonlight came through the window and lit the tendrils of steam that rose up like ghosts from the water. Her eyes adjusted.

Something nagged at her, a sense of doom that some fact had been overlooked.

"It's nothing to worry about," Keat said. "I'm back," he called from the hallway. Then she saw his familiar form carrying a tray filled with a dozen candles flickering with little flames. He continued, "The power will be back on soon, I'm sure of it. I thought we'd have some fun with it."

Penrose watched as he approached the tub, sat beside her and set the tray down. "You look beautiful in the candlelight," he said. "Like a fiery angel."

Candles.

She said nothing, merely watched silently, in shock, as he lifted a candle, placed it in the water and gently nudged it in her direction. Oh, she thought, fate was cruel. Things were repeating. Dear God, things were repeating.

It twirled out straight toward Penrose. Keat took a few more candles and scattered them over the water.

"Stop," she said in a quivering voice. She was instantly split in two centuries. "Please, stop." She froze, barely even able to draw breath. Panic rose inside of her, and she couldn't understand why. She couldn't let those candles go out—with all her heart she knew they couldn't go dark. If those candles went dark, something very bad would happen. "Please, take the candles from the water. Please."

"Penrose," he said with a look of concern on his face. "What is it?"

How could she explain it to him? That she and Carrick had placed candles on the dark water, and that the indifferent darkness had snuffed them out? She looked at him with every ounce of emotion she had, willing him to understand. "Please," she whispered in a voice that didn't sound like her own.

"Sure," he said, "no problem." He scooped his hand into the water to lift a candle. The motion created a wave that rippled out, reaching first the nearest candles, which wobbled and then flipped.

"No. No. No," she said softly, and covered her mouth with her hand. Other candles began tipping into the water and flipping over. She closed her eyes. "Make it stop. Please. They can't go out!"

"They're just batteries. Open your eyes. There's nothing to be scared of. They won't go out."

She opened her eyes the tiniest bit and peered out through the fringe of her eyelashes. A fuzzy yellow glow greeted her, and then her eyes flew wide open. And she saw the miraculous sight of the candles hanging upside down, yet still burning. The little flames flickered, illuminating the dark water and casting wavy rays of yellow light on her skin.

"Look," he said. "I'll show you. I'll turn it over." He reached for a candle, his hand sliding under the water and brushing against her thigh. It left a trail of heat on her skin. "It's okay, look," he said. He turned the candle right side up, and the strange light still burned perfectly.

"You don't understand," she whispered, and shook her head, unwilling to believe what was happening. She spoke without thinking. "What if this is our brief chance at heaven?" she said, remembering the words that were once spoken to her by a different Arundell man. Carrick's words. The words seemed to hang over the water of the bath.

It was not Carrick who replied, though. It was Keat. "If this is our nirvana, then I've died happy, Penrose."

The world had turned inside out. She was staring at candles that burned under the water. They were a different kind of fire.

She looked up at Keat. He was a different kind of man. Not a dark twin to Carrick. And what if this really was her brief nirvana? What if this was the only happiness she could grasp? Wouldn't Carrick want it for her? Of course he would. Carrick himself had said, "Fire has no choice but to grab its moment, whatever moment it's given, and burn."

A different century. A different kind of fire. A different man, one she couldn't help but to burn for. Was this the moment she'd been given? It was. She turned to Keat and said, "Take me to bed now."

"My pleasure," he replied, and reached down for her.

They went to his bedroom, and he laid her dripping wet on the bed. By the light of the fire, he saw her. She was magnificent, Keat thought. The sight of her body was a shock to his system. He sucked in his breath like a dying man. He was so used to plucked and perfected women.

Christ, he wanted her, wanted her like no other woman before. His cock was stiff and ready to bury itself inside of her.

She reached up to him and touched his stomach. He peeled his cold, wet jeans off and climbed into the bed.

Her skin was hot. His was cold. A groan came from some dark, primitive place within him. Their bodies slid against each other, exchanging high temperature and cold, settling on a burn that pleased both of them.

He kissed her. She had the sweetest little mouth he'd ever felt. Good God, her mouth could drive a man to insanity.

She whimpered and moaned, and her hands were everywhere on his body. There was a wildness in her that reminded him of a winter storm, fierce and determined. He moved with deliberate slowness, taking her mouth slowly with his own, thrusting his cock against her bare thigh. He kissed her for so long that her mouth became swollen from his kisses. Now she was no longer fierce but softened, ripe and willing. Every time his hands touched her body, she arched her back and opened her legs.

He was torturing himself. It took all his will not to slip his hand over her downy hair and between her legs. Once he felt her hot and wet and waiting, he would be unable to resist. And he wanted this to last, because he felt alive. Wholly alive. Her body bloomed under his hands. His touch coaxed moans and whimpers from her.

With other women, he was mechanical, like a robot. With her, he was alive.

* * *

Penrose wanted him. She closed her eyes. She wanted to savor his touch and block out everything else except the trail of heat he left along her skin. Her awareness followed his fingertips.

He came to her breasts first, caressed them and brought her nipples to fine points. Then his hands traveled over her stomach, lingering and gripping her pelvic bone. She thrust upward, inviting him lower. But he denied her, skimming lightly over her curls and down her thighs.

Need consumed her. She wanted to be taken by him. Claimed. The rest could wait.

"Now, Keat," she begged him when she couldn't take it any longer.

As he settled over her, she realized that there would be two moments in her life. Before and after, and she was in the very last moments of before. "Hurry," she whispered, not wanting to chance fate, grabbing his hips and urging him on. She was ready for the after. For the ever after.

He spread her legs, positioned himself at her entrance and then thrust inside.

Heat consumed her, a deep passion made fierce what they had endured together.

"Yes," she whispered, trailing the word in a long sigh. It felt as if she'd waited a century for this moment.

How strange that she felt so comfortable with Keat, Penrose marveled. It was a different century, after all. Of course, it wasn't simply the change on the calendar. But the feeling she had when she was next to him was a timeless contentment. It didn't matter what the calendar said when she was next to him. She felt whole. For an entire week, they indulged themselves in the bedroom, spending long, lingering mornings twisting in the sheets before they made their way downstairs to eat breakfast.

Penrose often accompanied him to the workshop. At first, she watched him and did small jobs, her mouth open in awe at every bit of technology the robots had inside of them. After a few days, she began to ask questions and then graduated to offering her opinions. Which were usually wrong. But it was still exciting to discuss ideas with Keat. He reminded her of Carrick in that he loved a good discussion about inventing.

Every moment felt sweet but stolen. All of her emotions for Keat came with the small but still-present baggage of guilt attached. Everyone she knew was gone. Carrick was long dead, and though her emotions were poignant, they'd certainly dimmed. Her short time with him felt almost like a dream. He was gone, but she vowed to never let his memory die away.

Some of her favorite moments were in the bathroom, sitting at the vanity and trying out new looks. Keat bought her magazines, and she flipped through the pages, looking at the glossy photos with awe. She experimented.

Sometimes, when she emerged from the shower and looked at herself in the mirror, she barely recognized herself.

Later that week, Keat set up a movie on the large-screen television, grabbed some blankets and settled on the couch with Penrose to watch a movie. It was his new hobby—watching Penrose as she watched movies. Her reactions delighted him. For that night, he'd chosen *The Hobbit*.

When the movie started, he sat back and watched Penrose. She had no filter. She looked at him with absolute awe as she watched the strange creatures, peppering him with questions about how real they looked. Every emotion tore through her. She cried and laughed and screamed in fear. And every reaction entranced him.

He savored rather than distrusted her genuine delight at the world around them. He wanted to run from thing to thing and show them to her. He found new love in old, everyday items, and in visiting old ideas, he discovered new possibilities for his robots. She was like magic to him. He wasn't ever going to let her go. It didn't matter that he'd only known her a few weeks. His heart had longed a lifetime for her.

They drove into town later that week to do some shopping. On the way back home, she begged Keat to take her for a long drive. He indulged her, speeding up and down the roads, taking her deeper and deeper into the mountains. They drove for hours. He played music for her. All different kinds. She surprised him by liking pop music blared at high volume. They passed through a huge meadow covered in snow. Keat pulled the Range Rover to the side of the road and asked her, "Do you want to go play in the snow?"

She gazed out at the wide-open, perfectly untouched sea of white. She grinned wickedly. "Of course, I do," she said, and then, without hesitation, she opened the car door, stepped outside and ran straight into all that white powder.

Her breath came in great, steaming bursts. Cold air

sounded different than the warm summer air of Charleston. Keat yelled to her, but his voice was muted, and she kept on running. She'd been so trapped, so cooped up in the dark tunnel that the blindingly white open space felt like heaven. No. Better than heaven. It felt like life. With Keat at her side, she was fearless. She'd never been happier in her life than at that moment.

Something hit her back, and white powder exploded into a cloud all around her. She did a swift about-face, her hair whipping around. He ran toward her. Quickly, she scooped up a ball of snow and aimed it at Keat, who ran at full speed toward her. Her snowball didn't make it very far. It landed with a soft plop a few feet away from her. He ran faster, a solitary man in a winter wilderness. He took her breath away.

She scooped up another handful of snow and made her last stand. Widening her stance, she patted the ball tight as she'd seen him do and cocked her arm back. He barreled toward her, snow flying, his long legs eating up the ground between them. Her blood whooshed like mad in anticipation, and she focused on timing her snowball just right.

Counting out loud, she tried to pace his run to her throw. "One." Her hands packed the ball again. "Two." She trained her eyes on him. He was right there. "Three!" she shouted, throwing the ball.

Her timing was terrible. He was already in front of her by the time she let go. An explosion of white powder burst in front of her eyes. Before she even understood what happened, a tall, hard body enveloped her and then she was falling, falling.

The ground came up fast, but the snow was soft. His body was hard on top of hers. Warm, too. The snow stole all of the sounds and swallowed the whole world. Their breath was ragged, and he rolled her over so that she lay on top of him.

She leaned down to kiss him, draping her hair around his face. His lips were cold when hers touched his. A grunt of satisfaction rumbled from deep inside him. His hands wound through her hair, pulling her tight against him—and his tongue. That hot tongue slipped into her mouth.

Her whimper went nowhere. His mouth stifled it. Strong hands roamed her body, pressing against her and forcing her as close as possible to him. Grabbing her rump, he thrust her up and down on his very rigid cock.

"Oh," she said when she felt it through her jeans.

"*Oh* is right," he said. "See what you do to me? Winter has nothing on you, Penrose. You heat up any man's blood."

"Do I?" she asked, loving to hear those words from him and craving more.

"Take these pants off," he said. "I need you right now."

"Here?" she asked. "It's so cold." Her nipples were already hard points. Even her nose had numbed.

"I'll keep you warm."

She looked around, but all she could see in every direction was a white canvas. Only his black car stood out.

Only them. His hands began pushing her pants down her body.

"Off," he growled.

She complied, and happily, too. Her feet easily slipped out of the boots, and she stood towering above him, enjoying the view of his body stretched out right in front of her. Proof of his desire was the bulging in his denim pants and the intense look on his face.

He was so handsome. Everything had changed so much in the past week. As she stood before him, a little throb of anticipation pulsed between her legs. She shed her jacket, then her shirt, and quick as lightning she shimmied out of her jeans. She was getting better with wearing jeans.

"Oof," he said. "I've never been so damned cold and so damned hot at the same time. Get over here, Penrose."

She went and lay on top of him. His hands cupped her buttocks again. He urged her higher. "I want to taste you," he whispered. Rising up, she scooted higher, her knees burning in the snow. Her goose bumps tightened. Her stomach fluttered. She hovered with the most intimate part of her body right above his mouth.

A wicked smile teased on his lips. "This I like. No, this I love." He slipped two fingers between her legs and opened her lips. The bitter air swirled around her heat as the fingers of one hand slipped inside her and the other buried itself in the flesh of her backside. He held her firm. He wouldn't let her go. Or even move. His hands forced her down onto his mouth, and he locked her in place.

She cried out. His tongue. His mouth. Right there. She was forced to endure. To give in. To fly.

Her whimpers and moans, dampened by the heavy air, fell to the ground as soon as they left her lips. Dimly, she was aware of the world. A herringbone sky above. Pockets of melting snow dimpling the blanket around them. All bright images against his dark looks.

His lips were soft, pulling, sucking on her clitoris,

gentle and welcoming. But, beneath his lips, his tongue darted insistently, almost cruelly, flicking against her again and again. She bucked. Or tried to, but he held her still. As best she could, she rode him and thrust against him in minute motions.

A deeper need ruled her. She leaned down and twisted her hands around his head, dug her fingers into his hair. His eyes were closed, his mouth on fire. A delicious numbness gathered. Desperately, she tried to stay ahead of it, moving faster and faster until it overtook her, and in a fit of whimpers she went completely still. Then she fell forward, burying her hands in the icy snow, panting for breath as waves of pleasure flooded her.

He held perfectly still with his hands clutching her thighs. His mouth was gentle once more. Every touch of his tongue made her quiver, and he waited until the little waves passed. Only then did he release her.

Hovering over him on all fours, she said simply, "I never knew."

It took a moment for him to speak. He gripped her thighs and moved her lower onto his torso. She saw the glisten of her moisture on his lips as he spoke. "I never knew, either." He pulled his hands away, and she heard the sound of his zipper.

She lifted up so that he could lower his jeans.

"God," he said. "That's cold."

Moving her hips down his body until she was right over his hardness, she settled over him, legs wide, eyes on him, and pressed down.

Oh, that. It was a piercing. A hot and quick surrender and then he was buried. She couldn't move. She needed to stretch to accommodate him. He moaned and threw his arms to the side, clutching fistfuls of snow. He arched, contorted and hissed, "Dammit, Penrose. You're torturing me."

That was all she needed. She buried him deep in her belly and began circling her hips. She was sated, still numb and throbbing but no longer needy. So she taunted him—pulled back her hair, exposing her body to his gaze.

She rolled her hips around, watching his reaction. He looked driven, almost angry. It made her wild. She bit her lips and rolled again, stretching her breasts higher. Reveling in it.

A blur of motion. Icy hands at her hips. Grinding, demanding, forcing. On and on, bucking her around. He roared, primitive and claiming.

It was his turn to pant, to close his eyes. But not for long. He exploded in a roar. Only a moment later, he said, "I hate to do this—" he lifted her from his still-throbbing hardness "—but my ass is frozen solid."

They crammed into their wet and frigid clothes and laughed all the way back to the Range Rover. Now that their passion was sated, the cold announced itself with a vengeance. She shivered and walked as fast as she could, trying to force the jacket on. He ran, half-naked, and got to the car before her.

Once she reached the car, she was greeted by the sight of him pantless, sitting in the driver's seat, not even bothering to try to dress.

"They're heated seats," he explained with a wry grin on his face.

Chapter 21

After they returned home, they ate dinner and worked on the prototype. Penrose felt his eyes on her more than once. Finally, Keat went upstairs and called down to her from the landing, "Come on up, Penrose!"

"In a minute!" she replied. She had something she wanted to do. She had to look for it, but she finally found the white-out on Keat's table. Taking it upstairs with her, she padded down the hall until she came to the painting of Carrick as a child. With tender, gentle strokes, she painted his hair white and then stood back to look at him. It still wasn't quite right, but it made her feel better. The past mattered. These moments would matter, too.

She went to bed, and they made love by the light of the fireplace. The last thing she remembered before she'd fallen in the snow was the rising wind and heavy snowfall. She watched the flakes spin by the window until her eyes closed.

When she woke later, the fire in the bedroom had gone out, and the room was dark and chilly. Keat still slept beside her, happily hogging the covers.

A restlessness that she couldn't shake kept her awake. It was no use. She couldn't sleep. Carefully, she lifted Keat's arm and slipped away from his embrace. Putting on a robe and slippers, she went to the kitchen. After making herself a cup of tea, she sat at the table, letting the steaming mug warm her hands, and listened to wind circling around the house. The wind blew hard and seemed full of purpose, like a living thing, and it filled her with trepidation.

But it wasn't just the winter wind that scared her—it was the future. She wanted to be with Keat, and that hope warmed her more than the tea did. But everything was so different. *One step at a time*, she reminded herself.

Her dress still lay draped over the chair next to her, where she'd left it earlier in the week. Setting the mug down, she ran her finger along the dress. Everything had changed in the new century. Even her dress had been made new again. She sighed and suddenly wanted Keat next to her, and the reassuring warmth of his body.

She put the mug in the sink, turned off the light in the kitchen and, at the last minute, retrieved her dress from the back of the chair to take upstairs and hang in the closet. With her dress in one arm, she began to climb the stairs. As soon as her foot hit the first riser, a particularly fierce gale buffeted the house. It was a strange wind, a low growl. She stood on the stairs, hesitating, a tight nervousness taking hold.

There came a soft click. The tiniest noise, but one as familiar to her as her own heartbeat. The hair on the back of her neck rose and she slowly, reluctantly, turned around. Lightning flashed, and in the brief, flickering light, she saw a small, white head of hair emerging from the tunnel door.

"C.J.?" she said, hardly believing what she saw. It was him. It was C.J.

His face remained hidden in shadow, and a strange light came from the tunnel behind him. He turned toward her, hesitated for a moment, and then she saw his skinny body scurry back past the little door.

"No!" she shouted. Without hesitation, without so much as a thought, she rushed forward. Wearing a bathrobe, arms laden with her dress, she did what she promised Keat she'd never do. She entered the tunnel, and the darkness swallowed her whole.

Keat rolled over in bed. His hand reached out to find Penrose and grabbed nothing but empty sheets. He bolted upright in bed and looked around. The storm raged outside, and the howls sounded angry and vengeful. He rose from bed, slipped on a pair of jeans and walked down the hall.

"Penrose?" he called.

An eerie white light glowed up from the foyer, and he approached the landing with a deep sense of dread. When he reached the stairs, he saw the tunnel door open, strange light spilling from it and Penrose disappearing through the doorway. In that instant, he knew he loved her and couldn't live without her.

"No!" he roared, and flew down the stairs. "Come back!" he shouted at Penrose. It was too late. She was already gone. Without thinking, Keat landed hard on the floor and leaped forward, sliding into the tunnel to follow Penrose.

Penrose counted as the grandfather clock rang out ten chimes. Soft, reassuring sounds. But to her, hidden as she was in the tunnel, the sounds were anything but reassuring. Time had lost all meaning to her. She held her breath until the last chime died away, leaving only the ticking of the pendulum. The ticking was like a heartbeat, but the rhythm was unfamiliar. She didn't fear the darkness that surrounded her. No, she feared the light that snuck underneath the door, for she knew in her bones there would be a different world out there.

Waiting and hiding weren't options. Better to know than to wonder. She pushed open the door, stuck her head out and whispered urgently, "C.J.?"

There was no reply. She crawled from the tunnel, still holding the gown in her hand. The air hung thick and sweet and warm in the foyer. The sharp, tangy scent of yellow pine lingered and she heard the night calls of crickets.

She was home. *Home* meaning Arundell in Charleston. The scents and the sounds rolled over her, calling her back, though her memories felt distant. They were hard to recall, almost as if they belonged to someone else. Every breath she took felt stolen.

"C.J?" she said. "Carrick?" Saying his name made her nervous.

Yes, she knew she was back at Arundell, but in what time? The answer wasn't obvious. She took a few steps. Everything felt unreal, sights and sounds amplified. Out of habit, she began to walk toward the kitchen and the stairs that led to the workshop. Carrick. It was night. He would be down in the workshop right at that moment, working away. Why did she feel so scared, so unsettled? "Better to know. Better to know," she whispered.

Through the kitchen and down the stairs she slunk along, dress in her arms, and clinging to the shadows. At the foot of the stairs, the workshop came into view. The fireplace blazed with light and heat. But the room felt cold to her. The tables were piled high with odds and ends. Everything was familiar, but she couldn't shake the fear that clung to her insides.

In the middle of the room, standing with a childlike glory, Harris number one gleamed in the firelight. His gas-lamp eyes were dark. His power lay hidden and dormant, but she still warmed at the sight of him, knowing all of the potential inside of him. Not in his clunky body or his fiery eyes, but in the dreams he carried within him. The dreams and the vision of one man, the one man who had started everything. Then she realized she was back to the time before he fell and was destroyed. Knowing this made her feel a little better, but it still left many unanswered questions.

Carrick. There he was, sitting with his back to her, bent over a table, his white hair a wild halo. She brought her hand to her mouth and covered it to prevent her from crying out. Time meant nothing to her heart. Whether it was one beat or a million in the time since she'd last seen him, it didn't matter. She still had a fondness for him.

But it wasn't the same. Not anymore. Not after Keat. Layers of love and life collided in her mind, and she stared numbly as the man she never thought she'd see again as he toiled lovingly, obsessively, over some small component. It was bittersweet, the sight of him. Her feet began to move across the floor in his direction.

Then she stopped herself. Wait. She needed to think. She remembered the calendar that hung on the wall. It read August 18. She hadn't even started employment at the manor yet. In fact, she'd be arriving in the morning. In merely a few hours. And yet, there she stood. What did it mean? She didn't know.

He turned around suddenly. He wore his thick glasses and they made his eyes appear huge as he stared in her direction. The sight of those kaleidoscope eyes and their swirling colors made her want to cry. She was scared, too, unsure of what was happening. And Keat, oh, what about Keat? He'd be all alone, wondering if she'd ever return.

She froze, grateful for his limited eyesight. Some instinct told her she needed more information.

"Hello?" His familiar voice carried right to her heart. "C.J.? Is that you?" He stood up. His long, lean body rose to full height.

Her heart began to pound in her chest. He would think her a stranger. An intruder.

She had to leave, and right away. Turning, she ran up the stairs, careful to keep her footfalls light, her white gown still hanging in her arms. In a panic, she raced through the foyer, out the front door and into the night.

She tore down the gravel path that led away from Arundell Manor. Lightning and thunder crashed overhead and though it hadn't begun to rain, it would soon. There was only one place she wanted to go—to The Winding Stair, to get answers. More than anything, she needed answers. Could she just start afresh and simply circle back to the manor? The only way to know was to start at the very beginning.

The scents of the honeysuckle, gladiolas and jasmine that perfumed the air were as familiar to her as the back of her hand. Though she couldn't predict each gust of wind, the moment it came upon her she recalled it in full detail. Memories came back, far stronger than any déjà vu.

She stopped running and slipped out of her nightgown before hurriedly putting her dress on. It was humid out, and she was sweaty, so it was a struggle to don the gown. She fumbled with the buttons at her back and eventually had to settle for the top three remaining open. Her dress smelled of bleach, sharp in the perfumed summer air. She tossed the nightgown deep into the woods and wished that she'd worn her boots rather than the nighttime slippers. But they'd have to do.

As she walked through the woods, the moon bobbed between the trees, and a strange, persistent wind gusted against her. She leaned into the wind and pressed on, lost in her thoughts. She thought of Keat and Carrick both, and her memories of the men were twisted and tangled, overlapping in her mind.

Keat. It already felt as if he was slipping away from her. The future seemed far-off, a distant thing that she wouldn't see again. The impossible had happened twice. Perhaps it could happen a third time, and she would find Keat once again. She had to believe that.

And Carrick. How it tore her heart to see him, the emotions lost, never to be recovered. Even if she started again, how could she love him when Keat had her whole heart now? It was agonizing, and there was no easy answer.

It was late when she entered Charleston, the moon already halfway across the sky and peeking through the clouds. A haze covered the city, brought on by the rain, which had now lessened. That strange wind still blew, now at her back, curling the misty haze around her. She walked along the cobblestone streets, turning away from the few people who passed her by, unable to meet their gaze for, in a way, they were already dead.

Once you've been to the future, things change. Yes, everything was familiar, exactly as it should be. Yet she felt like a foreigner.

She walked until she reached the street that The Winding Stair Inn stood on. All of the buildings were dark except for one. Golden light from the streetlamps washed over the inn. Perhaps it was the way the light fell upon the glass, but the building seemed to shimmer for a brief moment, almost glimmering, and her eyes fell on a second-floor window. There, like a china doll, a woman with dark hair stood leaning against the window frame, looking up at the moon.

She watched as the woman—her—dropped the want ads. They fluttered to the ground. Oh, my God, she thought, realization dawning on her. She wore a white dress and her hair was now blond. Her gaze fell on the girl again—Penny—for she knew in her heart it was a different version of herself. Just like Harris the robot. Was she the newest model, or the oldest? Fate was cruel.

Chapter 22

Penrose opened the door to the pub. Charlie stood behind the bar, rag in hand. His head dipped in greeting. "Welcome back, dear," he said with a humble smile. "I said you can start again, and you can if you like."

Emerging into the modern-day Arundell had been enough to stretch her mind thin. This outright shattered every belief she ever knew. If she couldn't trust something as basic as her very existence, what could she trust?

She heard the scrape of a mug on wood and turned to see Mrs. Capshaw, her cheeks reddened after working in the kitchens. Penrose knew that because she'd worked beside the woman that very night, all those weeks ago. Weeks ago. No, minutes ago. The world was tilting, and she was sliding off it.

Without looking up from the warm cup of tea in her hand, Mrs. Capshaw said to her, "You're late. I was beginning to get worried." She turned to face Penrose, and there was little kindness in her expression. She had the fierce, calculating look she'd always had. "Time's wasting. Let's get on with it."

Penrose stormed to the table, shaking, and stood towering over the woman. "I'm late? Time's wasting?" Penrose said through clenched teeth, standing above her. She was so angry she could barely see straight. "You knew. The whole time, you knew."

"Of course I did," the woman said matter-of-factly, stirring her tea with a spoon and setting it aside. "I like the new hair color, by the way. I always forget how much blond hair complements your blue eyes until I see it again."

Penrose sank deeper into despair. *Until I see it again...* Her cheeks burned and her fingers tingled as she said, "And again? And again?"

Mrs. Capshaw smiled up at her. "On and on and on."

"What are you saying? What happened to me?" The horrible truth that was revealing itself seemed too big for her mind to swallow.

"What happened to you? That is a small question with a great big answer. Let me just say that my job is plugging leaks. And you, my dear Penny, are a leak."

Penrose took a step back. "I'm not Penny anymore," she said, lifting her chin. "Call me Penrose."

"How appropriate," said Mrs. Capshaw with a strange smile. "Because Penny is upstairs as we speak. But you're still a leak, whether you're Penny or Penrose. Think on it. A midnight baby. Born on such an auspicious day. A foot in two worlds. Cursed. And I of all people should know, for my story is similar. It's not your fault, dear. Fate hands out life sentences blindly. There's nothing you could have done."

Penrose sank into the chair beside her old landlady. If Mrs. Capshaw had dropped a boulder onto Penrose's head, she'd have been less surprised. It seemed too awful to consider. She put her head on her arms.

"Come now, Mrs. Capshaw. Must you be so cruel?" said Charlie from behind the bar. "What an awful way to break the news. Haven't we talked about this?"

"What does it matter, Charlie? It never changes. Never." She seemed so awfully practical about the whole thing.

"She and I—the same person—will be here, in the same room, at the same time?" Penrose asked in a weak voice. "When I...when I stole her position—"

Mrs. Capshaw put a hand on her shoulder, and Penrose lifted her head from the table, sitting up and violently shrugging the arm away. Mrs. Capshaw seemed unfazed. "You stole nothing. You gave a future to yourself. You gave a chance to yourself. You gave love. Hate me if you want, but I'm not the cause of it. I merely keep things in order. I'm a gatekeeper. There are plenty of us around. We tend to very few, but our job is of utmost importance."

Penrose felt the ground move underneath her, far stronger than any earthquake. "How...how can that be?"

"It just is. To question it is to court madness. I should know. I did that once."

"What if I choose not to go through with it?" The question came out limp and weak as it left her lips.

Mrs. Capshaw laughed. "That's the last thing I worry about. Every single person in your shoes does exactly what they should. You simply won't be able to stop yourself. It will be a compulsion inside of you. It's after this moment I worry most about. That's when it gets dangerous." Her dark eyes swept up and down the length of Penrose's body. "Don't you feel it right at this moment? Pulling on you? Can you deny the girl upstairs? Yourself? All that, painful as it was—can you deny her the same chance you had? The same love?"

"I can't," she said. She shook her head. "I can't deny her." The pull inside her was so strong. She detested it fiercely but was powerless to fight it. Love, real love, deep and parental, thrummed inside her for the girl upstairs. Lost and alone. Unloved by all, except her. Being unloved was a crime above all things. Worse than being forgotten.

"Well, then, shall we get started?"

Without even thinking or trying, Penrose sat more proudly in the chair, smoothed down her cheeks and rubbed her tears away. Penny must see her looking her best.

Mrs. Capshaw stood up, her beady eyes resting on Penrose a moment too long. "Look," she said. "You're already falling right in line. I have good news for you. All is not lost. You want to return to where you came from, I assume?"

Her gaze shot up and hope burned in her eyes. "I do. Keat. I need Keat. And more. I want to somehow save everyone from the earthquake and get back to him—"

Mrs. Capshaw held up her hand. "The man you love—you might, just might, be able to return to. The other—that is something you cannot do," she said. "You can only save yourself. It's your only hope. If you fail, you are doomed."

"How am I doomed?" asked Penrose, wondering if things could ever get any worse.

"Take a good long look at me," Mrs. Capshaw said, rising to full height. "Take heed of my loveless eyes. I was once in your shoes, and I failed in my quest to return. I wanted so badly to save others, but instead I ruined everything. When it was over, I had two choices available to me." A look of anguish flashed across her face. "I chose the less courageous path. I should have chosen the braver but final path. Now I am trapped here forever. A gatekeeper for the lost. If you'd arrived in a more timely fashion, I could've told you my own tale of endless woe. I'll just say this. Listen to me well, Penrose Heatherton, and do exactly as I say. Everything depends on it."

"I made the wrong choice when you first approached me. I should've refused." It was a sad, soft confession. "My greed condemned me. It has made me suffer."

"Everyone suffers, Penrose. Everyone makes choices—bad or good, they're just choices. A path taken. A coin spent. You were no different, you committed no crime. You didn't ask to be put in this position. It's just that your choices stretched across centuries. They always will."

"At least tell me I can get back," asked Penrose. "I need to get back."

"You can. Possibly. Though, after a few days, you might not want to. Hearts change."

"No, they don't," Penrose replied hotly.

"Didn't your heart change when you slipped away from us?"

There was nothing to say in answer to that, for it was true. All she could think of was Keat, the man she had left behind. Or in the future, depending on how she looked at it. Either way, he was no longer with her. "Keat needs me," she whispered. "And I need him."

"Right now, I need you. But she—" Mrs. Capshaw jabbed her fingers in the direction of the upstairs bedroom "—needs you most of all. Do not fail me. Make her want what you have. And she will, oh, she will. For the compulsion that's sweeping over you right now, the compulsion to help her, the same will rush over her. She'll not be able to resist. Once she's on her way, I'll explain how you can get home and get back to Keat. So, let's get started." Mrs. Capshaw stood up. "Time's wasting. Always wasting. We have to hurry and do something about that hair," she said. "Oh. You've no bonnet. I always forget that."

"I never do," said Charlie, and he tossed a blue bonnet toward her. It landed perfectly on the table, in exactly the same position she first remembered seeing it as she descended the stairs.

"Now," said Mrs. Capshaw. "Here's what you'll do." Her gaze held Penrose's and seemed to be admonishing her, warning her to follow orders exactly. "When Penny comes in, you must play your part perfectly. You have one chance to close this loop. One chance to seal the hole, and everything you do from here on out impacts that. When Penny comes in you must not turn around, and you must never look at her. Keep your chin up and look happy. I'll do the rest. When I walk upstairs to speak with her, you are to speak to Charlie. Don't worry. You'll remember your words. Under no conditions are you to get any clever ideas. I'll take care of everything."

"You'll take care of everything," repeated Penrose

numbly. "You always were an enterprising woman, weren't you?"

"You'd have to be, in my position. Try to understand. That's all I ask." She went to the stairs and began climbing them, looking back at Penrose one last time.

"Don't worry, dear. She always has to scare the person. It works best that way. The good news is that it works."

"Always? It always works?"

"Well…" he said, his voice fading away to nothing.

"Charlie," she whispered. "I have to know. Why did you warn me against Carrick?"

"Ah, I had to try. I think of you as my own child and I keep trying to protect you from a broken heart. It never works, though."

She heard a noise upstairs. Hushed voices from the top of the landing.

At that moment, everything changed. As soon as she heard Penny's soft voice whispering, unsure and afraid, her entire being focused on the sound. Penny. No longer Penrose. Still, they were entwined. The same. Again, that strong rush of love and protective instincts surged through her.

She started to recall the words from that fateful night, and then she began to speak them. Repeating perfectly word for word. Charlie nodded, encouraging her and replying exactly as he should. She played her role. Back straight. Look proud and happy. It was like déjà vu but a thousand times stronger. She walked a razor's edge. She had to play it perfectly.

She felt Penny's presence on the stairs, the lingering, hotly jealous gaze on her back. *Don't worry,* she willed the woman to understand, *it will all work out. Maybe. Hopefully.*

She felt the cold hand of fate slide up her spine as Penny swept past her, and she suddenly knew what it must be like to have someone walk upon your grave. She collapsed, head down on the table, as soon as Penny stepped outside. Charlie patted her on the shoulder as he walked by. "There, there, dear. You did just right. Breathe easy." The door shut behind him and she was alone. She put her head down and sobbed openly.

The grief and uneasiness was a feeling she couldn't shake, no matter how she tried. The colors of the world were off now that she knew the truth. Everything seemed dangerous. Even something as simple as opening the door was fraught with peril. One misstep, a slipped boot, and down she'd go, and the future would be in jeopardy.

She couldn't explain that feeling, the sense that she needed to be cautious. It was just there, part of her, like the need to be careful when crossing a busy street or handling a hot pan. The fear was folded into her soul, yet she still had to function.

The door creaked as Mrs. Capshaw returned to the pub. "Oh, child," she said in a weary, ancient-sounding voice. "Come with me up the stairs and sleep. I'll explain the plan along the way. Trust me. You'll feel better in the morning."

Penrose put up no fight. She followed her landlady up the stairs, listening to the plan. She was to return to the house on the night of the earthquake and no matter what, she was to prevent Penny from entering the tunnel. She alone must enter it. When she reached her old room, she collapsed on the cot. After Mrs. Capshaw had left, she stared out at the moon. One moon. Two Penroses. She closed her eyes and waited for the nothingness to sweep her away.

But the nothingness never came. She slept fitfully, plagued by dreams of Carrick and Keat. When she rolled out of bed in the morning, the realization that right at that moment Penny was now arriving at Arundell hit her hard. All of the emotions were knotted inside her. Remembering Keat, she held on to the conviction that it was possible to return to him.

Afterward, she dressed and went down the winding staircase to the rear of the shop where the kitchen was and found Mrs. Capshaw. She felt like a traitor because there was something she had to do.

She had to go back to Arundell. Just one more time. To see Penny. To make sure she was okay. The need burned inside of her. Mrs. Capshaw seemed to sense it and had kept a ready eye on her all day, but Penrose was careful and concealed her intentions as best she could.

The opportunity came at a strange moment. Late that afternoon, a woman came striding into the pub, creating a ruckus as she tried to rent a room. Luckily, Charlie wasn't around. And when a grumbling Mrs. Capshaw escorted the woman upstairs, Penrose slipped from the pub.

Chapter 23

It was twilight as Penrose approached Arundell Manor. A raven cried out a coarse cackle from somewhere in the forest. She shuddered. It seemed a bad omen. When she first came to Arundell, the road had taken her closer to her future. Now, it took her closer to her past.

Emerging from the tree-lined path, she looked at the house. The sight of Arundell, its smooth marble glowing under the moon, a mansion of forty-one rooms and hidden passages crammed with secrets made her heart seize with gratitude. For when she fell into the gray area of destiny and everything had turned slippery and uncertain, it was the manor upon which she depended most.

A few windows glowed orange with light, and she thought of Carrick, C.J. and Penny inside the home. Suddenly, she couldn't move fast enough. Lifting her skirt, she ran. Carrick and Penny would be downstairs in the workroom. Penrose knew she was in dangerous territory, but she couldn't help it. She had to see them. Taking a wide path, she hugged the trees until she reached the gardens behind the house.

Penrose crept closer to the workshop until she saw inside clearly. The room blazed with light. The mechanical man stood imposingly, the center of attention in the room. Even from afar he looked magical.

Suddenly, the tall, lean figure of a man crossed in front of the window. Carrick. He was so handsome, his looks so arresting. She heard his impassioned, driven voice as he spoke to Penny. It moved her to listen to him talk about the mechanical man and hear his zeal and his intelligence. It bound him to her heart and memories, but he belonged to Penny now.

Penny sat at her desk, scribbling furiously in the journals. Carrick paced beside her. With the tiniest tick of her head, she looked up. A stolen glance of longing at the man she was just beginning to have feelings for.

Penrose ached to see them from a closer vantage point. The workshop was bright and hopeful and both of them full of ideas, right on the cusp of discovering each other. The realization hurt. Keat was lost to her forever. But Carrick was fresh and new to Penny. Even if they had a brief amount of time together, Carrick and Penny deserved every moment of happiness they could grab. She crept closer until she was just outside the door. Suddenly, she remembered that night. The blonde woman at the door. How had she forgotten?

She had to get away. Turning to run, she tripped and fell to the ground loudly. Immediately, she realized her error. Events began to unfold exactly as she remembered them; it was as if she played a part in one of Keat's movies. A part that she was powerless to step out of.

She said to herself, "Now the door will open, and I'll see Carrick." A moment later it did. He stood there, the light streaming from behind him. She froze, half-bent over the bell, her blond hair covering her face. Petrified to look up yet unable to stop herself, her gaze rose and their eyes met. Time ceased to matter.

Her emotions came roaring back—the hope, the intense longing for him, even the simple joy of being beside him. The feelings swarmed her and, standing right there, her heart broke into two pieces. One piece would always be at the Arundell Manor she knew and loved. The other piece would forever be with Keat, and nothing in the world could be done about it. It was a pain she would live with forever.

Penny stepped into the doorway just then. Her face ashen, her eyes wide as saucers, she looked like a child. Her fear was palpable as she stared at Penrose.

And Penrose hated to see her so afraid. She wanted to comfort Penny, to tell her it would be okay, even if it wasn't exactly the truth. The need to reassure Penny was so strong that Penrose couldn't fight it. Lifting her hand, she was about to speak when she remembered Mrs. Capshaw's stern warning. She walked a razor's edge. So, Penrose stepped back into the darkness and fled, knowing that Carrick would chase her.

Racing as fast as she could, she didn't dare look behind her. The trees flew by as she ran, and the ground blurred beneath her feet. It had been a mistake to come, and now she was afraid.

Perhaps Carrick wouldn't catch her. It was a foolish

wish. She already knew the end result, just not what happened between them.

She came around to the front of the house but before she reached the road, someone came from behind and tackled her. Down she went, hard and fast. A boot was lowered onto her spine and it held her against the ground. She twisted around and saw Carrick looming above her with the moon beside him, illuminating his harsh expression.

"Who are you?" he asked in a voice edged with anger as he looked at her. He peered closer. "And why are you familiar to me?"

She could barely breathe. "I'm… I'm," she began to say, but there was no way to explain who she was. "I'm no one," she finally said, giving up and letting her head drop to the ground again. "No one you know, Carrick."

"Then how do you know my name?"

"Does it matter?"

"Seeing as how you're under my boot, it matters very much."

The last thing she ever thought she'd feel with Carrick again was fear. But as his boot held her to the ground fear sizzled inside of her.

"Spit it out," he said. "How do you know her? Why did you wave at her?" He bent over her, leaned so close that their noses almost touched and said, "How do you know my name?"

Her hands clawed the air as she struggled to rise. "Let me up," she huffed. "Let me up and I'll explain."

There was a hand at her back, and, with a rustle of skirts she was standing. Disoriented, she smoothed her hair. The strange sensation of dreaming swept over. Everything seemed unreal. Vivid, but not real.

He stood a few feet away from her, scowling, his hands clenched at his sides. "You have three seconds to start talking," he said, taking one menacing step forward. His voice was familiar and yet threatening.

But even more familiar was the odd compulsion to move events along. She risked everything in these moments. Everything. The words found her, not the other way around. It was easy. She began to speak. "Penny stole something from me! She stole my job. My future. You!" she said, and paused.

"What the hell are you talking about?" he asked.

She took a deep breath. "Carrick, you once told me that we have only the briefest chance at happiness."

"I once told you? I just met you. Are you mad?"

How tired of that question she'd become. A bitter laugh escaped her. "It would be easier if I were mad. I'll just say it plainly. I'm caught in a time loop. I am her. Lost to time now. I am Penny."

"No, you are not. You are insane."

"You're just like someone else I know with that accusation. Set that thought aside and just listen." Her voice turned strong and certain. She began to talk, her words coming fast. "I know the painting where your mother had you colored in brown hair with a smile on your face, and I know the configuration of all the gears in your mechanical man. I know all of these things."

He crossed the space between her instantly and grabbed her arms hard. "I'll say it again. What the hell is going on?"

She cried out at his touch and spun away. "No, no, no," she said quickly. "Don't come any closer... I'm warning you. I walk a razor's edge." His grip made her uneasy. This was so very dangerous. She was a fool to have come. One wrong word…

He laughed. "Even you, crazy as you are, won't let me touch you."

"Wrong!" she said. "From the moment I saw you I thought you were beautiful. You have a wild, other-worldly look. And I am her! Penny feels those things for you." He must know that. If only one good thing would come of this disaster, let it be that their love could bloom and Penny could stay with him.

"This is insanity. Utter insanity. Then why don't you just tell me the future?"

"No. I cannot do that," she whispered, remembering the admonition to save herself and no one else. But couldn't she save the budding love and attraction between Penny and Carrick? It was worth a chance. "Already, I've told you too much. I can only say she wants you and desires you."

"My God." He was shaking his head, his brows drawn together. "You suffer from lunacy."

"Just hear me out. Then I'll leave."

"Speak then."

"I cannot say much. Only this. I'm left…" She wrung her hands together. "I'm a scavenger, left to follow along in destiny's shadow, seeking whatever shelter I can. And you want to talk to me about your misfortune. How the whole world hates you. Well, at least you have a world."

Everything came together inside of her. Fear and rage and more fear. "And besides," she said, hating that her emotions turned her voice shrill, but she couldn't stop it. "You have happiness waiting inside for you right now. Penny sits there thinking only of you."

He snorted. "Her? She wants nothing to do with me."

Her white-blond hair flew around her face as she shook her head. "You are blinder than I ever knew! She longs for you and thinks about you constantly." Her eyes met his, and with her soul she implored him. "If you trust only one thing I tell you, trust this—you may have only one little sliver to be with her. The briefest heaven. Carrick, grab it. Grab your happiness, your piece of heaven, while you can. Believe me. Your world could come apart at any moment. Nothing matters except those brief moments of love and happiness."

"Happiness. Love. What big words. Words I don't know the meaning of. Never did. And she is you? You are the same?"

"Yes!" She was wild, her hair blowing about her face. "I cared for you. I desired you. And now I'm lost to you. There's no hope for me here. I know my words sound foolish, but you of all people understand that unexplainable things can and do happen. At least do this—feel her lips on yours and then make your decision."

"If you desired me once and she desires me now, then prove it. Kiss me." He sneered at her, and she saw the pain, the challenge in his twisted features. "Prove your words. Because I know you won't even touch me. And she never will. Ever."

It all came down to this. She grabbed his hands, pressed them against her waist. "I can still remember the feel of your hands on my body. You were my lover. For a short time. But there's hope. You can have her forever if you listen to me. So listen."

"Speak." His voice had shifted.

"You may not believe that I traveled through time, and you don't have to. You only have to know that Penny wants you." She reached out and gripped his forearms. "So, yes, I will prove it to you."

A sneer pulled his lip tight. "Go ahead," he spit out.

"Gladly," she said, leaning up, her lips touching his. With that one kiss, she hoped to save all of their futures.

He stood still, not moving at all. But he did not pull away or stop her. She deepened the kiss, remembering the sweet times she'd had with him.

Suddenly, he boomed a response, smashed his hands through her hair, clutched her and drew her in with raw need.

She kissed him with a lifetime of anguish. Pouring into him everything she still yearned for with Keat but would never have again. He was gone to her. She could scream in anger of it. But she had Carrick. If only for a moment, she could remember, take shelter in it.

He overwhelmed her, yanking her tight against him.

She knew him at that moment. The real him. Emotion unchecked by fear. By rejection. She knew him to his soul for a quick instant. But she remembered, and it was a gift. A goodbye present. Because it didn't belong to her anymore. It belonged to Penny.

It all became so clear. One brief nirvana. It was all she had left with him, and she melted into him. Longing, pain, love, heartbreak all flooded her, and she spoke to him of these things with her lips. He responded in kind, passionate and wild. And then she shuddered, a heaving sigh that came from somewhere deep inside of her.

She pulled away, the hardest thing she'd ever done. "That. Look for that."

"What?" he asked in a husky voice.

"Look for that shudder, that response to you, and you'll know she wants you. Badly, too."

"I have to go," she said, pulling away from him. "Time is wasting." She was aware that this might be the last time they ever touched, the last time she felt his warm skin on hers. She backed away.

"Forgive me," she said. Was she speaking to him? Or to Keat? She didn't know.

"Wait!" he called out as she ran away.

She stopped running, reluctant to turn around. She looked up at the black velvet sky and the silvery moon. That was how they used to be. Penrose black as night, Carrick bright as the moon. Now they were two pale stars locked into distant positions, destined never to meet again. Without turning around, she said, "Please, Carrick, heed my words." Then she turned and ran away.

"Wait!" he called out after her.

But she couldn't look back. She moved through the thick air, pulling on the branches as she passed by, needing the feel of things to reassure her that everything was real. With her white hair and gown and her quick gait, she resembled a ghost slipping along the gravel path.

It was a long walk back to The Winding Stair. It seemed as though she walked beneath the rustling trees forever. Finally, she emerged from the forest and Charleston lay just ahead. Now that she wasn't beneath the canopy anymore, the milky-blue moonlight blinded her, and when her eyes adjusted, she saw a man sitting right in front of her on the side of the road. He sat defeated, head in hands, like a king reflecting after a great loss on the battlefield. Even seated, she recognized his body posture, tall, with straight shoulders. The familiar Arundell frame.

"Carrick?" she whispered, unable to believe that he had somehow moved so quickly that he could be ahead of her on the path.

"Keat," he replied raggedly. And then she noticed what her moon-blinded eyes had missed—his hair was jet-black. Just like that, her legs gave out.

Keat shot up to catch her, reaching her just in time. His arms encircled her, grasping her around the back and scooping her up. He folded her into his arms and embraced her. "Penrose," he said, breathing her in, winding his hands farther around her torso and grasping her even closer, as if he were afraid to let go.

It was impossible. But those arms felt like bands of truth supporting her. It was him. "Keat," she said in a breathless voice. "How did you—"

"The tunnel," he whispered, his head buried in her hair. "I followed you."

"What if something had happened? What if I lost you forever or you died?"

"I'd rather die than not know where you were. Than to be without you, Penrose." His grip tightened around her so hard that she gasped. "Penrose," he said. "I'm sorry that I never believed you." His voice was thick with regret. "You were right all along."

"I forgive you." Her words were given simply, freely.

"God, you were right. Until I experienced it, I couldn't fathom it. And look at me now. I have my whole life in order, but I'm helpless as a babe here. I've been wandering, trying to make sense of it all. I may have gone back in time, but I don't even know how to get from one place to another. Life is no simpler."

She knew exactly what he meant. "Oh, Keat, I'm in this century trying my hardest to return to you," she said. "Because I couldn't bear it, either. And now, you're here." She laughed, almost giddy, looking up at him and raining small, happy kisses on his cheeks.

His lips found hers and demanded more. Finally, he broke away and said, "When I came out of the tunnel, a little boy with pale hair chased me from the house, yelling and screaming at me."

"That was C.J.!" she exclaimed.

"I know. He shouted the most awful things at me. I ran like hell, Penrose." He sighed. "There's something I never told you. When I was a boy, I saw him—C.J.—he came to my room in the middle of the night. I thought he was a ghost. But he wasn't…he wasn't."

"I saw him in your house, too. I followed him into the tunnel. Do you know what that means?" she said in a rising voice. "It means that he can travel back and forth, and if he can, we can! It means we can, as well." She hugged him. "We can go back," she said, gripping him even tighter. Even though she was filled with hope, it was a long time until she felt whole again. Pulling away from him, she said, "Come on," and tugged at him. "Let's go. Mrs. Capshaw will be so glad to meet you! Let's go to The Winding Stair."

Penrose was dead wrong. Mrs. Capshaw was not glad in the slightest to meet Keat. "Penrose Heatherton, what have you done?" she hissed as she stood in her doorway eyeing Keat up and down. Curling away from him, she looked in his direction as if he were cursed.

"He followed me to our time," she replied. "I didn't bring him here."

Mrs. Capshaw sighed, a sound dangerously close to a growl. "The potential for a disaster just became a likelihood." Shaking her head, she took two steps back, allowing them to enter the pub. "Take him upstairs. Don't let him out and, whatever you do, keep him in your sights at all times."

The seriousness of her demeanor surprised Penrose. Keat took a step. "I think I can help," he offered.

"Help?" croaked Mrs. Capshaw. Holding up her hand, she pinched her fingers together. "You're this close to disaster, and the scales might have just tipped in the wrong direction. Everything is at risk right now. Every single thing. You risk the future merely by talking to me. You must hide, and only at the last moment can you come out."

She swung around, her heavy skirts swirling in the air. "Take him upstairs. Right now. And, for God's sakes, Penrose, keep him there."

Control had always been something Keat took for granted. He had an excess of it. But now he had none, and it scared him. From the second the tunnel swallowed him up, he'd been careening, unsure of everything. It was a nightmarish feeling, but it opened his eyes to the suffering Penrose went through.

He considered himself a man of science, but he had to set all of that aside to believe what he was seeing. He had to focus on feeling instead of thinking. It was a tough transition for him to make, but there was no other option.

If Penrose hadn't found him when she did, he would've been a doomed man. Though, he supposed, he would return to Arundell and lurk around the edges, needing to be near the one thing that was familiar. Just as Penrose had done. When she'd told him she would never leave the manor, he thought that remark strange, but now he knew what she meant.

Penrose explained the plans for returning and, for a man who was used to being in control, he felt very dependent on a thousand different variables, none of which he had any control over. It was the most vulnerable he'd ever felt in his entire life.

They slept and made love for days. If one good thing could be pulled from the experience, Keat reasoned, it was that their last days of certainty were filled with passion and love. After that, they would enter that door, and it was up to fate.

Chapter 24

Just like that, two weeks slid by, and on the day of the earthquake, Penrose woke at dawn with an unsettled feeling. She tossed and turned, unable to fall back asleep. Keat lay beside her all tangled in the sheets, sleeping like a baby. She sat up and ran her hands through her blond hair. A thousand small problems could pop up and prevent them from even getting to Arundell Manor. And, worse, once they arrived at the manor and the earthquake hit, anything could happen.

The variables swirled in her head, all the possibilities waiting to happen or—worse—go wrong. But the big unknown, the very scariest part of all, was the little door to the tunnel. What would greet them on the other side of the door?

She nudged him and he opened his eyes. "Keat," she said, "what if—"

"Stop." He said in a sleepy voice, cutting her off. "Don't torture yourself again. We've gone over this for days. Fate doesn't like to be second-guessed. Penrose, you need to have faith."

She laughed harshly. "Faith is not something to have. It's something to get rid of."

"Come here," he said, and pulled her down into the covers. "Do you think fate would bring us together from one hundred thirty years of distance—not once but twice—just to turn its back on you?" He ran a hand through his tousled hair. "No. No. Scratch that. Don't think. Feel. And if you can't feel it, just look at me. I have no worries. I'm with the woman I love. I fear nothing. Whatever fate hands us, she hands it to both of us, and we face it together."

His hand trailed along her spine, bumping along the little ridges of her backbone. "Come here and let me show you what faith is, how to let things progress without worrying about the outcome." His smile was lazy and wicked, as he drew her close to him. "Endings will happen naturally. Just follow along."

And he was right.

At four o'clock that evening, Penrose waited for Keat at the door of The Winding Stair. Mrs. Capshaw stood beside her, her jeweled hands interlinked with Penrose's.

"Take care, my dear," she said. "And I hope I don't see you again. And you know I mean that with the utmost sincerity."

"I know," replied Penrose, hugging her.

Keat and Mrs. Capshaw shook hands. "Be careful," she said.

"Always. And thank you," he said.

The sun still shone, though softly, when they began

their walk to Arundell. Gold fingerlings of light stretched between the trees and fell on the ground in bright circles. They walked along the dappled road, holding hands. Keat showed no nervousness; he was easy and free with his gait.

She thought of their home, the Arundell of the future. "Do you think we'll make it back to our home?" she asked.

"I'm hopeful we'll make it somewhere," he said. "But I'm certain that wherever we end up, we'll be together because I won't let go of your hand. And that's a promise."

They reached Arundell and passed through the gates as the moon began to rise in the sky. The tree-lined road stretched in front of them, and they strolled slowly under the canopy until the manor came into view.

Keat stopped walking. "What a sight to see."

And it *was* a sight to see. The white stone of Arundell glistened like a pearl. "It takes my breath away. In a way, I hate to leave it."

"I can certainly understand."

They went and stood behind the ancient oak tree that kept watch by the pond. It was fully dark by then, and they were well hidden in the shadows. "Now we wait," she said, and try as she might, she still couldn't quiet the grim apprehension she felt. But there were hints that something was amiss.

She noticed unusual happenings that she hadn't before. Small things like the curious absence of mosquitoes, and large things like the pungent smell of the marsh grass, stronger than she'd ever smelled before. She felt the earth readying itself, hunkering down before it let loose. The colors of the night were even richer.

The moon had never been so silver, the sky so black. The breeze slipped over her skin as if it were memorizing her. These things comforted her.

She said to Keat, remembering the first earthquake, "There will be a large sound, like an out-of-control train."

"I'm ready for it."

There came a tugging on her skirt and she turned to see C.J. standing beside her. "C.J.!" she exclaimed, gathering the boy in her arms. He went willingly and returned the hug fiercely. Then she remembered. He shouldn't know her. But it seemed as if he did. She thought of Mrs. Capshaw's warning. *The razor's edge.* She pulled away and stood up. "I can't hug you. I'm sorry."

"Penny," said C.J. He looked up at her, his expression grave. "It's all right. I know everything. I know about the two houses. You know the other Arundell? The scary one."

She wasn't surprised. She'd seen him, after all. So had Keat. She said, "I know the scary Arundell. Only it's not so scary once you get to know it." She ruffled his hair. For the first time, he seemed like a child, afraid and innocent, and not the angry boy with the genius intelligence she'd first met. "But I'm curious, how do you know?"

"I've known…forever." He gave her a wan smile. "At least it seems like forever. My life before. This is going to sound mighty wild to you—"

"Trust me. It won't." Keat came and stood beside her, watching the boy intently.

"Well, you see, I was born in 1850."

"It's 1886," she said gently, a strange foreboding coming over her.

A touch of the old C.J. slipped out. "I know. Of course I know!" He looked away with a pained expression. "I live with my parents. I have two brothers. The war hasn't started yet. I race to the walls and hide in them when anyone comes over."

"Oh, my God," she said. "You're Carrick, just like I'm Penny?"

He nodded fiercely. "I knew you were just like me!" he said. "When it first happened—there was a blue light, you see—"

"Of course," she said, nodding.

"And I ran toward it. It was so pretty, but when I went into the hole, I ended up here. And I hated it. It was so scary. I hated him." He wiped his eyes with the back of his hand. "I hid. I watched him. I listened. And one day when he caught me out of the tunnel, I made up a story that I knew he couldn't argue with. I kept trying to go back to my own time. Even that would have been better. Less scary, you know?"

She nodded.

"But every time I saw the blue light and went in the tunnel, it took me to the scary place. But I had to keep trying. I had to."

"It's all right now," she said, hugging C.J., the razor's edge be damned. She knew firsthand how frightening it was, and she was an adult—far better equipped to cope than a child.

"But I don't hate him so much anymore," he whispered in her ear. He pulled back and looked at her. "Because when you came everything changed. He changed. Life got so much better. I wasn't near as scared as before. I want Penny to stay," he said. "But I know what's going to happen. I remember the first earthquake. It was so strange that night, wasn't it?"

"It was."

"And when I saw the blue light, I had to take my chance. And you followed me. But when I came out of the tunnel it was different again. Not like before."

"How?" She was almost afraid to ask, but she had to know.

"It was like time went backward in the same place. That never happened. I always switched houses. It always sent me to the other house. And when I crawled out of the tunnel, you were walking up the path. On your first day of work. I watched you from the window." He made a hitched sound, and his lips curled down as he began to cry. "And I don't want her to go in the tunnel. I don't want Penny to disappear. I saw in the scary house, and you looked so familiar. But your hair was weird. I don't like it like that. All white," he said with an apologetic glance. "Then I saw him—" he jerked his head toward Keat, his voice wavering "—coming out of the tunnel. And now you're here. I knew something was brewing, so I took a chance and talked to you. But I'm scared."

"Don't be scared," she said, realizing that she had more faith than she thought she did. "And don't worry. We're going to do our best to make sure Penny stays with you. You see, I love her, too, and I want her to stay with Carrick. Forever."

His whole face lit up. "Really?"

"Really. But I need your help. When the earthquake comes, I need you to stay far, far away from the tunnel door. Can you do that for me?"

He nodded. Almost as if fate were listening, a far-off rumble began. Low and constant, the sound built upon itself as it drew closer. "Here we go," she said. The noise of the rattling earth muffled her words, but C.J. nodded. He understood.

Keat stepped up and held out a hand. Penrose saw unshed tears filling his eyes. "Young man," he said when the boy took his hand, "it's an honor to meet you."

C.J. looked up at him with a mixture of awe and confusion right as the ground beneath their feet trembled slightly and then stilled. The earth went completely silent. Not a cricket to be heard.

Their eyes met, each of them looking for reassurance. And then the earth let loose. A rumble coursed through the ground and it sank away from beneath them. They tumbled and fell. Keat shot up and pulled C.J. and then Penrose to standing, and they began to stagger toward the house.

The next minute—for it was no more than a minute—stretched out longer than a lifetime. The ground undulated like rippling water. Crunching, gnawing noises filled the air, and a smell, dank and loamy, like rotting secrets, swirled around them.

Penrose trained her eyes on the front door, fighting with all her might as the ground shifted in each direction. The front door broke free of its hinges and swung open, revealing the bright light of the crystal chandelier. The lights became a beacon, calling her forward, and she followed Keat, who was struggling to help C.J. up the front stairs.

She reached the landing. There was only a brief second to exchange glances before Keat reached out and clamped down on her hand, hard as steel, dragging her into the house. C.J. raced ahead, and she felt a swift rush of relief when he ran toward Penny at the end of the hall.

Penny. She looked confused standing there, not knowing that at that moment her future was being tacked down and made certain. She could stay with Carrick and help him become whole. She could keep falling in love with him. Penrose lifted her free hand, the quickest wave, before turning to the tunnel.

The door slapped open and shut and the blue light flashed onto the floor. "Are you ready?" asked Keat.

She nodded, realizing that she didn't have to grab her future. She could let it guide her because just then her future stood beside her, his hand firmly holding hers as he pulled her closer to the door.

Keat reached the door, sliding on his knees and expertly holding it open as he pushed Penrose through the opening. He never let go of her hand, and as the door shut behind them, she smiled, unafraid. Wherever fate led them, they would arrive together.

* * * * *

THE WORLD IS BETTER WITH

Romance

Harlequin has everything from contemporary, passionate and heartwarming to suspenseful and inspirational stories.

Whatever your mood, we have a romance just for you!

JUST CAN'T GET ENOUGH?

Join our social communities
and talk to us online.

You will have access to the latest
news on upcoming titles and special
promotions, but most importantly,
you can talk to other fans about your
favorite Harlequin reads.

Harlequin.com/Community

Facebook.com/HarlequinBooks

Twitter.com/HarlequinBooks

Pinterest.com/HarlequinBooks

Love the Harlequin book you just read?

Your opinion matters.

Review this book on your favorite book site, review site, blog or your own social media properties and share your opinion with other readers!

HARLEQUIN®

A Romance FOR EVERY MOOD™

**Stay up-to-date on all your
romance-reading news with the
Harlequin Shopping Guide,
featuring bestselling authors, exciting new
miniseries, books to watch and more!**

The newest issue will be delivered right to you
with our compliments! There are 4 each year.

Signing up is easy.

EMAIL

ShoppingGuide@Harlequin.ca

WRITE TO US

HARLEQUIN BOOKS
Attention: Customer Service Department
P.O. Box 9057, Buffalo, NY 14269-9057

OR PHONE

1-800-873-8635 in the United States
1-888-343-9777 in Canada

Please allow 4-6 weeks for delivery of the first issue by mail.